D0049377

# SHADOW OF THE GIANT

## TOR BOOKS BY ORSON SCOTT CARD

*The Folk of the Fringe*
*Future on Fire* (editor)
*Future on Ice* (editor)
*Lovelock* (with Kathryn Kidd)
*Maps in a Mirror: The Short Fiction of Orson Scott Card*
*Pastwatch: The Redemption of Christopher Columbus*
*Saints*
*Songmaster*
*The Worthing Saga*
*Wyrms*

THE TALES OF ALVIN MAKER
*Seventh Son*
*Red Prophet*
*Prentice Alvin*
*Alvin Journeyman*
*Heartfire*
*The Crystal City*

ENDER
*Ender's Game*
*Ender's Shadow*
*Shadow of the Hegemon*
*Shadow Puppets*
*Shadow of the Giant*
*Speaker for the Dead*
*Xenocide*
*Children of the Mind*

HOMECOMING
*The Memory of Earth*
*The Call of Earth*
*The Ships of Earth*
*Earthfall*
*Earthborn*

WOMEN OF GENESIS
*Sarah*
*Rebekah*
*Rachel & Leah**

*forthcoming

# SHADOW OF THE GIANT

A TOM DOHERTY ASSOCIATES BOOK
NEW YORK

This is a work of fiction. All the characters and events portrayed in this novel are either fictitious or are used fictitiously.

SHADOW OF THE GIANT



This book is printed on acid-free paper.

Edited by Beth Meacham

A Tor Book
Published by Tom Doherty Associates, LLC
175 Fifth Avenue
New York, NY 10010

www.tor.com



ISBN 0-312-85758-6 (regular edition)
EAN 978-0312-85758-5
ISBN 0-765-30749-9 (limited edition)
EAN 978-0765-30749-1
ISBN 0-765-31422-3 (international trade paperback edition)
EAN 978-0765-31422-2

First Edition: March 2005

Printed in the United States of America

0 9 8 7 6 5 4 3 2 1

To Ed and Kay McVey,
who are saving the world
one kindness at a time

# CONTENTS

# SHADOW OF THE GIANT

# 1

# MANDATE OF HEAVEN

From: Graff%pilgrimage@colmin.gov
To: Soup%battleboys@strategyandplanning.han.gov
Re: Free Vacation Offer

Destination of your choice in the known universe. And . . . we pick you up!

Han Tzu waited until the armored car was completely out of sight before he ventured out into the bicycle-and-pedestrian-packed street. Crowds could make you invisible, but only if you were moving in the same direction, and that's the thing Han Tzu had never really been able to do, not since he came home to China from Battle School.

He always seemed to be moving, not upstream, but crossways. As if he had a completely different map of the world from the one everyone around him was using.

And here he was again, dodging bikes and forward-pressing people on their ten thousand errands in order to get from the doorway of his apartment building to the door of the tiny restaurant across the street.

But it was not as hard as it would have been for most people. Han Tzu had mastered the art of using only his peripheral vision, so his eyes stared straight ahead. Without eye contact, the others on the street could not face him down, could not insist that he yield the right of way. They could only dodge him, as if he were a boulder in the stream.

He put his hand to the door and hesitated. He did not know why he had not been arrested and killed or sent for retraining already, but if he was photographed taking this meeting, then it would be easy to prove that he was a traitor.

Then again, his enemies didn't need evidence to convict—all they needed was the inclination. So he opened the door, listened to the tinkle of the little bell, and walked toward the back of the narrow corridor between booths.

He knew he shouldn't expect Graff himself. For the Minister of Colonization to come to Earth would be news, and Graff avoided news unless it was useful to him, which this would certainly not be. So whom would Graff send? Someone from Battle School, undoubtedly. A teacher? Another student? Someone from Ender's Jeesh? Would this be a reunion?

To his surprise, the man in the last booth sat with his back toward the door, so all Han Tzu could see was his curly steel-grey hair. Not Chinese. And from the color of his ears, not European. The pertinent fact, though, was that he was not facing the door and could not see Han Tzu's approach. However, once Han Tzu sat down, *he* would be facing the door, able to observe the whole room.

That was the smart way to do it—after all, Han Tzu was the one who would recognize trouble if it came in the door, not this foreigner, this stranger. But few operatives on a mission this dangerous would have the brass to turn their backs on the door just because the person they were meeting would be a better observer.

The man did not turn as Han Tzu approached. Was he unobservant, or supremely confident?

"Hello," the man said softly just as Han Tzu came up beside him. "Please sit down."

Han Tzu slid into the booth opposite him and knew that he knew this old man but could not name him.

"Please don't say my name," said the man softly.

"Easy," said Han Tzu. "I don't remember it."

"Oh, yes you do," said the man. "You just don't remember my face. You haven't seen me very often. But the leader of the Jeesh spent a lot of time with me."

Now Han Tzu remembered. Those last weeks in Command School—on Eros, when they thought they were in training but were really leading far-off fleets in the endgame of the war against the Hive Queens. Ender, their commander, had been kept separate from them, but they learned afterward that an old half-Maori cargo-ship captain had been working closely with him. Training him. Goading him. Pretending to be his opponent in simulated games.

Mazer Rackham. The hero who saved the human race from certain destruction in the Second Invasion. Everyone thought he died in the war, but he had been sent out on a meaningless voyage at near-lightspeed, so that relativistic effects would keep him alive so he'd be there for the last battles of the war.

He was ancient history twice over. That time on Eros as a part of Ender's Jeesh seemed like another lifetime. And Mazer Rackham had been the most famous man in the world for decades before that.

Most famous man in the world, but almost nobody knew his face.

"Everyone knows you piloted the first colony ship," said Han Tzu.

"We lied," said Mazer Rackham.

Han Tzu accepted that and waited in silence.

"There is a place for you as head of a colony," said Rackham. "A former Hive world, with mostly Han Chinese colonists and many interesting challenges for a leader. The ship leaves as soon as you board it."

That was the offer. The dream. To be out of the turmoil of Earth, the devastation of China. Instead of waiting to be executed by the angry and feeble Chinese government, instead of watching the Chinese people writhe under the heel of the Muslim conquerors, he could board a beautiful clean starship and let them fling him out into space, to a world where human feet had never stepped, to be the founding leader of a colony that would hold his name in reverence forever. He would marry, have children, and, in all likelihood, be happy.

"How long do I have to decide?" asked Han Tzu.

Rackham glanced at his watch, then looked back at him without answering.

"Not a very long window of opportunity," said Han Tzu.

Rackham shook his head.

"It's a very attractive offer," said Han Tzu.

Rackham nodded.

"But I wasn't born for such happiness," said Han Tzu. "The present government of China has lost the mandate of heaven. If I live through the transition, I might be useful to the new government."

"And that's what you were born for?" asked Rackham.

"They tested me," said Han Tzu, "and I'm a child of war."

Rackham nodded. Then he reached inside his jacket and took out a pen and laid it on the table.

"What's that?" asked Han Tzu.

"The mandate of heaven," said Rackham.

Han Tzu knew then that the pen was a weapon. Because the mandate of heaven was always bestowed in blood and war.

"The items in the cap are extremely delicate," said Rackham. "Practice with round toothpicks."

Then he got up and walked out the back door of the restaurant.

No doubt there was some kind of transport waiting there.

Han Tzu wanted to leap to his feet and run after him so he could be taken out into space and set free of all that lay ahead.

Instead he put his hand over the pen and slid it across the table, then put it into the pocket of his trousers. It was a weapon. Which meant Graff and Rackham expected him to need a personal weapon soon. How soon?

Han Tzu took six toothpicks out of the little dispenser that stood on the table against the wall, beside the soy sauce. Then he got up and went to the toilet.

He pulled the cap off the pen very carefully, so he didn't spill out the four feather-ended poison darts bunched in it. Then he unscrewed the top of the pen. There were four holes there, besides the central shaft that held the tube of ink. The mechanism was cleverly designed to rotate automatically with each discharge. A blow-gun revolver.

He loaded four toothpicks into the four slots. They fit loosely. Then he screwed the pen back together.

The fountain pen writing tip covered the hole where the darts would emerge. When he held the top of the pen in his mouth, the point of the writing tip served as the sighting device. Point and shoot.

Point and *blow*.

He blew.

The toothpick hit the back wall of the bathroom more or less where he was aiming, only a foot lower. Definitely a close-range weapon.

He used up the rest of the toothpicks learning how high to aim in order to hit a target six feet away. The room wasn't large enough for him to practice aiming at anything farther. Then he gathered up the toothpicks, threw them away, and carefully loaded the pen with the real darts, handling them only by the feathered part of the shaft.

Then he flushed the toilet and reentered the restaurant. No one was waiting for him. So he sat down and ordered and ate methodically. No reason to face the crisis of his life with an empty stomach and the food here wasn't bad.

He paid and walked out into the street. He would not go home. If he waited there to be arrested, he would have to deal with any number of low-level thugs who would not be worth wasting a dart on.

Instead, he flagged down a bicycle taxi and headed for the ministry of defense.

The place was as crowded as ever. Pathetically so, thought Han Tzu. There was a reason for so many military bureaucrats a few years ago, when China was conquering Indochina and India, its millions of soldiers spread out to rule over a billion conquered people.

But now, the government had direct control only over Manchuria and the northern part of Han China. Persians and Arabs and Indonesians administered martial law in the great port cities of the south, and large armies of Turks were poised in Inner Mongolia, ready to slice through Chinese defenses at a moment's notice. Another large Chinese army was isolated in Sichuan, forbidden by the government to surrender any portion of their troops, forcing them to sustain a multimillion-man force from the production of that single province. In effect, they were under siege, getting weaker—and more hated by the civilian population—all the time.

There had even been a coup, right after the ceasefire—but it was a sham, a reshuffling of the politicians. Nothing but an excuse for repudiating the terms of the ceasefire.

No one in the military bureaucracy had lost his job. It was the military that had been driving China's new expansionism. It was the military that had failed.

Only Han Tzu had been relieved of his duties and sent home.

They could not forgive him for having named their stupidity for what it was. He had warned them every step of the way. They had ignored every warning. Each time he had shown them a way out of their self-induced dilemmas, they had ignored his offered plans and proceeded to make decisions based on bravado, face-saving, and delusions of Chinese invincibility.

At his last meeting he had left them with no face at all. He had stood there, a very young man in the presence of old men of enormous authority, and called them the fools they were. He laid out exactly why they had failed so miserably. He even told them that they had lost the mandate of heaven—the traditional excuse for a change of dynasty. This was the unforgivable sin, since the present dynasty claimed not to be a dynasty at all, not to be an empire, but rather to be a perfect expression of the will of the people.

What they forgot was that the Chinese people still believed in the mandate of heaven—and knew when a government no longer had it.

Now, as he showed his expired i.d. at the gate of the complex and was admitted without hesitation, he realized that there was only one fathomable reason why they hadn't already arrested him or had him killed:

They didn't dare.

It confirmed that Rackham was right to hand him a four-shot weapon and call it the mandate of heaven. There were forces at work here within the defense department that Han Tzu could not see, waiting in his apartment for someone to decide what to do with him. They had not even cut off his salary. There was panic and confusion in the military and now Han Tzu knew that he was at the center of it. That his silence, his waiting, had actually been a pestle constantly grinding at the mortar of military failure.

He should have known that his *j'accuse* speech would have more effects than merely to humiliate and enrage his "superiors." There were aides standing against the walls listening. And *they* would know that every word that Han Tzu said was true.

For all Han Tzu knew, his death or arrest had already been ordered a dozen times. And the aides who had been given those orders no doubt could prove that they had passed them along. But they would also have passed along the story of Han Tzu, the former Battle Schooler who had been part of Ender's Jeesh. The soldiers ordered to arrest him would have also been told that if Han Tzu had been heeded, China would not have been defeated by the Muslims and their strutting boy-Caliph.

The Muslims won because they had the brains to put *their* member of Ender's Jeesh, Caliph Alai, in charge of their armies—in charge of their whole government, their religion itself.

But the Chinese government had rejected their own Enderman, and now were giving orders for his arrest.

In these conversations, the phrase "mandate of heaven" would certainly have been spoken.

And the soldiers, if they left their quarters at all, seemed unable to locate Han Tzu's apartment.

For all these weeks since the war ended, the leadership must already have come face to face with their own powerlessness. If the soldiers would not follow them on such a simple matter as arresting the political enemy who had shamed them, then they were in grave danger.

That's why Han Tzu's i.d. was accepted at the gate. That's why he was allowed to walk unescorted among the buildings of the defense department complex.

Not *completely* unescorted. For he saw through his peripheral vision that a growing number of soldiers and functionaries were shadowing him, moving among the buildings in paths parallel to his own. For of course the gate guards would have spread the word at once: He's here.

So when he walked up to the entrance of the highest headquarters, he paused at the top step and turned around. Several thousand men and women were already in the space between buildings, and more were coming all the time. Many of them were soldiers under arms.

Han Tzu looked them over, watching as their numbers grew. No one spoke.

He bowed to them.

They bowed back.

Han Tzu turned and entered the building. The guards inside the doors also bowed to him. He bowed to each of them and then proceeded to the stairs leading to the second floor office suites where the highest officers of the military were certainly waiting for him.

Sure enough, he was met on the second floor by a young woman in uniform who bowed and said, "Most respectfully, sir, will you come to the office of the one called Snow Tiger?"

Her voice was devoid of sarcasm, but the name "Snow Tiger" carried its own irony these days. Han Tzu looked at her gravely. "What is your name, soldier?"

"Lieutenant White Lotus," she said.

"Lieutenant," said Han Tzu, "If heaven should bestow its mandate upon the true emperor today, would you serve him?"

"My life will be his," she said.

"And your pistol?"

She bowed deeply.

He bowed to her, then followed her to Snow Tiger's office.

They were all gathered there in the large anteroom—the men who had been present weeks ago when Han Tzu had scorned them for having lost the mandate of heaven. Their eyes were cold now, but he had no friends among these high officers.

Snow Tiger stood in the doorway of his inner office. It was unheard of for him to come out to meet anyone except members of the Politburo, none of whom were present.

"Han Tzu," he said.

Han Tzu bowed slightly. Snow Tiger bowed almost invisibly in return.

"I am happy to see you return to duty after your well-earned vacation," said Snow Tiger.

Han Tzu only stood in the middle of the room, regarding him steadily.

"Please come into my office."

Han Tzu walked slowly toward the open door. He knew that Lieutenant White Lotus stood at the door, watching to make sure that no one raised a hand to harm him.

Through the open door, Han Tzu could see two armed soldiers flanking Snow Tiger's desk. Han Tzu stopped, regarding each of the soldiers in turn. Their faces showed nothing; they did not even look back at him. But he knew that they understood who he was. They had been chosen by Snow Tiger because he trusted them. But he should not have.

Snow Tiger took Han Tzu's pause as an invitation for him to enter the office first. Han Tzu did not follow him inside until Snow Tiger was seated at his desk.

Then Han Tzu entered.

"Please close the door," said Snow Tiger.

Han Tzu turned around and pulled the door all the way open.

Snow Tiger took his disobedience without blinking. What could he do or say without making himself seem pathetic?

Snow Tiger pushed a paper toward Han Tzu. It was an order, giving him command over the army that was slowly starving in Sichuan province. "You have proved your great wisdom many times," said Snow Tiger. "We ask you now to be the salvation of China and lead this great army against our enemy."

Han Tzu did not even bother to answer. A hungry, ill-equipped, demoralized, surrounded army was not going to accomplish miracles. And Han Tzu had no intention of accepting this or any other assignment from Snow Tiger.

"Sir, these are excellent orders," said Han Tzu loudly. He glanced at each of the soldiers standing beside the desk. "Do you see how excellent these orders are?"

Unused to being spoken to directly in such a high-level meeting, one of the soldiers nodded; the other merely shifted uncomfortably.

"I see only one error," said Han Tzu. His voice was loud enough to be heard in the anteroom as well.

Snow Tiger grimaced. "There is no error."

"Let me take my pen and show you," said Han Tzu. He took the pen from his shirt pocket and uncapped it. Then he drew a line through his own name at the top of the paper.

Turning around to face the open door, Han Tzu said, "There is no one in this building with the authority to command me."

It was his announcement that he was taking control of the government, and everyone knew it.

"Shoot him," said Snow Tiger behind him.

Han Tzu turned around, putting the pen to his mouth as he did.

But before he could fire a dart, the soldier who had refused to nod had blown out Snow Tiger's head, covering the other soldier with a smear of blood and brains and bone fragments.

The two soldiers bowed deeply to Han Tzu.

Han Tzu turned back around and strode out into the anteroom. Several of the old generals were heading for the door. But Lieutenant White Lotus had her pistol out and they all froze in place. "Emperor Han Tzu has not given the honorable gentlemen his permission to leave," she said.

Han Tzu spoke to the soldiers behind him. "Please assist the lieutenant in securing this room," he said. "It is my judgment that the officers in this room need time to contemplate upon the question of how China came into her current difficult situation. I would like them to remain in here until each of them has written a complete explanation of how so many mistakes came to be made, and how they think matters should have been conducted."

As Han Tzu expected, the suck-ups immediately went to work, dragging their compatriots back to their places against the walls. "Didn't you hear the emperor's request?" "We will do as you ask, Steward of Heaven." Little good it would do them. Han Tzu already knew perfectly well which officers he would trust to lead the Chinese military.

The irony was that the "great men" who were now humiliated and writing reports on their own mistakes were never the source of those errors. They only believed they were. And the underlings who had really originated the problems saw themselves as merely instruments of their commanders' will. But it was in the nature of underlings to use power recklessly, since blame could always be passed either upward or downward.

Unlike credit, which, like hot air, always rose.

As it will rise to me from now on.

Han Tzu left the offices of the late Snow Tiger. In the corridor, soldiers stood at every door. They had heard the single gunshot, and Han Tzu was pleased to see that they all looked relieved to learn that it was not Han Tzu himself who had been shot.

He turned to one soldier and said, "Please enter the nearest office and telephone for medical attention for the honorable Snow Tiger." To three others, he said, "Please help Lieutenant White Lotus secure the cooperation of the former generals inside this room who have been asked to write reports for me."

As they rushed to obey, Han Tzu gave assignments to the other soldiers and bureaucrats. Some of them would later be purged; others would be elevated. But at this moment, no one even thought of disobeying him. Within only a few minutes he had given orders to have the perimeter of the defense complex sealed. Until he was ready, he wanted no warning going to the Politburo.

But his precaution was in vain. For when he went down the stairs and walked out of the building, he was greeted by a roar from the thousands and thousands of military people who completely surrounded the headquarters building.

"Han Tzu!" they chanted. "Chosen of Heaven!"

There was no chance the noise would not be heard outside the complex. So instead of rounding up the Politburo all at once, he would have to waste time tracking them down as they fled to the countryside or tried to get to the airport or onto the river. But of one thing there could be no doubt: With the new emperor enthusiastically supported by the armed forces, there would be no resistance to his rule by any Chinese, anywhere.

That's what Mazer Rackham and Hyrum Graff had understood when they gave him his choice. Their only miscalculation was how completely the story of Han Tzu's wisdom had swept through the military. He hadn't needed the blowgun after all.

Though if he hadn't had it, would he have had the courage to act as boldly as he did?

One thing Han Tzu did not doubt. If the soldier had not killed Snow Tiger first, Han Tzu would have done it after—and would have killed both soldiers if they had not immediately submitted to his rule.

My hands are clean, but not because I wasn't prepared to bloody them.

As he made his way to the department of Planning and Strategy, where he would make his temporary headquarters, he could not help but ask himself: What if I had taken their initial offer, and fled into space? What would have happened to China then?

And then a more sobering question: What will happen to China *now?*

# 2

# MOTHER

From: HMebane%GeneticTherapy@MayoFlorida.org.us
To: JulianDelphiki%Carlotta@DelphikiConsultations.com
Re: Prognosis

Dear Julian,

I wish I had better news. But yesterday's tests are conclusive. Estrogen therapy has had no effect on the epiphyses. They remain open, even though you definitely do not have any defect in the estrogen receptors on the growth plates of your bones.

As to your second request, of course we will continue to study your DNA, my friend, whether any of your missing embryos are found or not. What was done once can be done again, and Volescu's mistakes may be repeated with some other genetic alteration in the future. But the history of genetic research is fairly consistent. It takes time to map and isolate an unusual sequence and then perform animal experiments in order to determine what each portion of it does and how to counteract its effects.

There is no way to expedite such research. If we had ten thousand working on the problem, they would perform the same experiments in the same order and it would take the same amount of time. Someday we will understand why your astonishing intellect is so incurably linked with uncontrolled growth. Right now, to be candid, it seems to be almost malicious on the part of nature, as if there were some law that the price for the unleashing of human intellect is either autism or giantism.

If only, instead of military training, you had been taught biochemistry so that at your present age you could be up to speed in this field. I have no doubt that you would be more likely to have the kind of insights we need than we of fettered intellect. That is the bitter irony of your condition and your personal history. Even Volescu could not have anticipated the consequence of his alteration of your genes.

I feel like a coward, delivering this information in an email instead of face to face, but you insisted on no delay and a written report. The technical data will, of course, be forwarded to you as the final reports become available.

If only cryogenics had not proven to be such a barren field.

Sincerely,
Howard

As soon as Bob left for his shift as night manager of the grocery store, Randi sat down in front of the screen and started the special on Achilles Flandres over again from the beginning.

It galled her to hear how they slandered him, but by now she was adept at tuning it out. Megalomaniac. Madman. Murderer.

Why couldn't they see him as he really was? A genius like Alexander the Great, who came *this* close to uniting the world and ending war forever.

Now the dogs would fight over the scraps of Achilles's achievements, while his body rested in an obscure grave in some miserable tropical village in Brazil.

And the assassin who had ended Achilles's life, who had thwarted his greatness, *he* was being honored as if there were something heroic about putting a bullet into the eye of an unarmed man. Julian Delphiki. Bean. The tool of the evil Hegemon Peter Wiggin.

Delphiki and Wiggin. Unworthy to be on the same planet with Achilles. And yet they claimed to be his heirs, the rightful rulers of the world.

Well, poor fools, you're the heirs of nothing. Because I know where Achilles's true heir is.

She patted her stomach, though that was a dangerous thing to do, what with her puking at a moment's notice ever since the pregnancy really took hold. She didn't show yet, and when she did, it was a fifty-fifty chance whether Bob would throw her out or keep her and accept the child as his own. Bob knew he couldn't father children—they'd had enough tests—and there was no point in pretending since he'd ask for a DNA test and then he'd know anyway.

And she had sworn never to tell that she had received an implant after all. She would have to pretend that she had had an affair with somebody and wanted to keep the baby. Bob would *not* like that at all. But she knew that her baby's life depended on keeping the secret.

The man who interviewed her at the fertility clinic had been adamant about that. "It doesn't matter whom you tell, Randi. The enemies of the great man know that this embryo exists. They'll be searching for it. They'll be watching all the women in the world who give birth within a certain timeframe. And any rumor that a baby was implanted rather than naturally conceived will bring them like hounds. Their resources are unlimited. They will spare no effort in their search. And when they find a woman that they even think *might* be the mother of his child, they will kill her, just in case."

"But there must be hundreds. Thousands of women who have babies implanted," Randi protested.

"Are you a Christian?" asked the man. "You've heard of the slaughter of the innocents? However many you have to kill, it's worth it to these monsters, as long as it means they can prevent the birth of this child."

Randi watched the stills of Achilles during his Battle School days and soon after, during his time at the asylum where his enemies had him confined after it became clear that he was a better commander than their precious Ender Wiggin. She had read it on the nets in many places, the fact that Ender Wiggin actually used plans devised by Achilles in order to beat the Buggers. They could glorify their phony little hero all they wanted—but everyone knew it was only because he was Peter Wiggin's little brother that Ender was given all the credit.

It was Achilles who had saved the world. And Achilles who had fathered the baby she had been chosen to bear.

Randi's only regret was that she could not be the biological mother as well, and that the child could not have been naturally conceived. But she knew that the bride of Achilles must have been very carefully chosen—a woman who could contribute the right genes so as not to dilute his brilliance and goodness and creativity and drive.

But *they* knew about the woman Achilles loved, and if she had been pregnant when he died, they would have torn the womb out of her so she could lie there in agony and watch them burn the fetus before her eyes.

So to protect the mother and the baby, Achilles had arranged for their embryo to be taken secretly and implanted in the womb of a woman who could be trusted to take the child to term and give him a good home and raise him with full awareness of his vast potential. To teach him secretly who he really was and whose cause he served, so he could grow up to fulfil his father's cruelly-blocked destiny. It was a sacred trust, and Randi was worthy of it.

Bob was not. It was that simple. Randi had always known that she married beneath herself. Bob was a good provider, but he hadn't the imagination to understand anything more important than making a living and planning his next fishing trip. She could just imagine how he would respond if she told him that not only was she pregnant, but the baby was not even hers.

Already she had found several places on the web where people were searching for "lost" or "kidnapped" embryos. She knew—the man who spoke to her had warned her—that these were likely to originate from Achilles's enemies, trolling for information that would lead them to . . . to her.

She wondered if maybe the very act of searching for people searching for embryos would alert them. The search companies claimed that no government had access to their databases, but it was possible that the International Fleet was intercepting all the messages and monitoring all the searches. People said that the I.F. was really under the control of the United States government, that America's isolationism was a façade and it ran everything through the I.F. Then there were the people who said that it was the other way around—the U.S. was isolationist because that was the way the I.F. wanted it, since most of the space technology they depended on was developed and built in the U.S.

It couldn't be an accident that Peter the Hegemon was American himself.

She would stop searching for information about kidnapped embryos. It was all lies and traps and tricks. She knew she would seem paranoid to anyone else, but that's only because they didn't know what she knew. There really were monsters in the world, and those who kept secrets from them had to live with constant vigilance.

There on the screen was that terrible picture. They showed it over and over again: Achilles's poor broken body lying on the floor in the Hegemon's palace, looking so peaceful, not a wound on his body. Some on the nets said that Delphiki didn't shoot him through the eye at all; that if he had, Achilles's face would have been powder-burned and there would have been an exit wound and blood all over.

No, Delphiki and Wiggin imprisoned Achilles and faked some kind of phony standoff with the police, pretending that Achilles was taking hostages or something, so they'd have an excuse for killing him. But in fact they gave him a lethal injection. Or poisoned his food. Or infected him with a hideous disease so he died writhing on the floor in agony while Delphiki and Wiggin looked on.

Like Richard III murdering those poor princes in the tower.

But when my son is born, Randi told herself, then all these false histories will be destroyed. The liars will be eliminated, and so will their lies.

Then this footage will be used in a *true* story. My son will see to that. No one will ever even hear the lies they're telling now. And Achilles will be known as the great one, even greater than the son who will have completed his life's work.

And I will be remembered and honored as the woman who sheltered him and gave him birth and raised him up to rule the world.

All I have to do to accomplish that is: nothing.

Nothing that calls attention to me. Nothing that makes me unusual or strange.

Yet the one thing she couldn't bear to do was *nothing*. Just to sit here, watching the television, worrying, fretting—it had to be harmful for the baby, to have so much adrenalin coursing through her system.

It was the waiting that was making her crazy. Not waiting for the baby—that was natural and she would love every day of her pregnancy.

It was waiting for her life to change. Waiting . . . for Bob.

Why should she wait for Bob?

She got up from the couch, switched off the television, went into the bedroom, and started packing her clothing and other things into cardboard boxes. She emptied out Bob's obsessive financial records in order to empty the boxes—let him amuse himself by sorting them out later.

Only after she had packed and taped up the fourth box did it occur to her that the *normal* pattern would have been to tell him about the baby and then make *him* move out.

But she didn't want a connection with him. Didn't want any dispute about paternity. She just wanted to be gone. Out of his ordinary, meaningless life, out of this pointless town.

Of course she couldn't just disappear. Then she'd be a missing person. She'd be added to databases. Someone would be alerted.

So she took her boxes of clothing and a few favorite pots, pans, and recipe books and loaded them into the car that she had owned before she married Bob and that was still in her name alone. Then she spent half an hour writing different versions of a letter to Bob explaining that she didn't love him anymore and was leaving and didn't want him to look for her.

No. Nothing in writing. Nothing that can be reported to anyone.

She got in the car and drove to the grocery store. On the way in from the parking lot she took a cart that someone had left blocking a parking space and pushed it into the store. Helping keep the parking lot clear of abandoned carts proved that she wasn't vindictive. She was a civilized person who wanted to help Bob do well in his business and his ordinary, ordinary, ordinary life. It would *help* him not to have such an extraordinary woman and child in that life.

He was out on the floor and instead of waiting in his office, she went in search of him. She found him supervising the unloading of a truck that was late because of a breakdown on the highway, making sure that the frozen foods were at a low enough temperature to be safely offloaded and shelved.

"Can you wait just a minute?" he said. "I know it's important or you wouldn't have come down here, but . . ."

"Oh, Bob, it won't take more than a second." She leaned close to him. "I'm pregnant and it's not yours."

Being a two-part message, it didn't entirely register right away. For a moment he looked happy. Then his face started to turn red.

She leaned in close again. "Don't worry, though. I'm leaving you. I'll let you know where to mail the divorce papers. Now, you get back to work."

She started to walk away. "Randi," he called after her.

"Not your fault, Bob!" she called over her shoulder. "Nothing was your fault. You're a great guy."

She felt liberated as she walked back through the store. Her mood was so generous and expansive that she bought a little container of lip balm and a bottle of water. The tiny amount of profit from the sale would be her last contribution to Bob's life.

Then she got into the car and drove south, because that way was a right turn coming out of the parking lot, and traffic was too heavy to wait for a chance to go left. She'd drive wherever the currents of the traffic led her. She wouldn't try to hide from anybody. She'd let Bob know where she was as soon as she decided she was there, and she'd divorce him in a perfectly ordinary way. But she wouldn't bump into anyone she knew or anyone who knew her. She would become effectively invisible, not like someone *trying* to hide, but like someone who had nothing to hide at all but who never became important to anyone.

Except to her beloved son.

# 3

# COUP

From: JulianDelphiki%milcom@hegemon.gov
To: Volescu%levers@plasticgenome.edu
Re: Why keep hiding when you don't have to?

Look, if we wanted you dead or punished, don't you think it would have happened already? Your protector is gone and there's not a country on Earth that will protect you if we lay out the facts of your "achievements."

What you did, you did. Now help us find our children, wherever you've hidden them.

Peter Wiggin had brought Petra Arkanian with him because she knew Caliph Alai. They had both been in Ender's Jeesh together. And it was Alai who had sheltered her and Bean in the weeks before the Muslim invasion of China—or liberation of Asia, depending on which propaganda mill you shopped at.

But now it seemed that having Petra with him meant nothing at all.

Nobody in Damascus acted as if it even mattered that the Hegemon had come like a supplicant to see the Caliph. Not that Peter had arrived with any publicity—this was a private visit, with him and Petra passing themselves off as a tourist couple.

Complete with bickering. Because Petra had no patience with him. Everything he did and said and even *thought* was wrong. And last night, when he finally demanded, "Tell me what you really hate about me, Petra, instead of pretending it's all this trivial stuff."

Her answer had been devastating: "Because the only difference I ever saw between you and Achilles was that you let others do your killing for you."

It was so patently unfair. Peter had devoted himself to trying to avoid war.

At least now he knew why she was so furious at him. When Bean went into the besieged Hegemony compound to face Achilles alone, Peter understood that Bean was putting his own life on the line and that it was extremely unlikely that Achilles would give him what he had promised—the embryos of Bean's and Petra's children that had been stolen from a hospital soon after in vitro fertilization.

So when Bean put a .22 slug through Achilles's eye and let it bounce around a few dozen times inside his skull, the only person who absolutely got everything he needed was Peter himself. He got the Hegemony compound back; he got all the hostages safely returned; he even regained his tiny army trained by Bean and led by Suriyawong, who had turned out to be loyal after all.

While Bean and Petra did not get their babies, and Bean was dying, Peter couldn't do a thing to help either of them except provide office space and computers for them to conduct their search. He also used all his connections to get them whatever cooperation he could from the nations where they needed access to records.

Right after Achilles's death, Petra had simply been relieved. Her irritation with Peter had developed—or merely resurfaced—in the weeks after, as she saw him trying to reestablish the prestige of the office of

Hegemon and try to put together a coalition. She began making snotty little comments about Peter playing in his "geopolitical sandbox" and "outstrutting the heads of state."

He should have expected that actually having her travel along with him would only make it worse. Especially because he wasn't following her advice about anything.

"You can't just show up," she told him.

"I have no choice."

"It's disrespectful. As if you think you can drop in on the Caliph. It's treating him like a servant."

"That's why I brought *you*," Peter patiently explained. "So you can see him and explain that the only way this can happen is if it's a secret meeting."

"But he already told me and Bean that we couldn't have access to him like we used to. We're infidels. He's Caliph."

"The Pope sees non-Catholics all the time. He sees *me*."

"The Pope isn't Muslim," said Petra.

"Just be patient," said Peter. "Alai knows we're here. Eventually he'll decide to see me."

"Eventually? I'm pregnant, Mr. Hegemon, and my husband is dying in a big way, ha ha ha, and you're wasting some of the time we have together and that pisses me off."

"I invited you to come. I didn't compel you."

"It's a good thing you didn't try."

But now it was out. In the open. Clear at last. Of course she was really irritated at all the things she complained about. But underneath it all was resentment about how Peter had let Bean do his killing for him.

"Petra," said Peter. "I'm not a soldier."

"Neither is Bean!"

"Bean is the finest military mind alive," said Peter.

"So why isn't he Hegemon?"

"Because he doesn't want to be."

"And you do. And *that's* why I hate you, since you asked."

"You know why I wanted this office and what I'm trying to do with it. You've read my Locke essays."

"I also read your Demosthenes essays."

"Those also needed to be written. But I intend to govern as Locke."

"You govern nothing. The only reason you even have your little army is because Bean and Suriyawong created it and decided to let you have the use of it. You only have your precious compound and all your staff because Bean killed Achilles and gave it back to you. And now you're back to putting on your little show of importance, but you know what? Nobody's fooled. You're not even as powerful as the Pope. He's got the Vatican and a billion Catholics. You've got nothing but what my husband gave you."

Peter didn't think this was quite accurate—he had labored for years to build up his network of contacts, and he had kept the office of Hegemon from being abolished. Over the years he had made it mean something. He had saved Haiti from chaos. Several small nations owed their independence or freedom to his diplomatic and, yes, military intervention.

But certainly he was on the verge of losing it all to Achilles—because of his own stupid mistake. A mistake that Bean and Petra had warned him about before he made it. A mistake that Bean had rectified only at a grave risk.

"Petra," said Peter, "you're right. I owe everything to you and Bean. But that doesn't change the fact that whatever you think of me and whatever you think of the office of Hegemon, I hold that office, and I'm trying to use it to avoid another bloody war."

"You're trying to use your office to make your office into 'dictator of the world.' Unless you can figure out a way to extend your reach out to the colonies and become 'dictator of the known universe.' "

"We don't actually have any colonies yet," said Peter. "The ships are all still in transit and will be until we're all dead. But by the time they arrive, I'd like them to send their ansible messages back home to an Earth that is united under a single democratic government."

"It's the democratic part I missed," said Petra. "Who elected you?"

"Since I don't have any actual authority over anybody, Petra, how can it possibly matter if I'm not legitimately authorized?"

"You argue like a debater," she said. "You don't actually have to have an idea, you just have to have a seemingly clever refutation."

"And you argue like a nine-year-old," said Peter. "Sticking your fingers in your ears and going 'La la la' and 'same to you.' "

Petra looked like she wanted to slap him. Instead she put her fingers in her ears and said, "Same to you" and "La la la."

He did not laugh. Instead he reached out a hand, intending to pull her arm away from her ear. But she whirled around and kicked his hand so hard that he thought she might have broken his wrist. As it was, he staggered and stumbled over the corner of the bed in his hotel room and ended up on his butt on the floor.

"There's the Hegemon of Earth," said Petra.

"Where's your camera? Don't you want this to be public?"

"If I wanted to destroy you, you'd be destroyed."

"Petra, I didn't send Bean into that compound. Bean sent himself."

"You let him go."

"Yes I did, and in any event I was proven right."

"But you didn't know he'd live. I was carrying his baby and you sent him in to *die*."

"Nobody sends Bean anywhere," said Peter, "and you know it."

She whirled away from him and stalked out of the room. She would have slammed the door, but the pneumatics prevented it.

He had seen, though. The tears in her eyes.

She didn't hate Peter. She wanted to hate him. But what she really was furious about was that her husband was dying and she had agreed to this mission because she knew it would be important. If it worked, it would be important. But it wasn't working. It probably wouldn't work.

Peter knew that. But he also knew that he had to talk to Caliph Alai, and he had to do it now if the conversation was to have any good effect. If possible, he'd like to have the conversation without risking the prestige of the office of Hegemon. But the longer they delayed, the greater the likelihood of word of his trip to Damascus getting out. And then if Alai rebuffed him, the humiliation would be public, and the office of Hegemon would be greatly diminished.

So Petra's judgment of him was obviously unfair. If all he cared about was his own authority, he wouldn't be here.

And she was clever enough to know that. *She* got into Battle School, didn't she? *She* was the only girl among Ender's Jeesh. That certified her as his superior—at least in the area of strategy and leadership. Surely she must see that he was putting the goal of preventing a bloody war above his own career.

As soon as he thought of this, he heard her voice inside his head, saying, "Oh, isn't that fine and noble of you, to put the lives of hundreds of thousands of soldiers ahead of your own indelible place in history. Do you think you get a prize for that?" Or else she'd say, "The only reason I'm along is specifically so you can avoid risking anything." Or else, "You've always been bold as a risk-taker—when the stakes are high enough and your own life isn't on the line."

This is great, Peter, he thought. You don't even need her in the room with you and you can still carry on an argument with her.

How did Bean stand her? No doubt she didn't treat him like this.

No. It was impossible to imagine that being nasty was something she could switch on and off. Bean *had* to have seen this side of her. And yet he stayed with her.

And loved her. Peter wondered what it would be like, to have Petra look at him the way she looked at Bean.

Then he corrected himself at once. Wonderful to have *a woman* look at him the way Petra looked at Bean. The last thing he wanted was a lovelorn Petra making googly eyes at him.

The telephone rang.

The voice made sure it was "Peter Jones" and then said, "Five in the morning, be downstairs outside the north lobby doors." Click.

Well, what brought *that* on? Something in Petra's and his argument? Peter had swept the room for bugs, but that didn't mean they couldn't have some low-tech device like somebody in the next room with his ear pressed against the wall.

What did we say to make them let me see the Caliph?

Maybe it was what he said about avoiding another bloody war.

Or perhaps it was because they heard him admit to Petra that maybe he didn't have any legitimate authority.

What if they recorded that? What if it suddenly surfaced on the web?

Then it would happen, and he'd do his best to recover from the blow, and either he'd succeed or he'd fail. No point fretting about it now. Somebody was meeting him at the north door of the lobby tomorrow morning before daylight. Maybe they'd lead him to Alai, and maybe he'd achieve what he needed to achieve, save all that he needed to save.

He toyed with the idea of not telling Petra about the meeting. After all, she had no pertinent office at all. She had no particular right to be at the meeting, especially after their quarrel tonight.

Don't be spiteful and petty, Peter told himself. One spiteful act brings too much pleasure—it just makes you want to do another, and another. And sooner each time.

So he picked up the phone and on the seventh ring she picked it up.

"I'm not going to apologize," she said curtly.

"Good," he said. "Because I don't want some smarmy I'm-sorry-you-got-so-upset fake apology. What I want is for you to join me at five A.M. at the north door of the lobby."

"What for?"

"I don't know," said Peter. "I'm just passing along what I was just told on the telephone."

"He's going to let us see him?"

"Or he's sending thugs to escort us back to the airport. How can I possibly know? You're the one who's his friend. You tell *me* what he's planning."

"I haven't the slightest idea," said Petra. "It's not like Alai and I were ever *close*. And are you sure they want me to come to the actual meeting? There are plenty of Muslims who would be horrified at the thought of an unveiled married woman speaking face to face with a man—even the Caliph."

"I don't know what they want," said Peter. "*I* want you at the meeting."

---

They were ushered into a closed van and driven along a route that Peter assumed was convoluted and deceptively long. For all he knew, the Caliph's headquarters was next door to their hotel. But Alai's people knew that without the Caliph there was no unity, and without unity Islam had no strength, so they were taking no chances on letting outsiders know where the Caliph lived.

They were driven far enough that they might be outside Damascus. When they emerged from the van, it was not in daylight, it was indoors . . . or underground. Even the porticoed garden into which they were ushered was artificially lighted, and the sound of running and trickling and falling water masked any faint noises that might have seeped in from outside and hinted where they were.

Alai did not so much greet them as notice their presence as he walked in the garden. He did not even face them, but sat a few meters away, facing a fountain, and began to speak.

"I have no desire to humiliate you, Peter Wiggin," he said. "You should not have come."

"I appreciate your letting me speak with you at all," Peter answered.

"Wisdom said that I should announce to the world that the Hegemon had come to see the Caliph, and the Caliph refused to see him. But I told Wisdom to be patient, and let Folly be my guide today in this garden."

"Petra and I are here to—"

"Petra is here," said Alai, "because you thought her presence might get you in to see me, and you needed a witness that I would be reluctant to kill, and because you want her to be your ally after her husband is dead."

Peter did not let himself glance at Petra to see how she took this sally from Alai. She knew the man; Peter did not. She would interpret his words as she saw fit, and nothing he could see in her face right now would help him understand anything. It would only weaken him to show he cared.

"I'm here to offer my help," said Peter.

"I command armies that rule over more than half the population of the world," said Alai. "I have united Muslim nations from Morocco to Indonesia, and liberated the oppressed peoples in between."

"It's the difference between 'conquered' and 'liberated' that I wanted to talk about."

"So you came to rebuke me, not to help after all," said Alai.

"I see I'm wasting my time," said Peter. "If we can't speak together without petty debate, then you are past receiving help."

"Help?" said Alai. "One of my advisers said to me, when I told them I wanted to see you, 'How many soldiers does this Hegemon have?' "

"How many divisions has the Pope?" quoted Peter.

"More than the Hegemon has," said Alai, "if the Pope should ask for them. As the old dead United Nations found out long ago, religion always has more warriors than some vague international abstraction."

Peter realized then that Alai was not speaking to him. He was speaking past him. This was not a private conversation after all.

"I do not intend to be disrespectful to the Caliph," said Peter. "I have seen the majesty of your achievement and the generosity of spirit with which you have dealt with your enemies."

Alai visibly relaxed. They were now playing the same game. Peter had finally understood the rules. "What is to be gained from humiliating those who believe they stand outside the power of God?" asked Alai. "God will show them his power in his own good time, and until then we are wise to be kind."

Alai was speaking as the true believers around him required him to speak—always asserting the primacy of the Caliphate over all non-Muslim powers.

"The dangers I came to speak of," said Peter, "will not ever come from me or because of the small influence I have in the world. Though I was not chosen by God, and there are few who listen to me, I also seek, as you seek, the peace and happiness of the children of God on Earth."

Now was the time, if Alai was completely the captive of his supporters, for him to rant about how it was blasphemous for an infidel like Peter to invoke the name of God or pretend that there could be peace before all the world was under the rule of the Caliphate.

Instead Alai said, "I listen to all men, but obey only God."

"There was a day when Islam was hated and feared throughout the world," said Peter. "That era ended long ago, before either of us were born, but your enemies are reviving those old stories."

"Those old lies, you mean," said Alai.

"The fact that no man can make the Hajj in his own skin and live," said Peter, "suggests that not all the stories are lies. In the name of Islam terrible weapons were acquired and in the name of Islam they were used to destroy the most sacred place on Earth."

"It is not destroyed," said Alai. "It is protected."

"It's so radioactive that nothing can live within a hundred kilometers," said Peter. "And you know what the explosion did to Al-hajar Al-aswad."

"The stone was not sacred in itself," said Alai, "and Muslims never worshipped it. We only used it as a marker to remember the holy covenant between God and his true followers. Now its molecules are powdered and spread over the whole Earth, as a blessing to the righteous and a curse to the wicked, while we who follow Islam still remember where it was, and what it marked, and bow toward that place when we pray."

It was a sermon he had surely said many times before.

"Muslims suffered more than anyone in those dark days," said Peter. "But that is not what most people remember. They remember bombs that killed innocent women and children, and fanatical self-murderers who hated any freedom except the freedom to obey the very narrowest interpretation of Shari'ah."

He could see Alai stiffen. "I make no judgment myself," Peter immediately said. "I was not alive then. But in India and China and Thailand and Vietnam, there are people who fear that the soldiers of Islam did not come as liberators, but as conquerors. That they'll be arrogant in victory. That the Caliphate will never allow freedom to the people who welcomed him and aided him in overcoming the Chinese conquerors."

"We do not force Islam on any nation," said Alai, "and those who claim otherwise are liars. We ask them only to open their doors to the teachers of Islam, so the people can choose."

"Forgive my confusion, then," said Peter. "The people of the world see that open door, and notice that no one passes through it except in one direction. Once a nation has chosen Islam, then the people are never allowed to choose anything else."

"I hope I do not hear the echo of the Crusades in your voice."

The Crusades, thought Peter, that old bugbear. So Alai really has joined himself to the rhetoric of fanaticism. "I only report to you what is being said among those who are seeking to ally against you in war," said Peter. "That war is what I hope to avoid. What those old terrorists tried, and failed, to achieve—a worldwide war between Islam and everyone else—may now be almost upon us."

"The people of God are not afraid of the outcome of such a war," said Alai.

"It's the process of the war that I hope to avoid," said Peter. "Surely the Caliph also seeks to avoid needless bloodshed."

"All who die are at the mercy of God," said Alai. "Death is not the thing to fear most in life, since it comes to all."

"If that's how you feel about the carnage of war," said Peter, "then I've wasted your time." Peter leaned forward, preparing to rise to his feet.

Petra put her hand on his thigh, pressing down, urging him to remain seated. But Peter had had no intention of leaving.

"But," said Alai.

Peter waited.

"But God desires the willing obedience of his children, not their terror."

It was the statement Peter had been hoping for.

"Then the murders in India, the massacres—"

"There have been no massacres."

"The *rumors* of massacre," said Peter, "which seem to be supported by smuggled vids and eyewitness accounts and aerial photographs of the alleged killing fields—I am relieved that such things would not be the policy of the Caliphate."

"If someone has slain innocents for no other crime than believing in the idols of Hinduism and Buddhism, then such a murderer would be no Muslim."

"What the people of India wonder—"

"You do not speak for the people of any place except a small compound in Ribeirão Preto," said Alai.

"What my informants in India tell me that the people of India wonder is whether the Caliph intends to repudiate and punish such murderers or merely pretend they didn't happen? Because if they cannot trust the Caliph to control what is done in the name of Allah, then they will defend themselves."

"By piling stones in the road?" asked Alai. "We are not the Chinese, to be frightened by stories of a 'Great Wall of India.' "

"The Caliph now controls a population that has far more non-Muslims than Muslims," said Peter.

"So far," said Alai.

"The question is whether the proportion of Muslims will increase because of teaching, or because of the slaughter and oppression of unbelievers?"

For the first time, Alai turned his head, and then his body, to face them. But it was not Peter he looked at. He only had eyes for Petra.

"Don't you know me?" he said to her.

Peter wisely did not answer. His words were doing their work, and now it was time for Petra to do what he had brought her to do.

"Yes," she said.

"Then tell him," said Alai.

"No," she said.

Alai sat in wounded silence.

"Because I don't know whether the voice I hear in this garden is the voice of Alai or the voice of the men who put him into office and control who may or may not speak to him."

"It is the voice of the Caliph," said Alai.

"I've read history," said Petra, "and so have you. The Sultans and Caliphs were rarely anything but holy figureheads, when they allowed their servants to keep them within walls. Come out into the world, Alai, and see for yourself the bloody work that's being done in your name."

They heard footsteps, loud ones, many footsteps, and soldiers trotted out of concealment. Within moments, rough hands held Petra and were dragging her away. Peter did not raise a hand to interfere. He only faced Alai, staring at him, demanding silently that he show who ruled in his house.

"Stop," said Alai. Not loudly, but clearly.

"No woman speaks to the Caliph like that!" shouted a man who was behind Peter. Peter did not turn. It was enough to know that the man had spoken in Common, not in Arabic, and that his accent bore the marks of a superb education.

"Let go of her," Alai said to the soldiers, ignoring the man who had shouted.

There was no hesitation. The soldiers let go of Petra. At once she came back to Peter's side and sat down. Peter also sat down. They were spectators now.

The man who had shouted, dressed in the flowing robes of an imitation sheik, strode up to Alai. "She uttered a *command* to the Caliph! A challenge! Her tongue must be cut out of her mouth."

Alai remained seated. He said nothing.

The man turned to the soldiers. "Take her!" he said.

The soldiers began to move.

"Stop," said Alai. Quietly but clearly.

The soldiers stopped. They looked miserable and confused.

"He doesn't know what he's saying," the man said to the soldiers. "Take the girl and then we'll discuss it later."

"Do not move except at my command," said Alai.

The soldiers did not move.

The man faced Alai again. "You're making a mistake," he said.

"The soldiers of the Caliph are witnesses," said Alai. "The Caliph has been threatened. The Caliph's orders have been countermanded. There is a man in this garden who thinks he has more power in Islam than the Caliph. So the words of this infidel girl are correct. The Caliph is a holy figurehead, who allows his servants to keep him within walls. The Caliph is a prisoner and others rule Islam in his name."

Peter could see in the man's face that he now realized that the Caliph was not just a boy who could be manipulated.

"Don't go down this road," he said.

"The soldiers of the Caliph are witnesses," said Alai, "that this man has given a command to the Caliph. A challenge. But unlike the girl, this man has ordered armed soldiers, in the presence of the Caliph, to disobey the Caliph. The Caliph can *hear* any words without harm, but when soldiers are ordered to disobey him, it does not require an imam to explain that treason and blasphemy are present here."

"If you move against me," the man said, "then the others—"

"The soldiers of the Caliph are witnesses," said Alai, "that this man is part of a conspiracy against the Caliph. There are 'others.' "

One soldier came forward and laid a hand on the man's arm.

He shook it off.

Alai smiled at the soldier.

The soldier took the man's arm again, but not gently. Other soldiers stepped forward. One took the man's other arm. The rest faced Alai, waiting for orders.

"We have seen today that one man of my council thinks he is the master of the Caliph. Therefore, any soldier of Islam who truly wishes to serve the Caliph will take every member of the council into custody and hold them in silence until the Caliph has decided which of them can be trusted and which must be discarded from the service of God. Move quickly, my friends, before the ones who are spying on this conversation have time to escape."

The man wrenched one hand free and in a moment held a wicked-looking knife.

But Alai's hand was already firmly gripping his wrist.

"My old friend," said Alai, "I know that you were not raising that weapon against your Caliph. But suicide is a grave and terrible sin. I refuse to allow you to meet God with your own blood on your hands." With a twist of his hand, Alai made the man groan with pain. The knife clattered on the flagstones.

"Soldiers," said Alai. "Make me safe. Meanwhile, I will continue my conversation with these visitors, who are under the protection of my hospitality."

Two soldiers dragged the prisoner away, while the others took off at a run.

"You have work to do," said Peter.

"I've just done it," said Alai. He turned to Petra. "Thank you for seeing what I needed."

"Being a provocateur comes naturally to me," she said.

"I hope we've been helpful."

"Everything you said has been heard," said Alai. "And I assure you that when it's actually in my power to control the armies of Islam, they will behave as true Muslims, and not as barbarian conquerors. Meanwhile, however, I'm afraid that bloodshed is likely, and I believe you will be safest here with me in this garden for the next half hour or so."

"Hot Soup has just taken over in China," said Petra.

"So I've heard."

"And he's taking the title of emperor," she added.

"Back to the good old days."

"A new dynasty in Beijing now faces the restored Caliphate in Damascus," said Petra. "It would be a terrible thing, for members of the Jeesh to have to choose up sides and wage war against each other. Surely that's not what Battle School was ever meant to accomplish."

"Battle School?" said Alai. "They may have identified us, but we already were who we were before they laid a hand on us. Do you think that without Battle School, I could not be where I am, or Han Tzu where he is? Look at Peter Wiggin—*he* didn't go to Battle School, but he got himself appointed Hegemon."

"An empty title," said Peter.

"It was when you got it," said Alai. "Just as my title was until two minutes ago. But when you sit in the chair and wear the hat, some people don't understand that it's just a play and start obeying you as if you had real power. And then you *have* real power. Neh?"

"Eh," said Petra.

Peter smiled. "I'm not your enemy, Alai," he said.

"You're not my friend, either," said Alai. But then he smiled. "The question is whether you'll turn out to be a friend to humanity. Or whether I will." He turned back to Petra. "And so much depends on what your husband chooses to do before he dies."

Petra nodded gravely. "He'd prefer to do nothing except enjoy the months or perhaps years he'll have with me and our child."

"God willing," said Alai, "that's all he'll be required to do."

A soldier came pounding across the flagstones. "Sir, the compound is secure and none of the council have escaped."

"I'm happy to hear that," said Alai.

"Three councilmen are dead, sir," said the soldier. "It could not be helped."

"I'm sure that's the truth," said Alai. "They are now in God's hands. The rest are in mine, and now I must try to do what God would have me do. Now, my son, will you take these two friends of the Caliph safely back to their hotel? Our conversation is finished, and I wish them to be free to leave Damascus, unhindered and unrecognized. No one will speak of their presence in this garden on this day."

"Yes, my Caliph," said the soldier. He bowed, and then turned to Peter and Petra. "Will you come with me, friends of the Caliph?"

"Thank you," Petra said. "The Caliph is blessed with true servants in this house."

The man did not acknowledge her praise. "This way," he said to Peter.

As they followed him back to the enclosed van, Peter wondered whether he might have unconsciously planned for the events that happened here today, or whether it was just dumb luck.

Or whether Petra and Alai planned it, and Peter was nothing more than their pawn, thinking foolishly that he was making his own decisions and conducting his own strategy.

Or are we, as the Muslims believe, only acting out the script of God?

Not likely. Any God worth believing in could make up a better plan than the mess the world was in now.

In my childhood I set my hand to improving the world, and for a while I succeeded. I stopped a war through words I wrote on the nets, when people didn't know who I was. But now I have the empty title of Hegemon. Wars are swirling back and forth across swathes of the Earth like a reaper's scythe, vast populations are seething under the whips of new oppressors, and I am powerless to change a thing.

# 4

# BARGAIN

From: PeterWiggin%private@hegemon.gov
To: SacredCause%OneMan@FreeThai.org
Re: Suriyawong's actions concerning Achilles Flandres

Dear Ambul,

At all times during Achilles Flandres's infiltration of the Hegemony, Suriyawong acted as my agent inside Flandres's growing organization. It was at my instructions that he pretended to be Flandres's staunch ally, and that was why, at the crucial moment when Julian Delphiki faced the monster, Suriyawong and his elite soldiers acted for the good of all humankind—including Thailand—and made possible the destruction of the man who, more than any other, was responsible for the defeat and occupation of Thailand.

This is the "public story," as you pointed out. Now I point out that in this case the public story also happens to be the complete truth.

Like you, Suriyawong is a Battle School graduate. China's new Emperor and the Muslim Caliph are both Battle School graduates. But they are two of those chosen to take part in my brother Ender's famous Jeesh. Even if you discount their actual brilliance as military commanders, the public perception of their powers is at the level of magic. This will affect the morale of your soldiers as surely as of theirs.

How do you suppose you will keep Thailand free if you reject Suriyawong? He is no threat to your leadership; he will be your most valuable tool against your enemies.

Sincerely,
Peter, Hegemon

Bean stooped to pass through the doorway. He wasn't actually tall enough to bang his head. But it had happened often enough, in other doorways that once would have given him plenty of room, that now he was overcautious. He didn't know what to do with his hands, either. They seemed too big for any job he might need them for. Pens were like toothpicks; his finger filled the trigger guard of many a pistol. Soon he'd have to butter his finger to get it out, as if the pistol were a too-tight ring.

And his joints ached. And his head hurt sometimes like it was going to split in two. Because, in fact, it was trying to do exactly that. The soft spot on the top of his head could not seem to expand fast enough to make room for his growing brain.

The doctors loved that part. To find out what it did to the mental function of an adult to have the brain grow. Did it disrupt memory? Or merely add to capacity? Bean submitted to their questions and measurements and scans and bloodlettings because he might not find all his children before he died, and anything they learned from studying him might help them.

But at times like this he felt nothing but despair. There was no help for him, and none for them, either. He would not find them. And if he did, he could not help them.

What difference has my life made? I killed one man. He was a monster, but I had it in my power to kill him at least once before, and failed to do it. So don't I share in the responsibility for what he did in the intervening years? The deaths, the misery.

Including Petra's suffering when she was his captive. Including our own suffering over the children he stole from us.

And yet he went on searching, using every contact he could think of, every search engine on the nets, every program he could devise for manipulating the public records in order to be ready to identify which births were of his children, implanted in surrogates.

For of that much he was certain. Achilles and Volescu had never intended to give the embryos back to him and Petra. That promise had only been a lure. A man of less malice than Achilles might have killed the embryos—as he pretended to do when he broke test tubes during their last confrontation in Ribeirão Preto. But for Achilles, killing itself was never a pleasure. He killed when he thought it was necessary. When he actually wanted to make someone suffer, he made sure the suffering lingered as long as possible.

Bean's and Petra's children would be born to mothers unknown to them, probably scattered throughout the world by Volescu.

But Achilles had done his work well. Volescu's travels were completely erased from the public record. And there was nothing about the man to make him particularly memorable. They could show his picture to a million airline workers and another million cab drivers throughout the world and half of them might remember seeing a man who looked "like that" but none of them would be sure of anything and Volescu's path could not be retraced.

And when Bean had tried to appeal to Volescu's lingering shreds of decency—which he hoped existed, against all evidence—the man had gone underground and now all Bean could hope for was that somebody, some agency somewhere, would find him, arrest him, and hold him long enough for Bean to . . .

To what? Torture him? Threaten him? Bribe him? What could possibly induce Volescu to tell him what he needed to know?

Now the International Fleet had sent him some officer to give him "important information." What could they possibly know? The I.F. was forbidden to operate on the surface of Earth. Even if they had agents who had discovered Volescu's whereabouts, why would they risk exposing their own illegal activities just to help Bean find his babies? They had made a big deal about how loyal they were to the Battle School graduates, especially to Ender's Jeesh, but he doubted it went *that* far. Money, that's what they offered. All the Battle School grads had a nice pension. They could go home like Cincinnatus and farm for the rest of their lives, without even having to worry about the weather or the seasons or the harvest. They could grow weeds and still prosper.

Instead, I stupidly allowed children of my deformed and self-destructive genes to be created *in vitro* and now Volescu has planted them in foreign wombs and I must find them before he and people like him can exploit them and use them up and then watch them die of giantism, like me, before they turn twenty.

Volescu knows. He would never leave it to chance. Because he still imagined himself to be a scientist. He would want to gather data about the children. To him, it was all one big experiment, with the added inconvenience of being illegal and based on stolen embryos. To Volescu, those embryos belonged to him by right. To him, Bean was nothing but the experiment that got away. Anything he produced was part of Volescu's long-term study.

An old man sat at the table in the conference room. It took Bean a moment to decide whether his skin was naturally dark or merely weathered into a barnwood color and texture. Both, probably.

I know him, thought Bean. Mazer Rackham. The man who saved humanity in the Second Bugger Invasion. Who should have been dead many decades ago, but who surfaced long enough to train Ender himself for the last campaign.

"They send *you* to Earth?"

"I'm retired," said Rackham.

"So am I," said Bean. "So is Ender. When does *he* come to Earth?"

Rackham shook his head. "Too late to be bitter about that," he said. "If Ender had been here, do you think there's any chance he would be both alive and free?"

Rackham had a point. Back when Achilles was arranging for all of Ender's Jeesh to be kidnapped, the greatest prize of all would have been Ender himself. And even if Ender had evaded capture—as Bean had done—how long before someone else tried to control him or exploit him in order to achieve some imperial ambition? With Ender, being an American as he was, maybe the United States would have stirred from its torpor and now, instead of China and the Muslim world being the main players in the great game, America would be flexing its muscles again and then the world really would be in turmoil.

Ender would have hated that. Hated himself for being part of it. It really was better that Graff had arranged to send him off on the first colony ship to a former Bugger world. Right now, each second of Ender's life aboard the starship was a week to Bean. While Ender read a paragraph of a book, a million babies would be born on Earth, a million old people and soldiers and sick people and pedestrians and drivers would die and humanity would move forward another small step in its evolution into a starfaring species.

Starfaring species. That was Graff's program.

"You're not here for the fleet, then," said Bean. "You're here for Colonel Graff."

"For the Minister of Colonization?" Rackham nodded gravely. "Informally and unofficially, yes. To inform you of an offer."

"Graff has nothing that I want. Before any starship could arrive on a colony world, I'd be dead."

"You'd undoubtedly be an . . . interesting choice to head a colony," said Rackham. "But as you said, your term in office would be too brief to be effective. No, it's a different kind of offer."

"The only things I want, you don't have."

"Once upon a time, I believe, you wanted nothing more than survival."

"It's not within your power to offer me."

"Yes it is," said Rackham.

"Oh, from the vast medical research facilities of the International Fleet there comes a cure for a condition that is suffered by only one person on Earth?"

"Not at all," said Rackham. "The cure will have to come from others. What we offer you is the ability to wait until it's ready. We offer you a starship, and lightspeed, and an ansible so you can be told when to come home."

Precisely the "gift" they gave Rackham himself, when they thought they might need him to command all the fleets when they arrived at the various Bugger worlds. The chance of survival rang inside him like the tolling of a great bell. He couldn't help it. If there was anything that had ever driven him, it was that hunger to survive. But how could he trust them?

"And in return, what do you want from me?"

"Can't this be part of your retirement package from the fleet?"

Rackham was good at keeping a straight face, but Bean knew he couldn't be serious. "When I come back, there's going to be some poor young soldier I can train?"

"You're not a teacher," said Rackham.

"Neither were you."

Rackham shrugged. "So we become whatever we need to be. We're offering you life. We'll continue to fund research on your condition."

"What, using my children as your guinea pigs?"

"We'll try to find them, of course. We'll try to cure them."

"But they won't get their own starships?"

"Bean," said Rackham. "How many trillions of dollars do you think your genes are worth?"

"To me," said Bean, "They're worth more than all the money in the world."

"I don't think you could pay even the interest on that loan."

"So I don't have as high a credit rating as I hoped."

"Bean, take this offer seriously. While there's still time. Acceleration is hard on the heart. You have to go while you're still healthy enough to survive the voyage. As it is, we'll be cutting it rather fine, don't you think? A couple of years to accelerate, and at the end, a couple more to decelerate. Who gives you four years?"

"Nobody," said Bean. "And you're forgetting. I have to come home. That's four more years. It's already far too late."

Rackham smiled. "Don't you think we've taken that into account?"

"What, you've figured out a way to turn while traveling at lightspeed?"

"Even light bends."

"Light is a wave."

"So are you, when you're traveling that fast."

"Neither of us is a physicist."

"But the people who planned our new generation of messenger ship are," said Rackham.

"How can the I.F. afford to build new ships?" asked Bean. "Your funding comes from Earth and the emergency is over. The only reason the nations of Earth even pay your salaries and continue to supply you is because they're buying your neutrality."

Rackham smiled.

"Somebody's paying you to keep developing new ships," said Bean.

"Speculation is pointless."

"There's only one nation that could afford to do that, and it's the one nation that could never keep it secret."

"So it's not possible," said Rackham.

"Yet you're promising me a kind of ship that couldn't exist."

"You go through acceleration in a compensatory gravity field, so there's no additional strain on your heart. That lets us accelerate in a week instead of two years."

"And if the gravity fails?"

"Then you're torn to dust in an instant. But it doesn't fail. We've tested it."

"So messengers can go from world to world without losing more than a couple of weeks of their lives."

"Of their *own* lives," said Rackham. "But when we send someone out on such a voyage, thirty or fifty lightyears, everyone they ever knew is dead long before they come back. Volunteers are few."

Everyone they ever knew. If he got on this starship, he'd leave Petra behind and never see her again.

Was he heartless enough for that?

Not heartless at all. He could still feel the pain of losing Sister Carlotta, the woman who saved him from the streets of Rotterdam and watched over for him for years, until Achilles finally murdered her.

"Can I take Petra with me?"

"Would she go?"

"Not without our children," said Bean.

"Then I suggest you keep searching," said Rackham. "Because even though the new technology buys you a bit more time, it's not forever. Your body imposes a deadline that we can't put off."

"And you'll let me bring Petra, if we find our children."

"If she'll go," said Rackham.

"She will," said Bean. "We have no roots in this world, except our children."

"Already they're children in your imagination," said Rackham.

Bean only smiled. He knew how Catholic it made him sound, but that's how it felt to him and Petra both.

"We ask only one thing," said Rackham.

Bean laughed. "I knew it."

"As long as you're waiting around anyway, searching for your children," said Rackham. "We'd like you to help Peter unite the world under the office of the Hegemon."

Bean was so astonished he stopped laughing. "So the fleet intends to meddle in earthside affairs."

"We aren't meddling at all," said Rackham. "You are."

"Peter doesn't listen to me. If he did, he would have let me kill Achilles back in China when we first had the chance. Peter decided to 'rescue' him instead."

"Maybe he's learned from his mistake."

"He thinks he learned from it," said Bean, "but Peter is Peter. It wasn't a mistake, it's who he is. He can't listen to anyone else if he thinks he has a better plan. And he always thinks he has a better plan."

"Nevertheless."

"I can't help Peter because Peter won't be helped."

"He took Petra along on his visit to Alai."

"His top secret visit that the I.F. couldn't possibly know about."

"We keep track of our alumni."

"Is that how you pay for your new-model starships? Alumni donations?"

"Our best graduates are still too young to be at the really high salary levels."

"I don't know. You have two heads of state."

"Doesn't it intrigue you, Bean, to imagine what the history of the world would have been like if there had been two Alexanders at the same time?"

"Alai and Hot Soup?" asked Bean. "It'll all boil down to which of them has the most resources. Alai has most at the moment, but China has staying power."

"But then you add to the two Alexanders a Joan of Arc here and there, and a couple of Julius Caesars, maybe an Attila, and . . ."

"You see Petra as Joan of Arc?" asked Bean.

"She could be."

"And what am I?"

"Why, Genghis Khan of course, if you choose to be," said Rackham.

"He has such a bad reputation."

"He doesn't deserve it. His contemporaries knew he was a man of might who exercised his power lightly upon those who obeyed him."

"I don't want power. I'm not your Genghis."

"No," said Rackham. "That's the problem. It all depends on who has the disease of ambition. When Graff took you into Battle School, it was because your will to survive seemed to do the same job as ambition. But now it doesn't."

"Peter's your Genghis," said Bean. "That's why you want me to help him."

"He might be," said Rackham. "And you're the only one who *can* help him. Anybody else would make him feel threatened. But you . . ."

"Because I'm going to die."

"Or leave. Either way, he can have the use of you, as he thinks, and then be rid of you."

"It's not as he thinks. It's what you want. I'm a book in a lending library. You lend me to Peter for a while. He turns me in, then you send me out on another chase after some dream or other. You and Graff, you still think you're in charge of the human race, don't you?"

Rackham looked off into the distance. "It's a job that, once you take it on, it's hard to let go. One day out in space I saw something no one else could see, and I fired a missile and killed a Hive Queen and we won that war. From then on, the human race was my responsibility."

"Even if you're no longer the best qualified to lead it."

"I didn't say I was the leader. Only that I have the responsibility. To do whatever it takes. Whatever I can. And what I can do is this: I can try to persuade the most brilliant military mind on Earth to help unify the nations under the leadership of the only man who has the will and the wit to hold them all together."

"At what price? Peter's not a great fan of democracy."

"We're not asking for democracy," said Rackham. "Not at first. Not until the power of nations is broken. You have to tame the horse before you can let it have its head."

"And you say you're just the servant of humanity," said Bean. "Yet you want to put a bridle and saddle on the human race, and let Peter ride."

"Yes," said Rackham. "Because humanity isn't a horse. Humanity is a breeding ground for ambition, for territorial competitors, for nations that do battle, and if the nations break down, then tribes, clans, households. We were bred for war, it's in our genes, and the only way to stop the bloodshed is to give one man the power to subdue all the others. All we can hope for is that it be a decent enough man that the peace will be better than the wars, and last longer."

"And you think Peter's the man."

"He has the ambition you lack."

"And the humanity?"

Rackham shook his head. "Don't you know by now how human you are?"

Bean wasn't going to go down that road. "Why don't you and Graff just leave the human race alone? Let them go on building empires and tearing them down."

"Because the Hive Queens aren't the only aliens out there."

Bean sat up.

"No, no, we haven't seen any, we have no evidence. But think about it. As long as humans seemed to be unique, we could live out our species history as we always had. But now we know that it's possible for intelligent life to evolve twice, and in very different ways. If twice, then why not three times? Or four? There's nothing special about our corner of the galaxy. The Hive Queens were remarkably close to us. There could be thousands of intelligent species in our galaxy alone. And not all of them as nice as we are."

"So you're dispersing us."

"As far and wide as we can. Planting our seed in every soil."

"And for that you want Earth united."

"We want Earth to stop wasting its resources on war, and spend them on colonizing world after world, and then trading among them so that the whole species can profit from what each one learns and achieves and becomes. It's basic economics. And history. And evolution. And science. Disperse. Vary. Discover. Publish. Explore."

"Yeah, yeah, I get it," said Bean. "How noble of you. Who's paying for all this now?"

"Bean," said Rackham. "You don't expect me to tell you, and I don't expect you to have to ask."

Bean knew. It was America. Big sleepy do-nothing America. Burned out from trying to police the world back in the twenty-first century, disgusted at the way their efforts earned them nothing but hatred and resentment, they declared victory and went home. They kept the strongest military in the world and closed their doors to immigration.

And when the Buggers came, it was American military might that finally blew up those first exploratory ships that scoured the surface of some of the best agricultural land in China, killing millions. It was America that mostly funded and directed the construction of the interplanetary warships that resisted the Second Invasion long enough for New Zealander Mazer Rackham to find the Hive Queen's vulnerability and destroy the enemy.

It was America that was secretly funding the I.F. now, developing new ships. Getting its hand into the business of interstellar trade at a time when no other nation on Earth could even attempt to compete.

"And how will it be in *their* interest for the world to be united, except under their leadership?"

Rackham smiled. "So now you know how deep our game has to be."

Bean smiled back. So Graff had sold his colony program to the Americans—probably on the basis of future trade and a probable American monopoly. And in the meantime, he was backing Peter in the hope that he could unite the world under one government. Which would mean, eventually, a showdown between America and the Hegemon.

"And when the day comes," said Bean, "when America expects the

I.F., which it's been paying for and researching for, to come to its aid against a powerful Hegemon, what will the I.F. do?"

"What did Suriyawong do when Achilles ordered him to kill you?"

"Gave him a knife and told him to defend himself." Bean nodded. "But will the I.F. obey you? If you're counting on the reputation of Mazer Rackham, remember that hardly anybody knows you're alive."

"I'm counting on the I.F. living up to the code of honor that every soldier has drummed into him from the start. No interference on Earth."

"Even as you break that code yourself."

"We're not interfering," said Rackham. "Not with troops or ships. Just a little information here and there. A dollop of money. And a little, tiny bit of recruitment. Help us, Bean. While you're still on Earth. The minute you're ready to go, we'll send you, no delays. But while you're here . . ."

"What if I don't believe Peter's as decent a man as you think he is?"

"He's better than Achilles."

"So was Augustus," said Bean. "But he laid the foundation for Nero and Caligula."

"He laid a foundation that survived Caligula and Nero and lasted for a millennium and a half, in one form or another."

"And you think that's Peter?"

"We do," said Rackham. "I do."

"As long as you understand that Peter won't do a thing I say, won't listen to me or anyone, and will go on making idiotic mistakes that I can't prevent, then . . . yes. I'll help him, as much as he'll let me."

"That's all we ask."

"But I'll still give my first priority to finding my children."

"How about this," said Rackham. "How about if we tell you where Volescu is?"

"You know?"

"He's in one of our safe houses," said Rackham.

"He accepted the protection of the I.F.?"

"He thinks it's part of Achilles's old network."

"*Is* it?"

"Somebody had to take over his assets."

"Somebody could only do that if they knew where his assets were."

"Who do you think maintains all the communications satellites?" asked Rackham.

"So the I.F. is spying on Earth."

"Just as a mother spies on her children at play in the yard."

"Good to know you're looking out for us, Mummy."

Rackham leaned foward. "Bean, we make our plans, but we know we might fail. Ultimately, it all comes down to this. We've seen human beings at their best, and we think our species is worth saving."

"Even if you have to have the help of non-humans like me."

"Bean, when I spoke of human beings at their best, whom do you think I was talking about?"

"Ender Wiggin," said Bean.

"And Julian Delphiki," said Rackham. "The other little boy we trusted to save the world."

Bean shook his head and stood up. "Not so little now," said Bean. "And dying. But I'll take your offer because it gives me a hope for my little family. And apart from that, I have no hope at all. Tell me where Volescu is, and I'll go see him."

"You'll have to secure him yourself," said Rackham. "We can't have I.F. agents involved."

"Give me the address and I'll do the rest."

Bean ducked again to leave the room. And he was trembling as he walked through the park, back toward his office in the Hegemony compound. Huge armies prepared to clash, in a struggle for supremacy. And off to one side, not even on the surface of Earth, there were a handful of men who intended to turn those armies to their own purposes.

They were Archimedes, preparing to move the Earth because they finally had a lever big enough.

I'm the lever.

And I'm not as big as they think I am. Not as big as I seem. It can't be done.

Yet it might just be worth doing.

So I'll let them use me to try to pry the world of men loose from its age-old path of competition and war.

And I'll use them to try to save my life and the lives of my children who share my disease.

And the chance of both projects succeeding is so slim that the odds are much better of the Earth being hit by a disastrously huge meteor first.

Then again, they probably already have a plan to deal with a meteor strike. They probably have a plan for everything. Even a plan they can turn to if . . . when . . . I fail.

# 5

# SHIVA

From: Figurehead%Parent@hegemon.gov
To: PeterWiggin%Private@hegemon.gov
Password: ********
Re: Speaking as a mother

After all these years of posing as the Madonna in your little Pietà, it occurs to me that I might whisper something in your oh-so busy ear:

Ever since Achilles's little kidnapping venture, the not-so-secret weapon in everyone's arsenal is whatever array of Battle School graduates they're able to acquire, keep, and deploy. Now it's even worse. Alai is Caliph in fact as well as name. Han Tzu is emperor of China. Virlomi is . . . what, a goddess? That's what I hear, coming out of India.

Now they will go to war against each other.

What are YOU doing? Betting on the winner and choosing up sides?

Quite apart from the fact that many of these children were Ender's friends and fellow soldiers, the whole human race owes them our very survival. We took away their childhood. When do they get a life they can call their own?

Peter, I've read history. Men like Genghis and Alexander were deprived of a normal childhood and absolutely focused on war and you know what? It deformed them. They were unhappy all the days of their lives. Alexander didn't know who he was when he stopped conquering people. If he stopped moving forward, slaughtering all the way, he died.

So how about setting these children free? Have you given any thought to that? Talk to Graff. He'll listen to you. Give these children an out. A chance. A life.

If for no other reason than because they're Andrew's friends. They're *like* Andrew. They didn't choose themselves for Battle School.

You, on the other hand, didn't go to Battle School. You volunteered to save the world. So you have to stay and see it through.

Your loving and ever-supportive mother

A woman's face appeared on the screen. She was dressed in the simple work-stained clothing of a Hindu peasant woman. But she bore herself like a lady of the highest caste—a concept that still had meaning, despite the long-ago banning of all outward markers of caste.

Peter did not know her. But Petra did. "It's Virlomi."

"All this time," said Bean, "she hasn't shown her face. Till now."

"I wonder," said Petra, "how many thousands of people in India already know her face."

"Let's listen," said Peter. He moused the PLAY button.

"No one is faithful to God who has no choice. That is why Hindus are truly faithful, for they may choose not to be Hindus and no harm comes to them.

"And that is why there are no true Muslims in the world, because they may not choose to cease to be Muslims. If a Muslim tries to become a Hindu or a Christian or even a simple unbeliever, some fanatical Muslim will kill him."

Pictures were flashed on the screen of beheaded bodies. Well-known images, but still potent as propaganda.

"Islam is a religion that has no believers," she said. "Only people who are compelled to call themselves Muslims and live as Muslims under fear of death."

Standard pictures of Muslims en masse, bowing down to pray—the very footage that was often used to show the piety of Muslim populations. But now, framed as Virlomi had framed it, the images seemed to be those of puppets, acting in unison out of fear.

Her face reappeared on the screen. "Caliph Alai: We welcomed your armies as liberators. We sabotaged and spied and blocked Chinese supply routes to help you defeat our enemy. But your followers seem to think they conquered India rather than liberating us. You did not conquer India. You will never conquer India."

Now there was new footage: Ragged Indian peasants bearing modern Chinese arms, marching like old-fashioned soldiers.

"We have no need of false Muslim soldiers. We have no need of false Muslim teachers. We will never accept any Muslim presence on Indian soil until Islam becomes a true religion and allows people the freedom to choose *not* to be Muslim, without any penalty."

Virlomi's face again. "Do you think your mighty armies can conquer India? Then you do not know the power of God, for God will always help those who defend their homeland. Any Muslim that we kill on Indian soil will go straight to hell, for he does not serve God, he serves Shaitan. Any imam who tells you otherwise is a liar and a shaitan himself. If you obey him, you will be condemned. Be true Muslims and go home to your families and live at peace, and let us live in peace with our own families, in our own land."

Her face looked calm and sweet as she uttered these condemnations and threats. Now she smiled. Peter thought she must have practiced the smile for hours, for days in front of a mirror, because she absolutely looked like a god, even though he had never seen a god and did not know how one should look. She was radiant. Was it a trick of the light?

"My blessing upon India. I bless the Great Wall of India. I bless the soldiers who fight for India. I bless the farmers who feed India. I bless the women who give birth to India and raise India to manhood and womanhood. I bless the great powers of the Earth who unite to help us regain our stolen freedom. I bless the Indians of Pakistan who have embraced the false religion of Islam: Make your religion true by going home and letting us choose not to be Muslim. Then we will live at peace with you, and God will bless you.

"My blessing above all blessings on Caliph Alai. O noble of heart, prove that I am wrong. Make Islam a true religion by giving freedom to all Muslims. Only when Muslims can choose *not* to be Muslims are there any Muslims on Earth. Set your people free to serve God instead of being captives of fear and hate. If you are not the conqueror of India, then you will be the friend of India. But if you intend to be the conqueror of India, then you will make yourself nothing in the eyes of God."

Great tears rolled out of her eyes and down her cheeks. This was all done in a single take, so the tears were real enough. What an actress, thought Peter.

"Oh, Caliph Alai, how I long to embrace you as a brother and friend. Why do your servants make war on me?"

She made a strange series of movements with her hands, then drew three fingers backhanded across her forehead.

"I am Mother India," she said. "Fight for me, my children."

Her image remained on the screen as all motion stopped.

Peter looked from Bean to Petra and back again. "So my question is simple enough. Is she insane? Does she really believe she's a god? And will this work?"

"What was that business at the end, with the fingers on her forehead?" asked Bean.

"She was drawing the mark of Shiva the Destroyer on her forehead," said Peter. "It was a call to war." He sighed. "They'll be destroyed."

"Who?" said Petra.

"Her followers," said Peter.

"Alai won't let them," said Bean.

"If he tries to stop them, he'll fail," said Peter. "Which may be what she wants."

"No," said Petra. "Don't you see? The Muslim occupation of India absolutely counts on supplying their armies from Indian produce and Indian revenues. But Shiva will be there first. They'll destroy their own crops rather than let the Muslims have it."

"Then they'll die in famine," said Peter.

"And they'll absorb many bullets," said Petra, "and beheaded Hindu bodies will litter the ground. But then the Muslims will run out of bullets and they'll discover that they can't get more because the roads are blocked. And for every Hindu they killed, there will be ten more to overwhelm them with their bare hands. Virlomi understands her nation. Her people."

"And all of this you understand," said Peter, "because you were a prisoner in India for a few months?"

"India has never been led into war by a god," said Petra. "India has never gone to war with perfect unity."

"A guerrilla war," insisted Peter.

"You'll see," said Petra. "Virlomi knows what she's doing."

"She wasn't even part of Ender's Jeesh," said Peter. "Alai was. So he's smarter, right?"

Petra and Bean looked at each other.

"Peter, it's not about brains," said Bean. "It's about playing the hand you're dealt."

"Virlomi has the stronger hand," said Petra.

"I don't see it," said Peter. "What am I missing?"

"Han Tzu won't just sit there while the Muslim armies try to subdue India. The Muslim supply lines either run across the vast Asian desert or through India or by sea from Indonesia. If the Indian supply lines are cut, how long can Alai hold his armies there in numbers sufficient to keep Han Tzu contained?"

Peter nodded. "So you think Alai will run out of food and bullets before Virlomi runs out of Indians."

"I think," said Bean, "that what we just saw was a marriage proposal."

Peter laughed. But since Bean and Petra weren't laughing . . . "What are you talking about?"

"Virlomi *is* India," said Bean. "She just said so. And Han Tzu *is* China. And Alai *is* Islam. So will it be India and China against the world, or Islam and India against the world? Who can sell that marriage to their own people? Which throne will sit beside the throne of India? Whichever one it is, that's more than half the population of the world, united."

Peter closed his eyes. "So we don't want either to happen."

"Don't worry," said Bean. "Whichever happens, it won't last."

"You're not always right," said Peter. "You can't see that far ahead."

Bean shrugged. "Doesn't matter to me. I'll be dead before it all shakes out."

Petra growled and stood up and paced.

"I don't know what to do," said Peter. "I tried to talk to Alai, and all I did was provoke a coup. Or rather, Petra did that." He couldn't hide his annoyance. "I wanted him to control his people, but they're out of control. They're roasting cows in the streets of Madras and Bombay and then killing the Hindus who riot. They're beheading any Indian that someone accuses of being a lapsed Muslim—or even the *grandchild* of lapsed Muslims. Do I just sit here and watch the world collapse into war?"

Petra snapped at him. "I thought that was part of your plan. To make yourself seem indispensable."

"I don't have a great plan," said Peter. "I just . . . respond. And I'm asking you about it instead of figuring things out on my own because the last time I ignored your advice it was a disaster. But now I find out you don't actually have any advice. Just predictions and assumptions."

"I'm sorry," said Bean. "It didn't cross my mind you were asking for advice."

"Well, I am," said Peter.

"Here's my advice," said Bean. "Your goal isn't to avoid war."

"Yes it is," said Peter.

Bean rolled his eyes. "So much for listening."

"I'm listening," said Peter.

"Your goal is to establish a new order in which war between nations becomes *impossible*. But to get to that utopian place, there's going to have to *be* enough war that people will *know* the thing they're desperate to avoid."

"I'm not going to encourage war," said Peter. "It would discredit me completely as a peacemaker. I got this job because I'm Locke!"

"If you stop objecting and listen," said Petra, "you'll eventually get Bean's advice."

"I'm the great strategist, after all," said Bean with a wry smile. "And the tallest man in the Hegemony compound."

"I'm listening," said Peter again.

"You're right, you can't encourage war. But you also can't afford to try to stop wars that can't be stopped. If you're seen to try and *fail*, you're weak. The reason Locke was able to broker a peace between the Warsaw Pact and the West was that neither side wanted war. America wanted to stay home and make money, and Russia didn't want to run the risk of provoking I.F. intervention. You can only negotiate peace when both sides want it—badly enough to give up something in order to get it. Right now, nobody wants to negotiate. The Indians can't—they're occupied, and their occupiers don't believe they pose a threat. The Chinese can't—it's politically impossible for a Chinese ruler to settle for any boundary short of the borders of Han China. And Alai can't because his own people are so flushed with victory that they can't see any reason to give anything up."

"So I do nothing."

"You organize relief efforts for the famine in India," said Petra.

"The famine that Virlomi is going to cause."

Petra shrugged.

"So I wait until everybody's sick of war," said Peter.

"No," said Bean. "You wait until the exact moment when peace is possible. Wait too long, and the bitterness will run too deep for peace."

"How do I know when the time is right?"

"Beats me," said Bean.

"You're the smart ones," said Peter. "Everyone says so."

"Stop the humble act," said Petra. "You understand perfectly what we're saying. Why are you so angry? Any plan we make now will crumble the first time somebody makes a move that isn't on our script."

Peter realized that it wasn't them he was angry at. It was his mother and her ridiculous letter. As if he had the power to "rescue" the Caliph and the Chinese emperor and this brand new Indian goddess and "set them free" when they had all clearly maneuvered themselves into the positions they were in.

"I just don't see," said Peter, "how I can turn any of this to my advantage."

"You just have to watch and keep meddling," said Bean, "until you see a place where you can insert yourself."

"That's what I've *been* doing for years."

"And very well, too," said Petra. "Can we go now?"

"Go!" said Peter. "Get your evil scientist. I'll save the world while you're out."

"We expect no less," said Bean. "Just remember that you asked for the job. We didn't."

They got up. They started for the door.

"Wait a minute," said Peter.

They waited.

"I just realized something," Peter said.

They waited some more.

"You don't care."

Bean looked at Petra. Petra looked at Bean. "What do you mean we don't care?" said Bean.

"How can you say that?" said Petra. "It's war, it's death, it's the fate of the world."

"You're treating it like . . . like I was asking advice about a cruise. Which cruise line to go on. Or . . . or a poem, whether the rhymes are good."

Again they looked at each other.

"And when you look at each other like that," said Peter. "It's like you're laughing, only you're too polite to show it."

"We're not polite people," said Petra. "Especially not Julian."

"No, that's right, it's not that you're polite. It's that you're so much wrapped up in each other that you don't *have* to laugh, it's like you already laughed and only you two know about it."

"This is all so interesting, Peter," said Bean. "Can we go now?"

"He's right," said Petra. "We aren't involved. Like he is, I mean. But it's not that we don't care, Peter. We care even more than you do. We just don't want to get involved in *doing* anything about it because. . . ."

They looked at each other again and then, without saying another word, they started to leave.

"Because you're married," said Peter. "Because you're pregnant. Because you're going to have a baby."

"Babies," said Bean. "And we'd like to get on with trying to find out what happened to them."

"You've resigned from the human race is what you've done," said

Peter. "Because you invented marriage and children, suddenly you don't have to be part of anything."

"Opposite," said Petra. "We've *joined* the human race. We're like most people. Our life together is everything. Our children are everything. The rest is—we do what we have to. Anything to protect our children. And then beyond that, what we have to. But it doesn't matter to us as much. I'm sorry that bothers you."

"It doesn't bother me," said Peter. "It did before I understood what I was seeing. Now I think . . . sure, it's normal. I think my parents are like that. I think that's why I thought they were stupid. Because they didn't seem to care about the outside world. All they cared about was each other and us kids."

"I think the therapy is proceeding nicely," said Bean. "Now say three Hail Marys while we get on with our limited domestic concerns, which involve attack helicopters and getting to Volescu before he makes another change of address and identity."

And they were gone.

Peter seethed. They thought they knew something that nobody else knew. They thought they knew what life was about. But they could only *have* a life like that because people like Peter—and Han Tzu and Alai and that wacko self-deifying Virlomi—actually concentrated on important matters and tried to make the world a better place.

Then Peter remembered that Bean had said almost exactly what his mother said. That Peter chose to be Hegemon, and now he had to work it out on his own.

Like a kid who tries out for the school play but he doesn't like the part he's been given. Only if he backs out now the show can't go on because he has no understudy. So he's got to stick it out.

Got to figure out how to save the world, now that he's got himself made Hegemon.

Here's what I want to have happen, thought Peter. I want every damn Battle School graduate off Earth. *They* are the complicating factor in every country. Mother wants them to have a life? Me too—a nice long life on another planet.

But to get them offplanet would require getting the cooperation of Graff. And Peter had the sneaking suspicion that Graff didn't actually want Peter to be an effective, powerful Hegemon. Why should Graff accept the Battle School kids into colony ships? They'd be a disruptive force in any colony they were in.

What about this? A colony of nothing *but* Battle School grads. If they bred true, they'd be the smartest military minds in the galaxy.

Then they'd come home and take over Earth.

OK, not that.

Still, it was the seed of a good idea. In the eyes of the people, it was the Battle School that won the war against the Buggers. They all wanted their armies to be led by Battle Schoolers. Which was why the Battle Schoolers were virtually the slaves of their nations' military.

So I'll do as Mother suggested. I'll set them free.

Then they can all marry like Bean and Petra and live happily ever after while other people—responsible people—did the hard work of running the world.

---

In India, the response to Virlomi's message was immediate and fierce. That very night, in a dozen incidents scattered across India, Muslim soldiers committed acts of provocation—or, as they saw it, retaliation or defiance to Virlomi's blasphemous, outrageous accusation. Thereby, of course, proving those accusations in the eyes of many.

But it wasn't riots they faced this time. It was an implacable mob determined to destroy them no matter what the cost. It was Shiva. So yes, the streets were littered with the dead bodies of Hindu civilians. But the Muslim soldiers' bodies could not be found. Or at least, could not be reassembled.

Reports of the bloodshed flowed into Virlomi's mobile headquarters. Including plenty of video. She had a selected version out on the web within hours. Lots of pictures of Muslims committing acts of provocation, and then firing on the rioters. No footage of human waves swarming over the machine-gun-firing Muslim soldiers and tearing them to pieces. What the world would *see* was Muslims offending Hindu religion and then massacring civilians. They would only hear about the fact that among the Muslim soldiers, there were no survivors.

---

Bean and Petra boarded attack helicopters and headed out across the ocean to Africa. Bean had heard from Rackham and knew where Volescu was.

# 6
# EVOLUTION

From: CrazyTom%WackoMack@sandhurst.england.gov
To: Magic%Legume@IComeAnon.com
Forwarded and Posted by IcomeAnon
Encrypted using code ********
Decrypted using code ***********
Re: England and Europe

I hope you're still using this address, now that you're official and not hiding from Mr. Tendon anymore. I don't think this should go through channels.

I keep getting these feelers from Wiggin. I think HE thinks he's got some special affinity for members of the Jeesh, just because he's Ender's brother. Does he? I know he's got his fingers in everything—the items the Hegemony seems to know before we do are sometimes quite amazing—but does he have his fingers in us?

He's asked me for an assessment of the European willingness to surrender sovereignty to a world government. Given that the whole history of the past two hundred years consists of Europe flirting with a real European government, and always backing away, I wonder if the question comes from an idiot child or a deep thinker who knows more than I do.

But if you think his question is a legitimate one, then let me say that surrendering sovereignty to any existing world or regional body is laughable. Only little countries like Benelux or Denmark or Slovenia are eager to join. It's like communes—people with nothing are always willing to share. Even though Europe now speaks a version of English as its native tongue (except a few diehard enclaves) we are as far from unity as ever.

Which is not to say that under the right pressure, at the right time, each proud nation of Europe might not trade sovereignty for safety.

Tom

It would have to be Fortress Rwanda, of course. The Switzerland of Africa, they called it sometimes—but it only maintained its independence and neutrality because meter for meter, it was probably the most fortified nation on Earth.

They could never have fought their way into Rwandan airspace. But a chatty phone call from Peter to Felix Starman, the prime minister, won them a safe passage for two Hegemony jet choppers and twenty soldiers—along with uploads of detailed maps of the medical center where Volescu was operating.

Under another name, of course. For Rwanda had been one of the places where Achilles maintained safe houses and spy cells. What Volescu could not have known was that Peter's computer experts had been able to enter Achilles's clandestine computer network through Suriyawong's computer, and cell by cell, Achilles's organization had either been coopted, subverted, or destroyed.

Volescu was depending on a Rwandan cell that had been reported to the Rwandan government. Felix Starman had chosen to continue to operate the cell through intermediaries, so the members of the cell did not realize that they were actually working for the Rwandan government.

So it was no small thing for Starman—who insisted that his self-chosen name should be translated, so that everyone was aware of the rather odd image he wished to convey—to give up this asset. While Bean and Petra took Volescu, the Rwandan police would be arresting all the other members of Achilles's organization. They even promised that Hegemony experts could monitor the Rwandan deconstruction of the Achillean computers.

The beat-beat-beat of chopper blades was as good as a police siren when it came to announcing their approach, so they set down a kilometer away from the medical center. Four soldiers on each chopper were equipped with slimline motorcycles, and they took off to secure all the vehicle exit points. The rest advanced through the yards and parking lots of houses, apartment buildings, and small businesses.

Since the entire population of Rwanda was trained as soldiers, they knew enough to stay indoors as they watched the dark-green-clad soldiers of the Hegemony jog cross-lots, from cover to cover. They might try to telephone the government to find out what was happening, but cellphones were getting a "we're making your service better, please have patience" message and landlines were hearing that "all circuits are busy."

Petra was pregnant enough now that she didn't jog along with the troops. And Bean was so distinctively large that he, too, remained in the choppers with the pilots. But Bean had trained these men and had no doubt of their ability. Besides, Suriyawong, still trying to rehabilitate himself even though Bean had assured him that he had his full trust, was eager to show that he could fulfil the mission perfectly without Bean's direct supervision.

So it was only fifteen minutes before Suriyawong texted them "fa," which either meant *fait accompli* or the fourth note of the musical scale, depending on what mood Bean was in. This time when he saw the message he sang it out, and the choppers rose into the air.

They came down in the parking lot of the medical complex. As befitted a rich country like Rwanda, it was state of the art; but the architecture was designed to make the place feel homelike to its patients. So it looked for all the world like a village, with every room that did not need a controlled environment open to whatever breezes blew.

Volescu was being held in the climate-controlled lab where he was arrested. He nodded gravely to Bean and Petra when they came inside. "How nice to see you again," he said.

"Was anything you told us true?" asked Petra. Her voice was calm, but she wasn't going to pretend that pleasantries were in order.

Volescu gave a little smile and shrug. "Doing what the boy wanted seemed to be a good idea at the time. He promised me . . . this."

"A place to conduct illegal research?" asked Bean.

"Oddly enough," said Volescu, "in our new days of freedom now that the Hegemony is powerless, my research is not illegal here. So I don't have to be prepared to dispose of my subjects at a moment's notice."

Bean looked at Petra. "He still says 'dispose of' instead of 'murder.' "

Volescu's smile grew sad. "How I wish I had all your brothers," he said. "But that's not why you're here. I already served my time and was legally released."

"We want our babies back," said Petra. "All eight of them. Unless there are more."

"There were never more than eight," said Volescu. "I was observed the whole time, as you arranged, and there is no way I could have faked the number. Nor could I have faked the destruction of the three discards."

"I've already thought of several," said Bean. "The most obvious being that the three you pretended to find had Anton's Key turned had already been taken away. What you destroyed were someone else's embryos. Or nothing at all."

"If you know so much, why do you need me?" asked Volescu.

"Eight names and addresses," said Bean. "The women who are bearing our babies."

"Even if I knew," said Volescu, "what purpose would be served by telling? None of them have Anton's Key. They aren't worth studying."

"There *is* no nondestructive test," said Petra. "So you don't know which of them had Anton's Key turned. You would have kept them all. You would have implanted them all."

"Again, since you know more than I do, by all means tell me when you find them. I'd love to know what Achilles did with the five survivors."

Bean walked up to his biological half-uncle. He towered over him.

"My," said Volescu. "What big teeth you have."

Bean took him by the shoulders. Volescu's arms seemed so small and fragile within the grasp of Bean's huge hands. Bean probed and pressed with his fingers. Volescu winced.

Bean's hands wandered idly along Volescu's shoulders until his right hand nested the back of the man's neck, and his thumb played with the point of Volescu's larynx. "Lie to me again," whispered Bean.

"You'd think," said Volescu, "that someone who used to be small would know better than to be a bully."

"We all used to be small," said Petra. "Let go of his neck, Bean."

"Let me crush his larynx just a little."

"He's too confident," said Petra. "He's very sure we'll never find them."

"So many babies," said Volescu genially. "So little time."

"He's counting on us not torturing him," said Bean.

"Or maybe he wants us to," said Petra. "Who knows how his brain works? The only difference between Volescu and Achilles is the size of their ambitions. Volescu's dreams are so very, very small."

Volescu's eyes were welling up with tears. "I still think of you as my only son," he said to Bean. "It grieves me that we don't communicate any better than this."

Bean's thumb massaged the skin of Volescu's throat in circles around the point of his larynx.

"It surprises me that you can always find a place to do your sick little brand of science," said Petra. "But this lab is closed now. The Rwandan government will have its scientists go over it to find out what you were doing."

"Always I do the work while others get the credit," said Volescu.

"Do you see how I nearly encircle his throat with just one hand?" said Bean.

"Let's take him back to Ribeirão Preto, Julian."

"That would be nice," said Volescu. "How are my sister and her husband doing? Or do you see them anymore, now that you've got to be so important?"

"He's talking about my family," said Bean, "as if he were not the monster who cloned my brother illegally and then murdered all but one of the clones."

"They've gone back to Greece," said Petra. "Please don't kill him, Bean. Please."

"Remind me why."

"Because we're good people," said Petra.

Volescu laughed. "You live by murder. How many people have you both killed? And if we add in all the Buggers you slaughtered out in space. . . ."

"All right," said Petra. "Go ahead and kill him."

Bean tightened his fingers. Not that much, really. But Volescu made a strangled sound in his throat and in moments his eyes were bugging out.

At that moment Suriyawong entered the lab. "General Delphiki, sir," he said.

"Just a minute, Suri," said Petra. "He's killing somebody."

"Sir," said Suriyawong. "This is a war materials lab."

Bean relaxed his grip. "Still genetic research?"

"Several of the other scientists working here had misgivings about Volescu's work and the sources of his grants. They were collecting evidence. Not much to collect. But everything points to Volescu breeding a common-cold virus that would carry genetic alterations."

"That wouldn't affect adults," said Bean.

"I shouldn't have said war materials," said Suriyawong, "but I thought that would stop your little game of strangulation faster."

"What is it, then?" asked Bean.

"It's a project to alter the human genome," said Suriyawong.

"We know that's what he worked with," said Petra.

"But not with viruses as carriers," said Bean. "What were you doing here, Volescu?"

Volescu choked out some words. "Fulfilling the terms of my grants."

"Grants from whom?"

"The grant granters," said Volescu.

"Lock this place down," said Bean to Suriyawong. "I'll call the Hegemon to request a Rwandan perimeter guard."

"I think," said Petra, "that our brilliant scientist friend had some bizarre notion of remaking the human race."

"We need Anton to look at what this sick little disciple of his was doing," said Bean.

"Suri," said Petra. "Bean wasn't really going to murder him."

"Yes I was," said Bean.

"I would have stopped him," said Petra.

Suri barked out a little laugh. "Sometimes people need killing. So far, Bean's record is one for one."

---

Petra stopped going along on the interviews with Volescu. They could hardly be called interrogations—direct questions led nowhere, threats seemed to mean nothing. It was maddening and stressful and she hated the way he looked at her. Looked at her belly, which was showing her pregnancy more and more every day.

But she still kept on top of what they were calling, for lack of a better name, the Volescu project. The head of electronic security, Ferreira, was working most intensely on trying to track down everything Volescu had been doing with his computer and tracking his various identities through the nets. But Petra made sure that the database searches and indexes that they already had under way continued. These babies were out there somewhere, implanted in surrogate mothers, and at some point they were going to give birth. Volescu wouldn't risk their lives by forbidding the mothers access to good medical care—in fact, that was bound to be a minimum. So they would be born in hospitals, their births registered.

How they would find these babies in the millions that would be born in that timeframe, Petra couldn't begin to guess. But they'd collect the data and index it on every conceivably useful variable so it was there to work with when they finally figured out some identifying marker.

Meanwhile, Bean conducted the interviews with Volescu. They were yielding some information that proved accurate, but it was hard for Bean to decide whether Volescu was unconsciously letting useful information slip, or deliberately toying with them by bleeding out little bits of information that he knew would not be terribly useful in the end.

When he wasn't with Volescu, Bean was with Anton, who had come away from retirement and accepted a heavy level of drugs to control his aversive reaction to working in his field of science. "I tell myself every day," he said to Bean, "that I'm not doing science, I'm merely grading a student's assignments. It helps. But I still throw up. This is not good for me."

"Don't push any harder than you can."

"My wife helps me," said Anton. "She's very patient with this old man. And you know what? She's pregnant. In the natural way!"

"Congratulations," Bean said, knowing how hard this was for Anton, whose sexual desires did not tend in the same direction as his reproductive plans.

"My body knows how, even at this old age." He laughed. "Doing what comes unnaturally."

But his personal happiness aside, the picture Anton began to paint looked worse and worse. "His plan was simple enough," said Anton. "He planned to destroy the human race."

"Why? That makes no sense. Vengeance?"

"No, no. Destroy and *replace*. The virus he chose would go straight to the reproductive cells in the body. Every sperm, every ovum. They infest, but they don't kill. They just snip and replace. All kinds of changes. Strength and speed of an East African. A few changes I don't understand because nobody's really mapped that part of the genome—not for function. And some I don't even know where they fit on the human genome. I'd have to try them out and I can't do that. That would be real science. Someone else. Later."

"You're sidestepping the big change," said Bean.

"My little key," said Anton. "His virus turns the key."

"So he has no cure. No way to switch the key for intellectual ability without also triggering this perpetual growth pattern."

"If he had it, he'd use it. There's no advantage not to."

"So it *is* a biological weapon."

"Weapon? Something that affects only your children? Makes them die of giantism before they're twenty? Oh, that would make armies run in panic."

"What then?"

"Volescu thinks he's God. Or at least he's playing dress-up with God's clothing. He's trying to jump the whole human race to the next stage of evolution. Spread this disease so that *no* normal children can be born, ever again."

"But that's insane. Everybody dying so young—"

"No, no, Julian. No, not insane. Why do humans live so long?

Mathematicians and poets, they burn out in their mid-twenties anyway. We live so long because of grandchildren. In a difficult world, grandparents can help ensure the survival of their grandchildren. The societies that kept their old people around and listened to them and respected them—that *fed* them—always do better. But that's a community on the edge of starvation. Always at risk. Are we at risk so much today?"

"If these wars keep getting worse—"

"Yes, war," said Anton. "Kill off a whole generation of men, yet the grandfathers keep their sexual potency. They can propagate the next generation even if the young ones are dead. But Volescu thinks we're ready to move beyond planning for the deaths of young men."

"So he doesn't mind having generations that are less than twenty years."

"Change society's patterns. When were you ready to assume an adult role, Bean? When was your brain ready to go to work and change the world?"

"Age ten. Earlier, if I'd had good education."

"So you get good education. All our schools change because children are ready to learn at age three. Age two. By age ten, if Volescu's gene change takes place, the new generation is completely ready to take over for the old. Marry as early as possible. Breed like bunnies. Become giants. Irresistible in war. Until they keel over from heart attacks. Don't you see? Instead of spending the young men in violent death, we send the old men—the eighteen-year-olds. While all the work in science, technology, building, planting, everything—all done by the young men. The ten-year-olds. All of them like you."

"Not human anymore."

"A different species, yes. The children of Homo sapiens. Homo lumens, maybe. Still capable of interbreeding, but the old style of human—they grow to be old, but they are never big. And they are never very smart. How can they compete? They are gone, Bean. Your people rule the world."

"They wouldn't be my people."

"It's good that you're loyal to old humans like me. But you are something new, Bean. And if you have any children with my little key turned, no, they won't be fast like what Volescu has designed, but they'll be brilliant. Something new in the world. When they can talk to each other, instead of being alone like you, will you be able to keep up with them? Well, maybe yes, for *you*. But will *I* be able to keep up with them?"

Bean laughed bitterly. "Will Petra? That's what you're saying."

"You had no parents to be humiliated when they found out that you were learning faster than they can teach."

"Petra will love them just as much."

"Yes, she will. But all her love won't turn them human."

"And here you told me that I'm definitely human. Not true after all."

"Human in your loves, your hungers. In what makes you good and not evil. But in the speed of your life, the intellectual heights, are you not alone in this world?"

"Unless that virus is released."

"How do you know it won't still be released?" asked Anton. "How do you know he hasn't already completed a batch and disseminated it? How do you know he didn't infect himself and now he spreads it wherever he goes? In these past weeks since he got here, how many people in the Hegemony compound have had a cold? Sniffly nose, itchy penis, tender nipples—yes, he used *that* virus as his base, he has a sense of humor, an ugly kind."

"I haven't checked on the subtler symptoms, but we've had the normal number of colds."

"Probably not," said Anton. "He probably didn't make himself a carrier. What would be the point? He wants other people to spread it."

"You're saying that it's already out there."

"Or he has a website that he has to check every week or every month. And then one month he doesn't do it. So a signal is sent out to some of Achilles's old network. The virus gets broken out and used. And all Volescu had to do to trigger it was . . . be a captive with no access to computers."

"Was his research that complete? *Could* he have a working virus?"

"I don't know. All his records were changed when he moved. When you sent him a message, you told me about that, yes? You sent him a message and he moved to Rwanda. Before that maybe he had an earlier version of the virus. Maybe not. Maybe this is the first time he put the changed human genes into the virus. If that's the case, then no, it has not been released. But it could be. It's ready. Ready *enough*. Maybe you caught him just in time."

"And if it *is* out there, what?"

"Then I hope the baby my wife is pregnant with, I hope it's one like you, and not one like me."

"Why?"

"Your tragedy, Bean, is that you are the only one. If all the world will soon be like you, then you know what that makes you."

"A damn fool."

"It makes you Adam."

Anton was unbearably complaisant about this. What Bean was, what was happening to him, he wouldn't wish that on anyone. Not his child, and not Anton's. But Anton could be forgiven for his idiotic wish. He had not been so small; he had not been this large. He could not know how . . . how larval the early stage was.

Like silkworms, the larva of my species does all the work of its life while it's young. Then the big butterfly, that's what people see, but all it has left to do in its life is get laid, then lay eggs, then die.

Bean talked it through with Petra, and then they went to Ferreira and Peter. Now the computer search was geared—with some urgency—toward detecting any kind of dead-man switch that Volescu was signing on to every day or every week. No doubt the dead-man switch was set to destroy itself as soon as its message was sent. Which meant that if it *was* already sent, it wouldn't be there anymore. But somewhere there were tracks. Backups. Records of one kind or another. Nobody traveled the networks clean.

Not even Bean. He had made himself untraceable by constantly changing everything. But Volescu had stayed rooted in a lab here or a lab there, as long as he could. He might not have been as careful in his maneuvers through the nets. After all, Volescu might think he was brilliant, but he was no Bean.

# 7

# AN OFFER

From: PeterWiggin%private@hegemon.gov
To: Vlad%Impaled@gcu.ru.gov
Re: my brother's friends

I'd like to have a chance to talk with you. Face to face. For my brother's sake. On neutral territory.

Peter arrived in St. Petersburg ostensibly to be an observer and consultant at the Warsaw Pact trade talks that were part of Russia's ongoing effort to set up an economic union to rival the western European one. And he did attend several meetings and kept his suite humming with conversations. Of course, his agenda was quite different from the official one, and he made good headway with—as expected—representatives from some of the smaller or less prosperous countries. Latvia. Estonia. Slovakia. Bulgaria. Bosnia. Albania. Croatia. Georgia. Every piece in the puzzle counted.

Not every piece was a country. Sometimes it was an individual.

That's why Peter found himself walking in a park—not one of the magnificent parks in the heart of St. Petersburg, but a smallish park in Kohtla-Järve, a town in northeastern Estonia with delusions of city-hood. Peter wasn't sure why Vlad had chosen a town that involved crossing borders—nothing could have made their encounter more obvious. And being in Estonia meant there'd be two intelligence services watching them, Estonia's *and* Russia's. Russia hadn't forgotten history: They still watched over Estonia using their domestic spy service rather than the foreign one.

This park was, perhaps, the reason. There was a lake—no, a pond, a skating pond in winter, Peter was sure, since it was almost perfectly round and over-equipped with benches. Now, in the summer, it was undoubtedly advertised with a "suck blood and lay eggs all in one place" campaign among the mosquitos, which had shown up in profusion.

"Close your eyes," said Vlad.

Peter expected some kind of spy ritual and, sighing, complied. His sigh left his mouth open, however, just enough to get a good taste of the insect repellant that Vlad sprayed in his face.

"Hands," said Vlad. "Tastes bad but doesn't kill. Hands."

Peter held out his hands. They were sprayed, too.

"Don't want you to lose more than a pint during our conversation. Horrible place. Nobody comes here in summer. So it isn't prewired. Lots of clear meadows. We can see if anybody's watching us."

"Are you that closely watched?"

"Russian government not as understanding as Hegemon. Suriyawong stays in your confidence because you believe he always opposed Achilles. But me? Not trusted. So if you think I have influence, very wrong thinking, my friend."

"Not why I'm here."

"Yes, I know, you're here for the trade talks." Vlad grinned.

"Not much point to trade talks when smuggling and bribery make any kind of customs collection a joke anyway," said Peter.

"I'm glad you understand our way of doing things," said Vlad. "Trust no one that you haven't bribed within the last half hour."

"Don't tell me you really have that thick a Russian accent, by the way," said Peter. "You grew up on Battle School. You should speak Common like a native."

"I do," said Vlad—still in a thick Russian accent. "Except when my future depends on giving people no reason to remember how different I am. Accents are hard to learn and hard to hold on to. So I will maintain it now. I am not by nature a good actor."

"May I call you Vlad?"

"May I call you Peter?"

"Yes."

"Then yes also. Lowly strategic planner cannot be more formal than Hegemon of whole world."

"You know just how much of the world I'm Hegemon over," said Peter. "And as I said, that's not why I'm here. Or not directly."

"What then? You want to hire me? Not possible. They may not trust me here, but they certainly don't want me going anywhere else. I'm a hero of the Russian people."

"Vlad, if they trusted you, what do you think you'd be doing right now?"

Vlad laughed. "Leading the armies of Mother Russia, as Alai and Hot Soup and Virlomi and so many others are already doing. So many Alexanders."

"Yes, I've heard that comparison," said Peter. "But I see it another way. I see it as being the arms race that led up to World War I."

Vlad thought for a moment. "And we Battle School brats are the arms race. If one nation has it, then another must have more. Yes, that's what Achilles's little venture in kidnapping was about."

"My point is: Having a Battle School graduate—particularly one of Ender's Jeesh—makes war more, not less, probable."

"I don't think so," said Vlad. "Yes, Hot Soup and Alai are in the thick of things, but Virlomi wasn't in the Jeesh. And the rest of the Jeesh—Bean and Petra are with you, struggling for world peace, yes? Like beauty pageant contestants? Dink is in a joint Anglo-American project which means he has had his balls cut off, militarily speaking. Shen is marking time in some ceremonial position in Tokyo. Dumper is a monk, I think, or whatever they call them. A shaman. In the Andes somewhere. Crazy Tom is at Sandhurst confined to a classroom. Carn Carby is in Australia where they may or may not have a military but nobody cares. And Fly Molo . . . well, he's a busy boy in the Philippines. But not their president or even an important general."

"That squares with my tally, though I think Carn would argue with you about the value of the Australian military."

Vlad waved the objection aside. "My point is, most nations that have this 'treasured national resource' are far more concerned to keep us under observation and away from power than to actually use us to make war."

Peter smiled. "Yes. Either they have you up to your elbows in blood, or they have you locked in a box. Anybody happily married?"

"We're none of us even twenty-five yet. Well, maybe Dink. He always lied about his age. Most of us are in our teens or barely out of them."

"They're afraid of you. All the more so now, because the nations that actually *used* their Jeesh members in war are now governed by them."

"If you can call 'worldwide Islam' a nation. I, personally, call it a riot with scripture."

"Just don't say that in Baghdad or Tehran," said Peter.

"As if I could ever go to those places."

"Vlad," said Peter. "How would you like to be free of all this beauty?"

Vlad hooted with laughter. "So you're here representing *Graff*?"

Peter was taken aback. "Graff came to you?"

"Be head of a colony. Get away from it all. All-expenses-paid vacation . . . that takes the rest of your life!"

"Not a vacation," said Peter. "Very hard work. But at least you *have* a life."

"So Peter the Hegemon wants Ender's Jeesh offplanet. Forever."

"Do you want my job?" said Peter. "I'll resign it today if I thought it would go to you. You or any member of Ender's Jeesh. You want it? Think you can *hold* it? Then it's yours. I only have it because I wrote the Locke essays and stopped a war. But what have I done lately? Vlad, I don't see you as a rival. How could I? What freedom do you have to oppose me?"

Vlad shrugged. "All right, so your motives are pure."

"My motives are realistic," said Peter. "Russia is not using you right now, but they haven't killed you or locked you up. If they ever decide that war is desirable or necessary or unavoidable, how long before you get promoted and put into the thick of things? Especially if the war goes badly for a while. You are their nuclear arsenal."

"Not really," said Vlad. "Since my brain is supposed to be the payload of this particular missile, and my brain was defective enough to *seem* to trust Achilles, then I must not be as good as the other Jeesh members."

"In a war against Han Tzu, how long before you commanded an army? Or at least were put in charge of strategy?"

"Fifteen minutes, give or take."

"So. Is Russia more or less likely to go to war, knowing they have you?"

Vlad smiled a little and ducked his head. "Well, well. So the Hegemon wants me out of Russia so Russia won't be so adventurous."

"Not quite so simple," said Peter. "There'll come a day when much of the world will have merged their sovereignty—"

"By which you mean they will have surrendered it."

"Into one government. It won't be the big nations. Just a bunch of little ones. But unlike the United Nations and the League of Nations and even the Hegemony in its previous form, it will *not* be designed to keep the central government as powerless as possible. The nations in this league will maintain no separate army or navy or air force. They will not have separate control over their own borders—and they will collect no customs. Nor will they maintain a separate merchant marine. The Hegemony will have power over foreign policy, period, without rival. Why would Russia ever join such a confederacy?"

"It never would."

Peter nodded. And waited.

"It never would unless it thought that it was the only safe thing to do."

"Add the word 'profitable' into that sentence and you'll be closer to right."

"Russians are not Americans like you, Peter Wiggin. We don't do things for profit motive."

"So all those bribes go into charitable causes."

"They keep the bookmakers and prostitutes of Russia from starving," said Vlad. "Altruism at its finest."

"Vlad," said Peter. "All I'm saying is, think about this. Ender Wiggin did two great deeds for humanity. He wiped out the Buggers. And he never returned to Earth."

Vlad turned on Peter with real fire in his eyes. "Do you think I don't know who arranged for that?"

"I advocated it," said Peter. "I wasn't Hegemon then. But do you dare to tell me I was wrong? What would have happened if Ender himself were here on Earth? Everybody's hostage. And if his homeland managed to keep him safe, what then? Ender Wiggin, the Bugger-slayer, now at the head of the armed forces of the dreaded United States. Think of the jockeying, the alliances, the preemptive attacks, all because this great and terrible weapon was in the hands of the nation that still thinks it has the right to judge and govern all the world."

Vlad nodded. "So it's just a happy coincidence that it left you without a rival for the Hegemony."

"I have rivals, Vlad. The Caliph has millions of followers who believe that he's the one God chose to be ruler over the earth."

"Aren't you making the same offer to Alai?"

"Vlad," said Peter. "I don't expect to persuade you. Only to inform you. If there comes a day when you think your best hope of safety is to leave Earth, post a note to me at the website I'll link to you in an email. Or if you realize that the only chance your nation has of peace is for all its Battle School grads to disappear from Earth, tell me, and I'll do all I can to get them safely out and off."

"Unless I go to my superiors and tell them all that you just told me."

"Tell them," said Peter. "Tell them and lose the last shreds of freedom that you have."

"So I won't tell them," said Vlad.

"And you'll think about it. It will be there in the back of your mind."

"And when all the Battle School grads are gone," said Vlad, "there will be Peter. Brother of Ender Wiggin. The natural ruler of all humankind."

"Yes, Vlad. The only chance we have of unity is to have a strong consensus leader. Our George Washington."

"And that's you."

"It could be a Caliph, and we'd have a future as a Muslim world. Or we might all be made into vassals of the Middle Kingdom. Or—tell me, Vlad—should we prefer to be ruled over by the government that now treats you so kindly?"

"I'll think about this," said Vlad. "And *you* think about something else. Ambition was part of the basis by which we were chosen for Battle School. Just how self-sacrificing do you think we'll be? Look at Virlomi. As shy a person as Battle School could possibly admit. But to achieve her purpose, she made herself into a god. And she does seem to play the part with enthusiasm, doesn't she?"

"Ambition balanced against survival instinct," said Peter. "Ambition leads you to great risk. But ambition never leads you to certain destruction."

"Unless you're a fool."

"There are no fools in this park today," said Peter. "Unless you count the spies lying underwater breathing through straws in order to overhear our conversation."

"It's the best the Estonians can do," said Vlad.

"I'm glad to know that Russians haven't forgotten their sense of humor."

"Everybody knows a few dozen Estonian jokes."

"Who do Estonians tell jokes about?" asked Peter.

"Estonians, of course. Only they don't realize that they're jokes."

Laughing, they left the park and headed back, Peter to his chauffered car, Vlad to the train back to St. Petersburg.

---

Some Battle School graduates came to Ribeirão Preto to hear Peter's invitation. Others, Peter contacted through mutual friends. Members of Ender's Jeesh, Peter met with directly. Carn Carby in Australia. Dink Meeker and Crazy Tom in England. Shen in Tokyo. Fly Molo in Manila. And Dumper amid a council of Quechuas in the ruins of Macchu Picchu, his unofficial headquarters as he worked steadily to organize the Native Americans of South America.

None of them accepted his offer. All of them listened and remembered.

Meanwhile, the guerrilla fighting in India grew more savage. More and more Persian and Pakistani troops were withdrawn from China. Until the day came when there was no one penning in the starving Chinese army in Sichuan province. Han Tzu set it in motion.

The Turks withdrew to Xinjiang province. The Indonesians got back in their boats and withdrew to Taiwan. The Arabs joined in the occupation of India. Han China was free of foreign occupiers, without the Emperor firing a shot.

At once, the Americans and Europeans and Latin Americans were back, buying and selling, helping China recover from empty wars of conquest. While the Muslim nations continued to bleed weapons and wealth and men in the ever-more-brutal war to control India.

Meanwhile, a new pair of essayists emerged on the nets.

One styled himself "Lincoln" and spoke of the need to put an end to bloody wars and oppression, and to secure the rights and freedoms of all societies by giving an honest, law-abiding world government exclusive control of all weapons of war.

The other called himself "Martel," harking back to Charles the Hammer, who stopped the Muslim advance into Europe at Poitiers. Martel kept pounding at the grave danger the world faced from the existence of a Caliph. The Muslims, who now made up more than a third of the population of some European countries, would be emboldened, seize power, and force all of Europe to live under brutal Muslim law.

There were some commentators who saw in these two new essayists a similarity to the days when Locke and Demosthenes dueled, with a similar division between statesmanlike peace-seeking and warnings of war. Those had turned out to be written by Peter and Valentine Wiggin. Only once did Peter answer a question about "Lincoln": "There are several ways the world could be united. I'm glad that I'm not the only one who hopes it will be through a liberal democracy rather than a conquering despotism."

And only once did Peter comment when questioned about "Martel": "I don't believe it helps the cause of peace in the world to stir up the kind of fear and hatred that leads to expulsions and genocide."

Both answers only added to the credibility of the two essayists.

# 8

# ENDER

From: Rockette%Armenian@hegemon.gov
To: Noggin%Lima@hegemon.gov
Re: I'm having fun so don't carp

Beloved husband,

What ELSE can I do while I'm sitting around with a belly the size of a barn except type? It's actually hard work, considering the keyboard is at arm's length. And it's not as if anti-Muslim propaganda is harder than breathing. I'm Armenian, O Father of the Balloon I'm Carrying Around Inside My Abdomen. We learn about how Muslims—Turks in particular, of course—have been slaughtering Armenian Christians from time immemorial. How they can never be trusted. And guess what? When I look for evidence, ancient and contemporary, I don't have to get out of my chair.

So I will continue to write the Martel essays and continue to laugh while they accuse Peter of writing them. Of course I

AM doing it at his request, which is what I understand Valentine did for him when she wrote Demosthenes's essays back when we were all in school. But you know that nobody will listen to his Lincoln stuff unless they're also terrified. Either terrified of Muslims taking over the world (id est, more particularly, their neighborhood) or terrified of the hideous bloodshed that would ensue if nations with Muslim minorities actually started restricting them or expelling them.

Besides, Bean, I think that what I'm saying is true. Alai means well but he clearly is not in control of his fanatical supporters. They really are murdering people and calling it "executions." They really are trying to rule over India. They really are agitating and rioting and committing the odd atrocity in Europe right now, pushing to have European nations declare for the Caliph and cease trading with China, which really is supplying Virlomi.

And now this essay will end because the stomach aches I've been having are clearly not stomach aches. This baby thinks it's coming, two months prematurely. Please get back here right away.

Peter waited outside the delivery room with Anton and Ferreira.

"Does this premature birth mean anything?" he asked Anton.

"They wouldn't let the doctors amnio the baby," said Anton, "so I didn't have any reliable genetic material to work with. But we know that in the early stages, maturity is highly accelerated. It seems possible to me that premature birth is consistent with the key being turned."

"My thought," said Peter, "is that this might be the break we need to find the other babies and unravel Volescu's network."

"Because the others might be premature too?" asked Ferreira.

"I think Volescu had a deadman switch and sometime after he was arrested, a warning went out and all the surrogate mothers bolted. That wouldn't help us before, because we didn't know when the signal went out, and pregnant women may be one of the more stable demographic groups, but they do move around by the hundreds of thousands."

Ferreira nodded. "But now we can try to correlate premature births with abrupt moves at the same time as other women with similarly premature births."

"And then check funding. They'll have the best possible hospital care, and somebody's paying for it."

"Unless," said Anton, "this baby is premature because Petra herself has some kind of problem."

"There's no history of premature births in her family," said Peter. "And the baby has been developing quickly. Not in size, mind you—but the parts were all in place before schedule. I think this baby is like Bean. I think the key is turned. So let's use it as a key to finding where Volescu went and where those viruses might be waiting to be released."

"Not to mention finding Bean's and Petra's babies," said Anton.

"Of course," said Peter. "That's the main purpose." He turned to the managing nurse. "Have someone call me when we know anything about the condition of the mother and baby."

---

Bean sat down beside Petra's bed. "How do you feel?"

"Not as bad as I expected," she said.

"That's one good thing about premature delivery," he said. "Smaller baby, easier birth. He's doing fine. They're only keeping him in neonate intensive care because of his size. All his other organs are working."

"He's got . . . he's like you."

"Anton is supervising the analysis right now. But that's my guess." He held her hand. "The thing we wanted to avoid."

"If he's like you," she said, "then I'm not sorry."

"If he's like me," said Bean, "then it means Volescu really didn't have any kind of test. Or he had one, and discarded the babies that were normal. Or maybe they're all like me."

"The thing you wanted to avoid," she whispered.

"Our little miracles," said Bean.

"I hope you're not too disappointed. I hope you. . . . Think of it as a chance to see what your life might have been like if you had grown up with parents, in a home. Not barely escaping with your life and then scrabbling to survive on the streets of Rotterdam."

"At the age of one."

"Think what it will be like to raise this baby surrounded by love, teaching him as fast as he wants to learn. All those lost years, recovered for our baby."

Bean shook his head. "I hoped the baby would be normal," he said. "I hoped they'd all be normal. So I wouldn't have to consider this."

"Consider what?"

"Taking the baby with me."

"With you where?" asked Petra.

"The I.F. has a new starship. Very secret. A messenger ship. It uses a gravity field to offset acceleration. Up to lightspeed in a week. The plan is that once we find the babies, I take the ones like me and we take off and keep traveling until they find the cure for this."

"Once you're gone," said Petra, "why do you think the fleet will bother even looking for a cure?"

"Because they want to know how to turn Anton's Key without the side effects," said Bean. "They'll keep working on it."

Petra nodded. She was taking this better than Bean expected.

"All right," she said. "As soon as we find the babies. Then we go."

"We?" said Bean.

"I'm sure, in your normal legumocentric view of the universe, it didn't cross your mind that there's no reason I shouldn't go along with you."

"Petra, it means being cut off from the human race. It's different for me because I'm *not* human."

"That again."

"What kind of life is that for the normal babies? Growing up confined to a starship?"

"It would only seem like weeks, Bean. How grown up will they be?"

"You'd be cut off from everything. Your family. Everybody."

"You stupid man," she said. "*You* are everybody now. You and our babies."

"You could raise the normal babies . . . normally. With grandparents. A normal life."

"A fatherless life. And their siblings off on a starship, so they'll never even meet. I don't think so, Bean. Do you think I'm going to give birth to this little boy and then let somebody take him away from me?"

Bean stroked her cheek, her hair. "Petra, there's a whole bunch of rational arguments against what you're saying, but you just gave birth to my son, and I'm not going to argue with you now."

"You're right," said Petra. "By all means, let's avoid this discussion until I've nursed the baby for the first time and it becomes even more impossible for me to consider letting you take him away from me. But I'll tell you this right now. I will never change my mind. And if you maneuver things so you sneak off and steal my son from me and leave me a widow without even my child to raise, then you're worse than Volescu. When he stole our children, we knew he was an amoral monster. But you—you're my husband. If you do that to me, I'll pray that God puts you in the deepest part of hell."

"Petra, you know I don't believe in hell."

"But knowing that I'm praying such a thing, *that* will be hell for you."

"Petra, I won't do anything you don't agree to."

"Then I'm coming with you," she said, "because I'll never agree to anything else. So it's decided. There's no discussion to have later when I'm rational. I'm already as rational as I'll ever be. In fact, there's no rational reason why I shouldn't come along if I want to. It's an excellent idea. And being raised on a starship has to be better than being orphaned on the streets of Rotterdam."

"No wonder they named you after rock," said Bean.

"I don't give up and I don't wear down. I'm not just rock, I'm *diamond*."

Her eyelids were heavy.

"Go to sleep now, Petra."

"Only if I can hold on to you," she said.

He took her hand; she gripped it fiercely. "I got you to give me a baby," she said. "Don't think for a minute I'm not going to get my way in this, too."

"I promised you already, Petra," said Bean. "Whatever we do, it'll be because you agree that it's the right thing."

"Think you *want* to leave me. Voyage to . . . nowhere. Think nowhere's *better* than living with me. . . ."

"That's right, baby," said Bean, stroking her arm with his other hand. "Nowhere is better than living with you."

They had the baby christened by a priest. He came into neonate intensive care; not the first time he'd done it, of course, baptizing distressed newborns before they died. He seemed relieved to learn that this baby was strong and healthy and likely to survive, despite how tiny he was.

"Andrew Arkanian Delphiki, I baptize you in the name of the Father, the Son, and the Holy Ghost."

It was quite a crowd gathered around the neonate incubator to watch. Bean's family, Petra's family, and of course Anton and Ferreira and Peter and the Wiggin parents and Suriyawong and those members of Bean's little army who weren't actually on assignment. They had to wheel the incubator cart out into a waiting room to have space enough to hold everybody.

"You're going to call him Ender, aren't you," said Peter.

"Until he makes us stop," said Petra.

"What a relief," said Theresa Wiggin. "Now you won't have to name a child of your own after your brother, Peter."

Peter ignored her, which meant that her words had really stung.

"The baby is named for Saint Andrew," said Petra's mother. "Babies are named for saints, not soldiers."

"Of course, Mother," said Petra. "Ender and our baby were *both* named for Saint Andrew."

---

Anton and his team learned that yes, the baby definitely had Bean's syndrome. The Key was turned. And having two sets of genes to compare confirmed that Bean's genetic modification bred true. "But there's no reason to suppose that all the babies will have the modification," he reported to Bean, Petra, and Peter. "The likelihood is that the trait is dominant, however. So any child who has it should be on the fast track."

"Premature birth," said Bean.

"And we can guess that statistically, half the eight babies should have the trait. Mendel's law. Not ironclad, because randomness is involved. So there might be only three. Or five. Or more. Or this might be the only one. But the likeliest thing—"

"We know how probability works, Professor," said Ferreira.

"I wanted to emphasize the uncertainty."

"Believe me," said Ferreira, "uncertainty is my life. Right now we've found either two dozen or nearly a hundred groups of women who gave birth within two weeks of Petra, and who moved at the same time as others in their group, since the day Volescu was arrested."

"How can you not even know how many groups you have?" asked Bean.

"Selection criteria," said Petra.

"If we divide them into groups that left within six hours of each other, then we get the higher total. If we divide them into groups that left within two days of each other, the lower total. Plus we can shift the timeframes and the groups also shift."

"What about prematurity in the babies?"

"That supposes that the doctors are aware that the babies are premature," said Ferreira. "Low birth weight is what we went for. We eliminated any babies that were higher than the low end of normal. Most of them will be premature. But not all."

"And all of this," said Petra, "depends on all the babies being on the same clock."

"It's all we can go on," said Peter. "If it turns out that Anton's Key doesn't make them all trigger delivery after about the same gestation time . . . well, it's no more of a problem than the fact that we don't know when the other embryos were implanted."

"Some of the embryos might have been implanted much more recently," said Ferreira. "So we're going to keep adding women to the database as they give birth to low-birthweight children and turn out to have moved at about the time Volescu was arrested. You realize how many variables there are that we don't know? How many of the embryos have Anton's Key. When they were implanted. *If* they were all implanted. *If* Volescu even had a deadman switch."

"I thought you said he did."

"He did," said Ferreira. "We just don't know what the switch was about. Maybe it was for release of the virus. Maybe for the mothers to move. Maybe both. Maybe neither."

"A lot of things we don't know," said Bean. "Remarkable how little we got from Volescu's computer."

"He's a careful man," said Ferreira. "He knew perfectly well that he'd be caught someday, and his computer seized. We learned more than he could have imagined—but less than we had hoped."

"Just keep looking," said Petra. "Meanwhile, I have a baby-shaped suction cup to go attach to one of the tenderest parts of my body. Promise me that he won't develop teeth early."

"I don't know," said Bean. "I can't remember not having them."

"Thanks for the encouragement," said Petra.

---

Bean got up in the night, as usual, to get little Ender so Petra could nurse him. Tiny as he was, he had a pair of lungs on him. Nothing small about his voice.

And, as usual, once the baby started suckling, Bean watched until Petra rolled over to feed the baby on the other side. Then he slept.

Until he awoke again. Usually he didn't, so for all he knew it was like this every time. Because Petra was still nursing the baby, but she was also crying.

"Baby, what's wrong?" said Bean, touching her shoulder.

"Nothing," she said. She wasn't crying anymore.

"Don't try to lie to me," said Bean. "You were crying."

"I'm so happy," she said.

"You were thinking about how old little Ender will be when he dies."

"That's silly," she said. "We're going off in a starship until they find a cure. He's going to live to be a hundred."

"Petra," said Bean.

"What. I'm not lying."

"You're crying because in your mind's eye you can already see the death of your baby."

She sat up and lifted the now-sleeping baby to her shoulder. "Bean, you really are bad at guessing things like this. I was crying because I thought of you as a little baby, and how you didn't have a father to go and get you when you cried in the night, and you didn't have a mother to hold you and feed you from her own body, and you had no experience of love."

"But when I finally found out what it was, I got more of it than any man could hope for."

"Damn right," said Petra. "And don't you forget it."

She got up and took the baby back to the bassinet.

And tears came to Bean's eyes. Not pity for himself as a baby. But remembering Sister Carlotta, who had become his mother and stayed with him long before he learned what love was and was able to give any back to her. And some of his tears were also for Poke, the friend who took him in when he was in the last stages of death by malnutrition in Rotterdam.

Petra, don't you know how short life is, even when you don't have some disease like Anton's Key? So many people prematurely in their graves, and some of them I put there. Don't cry for me. Cry for my brothers who were disposed of by Volescu as he destroyed evidence of his crimes. Cry for all the children that no one ever loved.

Bean thought he was being subtle, turning his head so Petra couldn't see his tears when she came back to bed. Whether she saw or not, she snuggled close to him and held him.

How could he tell this woman who had always been so good to him and loved him more than he knew how to return—how could he tell her that he had lied to her? He didn't believe that there would ever be a cure for Anton's Key.

When he got on that starship with the babies that had his same disease, he expected to take off and head outward into the stars. He would live long enough to teach the children how to run the starship. They would explore. They would send reports back by ansible. They would map habitable planets farther away than any other humans would want to travel. In fifteen or twenty years of subjective time they would live a thousand years or more in real time, and the data they collected would be a treasure trove. They would be the pioneers of a hundred colonies or more.

And then they would die, having no memory of setting foot on a planet, and having no children to carry on their disease for another generation.

And it would all be bearable, for them and for Bean, because they would know that back on Earth, their mother and their healthy siblings were living normal lives, and marrying and having children of their own, so that by the time their thousand-year voyage was over, every living human being would be related to them one way or another.

That's how we'll be part of everything.

So no matter what I promised, Petra, you're not coming with me, and neither are our healthy children. And someday you'll understand and forgive me for breaking my word to you.

# 9
# PENSION

From: PeterWiggin%personal@hegemon.gov
To: Champi%T'it'u@QuechuaNation.Freenet.ne.com
Re: The best hope of the Quechua and Aymara peoples

Dear Champi T'it'u,

Thank you for consenting to visit with me. Considering that I tried to call you "Dumper" as if you were still a child in Battle School and a friend of my brother, I'm surprised you didn't toss me out on the spot.

As I promised, I am sending you the current draft of the Constitution of the Free People of Earth. You are the first person outside the innermost circle of Hegemony officials to look at it, and please remember that it is only a draft. I would be grateful for your suggestions.

My goal is to have a Constitution that would be as attractive to nations that are recognized as states as to peoples that are still stateless. The Constitution will fail if the language is not identical for both. Therefore there are aspirations you would have to give up and claims you would have to relinquish. But I think you will see that the same will be true for the states that now occupy territory you claim for the Quechua and Aymara peoples.

The principles of majority, viability, contiguity, and compactness would guarantee you a self-governing territory, albeit one much smaller than your present claim.

But your present claim, while historically justifiable, is also unattainable without a bloody war. Your military abilities are sufficient to guarantee that the contest would be far more evenly matched than the governments of Ecuador, Peru, Bolivia, and Colombia would anticipate. But even if you won a complete victory, who would be your successor?

I speak candidly, because I believe that you are not following a delusion but embarking on a specific, attainable enterprise. The route of war might succeed for a time—and the operative word is "might," since nothing is certain in war—but the cost in blood, economic losses, and ill will for generations to come will be steep.

Ratifying the Hegemony Constitution, on the other hand, will guarantee you a homeland, to which those who insist on being governed only by Quechua and Aymara leaders and raising their children to be Quechua and Aymara speakers may migrate freely, without needing anyone's permission.

But take note of the irrevocability clause. I can promise you that this will be taken very seriously. Do not ratify this

Constitution if you and your people do not intend to abide by it.

As for the personal question you asked me:

I don't believe it matters whether I'm the one who unites the world under one government. No individual is irreplaceable. However, I am quite certain that it will need to be a person exactly like me. And at present, the only person who meets that requirement is me:

Committed to a liberal government with the highest degree of personal freedom. Equally committed to tolerating no breach of the peace or oppression of one people by another. And strong enough to make it happen and make it stick.

Join with me, Champi T'it'u, and you will not be an insurrectionary hiding out in the Andes. You'll be a head of a state within the Hegemony Constitution. And if you are patient, and wait until I have won the ratification of at least two of the nations at issue, then you and all the world can see how peacefully and equitably the rights of native peoples can be handled.

It only works if every party is determined to make the sacrifices necessary to ensure the peace and freedom of all other parties. If even one party is determined on a course of war or oppression, then someday that party will find itself bearing the full weight of the pressure the Free Nations can bring to bear. Right now that isn't much. But how long do you think it will take me to make it a considerable force indeed?

If you are with me, Champi T'it'u, you will need no other ally.

Sincerely,
Peter

Something was bothering Bean, nagging at the back of his mind. He thought at first that it was a feeling caused by his fatigue, getting so little uninterrupted sleep at night. Then he chalked it up to anxiety because his friends—well, Ender's and Petra's friends—were involved in a life-or-death struggle in India, which they couldn't possibly all win.

And then, in the middle of changing Ender's diaper, it came to him. Perhaps because of his baby's name. Perhaps, he thought bitterly, because of what he had his hands in.

He finished diapering the baby and left him in the bassinet, where Petra, dozing, would hear him if he cried.

Then he went in search of Peter.

Naturally, it wasn't easy to get in to see him. Not that there was so huge a bureaucracy in Ribeirão Preto. But it was large enough now that Peter could afford to pay for a few layers of protection. Nobody who just stood there being a guard. But a secretary here, a clerk there, and Bean found he had explained himself three times—at five-thirty in the morning—before he even got to see Theresa Wiggin.

And, now that he thought about it, he wanted to see her.

"He's on the phone with some European bigwig," she told him. "Either sucking up or getting sucked up to, depending on how big and powerful the country is."

"So that's why everybody's up early."

"He tries to get up early enough to catch a significant part of the working day in Europe. Which is hard, because it's usually only a few hours in the morning. *Their* morning."

"So I'll talk to you."

"Well, that's a puzzler," said Theresa. "Business so important that you'd get up at five-thirty to see Peter, and yet so unimportant that when you find out he's on a phone call, you can actually talk to me about it."

She said it with such verve that Bean might have missed the bitter complaint behind her words. "So he still treats you like a ceremonial mother?" asked Bean.

"Does the butterfly consult with the cocoon?"

"So . . . how do your other children treat you?" asked Bean.

Her face darkened. "This is your business?"

He wasn't sure if the question was pointed irony—as in, that's none of your business—or a simple question—this is what you came for? He took it the first way.

"Ender's my friend," said Bean. "More than anybody else except Petra. I miss him. I know there's an ansible on his ship. I just wondered."

"I'm forty-six years old," said Theresa. "When Val and Andrew get to their destination, I'll be . . . old. Why should they write to me?"

"So they haven't."

"If they have, the I.F. hasn't seen fit to inform me."

"They're bad at mail delivery, as I recall. They seem to think that the best family therapy method is 'out of sight, out of mind.' "

"Or Andrew and Valentine can't be bothered." Theresa typed something. "There. Another letter I'll never send."

"Who are you writing to?"

"Whom. You foreigners are wrecking the English language."

"I'm not speaking English. I'm speaking Common. There's no 'whom' in Common."

"I'm writing to Virlomi and telling her to wise up to the fact that Suriyawong is still in love with her and she has no business trying to play god in India when she could do it for real by marrying and having babies."

"She doesn't love Suri," said Bean.

"Someone else, then?"

"India. It's way past patriotism with her."

"Matriotism. Nobody thinks of India as the fatherland."

"And you're the matriarch. Dispensing maternal advice to Battle School grads."

"Just the ones from Ender's Jeesh who happen now to be heads of state or insurrectionary leaders or, in this case, fledgling deities."

"Just one question for you," said Bean.

"Ah. Back to the subject."

"Is Ender getting a pension?"

"Pension? Yes, I think so. Yes. Of course."

"And what is his pension doing while he's puttering along at lightspeed?"

"Gathering interest, I imagine."

"So you're not administering it?"

"Me? I don't think so."

"Your husband?"

"I'm the one who handles the money," said Theresa. "Such as it is. *We* don't get a pension. Come to think of it, we don't get a salary, either. We're just hangers-on. Camp followers. We're both on leave of absence at the University because it was too dangerous for potential hostages to be out where enemies could kidnap us. Of course, the main kidnapper is dead, but . . . here we stay."

"So the I.F. is holding on to Ender's money."

"What are you getting at?" asked Theresa.

"I don't know," said Bean. "I was wiping my little Ender's butt, and I thought, there's an awful lot of shit here."

"They drink and drink. The breast doesn't seem to get smaller. And they poop more than they could possibly get from the breast without shriveling it into a raisin."

"And then I thought, I know how much I'm getting in my pension, and it's kind of a lot. I don't actually have to work at anything as long as I live. Petra, too. Most of it we simply invest. Roll it back into investments. It's adding up fast. Pretty soon our income from invested pension is going to be greater than the original pension we invested. Of course, that's partly because we have so much inside information. You know, about which wars are about to start and which will fizzle, that sort of thing."

"You're saying that somebody ought to be watching over Andrew's money."

"I'll tell you what," said Bean. "I'll find out from Graff who's taking care of it."

"You want to invest it?" asked Theresa. "Going into brokering or financial management when Peter has finally achieved world peace?"

"I won't be here when Peter—"

"Oh, Bean, for heaven's sake, don't take me *seriously* and make me feel bad for acting as if you weren't going to die. I prefer not to think of you dying."

"I was only saying that I'm not a good person to manage Ender's . . . portfolio."

"So . . . who?"

"Wouldn't that be *whom?*"

She grimaced. "No it would not. Not even if you spoke English."

"I don't know. I've got no candidate."

"And so you wanted to confer with Peter."

Bean shrugged.

"But that would make no sense at all. Peter doesn't know anything about investing and . . . no, no, no. I see what you're getting at."

"How, when I'm not sure myself?"

"Oh, you're sure. You think Peter is financing some of this from Andrew's pension. You think he's embezzling from his brother."

"I doubt Peter would call it embezzling."

"What would he call it, then?"

"In Peter's mind, Ender's probably buying government bonds issued by the Hegemony. So when the Hegemon rules the world, Ender will get four percent per year, tax free."

"Even I know that would be a lousy investment."

"From a financial point of view. Mrs. Wiggin, Peter has the use of more money than the scant dues the few dues-paying nations still pay to the Hegemony."

"The dues go up and down," said Theresa.

"He tells you?"

"John Paul is closer to these things. When the world is worried about war, money flows into the Hegemony. Not a lot, just a little extra."

"When I first got here there were Peter, you two, and the soldiers I brought with me. A couple of secretaries. And a lot of debt. Yet Peter always had enough money to send us out in the choppers we brought with us. Money for fuel, money for ammunition."

"Bean, what will be gained if you accuse Peter of embezzling Ender's pension? You know Peter isn't making himself rich with it."

"No, but he *is* making himself Hegemon. Ender might need that money someday."

"Ender will never come back to Earth, Bean. How valuable will money be on the new world he's going to colonize? What harm is it causing?"

"So you're all right with Peter cheating his brother."

"*If* he's doing that. Which I doubt." Theresa's smile was tight and her eyes flashed just a little. Mother bear, guarding cub.

"Protect the son who's here, even if he's cheating the son who's gone."

"Why don't you go back to your place and take care of your own child instead of meddling with mine?"

"And the pioneers circle the wagons to protect from the arrows of the Native Americans."

"I like you, Bean. I'm also worried about you. I'll miss you when you die. I'll do my best to help Petra get through the hard times ahead. But keep your hippo-sized hands off my son. He has the weight of the world on his shoulders, in case you didn't notice."

"I think maybe I won't have that interview with Peter this morning after all."

"Delighted to be of service," said Theresa.

"Do avoid telling him I stopped by, will you?"

"With pleasure. In fact, I've already forgotten that you're here." She turned back to the computer and typed again. Bean rather hoped she was typing meaningless words and strings of letters because she was too angry to be writing anything intelligible. He even thought of peeking, just to see. But Theresa was a good friend who happened to be protective of her son. No reason to turn her into an enemy.

He sauntered away, his long legs carrying him much farther, much faster than a man walking so slowly should have gone. And even though he wasn't moving quickly, he still felt his heart pump faster. Just to walk down a corridor, it's as if he were jogging a little.

How much time? Not as much as I had yesterday.

---

Theresa watched him go and thought: I love that boy for being so loyal to Ender. And he's absolutely right to suspect Peter. It's just the sort of thing he'd do. For all I know, Peter got us back onto full salary at the University, too, only he didn't tell us and he's cashing our checks.

Then again, maybe he's secretly getting paid by China or America or some other country that values his services as Hegemon.

Unless they value his services as Lincoln. Or . . . as Martel. If he was really writing the Martel essays. Such a thing smacked of Peter's propaganda methods, but the writing sounded nothing like him, and it could hardly be Valentine this time. Had he found another surrogate writer?

Maybe somebody was contributing in a big way to "Martel's" cause and Peter was pocketing the money to advance his own.

But no. Word of such contributions would get out. Peter would never be so foolish as to accept money that might compromise him if it were found out.

I'll check with Graff, see whether the I.F. is paying out the pension to Peter. And if it is, I'll have to kill the boy. Or at least make my disappointed-in-you face and then curse about him to John Paul when we're alone.

---

Bean told Petra he was going to train with Suri and the boys. And he did—go where they were training, that is. But he spent his time in one of the choppers, making a scrambled and encrypted call to the old Battle School space station, where Graff was assembling his fleet of colony ships.

"Going to come visit me?" said Graff. "Want to take a trip into space?"

"Not yet," said Bean. "Not till I've found my lost kids."

"So you have other business to discuss?"

"Yes. But you'll immediately realize that the business I want to talk about is none of my business."

"Can't wait. No, got to wait. Call I can't turn down. Wait just a minute please."

The hiss of atmosphere and magnetic fields and radiation between the surface of the Earth and the space station. Bean thought of breaking off the connection and waiting for another time. Or maybe dropping the whole stupid line of inquiry.

Just as Bean was going to terminate the call, Graff came back on. "Sorry, I'm in the middle of tricky negotiations with China to let breeding couples emigrate. They want to send us some of their surplus males. I told him we were forming a colony, not fighting a war. But . . . negotiating with the Chinese. You think you hear yes, but the next day you find out they said no *very* delicately and then tittered behind their hands."

"All those years controlling the size of their population, and now they won't let go of a measly few thousand," said Bean.

"So you called me. What is it that's none of your business?"

"I get my pension. Petra gets hers. Who get's Ender's?"

"My, but you're to the point."

"Is it going to Peter?"

"What an excellent question."

"May I make a suggestion?"

"Please. As I recall, you have a history of making interesting suggestions."

"Stop sending the pension to anybody."

"I'm the Minister of Colonization now," said Graff. "I take my orders from the Hegemon."

"You're in bed so deep with the I.F. that Chamrajnagar thinks you're a hemorrhoid and wakes up scratching at you."

"You have a vast untapped potential as a poet," said Graff.

"My suggestion," said Bean, "is to get the I.F. to turn Ender's money over to a neutral party."

"When it comes to money, there *are* no neutral parties. The I.F. and the colony program both spend money as fast as it comes in. We have no idea where to begin an investment program. And if you think I'm trusting some earthside mutual fund with the entire savings of a war hero who won't even be able to inquire about the money for another thirty years, you're insane."

"I was thinking that you could turn it over to a computer program."

"You think we didn't think of that? The best investment programs are only two percent better at predicting markets and bringing a positive return on investment than closing your eyes and stabbing the stock listings with a pin."

"You mean with all the computer expertise and all the computer facilities of the Fleet, you can't devise a neutral program to handle Ender's money?"

"Why are you so set on software doing it?"

"Because software doesn't get greedy and try to steal. Even for a noble purpose."

"So what if Peter *is* using Ender's money—that's what you're worried about, right?—if we suddenly cut it off, won't he notice? Won't that set back his efforts?"

"Ender saved the world. He's entitled to have his full pension, when and if he ever wants it. There are laws to protect child actors. Why not war heroes traveling at lightspeed?"

"Ah," said Graff. "So you *are* thinking about what will happen when you take off in the scoutship we offered you."

"I don't need you to manage my money. Petra will do it just fine. I want her to have the use of the money."

"Meaning you think you'll never come back."

"You're changing the subject. Software. Managing Ender's investments."

"A semi-autonomous program that—"

"Not semi. Autonomous."

"There *are* no autonomous programs. Besides which, the stock market is impossible to model. Nothing that depends on crowd behavior can be accurate over time. What computer could possibly deal with it?"

"I don't know," said Bean. "Didn't that mind game you had us play predict human behavior?"

"It's very specialized educational software."

"Come on," said Bean. "It was your shrink. You analyzed the behavior of the kids and—"

"That's right. Listen to yourself. *We* analyzed."

"But the game also analyzed. It anticipated our moves. When Ender was playing, it took him places the rest of us never saw. But the game was always ahead of him. That was one cool piece of software. Can't you teach it to play Investment Manager?"

Graff looked impatient. "I don't know. What does an ancient piece of software have to do with . . . Bean, do you realize how much effort you're asking me to go to in order to protect Ender's pension? I don't even know that it needs protecting."

"But you *should* know that it doesn't."

"Guilt. You, the conscienceless wonder, are actually using guilt on me."

"I spent a lot of time with Sister Carlotta. And Petra's no slouch, either."

"I'll look at the program. I'll look at Ender's money."

"Just out of curiosity, what is the program being used for now that you don't have any kids up there?"

Graff snorted. "We have *nothing* but kids here. The adults are playing it now. The Mind Game. Only I promised them never to let the program do analyses on their gameplay."

"So the program *does* analyze."

"It does pre-analysis. Looking for anomalies. Surprises."

"Wait a minute," said Bean.

"You *don't* want me to have it run Ender's finances?"

"I haven't changed my mind about that. I'm just wondering—maybe it could look at a really massive database we've got here and analyze . . . well, find some patterns that we're not seeing."

"The game was created for a very specific purpose. Pattern finding in databases wasn't—"

"Oh, come on," said Bean. "That's *all* it did. Patterns in our behavior. Just because it assembled the database of our actions on the fly doesn't change the nature of what it was doing. Checking our behavior against the behavior of earlier children. Against our own normal behavior. Seeing just how crazy your educational program was making us."

Graff sighed. "Have your computer people contact my computer people."

"With your blessing. Not some foot-dragging fob-them-off-with-smoke-and-mirrors 'effort' that deliberately leads nowhere."

"You really care about what we do with Ender's money?"

"I care about Ender. Someday he may need that money. I once made a promise that I'd keep Peter from hurting Ender. Instead, I did nothing while Peter sent Ender away."

"For Ender's own good."

"Ender should have had a vote."

"He did," said Graff. "If he had insisted on going home to Earth, I would have let him. But once Valentine came up to join him, he was content."

"Fine," said Bean. "Has he given consent to have his pension pillaged?"

"I'll see about turning the mind game into a financial manager. The program is a complex one. It does a lot of self-programming and self-alteration. So maybe if we ask it to, it can rewrite its own code in order to become whatever you want it to be. It *is* magic, after all. This computer stuff."

"That's what I always thought," said Bean. "Like Santa Claus. You adults pretend he doesn't exist, but *we* know that he really does."

When he ended the conversation with Graff, Bean immediately called Ferreira. It was full daylight now, so Ferreira was actually awake. Bean told him about the plan to have the Mind Game program analyze the impossibly large database of vague and mostly useless information about the movements of pregnant women with low-birth-weight babies and Ferreira said he'd get right on it. He said it without enthusiasm, but Bean knew that Ferreira wasn't the kind of man to say he'd do something and not do it, just because he didn't believe in it. He'd keep his word.

How do I know that? Bean wondered. How do I know that I can trust Ferreira to go off on wild goose chases, once he gives his word to do it? While I know without even knowing that I know it, that Peter is partly financing his operations by stealing from Ender. That was bothering me for days before I understood it.

Damn, but I'm smart. Smarter than any computer program, even the Mind Game.

If only I could control it.

I may not have the capacity to consciously deal with a vast database and find patterns in it. But I could deal with the database of stuff I observe in the Hegemony and what I know about Peter and without my even *asking the question,* out pops an answer.

Could I always do that? Or is my growing brain giving me ever-stronger mental powers?

I really should look at some of the mathematical conundrums and see if I can find proofs of . . . whatever it is they can't prove but want to.

Maybe Volescu isn't so wrong after all. Maybe a whole world full of minds like mine . . .

Miserable, lonely, untrusting minds like mine. Minds that see death looming over them all the time. Minds that know they'll never see their children grow up. Minds that let themselves get sidetracked on issues like taking care of a friend's pension that he'll probably never need.

Peter is going to be so furious when he finds out that those pension checks aren't going to him anymore. Should I tell him it was my meddling? Or let him think the I.F. did it on their own?

And what does it say about my character that I am absolutely going to tell him I did it?

Theresa didn't actually see Peter until noon, when she and John Paul and their illustrious son sat down to a lunch of papaya and cheese and sliced sausage.

"Why do you always drink that stuff?" asked John Paul.

Peter looked surprised. "Guaraná? It's my duty as an American to never drink Coke or Pepsi in a country that has an indigenous soft drink. Besides which, I like it."

"It's a stimulant," said Theresa. "It fuzzes your brain."

"It also makes you fart," said John Paul. "Constantly."

"*Frequently* would be the more accurate term," said Peter. "And it's sweet of you to care."

"We're just looking out for your image," said Theresa.

"I only fart when I'm alone."

"Since he does it in front of us," said John Paul to Theresa, "what exactly does that make us?"

"I meant 'in private,' " said Peter. "And flatulence from carbonated beverages is odorless."

"He thinks it doesn't stink," said John Paul.

Peter picked up the glass and drained it. "And you wonder why I don't look forward to these little family get-togethers."

"Yes," said Theresa. "Family is so inconvenient for you. Except when you can spend their pension checks."

Peter looked back and forth between her and John Paul. "You aren't even *on* a pension. Either of you. You're not even fifty yet."

Theresa just looked at him like he was stupid. She knew that look drove him crazy.

But Peter refused to bite. He simply went back to eating his lunch.

His very incuriosity was proof enough to Theresa that he knew exactly what she was talking about.

"You mind telling me what this is about?" asked John Paul.

"Why, Andrew's pension," said Theresa. "Bean thinks that Peter's been stealing it."

"So naturally," said Peter with his mouth full, "Mother believes him."

"Oh, haven't you, then?" asked Theresa.

"There's a difference between investing and stealing."

"Not when you invest it in Hegemony bonds. Especially when a circle of huts in Amazonas has a higher bond rating than you."

"Investing in the future of world peace is a sound investment."

"Investing in *your* future," said Theresa. "Which is more than you did for Andrew. But now that Bean knows, you can be sure that source of funding will dry up very quickly."

"How sad for Bean," said Peter. "Since that was what was paying for his and Petra's search."

"It wasn't until you decided it was," said John Paul. "Are you really that petty?"

"If Bean decides unilaterally to cut off a funding source, then I have to reduce spending somewhere. Since spending on his personal quest has nothing to do with Hegemony goals, it seems only fair that the meddler's pet project be the first to go. It's all moot anyway. Bean has no claim on Ender's pension. He can't touch it."

"He's not going to touch it himself," said Theresa. "He doesn't want the money."

"So he'll turn it over to you? What will *you* do, keep it in an interest-bearing debit account, the way you do with your own money?" Peter laughed.

"He seems unrepentant," said John Paul.

"That's the problem with Peter," said Theresa.

"Only the one?" said Peter.

"Either it doesn't matter or it's the end of the world. No in between for him. Absolute confidence or utter despair."

"I haven't despaired in years. Well, weeks."

"Just tell me, Peter," said Theresa. "Is there no one you won't exploit to accomplish your purposes?"

"Since my purpose is saving the human race from itself," said Peter, "the answer is no." He wiped his mouth and dropped his napkin on his plate. "Thanks for the lovely lunch. I do enjoy our little times together."

He left.

John Paul leaned back in his chair. "Well. I think I'll tell Bean that if he needs any next-of-kin signatures for whatever he's doing with Andrew's pension, I'll be happy to help."

"If I know Julian Delphiki, no help will be needed."

"Bean saved Peter's whole enterprise by killing Achilles at great personal risk, and our son's memory is so short that he'll stop paying for the effort to rescue Bean's and Petra's children. What gene is it that Peter's missing?"

"Gratitude has a very short half-life in most people's hearts," said Theresa. "By now Peter doesn't even remember that he ever felt it toward Bean."

"Anything we can do about it?"

"Again, my dear, I think we can count on Bean himself. He'll expect retaliation from Peter, and he'll already have a plan."

"I hope his plan doesn't require appealing to Peter's conscience."

Theresa laughed. So did John Paul. It was the saddest kind of laughter, in that empty room.

# 10

# GRIEF

From: FelixStarman%backdoor@Rwanda.gov.rw
To: PeterWiggin%personal@hegemon.gov
Re: Only one question remains

Dear Peter,

Your arguments have persuaded me. In principle, I am prepared to ratify the Constitution of the Free People of Earth. But in practice, one key issue remains. I have created in Rwanda the most formidable army and air force north of Pretoria and south of Cairo. That is precisely why you regard Rwanda as the key to uniting Africa. But the primary motivation of my troops is patriotism, which cannot help but be tinged with Tutsi tribalism. The principle of civilian control of the military is, shall we say, not as preeminent in their ethos.

For me to turn over my troops to a Hegemon who happens to be not only white, but American by birth, would run a grave risk of a coup that would provoke bloodshed in the streets and destabilize the whole region.

That is why it is essential that you decide in advance who the commander of my forces will be. There is only one plausible candidate. Many of my men got a good look at Julian Delphiki. Word has spread. He is viewed as something of a god. His record of military genius is respected by my officer corps; his enormous size gives him heroic stature; and his partial African ancestry, which is, fortunately, visible in his features and coloring, makes him a man that patriotic Rwandans could follow.

If you send Bean to me, to stand beside me as the man who will assume command of Rwandan forces as they become part of the Free People's army, then I will ratify and immediately submit the issue to my people in a plebiscite. People who would not vote for a Constitution with you at its head will vote for a Constitution whose face is that of the Giant Julian.

Sincerely, Felix

Virlomi spoke on the cellphone with her contact. "All clear?" she asked.

"It's not a trap. They're gone."

"How bad is it?"

"I'm so sorry."

That bad.

Virlomi put away the phone and walked from the shelter of the trees into the village.

There were bodies lying in the doorway of every house they passed.

But Virlomi did not turn to the right hand or the left. They had to make sure they got the key footage first.

In the center of the village, the Muslim soldiers had spitted a cow and roasted it over a fire. The bodies of twenty or so Hindu adults surrounded the roasting pit.

"Ten seconds," said Virlomi.

Obediently, the vidman framed the shot and ran the camera for ten seconds. During the shot, a crow landed but did not eat anything. It merely walked a couple of steps and then flew again. Virlomi wrote her script in her head: The gods send their messengers to see, and in grief they fly away again.

Virlomi walked near the dead and saw that each corpse had a slab of half-cooked, bloody meat in its mouth. No bullets had been spent on the dead. Their throats were split and gaping open.

"Close up. These three, each in turn. Five seconds each."

The vidman did his work. Virlomi did not touch any of the bodies. "How many minutes left?"

"Plenty," said the vidman.

"Then take every one of them. Every one."

The vidman moved from body to body, taking the digital shots that would soon go out over the nets. Meanwhile, Virlomi now went from house to house. She hoped that there would be at least one person living. Someone they could save. But there was no one.

In the doorway of the village's largest house, one of Virlomi's men waited for her. "Please do not go in, Lady," he said.

"I must."

"You do not want this in your memory."

"Then it is exactly the thing that I must never forget."

He bowed his head and moved aside.

Four nails in a crossbeam had served the family as hooks for clothing. The clothing lay in a sodden mass on the floor. Except for the shirts that had been tied around the necks of four children, the youngest only a toddler, the eldest perhaps nine. They had been hung up on the hooks to strangle slowly.

Across the room lay the bodies of a young couple, a middle-aged couple, and an old woman. They had made the adults in the household watch the children die.

"When he is finished by the fire," said Virlomi, "bring him here."

"Is there enough light inside, Lady?"

"Take down a wall."

They took it down in minutes, and then light flooded into the dark place. "Start here," she told the vidman, pointing to the adults' bodies. Pan very slowly. And then pan, just a little faster, to what they were forced to watch. Hold on all four children. Then when I enter the frame, stay with me. But not so close that you can't see everything I do with the child."

"You cannot touch a dead body," said one of her men.

"The dead of India are my children," she said. "They cannot make me unclean. Only the ones who murdered them are made filthy. I will explain this to the people who see the vid."

The vidman started, but then Virlomi noticed the shadows of the watching soldiers in the frame and made him start over. "It must be a continuous take," she said. "No one will believe it if it is not smooth and continuous."

The vidman started again. Slowly he panned. When he had focused on the children for a solid twenty seconds, Virlomi stepped into the frame and knelt before the body of the oldest child. She reached up and touched the lips with her fingers.

The men could not help it. They gasped.

Well, let them, thought Virlomi. So would the people of India. So would the people of the whole world.

She stood and took the child in her arms, raising him up. With no tension on the shirt, it came away easily from the nail. She carried him across the room and laid him in the arms of the young father.

"O Father of India," she said, loudly enough for the camera, "I lay your child, the hope of your heart, in your arms."

She got up and walked slowly back to the children. She knew better than to look to see if the camera was with her. She had to act as if she didn't know the camera was there. Not that anyone would be fooled. But looking toward the camera reminded people that there were other observers. As long as she seemed oblivious of the camera, the viewers would forget that there must be a vidman and would feel as if only they and she and the dead were in this place.

She knelt before each child in turn, then rose and freed them from the cruel nails on which they once hung shawls or school bags. When she laid the second child, a girl, beside the young mother, she said, "O Mother of the Indian house, here is the daughter who cooked and cleaned beside you. Now your home is permanently washed in the pure blood of the innocent."

When she laid the third child, a little girl, across the bodies of the middle-aged couple, she said, "O history of India, have you room for one more small body in your memory? Or are you full of our grief at last? Is this one body at last too many to bear?"

When she took the two-year-old boy from his hook, she could not walk with him. She stumbled and fell to her knees and wept and kissed his distorted, blackened face. When she could speak again, she said, "Oh, my child, my child, why did my womb labor to bring you forth, only to hear your silence instead of your laughter?"

She did not stand again. It would have been too clumsy and mechanical. Instead, she moved forward on her knees across the rough floor, a slow, stately procession, so that each dip and lurch became part of a dance. She propped the little body on the corpse of the old woman.

"Great grandmother!" cried Virlomi. "Great grandmother, can't you save me? Can't you help me? Great grandmother, you are looking at me but you do nothing! I can't breathe, Great grandmother! You are the old one! It is your place to die before me, Great grandmother! It is my place to walk around your body and anoint you with ghi and water of the holy

Ganges. In my little hands there should have been a fistful of straw to do pranam for you, for my grandparents, for my mother, for my father!"

Thus she gave voice to the child.

Then she put her arm around the shoulder of the old woman and partly raised her body, so the camera could see her face.

"O little one, now you are in the arms of God, as I am. Now the sun will stream upon your face to warm it. Now the Ganges will wash your body. Now fire will purify, and the ashes will flow out into the sea. Just as your soul goes home to await another turn of the wheel."

Virlomi turned to face the camera, then gestured at all the dead. "Here is how I purify myself. In the blood of the martyrs I wash myself. In the stink of death do I find my perfume. I love them beyond the grave, and they love me, and make me whole."

Then she reached out toward the camera.

"Caliph Alai, we knew you out among the stars and planets. You were one of the noble ones then. You were one of the great heroes, who acted for the good of all humankind. They must have killed you, Alai! You must be dead, before you would let such things happen in your name!"

She beckoned, and the vidman zoomed in. She knew from experience with this vidman that only her face would be visible. She held herself almost expressionless, for at this distance any kind of expression would look histrionic.

"Once you spoke to me in the corridors of that sterile place. You said only one word. Salaam, you said. Peace, you said. It filled my heart with joy."

She shook her head once, slowly.

"Come forth from your hiding place, O Caliph Alai, and own your work. Or if it is not your work, then repudiate it. Join me in grieving for the innocent."

Because her hand could not be seen, she flicked with her fingers to tell the vidman to zoom away and include the whole scene again.

Now she let her emotions run free. She wept on her knees, then wailed, then threw herself across the bodies and howled and sobbed.

She let it go on for a full minute. The version for western eyes would have captions over this part, but for Hindus, the whole shocking scene would be allowed to linger, uninterrupted. Virlomi defiling herself upon the bodies of the unwashed dead; but no, no, Virlomi purified by their martyrdom. The people would not be able to look away.

Nor would the Muslims who saw it. Some would gloat. But others would be horrified. Mothers would see themselves in her grief. Fathers would see themselves in the corpses of the men who had been unable to save their children.

What none of them would hear was the thing she had not said: Not a single threat, not a single curse. Only grief, and a plea to Caliph Alai.

To the world at large, the video would excite pity and horror.

The Muslim world would be divided, but the portion that rejoiced at this video would be smaller each time it was shown.

And to Alai, it would be a personal challenge. She was laying responsibility for this at his door. He would have to come out of Damascus and take command himself. No more hiding indoors. She had forced his hand. Now to see what he would do.

---

The video swept around the world, first on the nets, then picked up by broadcast media—high-resolution files were conveniently provided for download. Of course there were charges that the whole thing was faked, or that Hindus had committed the atrocities. But no one really believed that. It fit too well with the record that Muslims had created for themselves during the Islamic wars that raged in the century and a half before the Buggers came. And it was unbelievable to imagine Hindus defiling the dead as these had been defiled.

Such atrocities were meant to strike terror in the hearts of the enemy. But Virlomi had taken this one and turned it into something else. Grief. Love. Resolve. And, finally, a plea for peace.

Never mind that she could have peace whenever she wanted, merely by submitting to Muslim rule. The world would understand that complete submission to Islam would not be peace, but the death of India and its replacement by a land of puppets. She had made this so clear in earlier vids that it did not need to be repeated.

They tried to keep the vid from Alai, but he refused to let them block what he saw on his own computer. He watched it over and over again.

"Wait until we can investigate and see if it's true," said Ivan Lankowski, the half-Kazakh aide he trusted to be closest to him, to see him when he was not acting the part of Caliph.

"I know that it's true," said Alai.

"Because you know this Virlomi?"

"Because I know the soldiers who claim to be of Islam." He looked at Ivan with tears streaming down his cheeks. "My time in Damascus is done. I am Caliph. I will lead the armies in the field. And men who act this way, I will punish with my own hand."

"That is a worthy goal," said Ivan. "But the kind of men who massacred that village in India and nuked Mecca in the last war, they're still out there. That's why your orders are not being obeyed. What makes you think you can reach your armies alive?"

"Because I truly am Caliph, and if God wants me to lead his people in righteousness, he will protect me," said Alai.

# 11
# AFRICAN GOD

From: H95Tqw0qdy9@FreeNet.net
Posted at site: ShivaDaughter.org
Re: Suffering daughter of Shiva, the Dragon grieves at the wounds he caused you.

May not the Dragon and the Tiger be lovers, and bring forth peace? Or if there is no peace, may not the Tiger and the Dragon fight together?

Bean and Petra were surprised when Peter came to see them in their little house on the grounds of the Hegemony compound. "You honor our humble abode," said Bean.

"I do, don't I," said Peter with a smile. "The baby's asleep?"

"Sorry, you don't get to watch me nurse him," said Petra.

"I have good news and bad news," said Peter.

They waited for him to tell them.

"I need you to go back to Rwanda, Julian."

"I thought the Rwandan government was with us," said Petra.

"It's not a raid," said Peter. "I need you to take command of the Rwandan military and incorporate it into the Hegemony forces."

Petra laughed. "You're kidding. Felix Starman is going to ratify your Constitution?"

"Hard to believe, but yes, Felix is ambitious the way I'm ambitious—he wants to create something that will outlive him. He knows that the best way for Rwanda to be safe and free is for there to be no armies in the world. And the only way for that to happen is to have a world government that will maintain the liberal values he has created in his Rwanda—elections, individual rights, the rule of law, universal education, and no corruption."

"We've read your Constitution, Peter," said Bean.

"He asked for you in particular," said Peter. "His men saw you when you took Volescu. They call you the African Giant now."

"Darling," said Petra to Bean. "You're a god now, like Virlomi."

"The question is whether you're woman enough to be married to a god," said Bean.

"I shade my eyes and it keeps me from going blind."

Bean smiled and turned to Peter. "Does Felix Starman know how long I'm not expected to live?"

"No," said Peter. "I regard that as a state secret."

"Oh no," said Petra. "Now we can't tell each other."

"How long will you expect me to stay?"

"Long enough for the Rwandan army to transfer its loyalty to the Free People."

"To you?"

"To the Free People," said Peter. "I'm not creating a cult of personality here. They have to be committed to the Constitution. And to defending the Free People who have accepted it."

"In practical terms, a date, please," said Bean.

"Until after the plebiscite, at least," said Peter.

"And I can go with him?" asked Petra.

"Your choice," said Peter. "It's probably safer there than here, but it's a long flight. You can write the Martel essays from anywhere."

"Julian, he's leaving it up to us. We're Free People now too!"

"All right, I'll do it," said Bean. "Now what's the good news?"

"That *was* the good news," said Peter. "The bad news is that we've had a sudden and unexpected shortfall in revenue. It will take months, at least, to make up what we abruptly stopped receiving. Therefore we're cutting back on projects that don't contribute directly to the goals of the Hegemony."

Petra laughed. "You have the cheek to ask us to help you, when you're cutting off funding for our search?"

"You see? You immediately recognized that your search was not contributing."

"You're searching, too," said Bean. "To find the virus."

"If it exists," said Peter. "In all likelihood, Volescu is teasing us, and the virus doesn't actually work and hasn't been dispersed."

"So you're going to bet the future of the human race on that?"

"No I'm not," said Peter. "But without a budget for it, it's beyond our reach. However, it is *not* beyond the reach of the International Fleet."

"You're turning it over to them?"

"I'm turning Volescu over to them. And they're going to continue the research into the virus he developed and where he might have dispersed it, if he did."

"The I.F. can't operate on Earth."

"They can if they're acting against an alien threat. If Volescu's virus works, and it's released on Earth, it would create a new species designed to completely replace humanity in a single generation. The Hegemon has issued a secret finding that Volescu's virus constitutes an alien invasion, which the I.F. has kindly agreed to track down and . . . repel for us."

Bean laughed. "Well, it seems we think alike."

"Really?" said Peter. "Oh, you're just flattering me."

"I already turned over our search to the Ministry of Colonization. And we both know that Graff is really functioning as a branch of the I.F."

Peter regarded him calmly. "So you knew I'd have to cut the budget for your search."

"I knew that you didn't have the resources no matter how much budget you have. Ferreira was doing his best, but ColMin has better software."

"Well, everything's working out happily for everyone, then," said Peter, standing up to go.

"Even for Ender," said Bean.

"Your baby's a lucky little boy," said Peter, "to have such attentive parents." And he was out the door.

---

Volescu looked tired when Bean went to see him. Old. Confinement wasn't good for him. He was not suffering physically, but he seemed to be growing wan as a plant kept in a closet without sun.

"Promise me something," said Volescu.

"What?" asked Bean.

"Something. Anything. Bargain with me."

"The one thing you want," said Bean, "you will never have again."

"Only because you're vindictive," said Volescu. "Ungrateful—you exist because I made you, and you keep me in this box."

"It's a good-sized room. It's air-conditioned. Compared to the way you treated my brothers. . . ."

"They were not legally—"

"And now you have my babies hidden away. And a virus with the potential to destroy the human race—"

"Improve it—"

"Erase it. How can you be given your freedom again? You combine grandiosity with amorality."

"Rather like Peter Wiggin, whom you serve so faithfully. His little toad."

"The word is 'toady,' " said Bean.

"Yet here you are, visiting me. Could it be that Julian Delphiki, my dear half-nephew, has a problem I could help him with?"

"Same questions as before," said Bean.

"Same answer," said Volescu. "I have no idea what happened to your missing embryos."

Bean sighed. "I thought you might want a chance to square things with me and Petra before you leave this Earth."

"Oh, come on," said Volescu. "You're threatening me with the death penalty?"

"No," said Bean. "You're simply . . . leaving Earth. Peter is turning you over to the I.F. On the theory that your virus is an alien invasion."

"Only if *you're* an alien invasion," said Volescu.

"But I am," said Bean. "I'm the first of a race of short-lived giant geniuses. Think how much larger a population the Earth can sustain when the average age at death is eighteen."

"You know, Bean, there's no reason for you to die young."

"Really? You have the antidote?"

"Nobody needs an antidote to destiny. Death from giantism comes from the strain on your heart, trying to pump so much blood through so many kilometers of arteries and veins. If you get away from gravity, your heart won't be overtaxed and you won't die."

"You think I haven't thought of that?" said Bean. "I'll still continue to *grow*."

"So you get large. The I.F. can build you a really big ship. A colony ship. You can gradually fill it up with your protoplasm and bones. You'd live for *years*, tied to the walls of the ship like a balloon. An enormous Gulliver. Your wife could come visit you. And if you get too big, well, there's always amputation. You could become a being of pure mind. Fed intravenously, what need would you have of belly and bowels? Eventually, all you really need is your brain and spine, and they need never die. A mind eternally growing."

Bean stood up. "Is that what you created me for, Volescu? To be a limbless crippled monster out in space?"

"Silly boy," said Volescu, "to ordinary humans you already *are* a monster. Their worst nightmare. The species that will replace them. But to me, you're beautiful. Even tethered to an artificial habitat, even limbless, trunkless, voiceless, you'd be the most beautiful creature alive."

"And yet you came within one toilet-tank lid of killing me and burning my body."

"I didn't want to go to jail."

"Yet here you are," said Bean. "And your next prison is out in space."

"I can live like Prospero, refining my arts in solitude."

"Prospero had Ariel and Caliban," said Bean.

"Don't you understand?" said Volescu. "*You're* my Caliban. And all your little children—they're my Ariels. I've spread them over the earth. You'll never find them. Their mothers have been taught well. They'll mate, they'll reproduce before their giantism becomes obvious. Whether my virus works or not, your children are my virus."

"So that's what Achilles plotted?"

"Achilles?" Volescu laughed. "That bloody-handed little moron? I told him your babies were dead. That's all he wanted. Fool."

"So they're not dead."

"All alive. All implanted. By now, perhaps, some of them born, since those with your abilities will be born two months premature."

"You knew that and didn't tell us?"

"Why should I? The delivery was safe, wasn't it? The baby was mature enough to breathe and function on its own?"

"What else do you know?"

"I know that everything will work out. Julian, look at yourself, man! You escaped at the age of *one*. Which means that seventeen months after conception, you were able to survive without parents. I don't have even the tiniest worry about the health of your babies, and neither should you. They don't need you, because you didn't need anybody. Let them go. Let them replace the old species, bit by bit, over the generations to come."

"No," said Bean, "I love the old species. And I hate what you did to me."

"Without 'what I did to you,' all you'd be is Nikolai."

"My brother is a wonderful person. Kind. And very smart."

"Very smart, but not as smart as you. Would you *really* trade with him? Would you really like to be as dull-witted as he is, compared to you?"

Whereupon Bean left, having no answer to Volescu's last question.

# 12

# ALLAHU AKBAR

From: Graff%pilgrimage@colmin.gov
To: Borommakot%pinto@IComeAnon.com
Forwarded and Posted by IcomeAnon
Encrypted using code ********
Decrypted using code ***********
Re: Investment Counselor

Your idea of converting the Fantasy Game software into an investment counselor is going surprisingly well. We haven't had time to do more than short-term testing, but so far it has outpicked all the experts. We are paying Ender's pension funds to it. As you suggested, we are making sure that all investments are under false identities; we are also making sure the software is hooked widely over the nets in endlessly self-varying forms. It will be effectively untraceable and unkillable unless someone is making a systematic international effort to wipe it out, which is unlikely to happen as long as no one suspects it's there.

Ender will have no need of this money on his colony, and he'll do a better job if he's not aware that it's there. The first time he enters the nets after his subjective twenty-first birthday, the software will reveal itself to him along with the extent of his investments. Given the amount of time in travel alone, Ender will come of age with a noticeable fortune. Considerably more, I might add, than even the most optimistic projections of the value of Hegemony bonds,

But Ender's finances are not an emergency, and your children are.

A different team is tweaking the database your Ferreira sent us so it yields us more useful information. It involves a lot of additional research, not by raw data-seeks, but by individual operators trawling various medical, voting, tax, real estate, moving company, transportation and other databases, some of them not legally available. Instead of getting thousands of positives, of which none is likely to be useful, we are now getting hundreds of positives of which some might actually go somewhere.

Sorry it takes time, but once we get a decent positive, we have to check it out, often with landside personnel. And for obvious reasons, we don't have many of those to work with.

Meanwhile, I suggest you keep in mind that our deal depends on your making Peter Hegemon in fact as well as name before you go. You asked me what my standard of success would be. You can go when: Peter has firm control over more than 50% of the world's population, or Peter has sufficient military force that he is assured of victory whether or not any potential opponent is led by Battle School graduates.

Therefore: Yes, Bean, we expect you to go to Rwanda. We are your best hope for your and your children's survival, and you are our best hope for assuring Peter will prevail and achieve unity and general peace. Your task begins with getting Peter that irresistible military force, and our task begins with finding your babies.

Like you, I hope both our tasks turn out to be achievable.

Alai had thought that once he took control of the complex in Damascus, he'd be free to rule as Caliph.

It didn't take long to learn otherwise.

All the men in his palace complex, including his bodyguards, obeyed him implicitly. But as soon as he tried to leave, even to ride around in Damascus, those he trusted most would begin to plead with him. "It's not safe," Ivan Lankowski would say. "When you got rid of the people controlling you here, it panicked their friends. And their friends include those who are commanding our armies everywhere."

"They followed my plan in the war," said Alai. "I thought they were loyal to the Caliph."

"They were loyal to victory," said Ivan. "Your plan was brilliant. And you . . . were in Ender's Jeesh. His closest friend. Of course they followed your plan."

"So they believed in me from Battle School, but not as Caliph."

"They believe in you as Caliph," said Ivan. "But more as the figurehead kind of Caliph who makes vague religious pronouncements and encouraging speeches, while you have wazirs and warlords to do all the nasty tedious work like making decisions and giving commands."

---

"How far does their control reach?" asked Alai.

"It's impossible to know," said Ivan. "Here in Damascus, your loyal servants have caught and eliminated several dozen agents. But I would not let you board an aircraft in Damascus—military or commercial."

"So if I can't trust Muslims, drive me over the Golan Heights into Israel, and let me fly on an Israeli jet."

"The same group that refuses to obey you in India is also saying that our accommodation with the Zionists was an offense against God."

"They want to start *that* nightmare all over again?"

"They long for the good old days."

"Yes, when Muslim armies were humiliated left and right, and the world feared Muslims because so many innocents were murdered in the name of God."

"You don't have to argue with *me*," said Ivan pleasantly.

"Well, Ivan," said Alai, "if I stay here, then someday my enemies will finish in India—either they'll win or they'll lose. Either way, they'll come here, made mad by victory or by defeat, it doesn't matter which. Either way, I'll be dead, don't you think?"

"Oh, definitely, sir. We do have to find a way to get you out of here."

"No plan?"

"All kinds of plans," said Ivan. "But they all involve saving your life. Not saving the Caliphate."

"If I run away, then the Caliphate is lost."

"And if you stay, then the Caliphate is yours until the day you die."

Alai laughed. "Well, Ivan, you've analyzed it well. So I have no choice. I have to go to my enemies and destroy them."

"I suggest you use a magic carpet," said Ivan, "as the most reliable form of transportation."

"You think only a genie could get me to India to face General Rajam?"

"Alive, yes."

"Then I must contact my genie," said Alai.

"Is this a good time?" asked Ivan. "With the madwoman's latest vid all over the nets and the media, Rajam is going to be a crazy man."

"That's the best time," said Alai. "By the way, Ivan, can you tell me why Rajam's nickname is 'Andariyy'?"

"Would it help if I told you that he chose the nickname 'thick rope' himself?"

"Ah. So it doesn't refer to his tenacity or strength."

"He would say it does. Or at least the tenacity of a particular part of his body."

"And yet . . . rope is limp."

"Thick rope isn't."

"Thick rope is as limp as any other," said Alai, "unless it's very short."

Ivan laughed. "I'll make sure to repeat this joke at Rajam's funeral."

"Just don't repeat it at mine."

"I will not be at your funeral," said Ivan, "unless it's a mass grave."

Alai went to his computer and began to compose a few emails. Within a half hour of sending them, he received a telephone call from Felix Starman of Rwanda.

"I'm sorry to tell you," said Felix, "that I cannot allow Muslim teachers into Rwanda."

"Fortunately," said Alai, "that isn't why I called."

"Excellent," said Felix.

"I am calling in the interest of world peace. And I understand you have already made your decision about who is the best hope of humankind for achieving that goal—no, say no names."

"Since I have no idea what you're talking about—"

"Excellent," said Alai. "A good Muslim always assumes that unbelievers have no idea." They both laughed. "All I ask is that you let it be known that there is a man crossing the Rub' al Khali on foot because his camel won't let him mount and ride."

"And you wish someone to help this poor wanderer?"

"God watches over all his creatures, but the Caliph cannot always reach out a hand to do God's will."

"I hope this poor unfortunate will be helped as soon as possible," said Felix.

"Let it be soon. I am ready at any time to hear good news of him."

They said their good-byes, and Alai got up and went in search of Ivan.

"Pack," he said.

Ivan raised his eyebrows. "What will you need?"

"Clean underwear. My most flamboyantly Caliph-like costume. Three men who will kill at my command and will not turn their weapons on me. And a loyal man with a video camera with a fully charged battery and plenty of film."

"Should the vidman be one of the loyal soldiers? Or a separate person?"

"Let all the loyal soldiers be part of the video crew."

"And shall I be one of these three?"

"That is for you to decide," said Alai. "If I fail, the men who are with me will surely die."

"Better to die quickly before the face of God's servant than slowly at the hands of God's enemies," said Ivan.

"My favorite Russian," said Alai.

"I'm a Kazakh Turk," Ivan reminded him.

"God was good to send you to me."

"And good when he gave you to all of the faithful."

"Will you say so when I have done all that I mean to do?"

"Always," said Ivan. "Always I am your faithful servant."

"You are a servant only to God," said Alai. "To me, you are a friend."

An hour later, Alai received an email that he knew was from Petra, despite the innocent signature. It was a request that he pray for a child that was undergoing an operation at the largest hospital in Beirut at seven o'clock the next morning. "We will begin our own prayers at five in the morning," said the letter, "so that dawn will find us praying."

Alai merely answered, "I will pray for your nephew, and for all those who love him, that he may live. Let it be as God wills, and we will rejoice in his wisdom."

So he would have to go to Beirut. Well, the drive was easy enough. The problem was doing it without alarming anyone that his enemies had set to spy on him.

When he left the palace complex, it was in a garbage truck. Ivan had protested, but Alai told him, "A Caliph who is afraid to be filthied on God's errand is unworthy to rule." He was sure this would be written down and, if he lived, would be included in a book of the wisdom of Caliph Alai. A book he hoped would be long and worth reading, instead of brief and embarrassing.

Dressed as a pious old woman, Alai rode in the back seat of a little old sedan driven by a soldier in civilian clothes and a false beard much longer than his real one. If he lost, if he was killed, then the fact that he dressed this way would be taken as proof that he was never worthy to be Caliph. But if he won, it would be part of the legend of his cleverness.

The old woman accepted a wheelchair to take her into the hospital, pushed by the bearded man who had driven her to Beirut.

On the roof, three men with ordinary, scuffed suitcases were waiting. It was ten minutes to five.

If someone in the hospital had noticed the disappearance of the old woman, or looked for the wheelchair, or wondered about the three men who had arrived separately, each carrying clothing for a family member to wear home, then word might already have gone out to Alai's enemies. If someone came to investigate, and they had to kill him, it would be as good as setting off an alarm by Rajam's own bed.

Three minutes before five, two young doctors, a man and a woman, came onto the roof, ostensibly to smoke. But soon they withdrew out of the sight of the men waiting with their suitcases.

Ivan looked at Alai questioningly. Alai shook his head. "They are here to kiss," he said. "They are afraid of us reporting them, that's all."

Ivan, being careful, got up and walked to where he could see them. He came back and sat down. "More than kissing," he whispered.

"They should not do that if they aren't married," said Alai. "Why do people always think that the only two choices are either to follow the harshest shari'ah or else discard all the laws of God?"

"You have never been in love," said Ivan.

"You think not?" said Alai. "Just because I can't meet any women does not mean I haven't loved."

"With your mind," said Ivan, "but I happen to know that with your body you have been pure."

"Of course I'm pure," said Alai. "I'm not married."

A medical chopper approached. It was exactly five o'clock. When it came close enough, Alai could see that it was from an Israeli hospital.

"Do Israeli doctors send patients to Beirut?" asked Alai.

"Lebanese doctors send patients to Israel," said Ivan.

"So must we expect that our friends will wait until this chopper leaves? Or are these our friends?"

"You have hidden in garbage and dressed as a woman," said Ivan. "What is riding in a Zionist helicopter compared to that?"

The chopper landed. The door opened. Nobody got out.

Alai picked up the suitcase that he knew was his because it was light—filled only with clothes instead of weaponry—and walked boldly to the door.

"Am I the passenger you came for?"

The pilot nodded.

Alai turned to look back toward where the couple had gone to kiss. He saw a flurry of motion. They had seen. They would speak of it.

He turned back to the pilot. "Can this chopper carry all five of us?"

"Easily," said the pilot.

"What about seven?"

The pilot shrugged. "We fly lower, slower. But we often do."

Alai turned to Ivan. "Please invite our young lovers to come with us." Then Alai climbed into the helicopter. In moments, he had the women's clothing off. Underneath, he was wearing a simple western business suit.

In moments, a pair of terrified doctors climbed into the helicopter at gunpoint, in various stages of deshabille. Apparently they had been warned to maintain absolute silence, because when they saw Alai and recognized him, the man went white and the woman began to weep while trying to refasten her clothing.

Alai came and knelt in front of her. "Daughter of God," he said, "I am not concerned about your immodesty. I am concerned that the man you offered your nakedness to is not your husband."

"We *will* be married," she said.

"Then when that happy day comes," said Alai, "your nakedness will bless your husband, and his nakedness will belong to you. Until then, I have this clothing for you." He handed her the costume he had worn. "I do not ask that you dress like this all the time. But today, when God has seen how your heart intended to sin, perhaps you might cover yourself in humility."

"Can she wait to dress until we're in the air?" asked the pilot.

"Of course," said Alai.

"Everybody strap down," said the pilot.

There weren't enough seats along the sides; the center was meant to hold a gurney. But Alai's driver grinned and insisted on standing. "I've ridden choppers into battle. If I can't keep my feet in a medical chopper, I deserve some bruises."

The chopper tilted as it rose into the air, but soon it found a workable equilibrium, and the woman unstrapped and awkwardly dressed herself. All the men looked away, except her companion, who helped her.

Meanwhile, Alai and the pilot conversed, making no attempt to lower their voices.

"I don't want these two with us for the main enterprise," said Alai. "But I don't want to kill them either. They need time to find their way back to God."

"They can be held in Haifa," said the pilot. "Or I can have them taken on to Malta, if that would suit you better."

"Haifa will do."

---

It wasn't a long journey, even flying low and slow. By the time they arrived, the doctors were quiet and looked penitent, holding hands and trying not to look at Alai too much. They landed on the roof of a hospital in Haifa, and the pilot turned off the engine and got out to converse for a moment with a man dressed like a doctor. Then he opened the door. "I have to lift off again," he said, "to make room for your transportation. So you need to come out now. Except those two."

The doctors looked at each other, frightened.

"They'll be safe?" asked Alai.

"Better if they don't see your transportation come and go," said the pilot. "It will soon be dawn and there's a little light. But they'll be safe."

Alai touched them both as he left the chopper.

He and his men watched as the medical chopper lifted off. Instantly, another chopper arrived, but this time a long-range battlejet, large enough to carry many soldiers into battle, and armed heavily enough to get them past a lot of obstacles.

The door opened, and Peter Wiggin stepped out.

Alai walked up to him. "Salaam," he said.

"And in you, too, let there be peace," said Peter.

"You look more like Ender than the public photographs show."

"I have them retouched by computer to make me look older and smarter," said Peter.

Alai grinned. "It was nice of you to give us a ride."

"When Felix told me the sad story of that lonely pedestrian in the Empty Quarter, I couldn't pass up the chance to help."

"I thought it would be Bean," said Alai.

"It's a whole bunch of men trained by Bean," said Peter. "But Bean himself is on another errand. In Rwanda, as it happens."

"So that's happening now?" asked Alai.

"Oh, no," said Peter. "We won't make a *move* until we see how your little adventure turns out."

"Then let's go," said Alai.

Peter invited Alai to take precedence, but then he himself entered before any of Alai's soldiers. Ivan made as if to protest, but Alai gestured for him to relax. Alai had already bet everything on Peter's being cooperative and trustworthy. Now was not the time to worry about assassination or kidnapping. Even though there were twenty Hegemony soldiers already inside, as well as a sizable amount of equipment. Alai recognized the Thai-looking commander as someone he knew from Battle School. Had to be Suriyawong. Alai nodded to him. Suriyawong nodded back.

Once they were under way and on jet power—this time without any embarrassed woman having to be officially rebuked and forgiven and dressed—Peter indicated the men who were with him.

"I assumed," said Peter, "that the lone hitchhiker our mutual friend told me about didn't need a large escort."

"Only enough to get me to where a certain thick rope is coiled like a snake."

Peter nodded. "I have friends currently trying to find his exact location."

Alai smiled. "I assume it's far from the front."

"If he's in Hyderabad," said Peter, "then he will be under extremely heavy guard. But if he's across the border in Pakistan, security will not be unusually heavy."

"Either way," said Alai, "I will not have your men exposed to danger."

"Or observed," said Peter. "It wouldn't do for too many people to know you were brought to real power with the help of the Hegemon."

"You do seem to be at hand whenever I make a play for power."

"This is the last time, if you win," said Peter.

"This is the last time either way," said Alai, then grinned. "Either the soldiers will follow me or they won't."

"They will," said Peter. "If they get the chance."

Alai indicated his small escort. "That's what my camera crew is here to ensure."

Ivan smiled and lifted his shirt enough to show that he was wearing a bulletproof vest and carrying grenades and clips and a machine pistol.

---

"Oh," said Peter. "I thought you had gained weight."

"We Battle School boys," said Alai, "we always have a plan."

"You're not going to fight your way in, then."

"We're going to walk in as if we expected to be obeyed," said Alai. "With cameras rolling. It's a simple plan. But it doesn't have to work for very long. That thick rope, it always did love a camera."

"A vain and brutal man, my sources say," said Peter. "And not stupid."

"We'll see," said Alai.

"I think you're going to succeed," said Peter.

"So do I."

"And when you do," said Peter, "I think you're going to do something about the things Virlomi has been complaining about."

"It's because of those things that I could not wait for a more opportune time. I must wash Islam clean of this bloody stain."

"I believe that with you as Caliph, the Free People of Earth can coexist with a united Islam," said Peter.

"I believe so as well," said Alai. "Though I can never say so."

"But what I want," said Peter, "is insurance that I can use in case you don't survive. Either today or at some future point, I want to make sure I don't have to face a Caliph I can't coexist with."

Peter handed Alai a couple of sheets of paper. It was a script. Alai began to read.

"If you die a natural death and pass on your throne to someone you have chosen, then I'll have no need of this," said Peter. "But if you were murdered or kidnapped or exiled or otherwise dethroned by force, then I want this."

"And what if *you* are killed or otherwise forcibly removed from office?" asked Alai. "What happens to this vid then, assuming I say these things for the camera?"

"Try to encourage your followers not to think that killing me would be good for Islam," said Peter, "and my soldiers and doctors will guard against any other possible causes of my untimely death."

"In other words, I just have to risk it," said Alai.

"Come now," said Peter, "the only way this vid will be useful is if you aren't around to repudiate it. And if I'm dead, it will have no value to my unworthy successor."

Alai nodded. "True enough."

He stood up, opened his suitcase, and dressed in the flamboyant costume of a Caliph as the Muslim people expected to see him. Meanwhile, Peter's vidman set up his equipment—and the backdrop, so it wouldn't be obvious it was taped on a battlecraft, surrounded by soldiers.

---

At the gate of the heavily guarded military complex at Hyderabad—once the headquarters of the Indian military, then of the Chinese occupiers, and now of the Pakistani "liberators"—three motorcycles pulled up, two of them carrying two men each, and the third a single rider with a satchel on the seat behind him.

They stopped well back from the gate, so no one would suppose it was an attempt at a suicide bombing. They all held up their hands so some trigger happy guard wouldn't take a shot at them while one of the men pulled a video camera out of the satchel and fitted a satellite feed to the top of it.

That got the attention of the guards, who immediately phoned for advice from someone in authority.

Only when the camera was ready did the man who had been alone on his cycle peel back the traveling coat that had covered him. The guards were almost blinded by the whiteness of his robes, and long before he had his kaffia-cloth and 'agal-rope in place on his head.

Even the guards who weren't close enough to recognize him by face guessed from the clothing and from the fact that he was a young black man that their Caliph had come to see them. None of the common soldiers and few of the officers suspected that General Rajam would not be happy to have a visit from the Caliph. So they raised their voices in cheers—some of them in an ululation meant to suggest the cries of Arab warriors riding into battle, though all the soldiers here were Pakistani.

---

The camera rolled as Alai raised his arms to receive the adulation of his people.

He strode through the checkpoint unmolested.

Someone brought him a jeep, but he refused and kept walking. But the vidman and his crew got into the jeep and rode along beside and then ahead of the Caliph. While the Caliph's aide, Ivan Lankowski, dressed in civilian clothes like the vid crew, explained to the officers who trotted alongside him that the Caliph was here to bestow upon General Rajam the honors he had earned. He expected General Rajam and those men he wished to have share this honor greet the Caliph in the open square before all of the Caliph's soldiers.

This word quickly spread, and before long, Alai's progress was accompanied by thousands of uniformed soldiers, cheering and calling his name. They kept a path clear for the vid crew, and those who thought they might be within line of sight of the camera made an especially exuberant show of their love for the Caliph, in case someone from home was watching and might recognize them.

Alai was reasonably confident that whatever Rajam might be planning, he wouldn't do it in front of a live satellite feed, with thousands of soldiers looking on. Rajam would have had Alai die in a plane crash on the way, or be assassinated somewhere far from Rajam himself. Now that he was here, Rajam would play a waiting game, to see what Alai was up to, meanwhile looking for some innocent-seeming way for Alai to be gotten rid of—killed, or trundled back to Damascus and kept under closer guard.

As Alai expected, Rajam waited for him at the top of the imposing stairs leading up to the finest-looking building in the compound. But Alai walked up only a few steps and stopped, turning his back on Rajam and facing the soldiers . . . and the camera. The light was good here.

The vid crew took their places at the bottom of the steps.

Alai held up his arms for silence and waited. The shouting died down.

"Soldiers of God!" he shouted.

A huge roar, but it subsided at once.

"Where is the general who has led you?"

Another cheer . . . but one that was noticeably less enthusiastic. Alai hoped that Rajam wouldn't be too resentful of the difference in their popularity.

Alai did not look—he counted on Ivan to signal him when Rajam was near. He saw Ivan beckoning to Rajam to take his place at Alai's left hand, directly in front of the camera.

Ivan signaled. Alai turned and embraced and kissed Rajam.

Stab me to death right now, Alai wanted to say. Because this is your last chance, you treasonous, murdering dog.

Instead, he spoke softly into Rajam's ear. "As my old friend Ender Wiggin used to say, Rajam, the enemy's gate is down."

Then he let go of the embrace, ignoring the puzzled look on Rajam's face, and took his hand, offering him to the cheering of the soldiers.

Alai raised his hands for silence and got it.

"God has seen all the deeds that have been done in his name here in India!"

Cheering. But also, on some faces, uncertainty. They had seen Virlomi's vid, including the most recent one. Some of them, the brightest of them, knew that they could not be sure what Alai meant by this.

"And God knows, as you all know, that nothing has been done in India except by the will of General Rajam!"

The cheering was definitely half-hearted.

"Now is the day God has appointed to pay the debt of honor that is owed!"

The cheer had barely started when the camera crew pulled out their machine pistols and filled Rajam's body with bullets.

At first many of the soldiers thought it was an assassination attempt on the Caliph, and there was a roar. Alai was glad to see that these were not the Muslim soldiers of history—few fled from the bullets, and many rushed forward. But Alai raised his arms and strode to a higher position, above the body of Rajam. At the same time, as he had instructed them, Ivan and the two men who were not holding the camera bounded up the steps and stood in line with Alai and raised their weapons above their heads.

"Allahu akbar!" they cried in unison. "Muhammed is his prophet! And Alai is Caliph!"

Again Alai raised his hands, and waited until he had relative silence and the rush toward the steps had ceased. Now there were soldiers all around him.

"The crimes of Andariyy Rajam have made a stink throughout the world! The soldiers of Islam came to India as liberators! In the name of God they came, as friends to our brothers and sisters in India! But Andariyy Rajam betrayed God and his Caliph by encouraging some of our people to commit terrible crimes!

"God has already declared the penalty for such crimes! Now I have come to cleanse Islam of such evil. Never again will any man or woman or child have reason to fear the army of God! I command all the soldiers of God to arrest any man who committed atrocities against the people we came to liberate! I command the nations of the world to give no shelter to these criminals. I command my soldiers to arrest any man who ordered such atrocities, and any man who knew of the atrocities but did nothing to punish the offenders. Arrest them and bear witness against them, and in the name of God I will judge them.

"If they refuse to submit themselves to my authority, then they are in rebellion against God. Bring them to me for judgment; if they do not resist you, and they are innocent, they have nothing to fear. In every city and fortress, in every camp and airfield, let my soldiers arrest the offenders and bring them to the officers who are loyal to God and the Caliph!"

Alai held his pose for a long ten seconds while the soldiers cheered. Then he saw the camera lowered, as some soldiers already dragged various men toward him and others ran for nearby buildings, in search of others.

It was a very rough kind of justice that was going to go on now, as the Muslim army tore itself apart. And it would be interesting to see where such men as Ghaffar Wahabi, the prime minister of Pakistan, aligned themselves. It would be a shame to have to use this army to subdue a Muslim government.

But Alai had to act quickly, even if it was messy. He could not afford to let any of the offenders get away to plot against him.

And as he watched the accused men being lined up in front of him, under the direction of Ivan and his men, who seemed unlikely to be killed today after all, Alai spoke inside his mind: There, Hot Soup! See how Alai adapted your trick to his purposes.

We still learn from each other, we soldiers of Ender's Jeesh.

As for you, Peter, keep your little vid. It will never be needed. For all men are only tools in the hand of God, and I, not you, am the tool God has chosen to unite the world.

# 13
# FOUND

From: Graff%pilgrimage@colmin.gov
To:PADelphiki@TutsiNet.rw.net
Re: Can you travel?

Since your husband is busy in Rwanda right now, I wonder if you are able to travel? We expect no physical danger apart from the normal rigors of air travel. But with little Ender still so young, you will probably want to leave him behind. Or not—if you wish to bring him, we will do our best to accommodate you.

We have confirmed the identity of one of your children. A daughter. Naturally, we are finding the children who share Bean's genetic condition first. We have already accessed blood samples from the child, taken at the hospital because the birth was premature. The genetic match is absolute: She is yours. In all likelihood this will be difficult for the erstwhile parents, especially for the mother, who, like the victim of the proverbial cuckoo, has just borne another female's child. I will understand completely if you prefer not to be present. Your presence, however, might also help them believe in the reality of the true mother of "their" child. Your call.

Petra was furious with Peter—and with Graff. These plotters, so sure they know what's best for everyone. If they were holding off on the announcement of ratification while the turmoil—no, the bloodbath—in the Muslim world continued, then why couldn't Bean come with her to pick up the first of their missing children to be found?

No, that was impossible, he needed to cement the allegiance of the Rwandan military, and so on and so on, as if it really mattered. And most maddening of all, why did Bean go along with it? Since when had Bean become *obedient?* "I have to stay," he said, over and over, without any further explanation, despite her demand for some kind of justification.

Was Bean a plotter too? But not against *her*, surely. Why would he conceal his thinking from her? What secrets would he keep?

But when it became clear that Bean would not come with her, Petra packed baby clothes, diapers, and a change of clothes for herself into a single bag, then scooped up little Ender and headed for Kayibanda Airport.

She was met there by Mazer Rackham. "You came to Kigali instead of meeting me there?" she said.

"Hello to you too," said Rackham. "We're not trusting commercial flights on this matter. We believe Achilles's network has been broken, but we can't risk having your baby kidnapped or you harmed en route."

So Achilles still bends us and costs us time and money, even after death. Or else he's just your excuse for making sure you supervise everything directly. Why are Bean's and my children so important to you? How do I know that you, too, don't have some plan to harness our children to the yoke of some noble world-saving project?

What she said aloud was, "Thank you."

They took off on a private jet that pretended to belong to one of the big solar desalinization companies that were developing the Sahara.

Nice to know which companies the I.F. is using as a cover for planetside operations.

They overflew the Sahara, and Petra couldn't help but be pleased at the sight of a restored Lake Chad and the vast irrigation project surrounding it. She had read that the desalination on the Libyan coast was now proceeding faster than evaporation, and that Lake Chad was already affecting weather in the surrounding area. But she had not been prepared to see so many kilometers of grassland, or the herds of animals grazing on it. The grass and vines were turning sand and sahel into fertile soil again. And the dazzling surface of Lake Chad was dotted with the sails of fishing boats.

They landed in Lisbon and Rackham took her first to a hotel, where she nursed Ender, cleaned herself up, then put the baby into a sling in front of her. Carrying him she went back down to the lobby, where Rackham met her and led her to the limo waiting outside.

To her surprise, she felt a sudden stab of fear. It had nothing to do with this car, or their destination today. She remembered the day in Rotterdam when Ender was implanted in her womb. Bean emerged from the hospital with her and the drivers of the first couple of taxis were smoking. So Bean made her get in the third one. He got into the first one himself.

The first two cabs had been part of a kidnapping and murder plot, and Bean only narrowly escaped death. The cab she entered was part of an entirely different plot—one to save her life.

"You know this driver?" asked Petra.

Mazer nodded gravely. "We leave nothing to chance," he said. "The driver is a soldier. One of ours."

So the I.F. had trained military personnel on Earth, wearing civilian clothes and driving limousines. Such a scandal.

They drove up into the hills, to a large and lovely home with an astonishing view of the city and the bay and, on a clear day, the Atlantic beyond. The Romans saw this place, ruled in this city. The Vandals took it, and then the Visigoths. The Moors got it next, and then the Christians took it back. From this city, sailing ships went out and rounded Africa and colonized in India and China and Africa and, eventually, Brazil.

And yet it was nothing more than a human city in a lovely setting. Earthquakes and fires had come and gone, but people still built in the hills and on the flat. Storms and calms and pirates and war had taken ship after ship, and yet people still put out to sea with nets or trade goods or guns. People made love and grew babies, in the mansions just as in the tiny houses of the poor.

She had come here from Rwanda, as humans had come out of Africa for fifty thousand years. Not as part of a tribe that climbed down into caves to paint their stories and worship their gods. Not as part of a wave of invaders. But . . . wasn't she here to take a baby out of a woman's arms? To claim that what came from this stranger's womb would belong to *her* from now on? Just as so many people had stood on the hills overlooking the bay and said, This is mine now, and it always was mine, regardless of the people who happen to think it belongs to them and have held this place all their lives.

Mine mine mine. That was the curse and power of human beings—that what they saw and loved, they had to have. They could share it with other people but only if they conceived of those people as being somehow their own. What we own is ours. What you own should also be ours. In fact, you own nothing, if we want it. Because you are nothing. We are the real people, you are only posing as people in order to try to deprive us of what God means us to have.

And now she understood for the first time the magnitude of what Graff and Mazer Rackham and, yes, even Peter were all trying to do.

They were trying to get human beings to define themselves as all belonging to one tribe.

It had happened briefly when they were threatened by creatures who truly were strangers; then the human race had felt itself to be one people, and united in order to repel an enemy.

And the moment victory was achieved, it all fell apart, and long-pent-up resentments erupted into war. First the old rivalry between Russia and the West. And when that was quelled by the I.F., and the old polemarch fell and was replaced by Chamrajnagar, the wars moved to different killing fields.

They even looked at the Battle School grads and said, Ours. Not free people, but the property of this nation or that.

And now those same children, once property, were at the heads of some of the most powerful nations. Alai, mortaring the bricks of his fragmented empire with the blood of his enemies. Han Tzu, restoring the prosperity of China as quickly as possible in order to emerge from defeat as a power in the world. And Virlomi, out in the open now, refusing to join any party, standing above politics, but Petra knew that she would not release her hold on power.

Hadn't Petra sat with Han Tzu and Alai and controlled fleets and squadrons in distant wars? They thought they were only playing a game—all of them thought that, except Bean, the secret-keeper—but they were saving the world together. They loved being together. They loved being one, under the leadership of Ender Wiggin.

Virlomi hadn't been with them then, but Petra remembered her as well, as the girl she turned to when she was a captive in Hyderabad. She had given her a message and Virlomi had taken the burden as if Petra were a real person; she had delivered it to Bean and had helped Bean to come and save her. Now Virlomi had created a new India out of the wreckage of the old; she had given them something more powerful than any mere elected government. She had given them a divine queen, a dream and a vision, and India was poised to become, for the first time, a great power commensurate with her great population and her ancient culture.

All three of them are making their nations great, in a time when the greatness of nations is the nightmare of humanity.

How will Peter ever gain mastery over them? How will he tell them, No, this city, that mountain, these fields, that lake, they do not belong to you or to any group or individual, they are part of Earth, and Earth belongs to all of us, a single tribe. One overgrown troop of baboons that have taken shelter in the shade of this planet's night, that draw their life from the heat of this planet's day.

Graff and his ilk did their work too well. They found all of the children best suited to rule; but part of the mix they selected for was ambition. And not just the desire to achieve or even surpass others—it was aggression, the desire to rule and control.

The need to have our own way.

I certainly have it. If I had not fallen in love with Bean and focused on our children, wouldn't I be one of them? Only I would be hampered by the weakness of my country. Armenia has neither the resources nor the national will to rule over great empires. But Alai and Han Tzu inherit centuries of empire and a sense of entitlement to rule. While Virlomi is making her own myth and teaching her people that their day of destiny has come.

Only two of these great children have stepped outside the pattern, the great game of slaughter and domination.

Bean was never selected for aggression. He was selected for brilliance alone. His mind far outshone any other. But he was not one of *us*. He could solve the strategic and tactical problems more easily than anyone—more easily than Ender. But he didn't care whether he ruled; he didn't care whether he won. When he had an army of his own, he never won a battle—all his effort was spent on training his soldiers and trying out his ideas.

That's why he was able to be the perfect shadow to Ender Wiggin. He did not need to surpass Ender. All he wanted was to survive. And, without knowing it, to belong. To love and be loved. Ender gave him that. And Sister Carlotta. And me. But he never needed to rule.

Peter is the other one. And he *does* need to rule, to surpass all others. Especially because he wasn't selected for Battle School. So what tames him?

Ender Wiggin? Is that it? Peter must be greater than his brother Ender. He can't do it by conquest because he isn't a match for these Battle

Schoolers. He can't take the field against Han Tzu or Alai—or Bean, or me, for that matter! Yet he must somehow be greater than Ender Wiggin, and Ender Wiggin saved the human race.

Petra stood at the edge of the hill, across the street from the house where her second child waited for her—a daughter she intended to take away from the woman who bore her. She looked out over the city and saw herself.

I am as ambitious as Hot Soup or Alai or any of them. Yet I fell in love with and determined to marry—against his will—the only Battle Schooler who had no ambition of his own. Why? Because I wanted to have the next generation. I wanted the most brilliant children. Even as I told him that I wanted none of them to have his affliction, in fact I wanted them to have it. To be like him. I wanted to be Eve to a new species. I wanted my genes to be part of the future of humanity. And they will be.

But Bean will also die. I knew that all along. I knew that I would be a young widow. In the back of my mind, I thought of that all along. What a terrible thing to realize about myself.

That's why I don't want him to take our babies away from me. I must have them all, the way conquerors have had to have this city. *I* must have them. That is my empire.

What kind of life will they have, with me for their mother?

"We can't put this off forever," said Mazer Rackham.

"I was just thinking."

"You're still young enough to believe that will get you somewhere," said Rackham.

"No," she said. "No, I'm older than you think. I know that I can't think my way out of being who I am."

"Why would you want to?" said Mazer Rackham. "Don't you know that you were always the best of them?"

She turned to him, suppressing the rush of pride, refusing to believe it. "That's nonsense. I'm the least. The worst. The one that broke."

"The one that Ender pressed hardest, relied on most. *He* knew. Besides, I didn't mean the best at war. I meant the best, period. The best at being human."

The irony of hearing him say that right after she realized just how selfish and ambitious and *dangerous* she was—she almost laughed. Instead she reached out and touched his shoulder. "You poor man," she said. "You think of us as your children."

"No," said Rackham, "that would be Hyrum Graff."

"Did you have children? Before your voyage?"

Rackham shook his head. But she couldn't tell if he was saying, No, I had no children, or No, I won't talk to you about this. "Let's go inside."

Petra turned around, crossed the narrow street, and followed him through the gate of the garden and up to the door of the house. It stood open in the early autumn sunlight. Bees hummed among the flowers of the garden but none came into the house; what business did they have in there, when all they needed was outside?

The man and woman waited in the dining room of their house. A woman in civilian clothes—who nevertheless seemed to Petra like a soldier—stood behind them. Perhaps watching to make sure they didn't try to run.

The wife sat in an armchair and held their newborn daughter. Her husband leaned on the table. His face was a mask of despair. The woman had been crying. So they already knew.

Rackham spoke at once. "I didn't want you to turn your baby over to strangers," he said to the man and woman. "I wanted you to see that the baby is going home to her mother."

"But she already has a baby," said the woman. "You didn't tell me that she already—"

"Yes he did," said the man.

Petra sat down in a chair across from the man, cornerwise from the woman. Ender wriggled a little but stayed asleep. "We meant to save the others, not to have them born all at once," said Petra. "I meant to bear them all myself. My husband is dying. I meant to keep having his children after he was gone."

"But don't you have more? Can't you spare this one?" The woman's voice was so piteous that Petra hated herself for saying no.

Rackham spoke before she could. "This child is already dying of the same condition that is killing her father. And her brother. That's why they were born prematurely."

This only made the woman cling more tightly to the baby.

"You'll have children of your own," said Rackham. "You still have the four fertilized embryos you already created."

The would-be father looked up at him blandly. "We'll adopt next time," he said.

"We're all very sorry," Rackham went on, "that these criminals stole the use of your womb to deliver another woman's child. But the child is truly hers, and if you adopt, you should have children that were willingly given up by their parents."

The man nodded. He understood.

But the woman had the baby in her arms.

Petra spoke up. "Would you like to hold her brother?" She reached down and lifted Ender out of the sling. "His name is Andrew. He's a month old."

The woman nodded.

Rackham reached down and took her daughter out of her arms. Petra handed Ender to her.

"My . . . the girl is . . . I call her Bella. My little Lourinha." She wept.

Lourinha? The baby's hair, such as it was, was brown. But apparently it didn't take much lightness of hair to earn the appellation "blonde."

Petra took the girl from Rackham's hands. She was even smaller than Ender, but her eyes were just as intelligent and searching. Ender's hair was as black as Bean's. Bella's hair was more like Petra's. It startled her, how happy it made her that the baby took after her.

"Thank you for bearing my daughter," said Petra. "I grieve for your grief, but I hope you can also rejoice at my joy."

Weeping, the woman nodded and clung now to Ender. She turned her face to the baby and spoke in a small babytalk voice. "Es tu feliz em ter irminha? Es tu felizinho?" Then she burst into tears and handed Ender to Rackham.

Standing, Petra laid Bella into the sling where Ender had been. Then she took Ender from Rackham and held him against her shoulder.

"I'm so sorry," said Petra. "Please forgive me for not letting you keep my baby."

The man shook his head. "Não ha de que desculpar," he said.

"Nothing to forgive," murmured the stern-looking woman who was apparently not just a guard, but also an interpreter.

The woman wailed in grief and leapt to her feet, upsetting the chair. She sobbed and babbled and clutched at Bella and covered her with kisses. But she didn't try to take the baby.

Rackham pulled Petra away as the guard and the husband pulled the mother back and held her, still wailing and sobbing, while Petra and Rackham left the house.

Back in the car, Rackham sat in back with Petra and took Ender out of her arms for the ride back to the hotel. "They really are small," he said.

"Bean calls Ender a toy person," said Petra.

"I can see why," said Rackham.

"I feel like a really polite kidnapper," said Petra.

"Don't," said Rackham. "Even though they were embryos when they were stolen from you, it was a kidnapping, and now you're getting your daughter back."

"But these people did nothing wrong."

"Think again," said Rackham. "Remember how we found them."

They moved, she remembered. When Volescu's deadman switch triggered a message, they moved. "Why would they knowingly—"

"The wife doesn't know. Our deal with the husband was that we wouldn't tell. He's completely sterile, you see. *Their* attempt at in vitro fertilization didn't take. That's why he took Volescu's offer and pretended to his wife that the baby was really theirs. He's the one that got the message and made up a reason for them to move to this house."

"He didn't ask where the baby came from?"

"He's a rich man," said Rackham. "Rich people tend to take it for granted that things they want simply come to them."

"The wife meant no harm, though."

"Neither did Bean, and yet he's dying," said Rackham. "Neither did I, and yet I was sent on a voyage that jumped me decades into the future, costing me everyone and everything. And you'll lose Bean, even though you've done nothing wrong. Life is full of grief, to exactly the degree we allow ourselves to love other people."

"I see," said Petra. "You're the Ministry of Colonization's resident philosopher."

Rackham grinned. "The consolations of philosophy are many, but never enough."

"I think you and Graff planned the whole history of the world. I think you chose Bean and Peter for the roles they're playing now."

"You're wrong," said Rackham. "Flat wrong. All that Graff and I ever did was choose the children we thought might win the war and try to train them for victory. We failed again and again until we found Ender. And Bean to back him up. And the rest of the Jeesh to help him. And when the last battle ended and we had won, Graff and I had to face the fact that the solution to the one problem was now the cause of another."

"The military geniuses you had identified would now tear the world apart with their ambition."

"Or be used as pawns to satisfy the ambitions of others, yes."

"So you decided to use them as pawns in your own game once again."

"No," said Rackham softly. "We decided to find a way to set most of them free to live human lives. We're still working on that."

"*Most* of us?"

"There was nothing we could do for Bean," said Rackham.

"I guess not," said Petra.

"But then something happened that we hadn't planned on," said Rackham. "Hadn't hoped for. He found love. He became a father. The one we could do nothing for, you made him happy. So, I have to admit, we feel a lot of gratitude to you, Petra. You could have been out there playing the game with the others." He chuckled. "We would never have guessed it. You're off the charts when it comes to ambition. Not quite like Peter, but close. Yet somehow you set it all aside."

She smiled as beatifically as she could.

If only you knew the truth, she thought.

Or maybe he does know, but telling her that he admires her is a way of manipulating her . . .

Nobody ever completely means what they say. Even when they think they're telling the truth, there's always something hidden behind their words.

It was dark when she got back to her own house in the military headquarters compound just outside Kigali. Mazer Rackham did not come inside with her. So she carried both babies, Ender in the sling again, and Bella at her shoulder.

Bean was there, waiting for her. He ran to her and took the new baby from her and pressed his cheek to the baby's cheek.

"Don't smother her, oaf," said Petra.

He laughed and kissed her. They sat together on the edge of the bed, holding the two children, and then trading, back and forth.

"Seven to go," said Petra.

"Was it hard?" asked Bean.

"I'm glad you weren't there," said Petra. "I'm not sure you would have been tough enough to go through with it."

# 14

# VIRLOMI'S VISITORS

From: ImperialSelf%HotSoup@ForbiddenCity.ch.gov
To: Suriyawong@hegemon.gov
Re: We have found Paribatra

Suriyawong, I am relieved to tell you that Paribatra, the former prime minister of Thailand, has been located. His health is not good but with proper attention it is believed that he will recover as well as can be expected for a man his age.

The former government had nearly perfected the art of making people disappear without actually killing them, but we are still tracking down other Thai exiles. I have great hopes of finding and releasing your family members.

You know that I opposed all these illegal actions against Thailand, its citizens, and its government. I have now moved at the first opportunity to undo as much of the damage as I can.

For internal political reasons I cannot release Paribatra directly to Ambul's Free Thai organization at this time, even though I fully expect that his group will be the core of the new government of Thailand and look forward to an early reconciliation.

As we free Paribatra into the care of the Hegemon, it seems appropriate that you who tried so hard to save Thailand should be the one to receive him.

Virlomi came to Hyderabad, and in front of the gate of the military complex where she once worked in virtual captivity, drawing up plans for wars and invasions she did not believe in, she now built a hut with her own hands.

Each day she went to a well and drew water, even though there were few villages in India that did not already have clean running water. Each dawn she buried her night soil even though most villages had working sewer systems.

Indians came to her by the hundreds, to ask her questions. When she was tired, she came out and wept for them and begged them to go home. They went, but the next morning others came.

No soldiers came near her, so there was no overt provocation to the Muslims inside the military compound. Of course, she was controlling the Indian military, which grew in strength every day, through her encrypted cellphones, which were swapped out daily for freshly charged ones by aides posing as ordinary supplicants.

Now and then someone from another land would come to see her. Her aides would whisper to them that she would not speak to anyone who was not barefoot, and if they wore western business suits she would offer them appropriate clothing, which they would not like, so it was better to be clad already in Indian clothing of their own choosing.

Three visitors came to her in one week of her vigil.

The first was Tikal Chapekar. Emperor Han had freed him, along with many other Indian captives. If he had expected some kind of ceremony when he returned to India, he was disappointed.

He assumed at first that the silence from the media was because the Muslim conquerors would not allow any mention of the return of the imprisoned Prime Minister to India.

So he went to Hyderabad to complain to the Caliph himself, who now ruled over his vast Muslim empire from within the walls of the military compound there. He was allowed to enter the compound, though while he waited in line at the checkpoint, he was curious about the hut a few dozen meters away, where a great many more Indians waited in line than waited to see the rulers of the nation.

"What is that hut?" he asked. "Do ordinary citizens have to go there first before coming to this gate?"

The gate guards laughed at his question. "You're an Indian, and you don't know that's where Virlomi lives?"

"Who is Virlomi?"

Now the guards grew suspicious. "No Hindu would say that. Who are you?"

He explained that he had been in captivity until just a few days ago, and was not aware of the news.

"News?" said one guard. "Virlomi isn't on the *news*. She makes her own news."

"Wish they'd just let us shoot her," muttered another.

"And then who would protect you as they tore us all limb from limb?" said another, quite cheerfully.

"So . . . who is she?" asked Chapekar.

"The soul of India is a *woman*," said the one who had wanted to shoot her. He said "woman" with all the contempt he could put into a single word. Then he spat.

"What office does she hold?" asked Chapekar.

"Hindus don't hold offices anymore," said another guard. "Not even you, former Prime Minister."

Chapekar felt a wave of relief. Someone had recognized his name.

"Because you forbid the Indian people to elect their own government?"

"We allow it," said the guard. "The Caliph declared an election but nobody came."

"No one voted?"

"No one ran for office."

Chapekar laughed. "India has been a democracy for hundreds of years. People run for office. People vote."

"Not when Virlomi asks them not to serve in any office until the Muslim overlords leave India."

Now Chapekar understood everything. She was a charismatic, like Gandhi, centuries ago. Rather a sad one, since she was imitating a primitive Indian lifestyle that hadn't been the rule through most of India in many lifetimes. Still, there was magic in the old icons, and with so many disasters befalling India, the people would look for someone to capture their imagination.

Gandhi never became ruler of India, however. That job was for more practical people. If he could just get the word out that he was back. Surely the Caliph would want a legitimate Indian government restored to help keep order.

After a suitable wait, he was ushered into a building. After another wait, he was brought to the anteroom of the Caliph's office. And finally he was brought into the Presence.

Except that the person he met with was not the Caliph at all, but his old adversary, Ghaffar Wahabi, who had been prime minister of Pakistan.

"I thought to see the Caliph," said Chapekar, "but I'm glad to see you first, my old friend."

Wahabi smiled and nodded, but he did not rise and when Chapekar made as if to approach him, hands restrained him. Still, they did not stop him from sitting in an armless chair, which was good, because Chapekar tired easily these days.

"I am glad to see that the Chinese have come to their senses and set their prisoners free. This new emperor they have is weak, a mere boy, but a weak China is better for all of us, don't you think?"

Chapekar shook his head. "The Chinese people love him."

"Islam has ground the face of China into the dust," said Wahabi.

"Has Islam ground the face of India into the dust as well?" asked Chapekar.

"There were excesses, under the previous military leadership. But Caliph Alai, may God preserve him, put a stop to that some time ago. Now the leader of the Indian rebels sits outside our gate, and we are untroubled, and she and her followers are unmolested."

"So now Muslim rule is benign," said Chapekar. "And yet when the Indian Prime Minister returns, there is not a word on television, not an interview. No car waiting for him. No office."

Wahabi shook his head. "My old friend," he said. "Don't you remember? As the Chinese surrounded and swallowed up your armies, as they swept across India, you made a great public pronouncement. You said, if I remember rightly, that there would be no government in exile. That the ruler of India from then on would be . . . and I say this with all modesty . . . me."

"I meant, of course, only until I returned."

"No you were very clear," said Wahabi. "I'm sure we can get someone to play you the vid. I can send for someone if you—"

"You are going to hold India without a government because—"

"India has a government. From the mouth of the Indus to the mouth of the Ganges, from the Himalayas to the waves that lap the shores of Sri Lanka, the flag of Pakistan flies over a united India. Under the divinely inspired leadership of Caliph Alai, may Allah be thanked for him."

"Now I understand why you suppress news of my coming," said Chapekar, rising to his feet. "You are afraid of losing what you have."

"What I have?" Wahabi laughed. "We are the government, but Virlomi rules India. You think *we* blacked out the news about you? *Virlomi* asked the Indian people not to look at television as long as the Muslim invaders retained their unwelcome presence in Mother India."

"And they obey her?"

"The drop in national power consumption is noticeable. No one interviewed you, old friend, because there *are* no reporters. And even if there were, why would they care about you? You don't rule India, and I don't rule India, and if you want to have anything to do with India, you'll take off your shoes and get in that line in front of the hut outside the gate."

"Yes," said Chapekar. "I'll do that."

"Come back and tell me what she says," said Wahabi. "I've been contemplating doing the same thing myself."

So Chapekar walked back out of the military compound and joined the line. When the sun set and the sky began to darken, Virlomi came out of the hut and wept with grief that she could not hear and speak to everyone personally. "Go home," she said. "I pray for you, all of you. Whatever is the desire of your heart, let the Gods grant it, if it would bring no harm to another. If you need food or work or shelter, go back to your city or your village and tell them that Virlomi is praying for that city, that village. Tell them that my prayer is this: Let the gods bless the people to exactly the degree that they help the hungry and jobless and homeless. Then help them make this prayer a blessing upon them instead of curse. *You* try to find someone less fortunate than you, and help him. In helping him, you will also rise."

Then she went back inside the hut.

The crowd dispersed. Chapekar sat down to wait until the morning.

One of the others who had been in the line said, "Don't bother. She never sees anyone who spends the night. She says that if she lets people gain an advantage by doing that, soon the plain will be covered with snoring Indians and she will never get any sleep!"

He and several others laughed, but Chapekar did not laugh. Now that he had seen his adversary, he was worried. She was beautiful and gentle-seeming, and moved with unspeakable grace. She had mastered it all—the perfect demagogue for India. Politicians had always shouted to whip an audience into a frenzy. But this woman spoke quietly, and made them hunger for her words, so she hardly had to say anything, and they felt blessed to hear her.

Still, she was only a lone woman. Chapekar knew how to command armies. More important, he knew how to get legislation through Congress and keep party members in line. All he needed to do was attach himself to this girl and soon he would be the real ruler of her party.

Now all he needed was to find a place to spend the night and come back in the morning to see her.

He was leaving when one of Virlomi's aides touched his shoulder. "Sir," said the young man, "the Lady has asked to see you."

"Me?"

"Aren't you Tikal Chapekar?"

"I am."

"Then you're the one she asked for." The young man eyed him up and down, then knelt, scooped up some dirt, and flung it at Chapekar's suit and began to rub it in.

"What are you doing! How dare you!"

"If I don't make you look like your suit is old and you have seen much suffering, then—"

"You idiot! My suit *is* old, and I have suffered in exile!"

"The Lady will not care, sir. But do as you wish. It's this or the loincloth. She keeps several in her hut, so she can humble proud men."

Chapekar glared at the young man, then squatted, scooped up dirt, and began rubbing it into his own clothing.

A few minutes later, he was inside the hut. It was lighted by three small flickering oil lamps. Shadows danced on the dried-mud walls.

She greeted him with a smile that seemed warm and friendly. Maybe this would go better than he had feared.

"Tikal Chapekar," she said. "I'm glad that our people are returning from captivity."

"The new emperor is weak," said Chapekar. "He thinks that he'll appease world opinion by letting his prisoners go."

She said nothing.

"You've done an excellent job of annoying the Muslims," he said.

She said nothing.

"I want to help you."

"Excellent," she said. "What weapons are you trained to use?"

He laughed. "No weapons."

"So . . . not as a soldier, then. Do you type? I know you can read, so I assume you can handle record keeping on our military computers."

"Military?" he asked.

"We're a nation at war," she said simply.

"But I'm not a soldier of any kind," said Chapekar.

"Too bad."

"I'm a governor."

"The Indian people are doing an excellent job of governing themselves right now. What they need are soldiers to drive out their oppressors."

"But you have government right here. Your aides, who tell people what to do. The one who covered me with dirt."

"They help people. They don't govern them. They give advice."

"And this is how you rule all of India?"

"I sometimes make suggestions, and my aides put the vid out over the nets," said Virlomi. "Then the people decide whether to obey me or not."

"You can reject government now," said Chapekar. "But someday you'll need it."

Virlomi shook her head. "I will never need government. Perhaps someday India will choose to have a government, but *I* will never need it."

"So you wouldn't stop me from urging exactly that course. On the nets."

She smiled. "Whoever comes to your site, let them agree or disagree with you as they see fit."

"I think you're making a mistake," said Chapekar.

"Ah," said Virlomi. "And you find this frustrating?"

"India needs better than a lone woman in a hut."

"And yet this lone woman in a hut held up the Chinese Army in the passes of the east, long enough for the Muslims to have their victory. And this lone woman led the guerrilla war and the riots against the

Muslim occupiers. And this lone woman brought the Caliph from Damascus to Hyderabad in order to seize control of his own army, which was committing atrocities against India."

"And you're very proud of your achievements."

"I'm pleased that the gods saw fit to give me something useful to do. I've offered you something useful, too, but you refuse."

"You've offered me humiliation and futility." He stood to go.

"Exactly the gifts I once had from your hand."

He turned back to her. "Have we met?"

"Have you forgotten? You once came to see the Battle School graduates who were planning your strategy. But you discarded all our plans. You despised them, and followed instead the plans of the traitor Achilles."

"I saw all your plans."

"No, you saw only the plans Achilles wanted you to see."

"Was that my fault? I *thought* they were from you."

"I foresaw the fall of India as Achilles's plans overextended our armies and exposed our supply lines to attack from China. I foresaw that you would do nothing except futile rhetoric—like the monstrous act of appointing Wahabi as ruler of India—as if the rule of India were yours to bequeath to another in your will. I saw—we all saw—how useless and vain and stupid you were in your ambition, and how easily Achilles manipulated you by flattery."

"I don't have to listen to this."

"Then go," said Virlomi. "I say nothing that doesn't play over and over again in the secret places in your heart."

He did not go.

"After I left, to notify the Hegemon of what was happening, so that perhaps my friends from Battle School could be saved from Achilles's plan to murder them all—when that errand was done, I set up resistance to Chinese rule in the mountains of the East. But back in Battle School, led by a brilliant and brave and beautiful young man named Sayagi, the Battle Schoolers drew up plans that would have saved India, if you had followed them. At risk of their own lives, they published it on the nets, knowing that Achilles would let none of it get to you if they submitted it through him. Did you see the plans?"

"I was not in the habit of getting my war plans from the nets."

"No. You got your plans from our enemy."

"I didn't know that."

"You should have known. It was plain enough what Achilles was. You saw what we saw. The difference is, we hated him, and you admired him—for exactly the same traits."

"I never saw the plans."

"You never asked the most brilliant minds in India for a shred of advice. Instead, you trusted a Belgian psychopath. And followed his advice to make unprovoked war on Burma and Thailand, pouring out war on nations that had done no harm to us. A man who embraces the voice of evil when it whispers in his ear is no less evil than the whisperer."

"I'm not impressed by your ability to coin aphorisms."

"Sayagi defied Achilles to his face, and Achilles shot him dead."

"Then he was foolish to do it."

"Dead as he is, Sayagi has more value to India than you have ever had or will ever have in all the days of your life."

"I'm sorry he's dead. But I'm not dead."

"You're mistaken. Sayagi lives on in the spirit of India. But you are dead, Tikal Chapekar. You are as dead as a man can be, and still breathe."

"So now it comes to threats."

"I asked my aides to bring you to me so I could help you understand what will now happen to you. There is nothing for you in India. Sooner or later you will leave and make a life for yourself somewhere else."

"I will never leave."

"Only on the day you leave will you begin to understand Satyagraha."

"Peaceful noncompliance?"

"Willingness to suffer, yourself and in person, for a cause you believe is right. Only when you are willing to embrace Satyagraha will you begin to atone for what you have done to India. Now you should go."

Chapekar did not realize anyone had been listening. He might have stayed to argue, but the moment she said those words, a man came into the hut and drew him out.

He had thought they would let him go, but they didn't, not until they led him into the town and sat him down in the back room of a small office and brought up a notice on the nets.

It was his own picture. A short vid taken as the young man tossed dirt onto him.

"Tikal Chapekar is back," said a voice.

The picture changed to show Chapekar in his glory days. Brief clips and stills.

"Tikal Chapekar brought war to India by attacking Burma and Thailand without any provocation, all to try to make himself a great man."

Now there were pictures of Indian victims of atrocities. "Instead, he was taken captive by the Chinese. He wasn't here to help us in our hour of need."

The picture of him with dirt being flung on him returned to the screen.

"Now he's back from captivity, and he wants to rule over India."

A picture of Chapekar talking cheerfully with the Muslim guards outside the gates of the compound. "He wants to help our Muslim overlords rule over us forever."

Again with the dirt-flinging.

"How can we rid ourselves of this man? Let us all pretend he doesn't exist. If no one speaks to him, waits on him, shelters him, feeds him, or helps him in any way, he will have to turn to the foreigners he invited into our land."

That was when they ran the footage of Chapekar turning the government of India over to Wahabi.

"Even in defeat, he invited evil upon us. But India will not punish him. India will simply ignore him until he goes away."

The program ended—with, of course, the dirt-flinging picture.

"Clever set-up," said Chapekar.

They ignored him.

"What do you want from me, so you won't publish that piece of trash?"

They ignored him.

After a while, he began to rage, and tried to fling the computer to the ground. That was when they restrained him and put him out of doors.

Chapekar walked down the street, looking for lodging. There were houses with rooms to rent. They opened the door when he called out, but when they saw his face, they closed the doors again.

Finally he stood in the street and shouted. "All I want is a place to sleep! And a bite to eat! What you would give a dog!"

But no one even told him to shut up.

Chapekar went to the train station and tried to buy a ticket out, using some of the money the Chinese had given him to help him make his way home. But no one would sell him a ticket. Whatever window he went to was closed in his face, and the line moved over to the next one, making no room for him.

At noon the next day, exhausted, hungry, thirsty, he made his way back to the Muslim military compound and, after being fed and clothed and given a place to bathe and sleep by his enemies, he was flown out of India, then out of Muslim territory. He ended up in the Netherlands, where public charity would support him until he found employment.

---

The second visitor followed no known road to come to the hut. Virlomi merely opened her eyes in the middle of the night, and despite the complete darkness, she could see Sayagi sitting on the mat near the door.

"You're dead," she said to him.

"I'm still awaiting rebirth," he said.

"You should have lived," Virlomi told him. "I admired you greatly. You would have been such a husband for me and such a father for India."

"India is already alive. She does not need you to give birth to her," said Sayagi.

"India does not know she's alive, Sayagi. To wake someone from a coma is to bring them to life as surely as a mother brings forth life when she bears a baby."

"Always have an answer, don't you? And the way you talk now—like a god. How did it happen, Virlomi? Was it when Petra chose you to confide in?"

"It was when I decided to take action."

"Your action succeeded," said Sayagi. "Mine failed."

"You should not have spoken to Achilles. You should simply have killed him."

"He said he had the building wired with explosives."

"And you believed him?"

"There were other lives besides mine. You escaped in order to save the lives of the Battle Schoolers. Should I then have thrown their lives away?"

"You misunderstand me, Sayagi. All I say now is, either you act or you don't act. Either you do the thing that makes a difference, or you do nothing at all. You chose a middle way, and when it comes to war, the middle way is death."

"Now you tell me."

"Sayagi, why have you come to me?"

"I haven't. I'm only a dream. You're awake enough to realize that. You're making up both sides of this conversation."

"Then why am I making you up? What do I need to learn from you?"

"My fate," said Sayagi. "So far all your gambits have worked, but that's because you have always played against fools. Now Alai is in control of one enemy, Han Tzu another, and Peter Wiggin is the most dangerous and subtle of all. Against these adversaries, you will not win so easily. Death lies down this road, Virlomi."

"I'm not afraid to die. I've faced death many times, and when the gods decide it's time for me to—"

"See, Virlomi? You've already forgotten that you don't believe in the gods."

"But I do, Sayagi. How else can I explain my string of impossible victories?"

"Superb training in Battle School. Your innate brilliance. Brave and wise Indians who awaited only a decisive leader to show them how to act like people worthy of their own civilization. And very, very stupid enemies."

"And couldn't it be the gods who arranged for me to have these things?"

"It was an unbroken network of causality leading back to the first human who wasn't a chimp. And farther back, to the coalescing of the planets around the sun. If you wish to call that God, go ahead."

"The cause of everything," said Virlomi. "The *purpose* of everything. And if there are no gods, then my own purposes will have to do."

"Making you the only god that actually exists."

"If I can call you back from the dead by the power of my mind alone, I'd say I'm pretty powerful."

Sayagi laughed. "Oh, Virlomi, if only we had lived! Such lovers we could have been! Such children we could have had!"

"You may have died, but I didn't."

"Didn't you? The real Virlomi died the day you escaped from Hyderabad, and this impostor has been playing the part ever since."

"No," said Virlomi. "The real Virlomi died the day she heard you had been killed."

"*Now* you say it. When I was alive, not one little kiss, nothing. I think you didn't even fall in love with me until I was safely dead."

"Go away," she said. "It's time for me to sleep."

"No," he said. "Wake up, light your lamp, and write down this vision. Even if it is only a manifestation of your unconscious, it's a fascinating one, and it's worth pondering over. Especially the part about love and marriage. You have some cockeyed plan to marry dynastically. But I tell you the only way you'll be happy is to marry a man who loves you, not one who covets India."

"I knew that," said Virlomi. "I just didn't think it mattered whether I was happy."

That's when Sayagi left her tent. She wrote and wrote and wrote.

But when she woke in the morning, she found that she had written nothing. The writing was also part of the dream.

It didn't matter. She remembered. Even if he denied that he was really the spirit of her dead friend and mocked her for believing in the gods, she did believe, and knew that he was a spirit in transit, and that the gods had sent him to her to teach her.

---

The third visitor did not have to have help from the aides. He came walking in from empty fields, and he already wore the garb of a peasant. However, he was not dressed as an Indian peasant. He wore the clothing of a Chinese rice-paddy worker.

He placed himself at the very end of the line and bowed himself to the dust. He did not move forward when the line moved forward. Every Indian he allowed to pass in front of him. And when dusk came and Virlomi wept and said good-bye to all, he did not go.

The aides did not come to him. Instead, Virlomi emerged from the hut and walked to him in the darkness, carrying a lamp.

"Get up," she said to him. "You're a fool to come here unescorted."

He stood up. "So I was recognized?"

"Could you have possibly looked more Chinese?"

"Rumors are flying?"

"But we're keeping them off the nets. For now. By morning, there's no controlling it."

"I came to ask you to marry me," said Han.

"I'm older than you," said Virlomi. "And you're the emperor of China."

"I thought that was one of my best features," said Han.

"Your country conquered mine."

"But *I* didn't. I gave the captives back and as soon as you say the word, I'll come here in state and get down on my knees in front of you—again—and apologize to you on behalf of the Chinese people. Marry me."

"What in the world do relations between our nations have to do with sharing a bed with a boy that I didn't have all that high an opinion of in Battle School?"

"Virlomi," said Han, "we can destroy each other as rivals. Or we can unite and together we'll have more than half the population of the world."

"How could it work? The Indian people will never follow you. The Chinese people will never follow me."

"It worked for Ferdinand and Isabella."

"Only because they were fighting the Moors. And Isabella and her people had to fight to keep Ferdinand from trampling on her rights as Queen of Castile."

"So we'll do even better," said Han. "Everything you've done has been flawless."

"As a good friend recently reminded me, it's easy to win when you're opposed by idiots."

"Virlomi," said Han.

"Now are you going to tell me that you love me?"

"But I do," said Han. "And you know why. Because all of us who were chosen for Battle School, there's only one thing we love and one thing we respect: We love brilliance and we respect power. You've created power out of nothing."

"I've created power out of the love and trust of my people."

"I love you, Virlomi."

"Love me . . . and yet you think that you're my superior."

"Superior? I've never led armies in battle. You have."

"You were in Ender's Jeesh," said Virlomi. "I wasn't. You'll always think I'm less than you because of that."

"Are you really telling me no? Or merely to try harder or come up with better reasons or prove my worth in some other way."

"I'm not going to set you to a series of lovers' tests," said Virlomi. "This isn't a fairy tale. My answer is no. Now and always. The dragon and the tiger don't have to be enemies, but how can a mammal and an egg-laying reptile ever possibly mate?"

"So you got my letter."

"Pathetically easy cipher. Anybody with half a brain could get it. Your code was just to type an obvious version of your nickname with your fingers moved one row higher on the keyboard."

"And yet only you, of all the thousands who access the nets, figured out it was from me."

Virlomi sighed.

"Just promise me this," said Han.

"No."

"Hear the promise first," said Han.

"Why should I promise you anything?"

"So I don't preemptively invade India again?"

"With what army?"

"I didn't mean *now*."

"What's the promise you want me to make?"

"That you won't marry Alai, either."

"A Hindu, marrying the Caliph of all Islam? I never knew you had such a sense of humor."

"He'll offer," said Han.

"Go home, Han. And, by the way, we saw the choppers arrive and let them pass. We also asked the Muslim oppressors not to shoot you down, either."

"I appreciated that. I thought it meant you liked me, at least a little."

"I do like you," said Virlomi. "I just don't intend to let you diddle me."

"I didn't know a mere diddle was on the table."

"Nothing's on the table. Back to your chopper, Boy Emperor."

"Virlomi, I beg you now. Let's be friends, at least."

"That would be nice. Someday, maybe."

"Write to me. Get to know me."

She shook her head, laughing, and walked back to her hut. Han Tzu walked back out into the fields as the night wind rose.

# 15

# RATIFICATION

From: RadaghasteBellini%privado@presidência.br.gov
To: PeterWiggin%private@hegemon.gov
Re: Please consider carefully

If your goal is to establish world peace, my friend, why would you begin our Constitution with a deliberate act of provocation against two widely separated nations, one of which might call upon the whole weight of Islam against you?

Is peace to be founded on war after all? And if you did not have Julian Delphiki commanding 100,000 friendly African troops, would you attempt it?

From: PeterWiggin%private@hegemon.gov
To: RadaghasteBellini%privado@presidência.br.gov
Re: We must make it real

History is strewn with the corpses of attempted world governments. We must demonstrate immediately that we are serious, that we are capable, and that we are transformative.

And without Delphiki, I would follow your more prudent counsel, because I would not count on our African troops.

---

The ceremony was simple enough. Peter Wiggin, Felix Starman, Klaus Boom, and Radaghaste Bellini stood on a platform in Kiyagi, Rwanda. There was no attempt to bring in crowds of citizens to cheer; neither was there any kind of military presence. The audience consisted entirely of reporters.

Copies of the Constitution were provided on the spot. Felix Starman explained the new government very briefly; Radaghaste Bellini informed them of the unified military command; Klaus Boom explained the principles under which new nations could be admitted to the Free People of the Earth.

"No nation will be admitted that does not already provide human rights, including a free and universal adult franchise." Then he dropped the bombshell. "Nor do we require that a nation already be recognized by any existing nation or body of nations, provided it meets our other requirements."

The reporters murmured to each other as Peter Wiggin walked to the dais and the map appeared on the screen behind him. As he named each country that had already secretly ratified the Constitution, it was lighted in pale blue on the map.

South America provided the largest swathes of blue, with Brazil lighting up half the continent, along with Bolivia, Chile, Ecuador, Suriname, and Guyana. In Africa, the blue was not so dominant, but it represented most of the African nations that had maintained stability and democracy for at least a hundred years: Rwanda, Botswana, Cameroon,

Mozambique, Angola, Ghana, Liberia. No two ratifying nations bordered on each other. No one missed the fact that South Africa and Nigeria were not participating, despite their long record of stability and freedom; nor did anyone fail to notice that no Muslim nation was included.

In Europe, the map was even sparser: The Netherlands, Slovenia, Czechland, Estonia, and Finland.

Elsewhere, blue was rare. Peter had hoped the Philippines would be ready for the announcement, but at the last minute the government chose to wait and see. Tonga had ratified; so had Haiti, the first nation where Peter's abilities had been tested. Several other small Caribbean nations were also blue.

"At the earliest opportunity," said Peter, "plebiscites will be held in all the ratifying nations. In the future, however, plebiscites will precede a nation's entry into the Free People of Earth. We will maintain capitals in three places: Ribeirão Preto, Brazil; Kiyagi, Rwanda; and Rotterdam in the Netherlands. However, because the official language of the FPE is Common, and few people find the pronunciation of Ribeirão Preto . . . comfortable . . ."

The reporters laughed, since they were the ones who had to bear the brunt of learning to pronounce the Portuguese nasals.

". . . therefore," Peter continued, "the Brazilian government has kindly allowed us to translate the name of the city for world government purposes. From now on, you may refer to the South American capital of the FPE as 'Blackstream,' one word."

"Will you do the same with Kiyagi!" shouted a reporter.

"Since you are able to pronounce it," said Peter, "we will not."

More laughter.

Peter's acceptance of the question, however, opened the floodgates, and they began calling out to him. He raised his hands. "In a minute, be patient."

They quieted down.

"There is a reason why we have chosen the name 'Free People of Earth' for our Constitution, instead of, say, 'United Nations.' "

Another laugh. They all knew why *that* name wouldn't be used.

"This Constitution is a contract among free citizens, not between nations. The old borders will be respected insofar as they make sense, but where they don't, adjustments will be made. And people who have long been deprived of legally recognized national boundaries and self-government will receive those things within the FPE."

Two new lights appeared, blinking a deeper blue. One cut a large swathe across the Andes. The other took a chunk out of southwestern Sudan.

"The FPE immediately recognizes the existence of the nations of Nubia, in Africa, and Runa, in South America. Plebiscites will be held immediately, and if the people of these regions vote to ratify the Constitution, then the FPE will act vigorously to protect their borders. You will notice that part of the territory of Runa has been voluntarily contributed by the nations of Bolivia and Ecuador as one of the terms of their entry into the FPE. The Free People of Earth salute the far-sighted and generous leaders of these nations."

Peter leaned forward. "The FPE will act vigorously to protect the electoral process. Any attempt to interfere with these plebiscites will be regarded as an act of war against the Free People of Earth."

There was the gauntlet.

The questioning afterward, as Peter had hoped, focused on the two new nations whose boundaries included territory belonging to nations that had not ratified—Peru and Sudan. Instead of being peppered with skeptical questions about the FPE itself, Peter had already settled the question of how serious they were. Taking on Peru was bad enough—no one doubted the ability of the FPE to crush the Peruvian military. It was Sudan. A Muslim country, which had given its allegiance to Caliph Alai.

"Are you declaring war against Caliph Alai?" demanded a reporter for an Arab news service.

"We declare war against no one. But the people of Nubia have a long history of oppression, atrocities, famine, and religious intolerance committed against them by the government of Sudan. How many times in the past two hundred years has international action caused Sudan to promise to do better? Yet in the aftermath of Caliph Alai's astonishing unification of the Muslim world, the outlaws and criminals in Sudan immediately took this as permission to renew their genocidal treatment of the Nubians. If Caliph Alai wishes to defend the criminals of Sudan even as he repudiates those of India, that is his choice. One thing is certain: Any right the Sudanese might once have claimed to rule over Nubia has long since expired. The Nubian people have been united by war and suffering into a nation that deserves statehood—and protection."

Peter ended the press conference soon afterward, announcing that Starman, Bellini, and Boom would each hold press conferences two days later in their home countries. "But the armed forces, border guards, and customs services of these nations are now all under the control of the FPE. There is no such thing as a Rwandan or Brazilian military. Only the military of the FPE."

"Wait!" cried one reporter. "There's no 'Hegemon' in this whole Constitution!"

Peter returned to the microphone. "Fast reading," he said.

Laughter, then expectant silence.

"The office of Hegemon was created to meet an emergency that threatened the entire Earth. I will continue as Hegemon under both the original authority under which I was selected for the office, and under temporary authorization from the FPE, until such time as no serious military threat against the Free People of Earth exists. At that time, I will resign my office and there will be no successor. I am the last Hegemon, and I hope to give up the office as quickly as possible."

Peter left again, and this time ignored the shouted questions.

---

As expected, Peru and Sudan didn't even declare war. Since they refused to recognize the legitimacy of the FPE *or* the new nations carved from their territory, whom would they declare war against?

Peruvian troops moved first, heading for known hideouts of Champi

T'it'u's revolutionary movement. Some of them were empty. But some of them were defended by highly trained Rwandan soldiers. Peter was using Bean's Rwandans so that it wouldn't be perceived as another war between Brazil and Peru; it had to be the FPE defending a member state's borders.

The Peruvian armies found themselves caught in well-laid traps, with sizable forces moving in across their lines of supply and communication.

It quickly became known throughout Peru that the Rwandan troops were better trained and better equipped than the Peruvian Army—and they were led by Julian Delphiki. Bean. The Giant.

Morale collapsed. Rwandan troops accepted the surrender of the entire Peruvian Army. The Peruvian Congress immediately voted almost unanimously to petition the FPE for membership. Radaghaste Bellini, as interim president of the South American region of the FPE, declined their offer, stating the principle that no territory would be added to the FPE by conquest or intimidation. "We invite the nation of Peru to hold a plebiscite, and if the people of Peru choose to join the Free People of Earth, we will welcome them to join with their brothers and sisters of Runa, Bolivia, Ecuador, and Chile."

It was over in two weeks, plebiscite and all: Peru was part of the FPE, and Bean and the bulk of the FPE's Rwandan troops were transported back across the Atlantic to Africa.

As a direct result of this decisive action, Belize, Cayenne, Costa Rica, and the Dominican Republic announced that they would hold plebiscites on the Constitution.

The rest of the world waited to see what would happen in Sudan.

---

Sudanese troops were already spread throughout Nubia; they were already engaged in military actions against the Nubian "rebels" who were resisting the renewed attempt to impose Shari'ah on the Christian and pagan region. So while there were plenty of acts of defiance against Peter's proclamation of Nubia's new status, there was no actual change.

Suriyawong, leading the elite core of the FPE military that he and

Bean had created years before and used so effectively since, conducted a series of raids designed to demoralize the Sudanese military and cut them off from their supplies. Ammunition dumps and arsenals were destroyed. Convoys were burned. But since Suri's choppers returned to Rwanda after every raid, there was no one for the Sudanese military to strike back against.

Then Bean returned with the bulk of the Rwandan soldiers. Burundi and Uganda both granted permission for him to transport his army across their territory.

As expected, the Sudanese army tried to strike at Bean's army inside the borders of Uganda, before they reached Nubia. Only then did they discover that this army was an illusion—there was nothing to strike but a bunch of old and empty trucks whose drivers fled at the first sign of trouble.

But it was a strike on Ugandan territory. Uganda not only declared war on Sudan, it also announced a plebiscite on the Constitution.

Meanwhile, Bean's army had already traversed the eastern reaches of Congo and were inside Nubia. And Suriyawong's strike force took over the two airbases to which the planes that had taken part in the attack on the decoy convoy had to return. The pilots landed without suspecting any problem, and were taken prisoner.

The trained jet pilots among Suriyawong's soldiers immediately took off again in Sudanese planes and carried out a demonstration bombing against the air defenses of Khartoum. And Bean's army made simultaneous attacks on all the Sudanese military bases inside Nubia. Unprepared to fight against a real army, the Sudanese forces surrendered or were overwhelmed within the day.

Sudan called on Caliph Alai to intervene and bring the wrath of Islam down on the heads of the infidel invaders.

Peter held an immediate press conference.

"The Free People of Earth do not conquer. The Muslim portions of Sudan will be respected, and all prisoners will be returned, as soon as we have the pledge of Caliph Alai and of the Sudanese government that they recognize Nubia as a nation and as part of the Free People of Earth. The Sudanese Air Force will be returned to Sudan, along with their air bases. We respect the sovereignty of Sudan and of all nations. But we will never recognize the right of any nation to persecute a stateless minority within their borders. When it is within our power, we will grant such minorities a state within the Constitution of the Free People of Earth and defend their national existence.

"Julian Delphiki is commander of all FPE forces within Nubia and temporarily occupying portions of Sudan. It would be a tragedy if two old friends from the war against the Buggers, Julian Delphiki and Caliph Alai, should face each other in combat over an issue as ridiculous as whether Sudan should have the right to continue persecuting non-Muslims."

Negotiators soon redrew the boundaries so that a significant portion of what Peter had originally declared to be Nubia would remain in Sudan. Of course, he had never expected to keep that territory and the Nubian leaders already knew that. But it was sufficient for Caliph Alai to save face. In the end, Bean and Suriyawong spent their efforts returning prisoners and protecting the convoys of non-Muslims who chose to leave their homes inside Sudanese territory and find new homes in their new nation.

In the aftermath of this clear victory, the FPE was so wildly popular in black Africa that nation after nation petitioned to hold a plebiscite. Felix Starman informed most of them that they had to reform their internal government first, providing human rights and elections. But the plebiscites in the democracies of South Africa, Nigeria, Namibia, Uganda, and Burundi proceeded immediately, and it was clear that the Free People of Earth had real existence as an intercontinental state with convincing military power and resolute leadership. As Colombia now accepted the borders of Runa and petitioned to become part of the FPE, it seemed inevitable now that all of Latin America and sub-Saharan Africa would be part of the FPE, and sooner rather than later.

---

There was movement elsewhere, too. Belgium, Bulgaria, Latvia, Lithuania, and Slovakia began to plan for their own plebiscites, as did the Philippines, Fiji, and most of the tiny island nations of the Pacific.

And of course the FPE capitals were flooded with pleas from minorities that wanted the FPE to grant them nationhood. Most of these had to be ignored. For now.

---

On the day that Sudan—under enormous pressure from Caliph Alai—recognized both Nubia and the FPE, Peter was surprised to see his office door open and his parents come in.

"What's wrong?" Peter asked.

"Nothing's wrong," said Mother.

"We came to tell you," said Father, "that we're very proud of you."

Peter shook his head. "It's only the first step on a long road. We don't have twenty percent of the world's population yet. And it will take time to integrate these new nations into the FPE."

"First step on the *right* road," said Father.

"A year ago, if somebody had put up a list of these nations," said Mother, "and said that they would ever unite into one coherent nation under a single Constitution, and surrender command of their armed forces to the Hegemon . . . is there anyone who would not have laughed?"

"It's all thanks to Alai and Virlomi," said Peter. "The atrocities committed by the Muslims in India, and the publicity Virlomi gave those actions, combined with all the recent wars . . ."

"Terrified everybody," said Father. "But the nations joining the FPE are *not* the ones that were most afraid. No, Peter, it was your Constitution. It was *you*—your achievements in the past, the promises you were making for the future . . ."

"It was the Battle Schoolers," said Peter. "Without Bean's reputation—"

"So you used the tools you had," said Mother. "Lincoln had Grant.

Churchill had Montgomery. It's part of their greatness that they weren't so jealous of their generals that they had to depose them."

"So you won't let me talk you out of this," said Peter.

"Your place in history was already assured by your work as Locke, before you ever became Hegemon," said Father. "But today, Peter, you became a great man."

They stood in the doorway for long moment.

"Well, that's what we came to say," said Mother.

"Thanks," said Peter.

They left, pulling the door closed behind them.

Peter went back to the papers on his desk.

And then discovered that he couldn't see them because of the tears blurring his eyes.

He sat up and found himself gasping. No, sobbing. Quietly—but his body was wracked with sobs as if he had just been relieved of a terrible burden. As if he had just learned that his terminal disease had spontaneously healed itself. As if he had just had a long-lost child returned to him.

Not once in that whole conversation had anybody said the name "Ender" or referred to him in any way.

It was a full five minutes before Peter got control of himself. He had to get up and wash his face in the tiny bathroom in his office before he could get back to work.

# 16

# JEESH

From: Weaver%Virlomi@MotherIndia.in.net
To: PeterWiggin%private@hegemon.gov
Re: Conversation

I have never met you, but I admire your achievements. Come visit me.

v

From: PeterWiggin%private@hegemon.gov
To: Weaver%Virlomi@MotherIndia.in.net
Re: Meeting

I also admire your achievements.

I will happily provide safe transportation for you to the FPE or any other site outside of India. While it is still under Muslim occupation I do not travel to India.

pw

From: Weaver%Virlomi@MotherIndia.in.net
To: PeterWiggin%private@hegemon.gov
Re: Place

I will not set foot on any country but India; you will not enter India.

Therefore: Colombo, Sri Lanka. I will come in a boat. Mine will not be comfortable. If you bring a better one, we'll enjoy our visit much more.

V

Fly Molo met Bean at the Manila airport and did his best not to look shocked at how tall Bean was.

"You said your business was personal," said Fly. "Forgive my suspicious nature. You are the head of FPE armed forces, and I am head of Filipino armed forces, and yet we have nothing to discuss?"

"I'm assuming that your military is superbly trained and well equipped."

"Yes," said Fly.

"Then until it's time for us to deploy somewhere, our planning and logistics departments have far more to say to each other than you or I do. Officially speaking."

"So you're here as a friend."

"I'm here," said Bean, "because I have a child in Manila. A boy. They tell me his name is Ramón."

Fly grinned. "And yet this is your first time here? Who was the mother, a flight attendant?"

"The baby was stolen from me, Fly. As an embryo. In vitro fertilization. The child is mine and Petra's. It's especially important to us, because it's the first we know of that definitely does not have my condition."

"You mean it isn't ugly?"

Bean laughed. "You've done well here in the Philippines, my friend."

"It's easy. Somebody argues with me, I just say, 'I was in Ender's Jeesh,' and they shut up and do what I say."

"It's just like that for me, too."

"Except for Peter."

"Especially Peter," said Bean. "I'm the power behind the throne, didn't you know? Don't you read the papers?"

"I notice the papers love to mention your zero-wins record as a commander in Battle School."

"Some achievements are so extraordinary," said Bean, "that you never live them down."

"How's Petra?" asked Fly. And they talked about people they both knew and reminisced about Battle School and Command School and the war with the Buggers until they got to a private home in the hills east of Manila.

There were several cars in front. Two soldiers wearing their new FPE uniforms stood at either side of the door.

"Guards?" asked Bean.

Fly shrugged. "Not my idea."

They did not have to prove who they were. And when they got inside, they realized that this was not the meeting either of them expected.

It was a reunion, apparently, of Ender's Jeesh—those that were available. Dink, Shen, Vlad on one side of a long table. Crazy Tom, Carn Carby, and Dumper—Champi T'it'u—on the other. And at the head of the table, Graff and Rackham.

"Now all are here that were invited," said Graff. "Please, Fly, Bean, take your seats. Bean, I trust that you will tell Petra all that goes on here. As for Han Tzu and Caliph Alai, they're now heads of state and don't travel easily or surreptitiously. However, everything we say to you will be said to them."

"I know some people who'd like to bomb this room," said Vlad.

"There's still someone unaccounted for," said Shen.

"Ender is voyaging safely. His ship is functioning perfectly. His ansible works well. Remember, though, that for him it has been scarcely a year since this group destroyed the Hive Queens. Even if you could talk to him, he would seem . . . young. The world has changed, and so have you." Graff glanced back at Rackham. "Mazer and I are deeply concerned, about you and about the world as a whole."

"We're doing all right," said Carn Carby.

"And thanks to Bean and Ender's big brother, maybe the world is, too," said Dumper. He said it a little defiantly, as if he expected to be argued with.

"I don't give a rat's ass about the world," said Bean. "I'm being blackmailed into helping Peter. And *not* by Peter."

"Bean is referring to a bargain he entered into with me of his own free will," said Graff.

"What's this meeting about?" asked Dink. "You're not our teacher any more." He glanced up at Rackham. "You're not our commander, either. We haven't forgotten how you both lied to us continually."

"We never *could* convince you of our sincere devotion to your welfare back in school, Dink," said Graff. "So as Dink requests, I won't waste time on preliminaries. Look around this table. How old are you?"

"Old enough to know better," muttered Carn.

"What are you, Bean, sixteen?" asked Fly.

"I was never actually born," said Bean, "and the records of my decanting were destroyed when I was about a year old. But sixteen is probably close."

"And all the rest of us must be around twenty, give or take," said Fly. "What's your point, Colonel Graff?"

"Call me Hyrum," said Graff. "I'd like to think we're colleagues now."

"Colleagues in *what*," muttered Dink.

"Back when you last met," said Graff, "when Achilles arranged for your kidnapping in Russia—you were already held in high esteem throughout the world. You were regarded as having . . . potential. Since then, however, one of your number has become Caliph, unified the un-unifiable Muslim world, and masterminded the conquest of China and the . . . liberation of India."

"Alai's lost his mind, that's what he's done," said Carn.

"And Han Tzu is Emperor of China. Bean is commander of the undefeated armies of the FPE, plus being known as the man who finally brought Achilles down. All in all, what once was viewed as potential is now regarded as a certainty."

"So what have you assembled here?" said Crazy Tom. "The losers?"

"I've assembled the people that national governments will turn to to stop Peter Wiggin from uniting the world."

They looked around at each other.

"Nobody's talked to *me* yet," said Fly Molo.

"But they turned to you to put down the Muslim rebellion in the Philippines, didn't they?" said Rackham.

"We're citizens of our countries," said Crazy Tom.

"Mine rents me out," said Dink. "Like a taxi."

"Because you always get along so well with authority," said Crazy Tom.

"Here's what will happen," said Graff. "Some combination of China, India, and the Muslim world destroy each other. Whichever one emerges on top, Bean destroys on the battlefield on behalf of the FPE. Does anyone doubt he can do it?"

Bean raised his hand.

No one else did.

And then Dink did.

"He's not hungry," he said.

No one argued with him.

"Now, what could Dink possibly mean by that?" said Graff. "Any ideas?"

No one seemed to have any.

"You don't want to say it, but I will," said Graff. "It's well known that Bean scored higher on the Battle School tests than anyone else in history. No one else was *close*. Well, Ender, but 'close' is such a relative term. Let's say Ender scored *closest.* But we don't know how close because Bean was off the charts."

"How?" said Dink. "He answered questions you didn't ask?"

"Exactly," said Graff. "That's what Sister Carlotta showed me. He had time to spare in taking the tests. He commented on them and mentioned how the test could have been improved. He was unstoppable. Irresistible. That's what the world knows about Julian Delphiki. And yet when we put him in charge of all of you on Eros, in Command School, while we were waiting for Ender to make up his mind about whether to continue his . . . education—how did that go?"

Again silence.

"Oh, why must we pretend that things weren't as they were?" said Graff.

"We didn't like it," said Dink. "He was younger than all of us."

"So was Ender," said Graff.

"But we knew Ender," said Crazy Tom.

"We loved Ender," said Shen.

"Everybody loved Ender," said Fly.

"I can give you a list of people who hated him. But *you* loved him. And you didn't love Bean. Why is that?"

Bean barked out a laugh. The others looked at him. Except the ones who were embarrassed and looked away. "I never learned how to be cuddly," said Bean. "In an orphanage that would have got me adopted, but on the street, it would have got me killed."

"Nonsense," said Graff. "Cuddly wouldn't have cut it with this group anyway."

"And you actually *were* cuddly," said Carn. "No offense, but you were spunky."

"If that's your word for 'bratty little asshole,' " said Dink mildly.

"Now now," said Graff. "You didn't dislike Bean personally. Most of you. But you didn't like serving under him. And you can't say that it's because you were too independent to serve under anybody, because you gladly served under Ender. You gave Ender everything you had."

"More than we had," said Fly.

"But not Bean." Graff said it like it was proof of something.

"Is this a therapy group?" asked Dink.

Vlad spoke up. "Of course it is. He wants us to reach the same conclusion he's already reached."

"Do you know what it is?" asked Graff.

Vlad took a breath. "*Hyrum* thinks that the reason we didn't follow Bean the way we followed Ender was because we knew something about Bean that the rest of the world doesn't know. And because of that, we're likely to be willing to challenge him in battle, while the rest of the world would just give up and surrender to him because of his reputation. Isn't that about it?"

Graff smiled benignly.

"But that's stupid," said Dumper. "Bean really *is* a good commander. I've seen him. Commanding his Rwandans in our campaign in Peru. It's true that the Peruvian Army wasn't well led or well trained, but those Rwandans—they worshipped Bean. They would have marched off a cliff if he asked them to. When he twitched, they sprang into action."

"And your point is?" asked Dink.

"My point is," said Dumper, "*we* didn't follow him well, but other people do. Bean's the real thing. He's still the best of us."

"I haven't seen his Rwandans," said Fly, "but I've seen him with the men he and Suriyawong trained. Back when the forces of the Hegemon were a hundred guys and two choppers. Dumper's right. Alexander the Great couldn't have had soldiers more devoted and more effective."

"Thanks for the testimonials, boys," said Bean, "but you're missing Hyrum's point."

" 'Hyrum,' " muttered Dink. "Aren't we cozy."

"Just tell them," said Bean. "They know it, but they don't know that they know it."

"You tell them," said Graff.

"Is this a Chinese reeducation camp? Do we have to indulge in self-criticism?" Bean laughed bitterly. "It's what Dink said right at the start. I'm not hungry. Which might seem stupid, considering I spent my whole infancy starving to death. But I'm not hungry for *supremacy.* And all of you are."

"That's the great secret of the tests," said Graff. "Sister Carlotta gave the standard battery of tests we used. But there was an additional test. One that I gave, or one of my most trusted aides. A test of ambition. Competitive ambition. You all scored very, very high. Bean didn't."

"Bean's not ambitious?"

"Bean wants victory," said Graff. "He likes to win. He *needs* to win. But he doesn't need to beat anybody."

"We all cooperated with Ender," said Carn. "We didn't have to beat *him.*"

"But you knew he would lead you to victory. And in the meanwhile, you were all competing with each other. Except Bean."

"Only because he was better than any of us. Why compete if you've won?" said Fly.

"If any one of you came up against Bean in battle, who would win?"

They rolled their eyes or chuckled or otherwise showed their derision for the question.

"That would depend," said Carn Carby, "on the terrain, and the weather, and the sign of the zodiac. Nothing's sure in war, is it?"

"There wasn't any weather in the Battle Room," said Fly, grinning.

"You can conceive of beating Bean, can't you?" said Graff. "And it's possible. Because Bean is only better than the rest of you if all else is equal. Only it never is. And one of the most important variables in war is the hunger that makes you take ridiculous chances because you intuit that there's a path to victory and you have to take that path because anything other than winning is inconceivable. Unbearable."

"Very poetic," said Dink. "The romance of war."

"Look at Lee," said Graff.

"Which one?" said Shen. "The Chinese or the American?"

"Lee L-E-E the Virginian," said Graff. "When the enemy was on Virginia soil, he won. He took the chances he needed to take. He sent Stonewall Jackson out on a forest path at Chancellorsville, dividing his forces and exposing himself dangerously against Hooker, exactly the sort of reckless commander who could have exploited the opportunity if he'd realized it."

"Hooker was an idiot."

"We say that because he lost," said Graff. "But would he have lost if Lee had not taken the dangerous move he took? My point isn't to re-fight Chancellorsville. My point is—"

"Antietam and Gettysburg," said Bean.

"Exactly. As soon as Lee left Virginia and entered Northern territory, he wasn't hungry anymore. He believed in the cause of defending Virginia, but he did *not* believe in the cause of slavery, and he knew that's what the war was about. He didn't want to see his state defeated, but he didn't want to see the southern cause win. All unconsciously. He didn't know this about himself. But it was true."

"It had nothing to do with the North's overwhelming force?"

"Lee lost at Antietam against the second stupidest and *most* timid commander the North had, McClellan. And Meade at Gettysburg wasn't terribly imaginative. Meade saw the high ground and he took it. And what did Lee do? Based on how Lee acted in all his Virginia campaigns, what would you have expected Lee to do?"

"Refuse to fight on that ground," said Fly. "Maneuver. Slide right. Steal a march. Get between Meade and Washington. Find a battlefield where the Unions would have to try to force *his* position."

"He *was* low on supplies," said Dink. "And he didn't have the information from his cavalry."

"Excuses," said Vlad. "No excuses in war. Graff is right. Lee didn't act like Lee, once he left Virginia. But that's Lee. What does that have to do with Bean?"

"He thinks," said Bean, "that when I don't believe in a cause, I can be beaten. That I would beat myself. The trouble is that I *do* believe in the cause. I think Peter Wiggin is a decent man. Ruthless, but I've seen how he uses power, and he doesn't use it to hurt anybody. He really is trying to create a world order that leads to peace. I want him to win. I want him to win *quickly*. And if any of you think you can stop me."

"We don't have to stop you," said Crazy Tom. "We just have to hold out till you're dead."

Utter silence.

"There it is," said Graff. "There's the whole point of this meeting. Bean only has a little while. So while he lives, the Hegemon is perceived as unbeatable. But the moment he's gone, what then? Dumper or Fly would probably be appointed commander after him, since they're already inside the FPE. But every one of you at this table would feel perfectly free to take on either of them, am I right?"

"Hell, *Hyrum*," said Dink, "we'd take on Bean."

"And so the world would be torn apart, and the FPE, even if it was victorious, would stand on the bodies of millions of soldiers who died because of *your competitive ambition*." He looked fiercely around the table.

"Hey," said Fly, "we haven't killed anybody yet. Talk to Hot Soup and Alai about that."

"Look at Alai," said Graff. "It took him two purges to get real control over the Islamic forces, but now he has it, and what has he done? Has he left India? Has he withdrawn from Xinjiang or Tibet? Have the Indonesian Muslims left Taiwan? He remains face to face with Han Tzu. Why is that? It makes no sense. He can't hold India. He couldn't rule over China. But he has Genghis dreams."

"It always comes back to Genghis," said Vlad.

"You all want the world united," said Graff. "But you want to do it yourselves, because you can't stand the thought of anyone else standing on top of the hill."

"Come on," said Dink. "In our hearts we're all Cincinnatus. We can hardly wait to get back to the farm."

They laughed.

"At this table sits fifty years of bloody war," said Graff.

"What about it?" said Dink. "We didn't invent war. We're just good at it."

"War gets invented every time there's somebody so hungry for domination that he can't leave peaceful nations alone. It is precisely people like you that invent war. Even if you have a cause, like Lee did, would the South have struggled on for all those bloody years of Civil War if they hadn't had the firm belief that no matter what happened, 'Marse Robert' would save them? Even if you don't make the decision for war, nations will enter into wars only because they have *you*."

"So what's your solution, Hyrum?" said Dink. "You have little cyanide pills for us all to swallow so we can save the world from ourselves?"

"It wouldn't help," said Vlad. "Even if what you're saying is true, there are other Battle School graduates. Look at Virlomi—she's outmaneuvered everybody."

"She hasn't outmaneuvered Alai yet," said Crazy Tom. "Or Hot Soup."

Vlad insisted on his point. "Look at Suriyawong. *That's* who Peter will turn to after Bean . . . retires. We weren't the only kids at Battle School."

"Ender's Jeesh," said Graff. "You're the ones who saved the world. You're the ones with the magic. And there are hundreds and hundreds of Battle School grads on Earth. Nobody is going to think that just because they happen to have one or two or five, they can conquer the world. Which *one* of them would it be?"

"So you want to be rid of us all," said Dink. "And that's why you brought us here. We're not leaving here alive, are we?"

"Lighten up, Dink," said Graff. "You can all go home as soon as this meeting is over. ColMin doesn't assassinate people."

"Now, that's an interesting point," said Crazy Tom. "What *does* ColMin do? It packs people into starships like sardines, and then it sends them off to colony worlds. And they'll never come back, not to the world they left. Fifty years out, fifty years back. The world would have forgotten all of us by then, even if we went to a colony and came right home. Which of course he wouldn't let us do."

"So this isn't an assassination," said Dink, "it's another damn kidnapping."

"It's an offer," said Rackham, "which you can accept or decline."

"I decline," said Dink.

"Hear the offer," said Rackham.

"Hear this," said Dink, with a gesture.

"I offer you command of a colony. Each one of you. No rivals. We don't know of any enemy armies for you to face, but there will be worlds full of danger and uncertainty, and your abilities will be highly adaptable. People will follow you—people older than you—partly because you *are* Ender's Jeesh, and partly because—*mostly* because—of your own abilities. They'll see how quickly to grasp important information, rank it by priority, foresee consequences, and make correct decisions. You'll be the founders of new human worlds."

Crazy Tom put on a babytalk voice. "Wiw dey name da pwanets aftew us?"

"Don't be such a dullbob," said Carn.

"Sowwy."

"Look, gents," said Graff. "We saw what happened to the Hive Queens. They bunched up on one planet and they got wiped out in a single blow. Any weapon we can invent, an enemy can also invent and use against us."

"Come on," said Dink. "The Hive Queens spread out and colonized as many planets as you're colonizing—in fact, all you're doing is sending ships to colonize the worlds they already settled because they're the only ones you know about that have an atmosphere we can breathe and flora and fauna we can eat."

"Actually, we're taking our own flora and fauna with us," said Graff.

"Dink's right," said Shen. "Dispersal didn't work for the Hive Queens."

"Because they didn't disperse," said Graff. "They had Buggers on all the planets, but when you boys blew up their home world, *all* the Hive Queens were there. They put all their eggs in one basket. We're not going to do that. Partly because the human race isn't just a handful of queens and a whole bunch of workers and drones, every damn one of us is a Hive Queen and has the seeds of recapitulating the whole of human history. So dispersing humanity *will* work."

"Like coughing in a crowd spreads the flu," said Crazy Tom cheerfully.

"Exactly," said Graff. "Call us a disease, I don't care—I *am* a human, and I want us to spread everywhere like an epidemic, so we can *never* be stamped out."

Rackham nodded. "And to accomplish that, he needs his colonies to have the best possible chance of survival."

"Which means you," said Graff. "If I can get you."

"So we make your colonies work," said Carn, "*and* you get us off Earth, too, so Peter can end all war and bring the millennial reign of Christ."

"Whether Christ comes or not isn't my business," said Graff. "All I care about is saving human beings. Collectively and individually."

"Aren't you the noble one."

"No," said Graff. "I created you. Not you individually—"

"Good thing you said that," said Carn, "because my dad would have had to kill you for that aspersion on my mother."

"I found you. I tested you. I assembled you. I made the whole world aware of you. The danger you represent, I created it."

"So you're really trying to atone for your mistakes."

"It wasn't a mistake. It was essential to winning the last war. But it's not unusual in history for the solution to one problem to become the root of the next one."

"So this meeting is clean-up," said Fly.

"This meeting is to offer you a chance to do something that will satisfy your own irresistible craving for supremacy, while ensuring the survival of the human race, both here on Earth and out there in the galaxy."

They thought about that for a moment.

Dumper was the first to speak. "I've already chosen my life's work, Colonel Graff."

"It's *Hyrum*," Dink whispered loudly. "Because he's our buddy."

"You chose it," said Graff, "and you accomplished it. Your people have a nation, and you're part of the FPE. That struggle is over for you. All that's left is for you to chafe under Peter Wiggin's rule until you either rebel against him or become his military commander—and then his replacement as Hegemon. Ruling the world. Am I close?"

"I have no such plans," said Dumper.

"But it resonates with you," said Graff. "Don't pretend otherwise. I know you boys. You're not crazy. You're not evil. But *you can't stop*."

"That's why you didn't invite Petra," said Bean. "Because then you couldn't have said 'you boys' all the time."

"You forget," said Dink, "we're his colleagues now. So we can call him and Rackham 'you boys' too."

Graff stood up from his seat at the head of the table. "I've made the offer. You'll think about it whether you mean to or not. You'll watch events unfold. You all know how to contact me. The offer is open. We're done here for today."

"No we're not," said Shen. "Because you aren't doing anything about the real problem."

"Which is?"

"We're just potential warmongers and baby killers," said Shen. "You're not doing a thing about Hot Soup and Alai."

"And Virlomi," added Fly Molo. "If you want somebody who's dangerous, it's *her*."

"They will get the same offer as you," said Rackham. "In fact, one of them already has."

"Which one?" asked Dink.

"The one who was in a position to hear it," said Graff.

"Hot Soup, then," said Shen. "Because you couldn't even get in to meet Mr. Caliph."

"What smart fellows you all turned out to be," said Graff.

" 'Waterloo was won,' " quoted Rackham, " 'on the playing fields of Eton.' "

"What the hell does *that* mean?" asked Carn Carby. "You never even went to Eton."

"It was an analogy," said Rackham. "If you hadn't spent your entire childhood playing war games, you'd actually know something. You're all so uneducated."

# 17

# BOATS

From: Champi%T'it'u@Runa.gov.qu
To: WallabyWannabe%BoyGenius@stratplan/mil.gov.au
Re: "Good Idea"

Of course Graff's "offer" sounded like a good idea to YOU. You live in Australia.

—Dumper

From: WallabyWannabe%BoyGenius@stratplan/mil.gov.au
To: Champi%T'it'u@Runa.gov.qu
Re: Ha ha

People who live on the moon—pardon me, the Andes—shouldn't joke about Australia.

—Carn

From: Champi%T'it'u@Runa.gov.qu
To: WallabyWannabe%BoyGenius@stratplan/mil.gov.au
Re: "Who was joking?"

I've seen Australia and I've lived on an asteroid and I'd take the asteroid.

—Dumper

From: WallabyWannabe%BoyGenius@stratplan/mil.gov.au
To: Champi%T'it'u@Runa.gov.qu
Re: Asteroid

Australia doesn't need life support like an asteroid or coca like the Andes to be livable. Besides, you only liked the asteroid because it was named Eros and that's as close to sex as you've ever gotten.

—Carn

From: Champi%T'it'u@Runa.gov.qu
To: WallabyWannabe%BoyGenius@stratplan/mil.gov.au
Re: At least

At least I have a sex. Male, by the way. Open your fly and check to see what you are. (You grip the handle of the zipper and pull downward.) (Oh, wait, you're in Australia. Upward, then.)

—Dumper

From: WallabyWannabe%BoyGenius@stratplan/mil.gov.au
To: Champi%T'it'u@Runa.gov.qu
Re: Let's see . . . zipper . . . fly . . . pull . . .

Ouch! Ow! Oweeee!

—Carn

The sailors were so nervous to have The Lady aboard their dhow that it was a wonder they didn't swamp the boat just getting out to sea. And sailing was slow, with lots of tacking; even turning the ship seemed to require as much work as the reinvention of navigation. Virlomi showed none of her impatience, though.

It was time for the next step—for India to reach for the world stage. She needed an ally to free her nation from the foreign occupiers. Even though the atrocities had ended—nothing filmable now—Alai persisted in keeping his Muslim troops all over India. Waiting for Hindu provocations. Knowing that Virlomi couldn't control her people as tightly as Alai now controlled his troops.

But she wasn't going to bring Han Tzu into the picture. She had fought too hard to get the Chinese out of India to invite them back again. Besides, even though they had no religion to force on people like Alai's Muslims, the Chinese were just as arrogant, just as sure they were entitled to rule the world.

And these Jeeshboys, they were *so* sure they could be her masters. Didn't they understand that her whole life was a repudiation of their sense of superiority? They had been chosen to wage war against aliens. The gods fought on their side in that war. But now the gods fought on Virlomi's side.

She hadn't been a believer when she began. She exploited her knowledge of the folk religion of her people. But over the weeks and months and years of her campaign against China and then against the Muslims, she had seen how everything bent and turned to fit her plans. Everything she thought of worked; and since there were tests proving that Alai and Han Tzu were smarter than she was, it must be that entities wiser than they were providing her with her ideas.

There was only one person now who could give her the help she needed, and only one man in the world whom it would not demean her to marry. After all, when she married it would be all India marrying; and whatever children she bore would be the children of a god, at least in the eyes of the people. Since parthenogenesis was out of the question, she needed a husband. And that's why she had summoned Peter Wiggin.

Wiggin, the brother of the great Ender. The *older* brother. Who then could doubt that her children would carry the best genes available on Earth? They would found a dynasty that could unite the world and rule forever. By marrying her, Peter would be able to add India to his FPE, transforming it from a sideshow into more than half the population of the world. And she—and India—would be raised above any other nation. Instead of being the leader of a single nation, like China, or the head of a brutal and backward religion, like Alai, she would be the wife of the enlightened Locke, the Hegemon of Earth, the man whose vision would bring peace to all the world at last.

Peter's boat wasn't huge—clearly he wasn't a wasteful man. But it wasn't a primitive fisherman's dhow; Peter's boat had modern lines and it looked as if it was designed to rise up and fairly fly over the waves. *Speed.* No time to waste in Peter Wiggin's world.

She had once belonged to that world. For years now she had slowed herself down to the pace of life in India. She had walked slowly when people were watching her. She had to maintain the simple grace they expected of someone in her position. And she had to hold silence while men argued, speaking only as much as was appropriate for her to say. She could not afford to do anything to diminish herself in their eyes.

But she missed the speed of things. The shuttles that took her to and from Battle School and Tactical School. The clean polished surfaces. The quickness of games in the Battle Room. Even the intensity of life in Hyderabad among other Battle Schoolers before she fled to let Bean know where Petra was. It was closer to her true inclinations than this pose of primitiveness.

You do what victory requires. Those with armies, train the armies. But when Virlomi started, she had only herself. So she trained and disciplined herself to seem as she needed to seem.

In the process, she had become what she needed to *be*.

But that didn't mean she had lost her ability to admire the sleek, fast vessel that Peter had brought to her.

The fishermen helped her out of the dhow and into the rowboat that would take her between the two vessels. Out in the Gulf of Mannar, there were undoubtedly much heavier waves, but the little islands of Adam's Bridge protected the water here, so it was only slightly choppy.

Which was just as well. There was a faint nausea that had been with her ever since she got aboard. Vomiting was not something she needed to show these sailors. She hadn't expected seasickness. How could she have known she was susceptible? Helicopters didn't bother her, or cars on winding roads, or even freefall. Why should a bit of chop on the water nearly do her in?

The rowboat was actually better than the dhow. More frightening, but less nauseating. Fear she could deal with. Fear didn't make her want to throw up. It only made her more determined to win.

Peter himself was at the side of his boat, and it was his hand that she took to help her climb aboard. That was a good sign. He wasn't trying to play games and force her to come to him.

Peter had her men tie the dinghy to his craft, and then brought them aboard to rest in relative comfort on the deck while she went inside the main cabin with Peter.

It was beautifully and comfortably decorated, but not overly large or pretentious. It struck just the right note of restrained opulence. A man of taste.

"It's not my boat, of course," said Peter. "Why would I waste FPE money on owning a boat? This is a loan."

She said nothing—after all, saying nothing was part of who she was now. But she was just a little disappointed. Modesty was one thing; but why did he feel compelled to tell her that he didn't own it, that he was frugal? Because he believed her image of seeking traditional Indian simplicity—no poverty—as something she really meant, and not just something she staged in order to hold on to the hearts of the Indian people.

Well, I could hardly expect him to be as perceptive as me. He wasn't admitted to Battle School, after all.

"Have a seat," he said. "Are you hungry?"

"No thank you," she said softly. If only he knew what would happen to any food she tried to eat at sea!

"Tea?"

"Nothing," she said.

He shrugged—with embarrassment? That she had turned him down? Really, was he such a *boy* as that? Was he taking this personally?

Well, he was supposed to take it personally. He just didn't understand how or why.

Of course he didn't. How could he imagine what she came to offer him?

Time to be Virlomi. Time to let him know what this meeting was about.

He was standing near a bar with a fridge, and seemed to be trying to choose between inviting her to sit with him at the table or on the soft chairs bolted to the deck.

She took two steps and she was with him, pressing her body against his, entwining the arms of India under his and around his back. She stood on her toes and kissed his lips. Not with vigor, but softly and warmly. It was not a girl's chaste kiss; it was a promise of love, as best she knew how to show it. She had not had that much experience before Achilles came and made Hyderabad a chaste and terrifying place to work. A few kisses with boys she knew. But she had learned something of what made them excited; and Peter was, after all, scarcely more than a boy, wasn't he?

And it seemed to work. He certainly returned the kiss.

It was going as she expected. The gods were with her.

"Let's sit down," said Peter.

But to her surprise, what he indicated was the table, not the soft chairs. Not the wide one, where they could have sat together.

The table, where they would have a slab of wood—*something* cold and smooth, anyway—between them.

When they were seated, Peter looked at her quizzically. "Is that really what you came all this way for?"

"What did you think?" she said.

"I hoped it had something to do with India ratifying the FPE Constitution."

"I haven't read it," she said. "But you must know India doesn't surrender its sovereignty easily."

"It'll be easy enough, if *you* ask the Indian people to vote for it."

"But, you see, I need to know what India gets in return."

"What every nation in the FPE receives. Peace. Protection. Free trade. Human rights and elections."

"That's what you give to Nigeria," said Virlomi.

"That's what we give to Vanuatu and Kiribati, too. And the United States and Russia and China and, yes, India, when they choose to join us."

"India is the most populous nation on Earth. And she's spent the past three years fighting for her survival. She needs more than mere protection. She needs a special place near the center of power."

"But I'm not the center of power," said Peter. "I'm not a king."

"I know who you are," said Virlomi.

"Who am I?" He seemed amused.

"You're Genghis. Washington. Bismarck. A builder of empires. A uniter of peoples. A maker of nations."

"I'm the breaker of nations, Virlomi," said Peter. "We'll keep the *word* nation, but it will come to mean what *state* means in America. An administrative unit, but little more. India will have a great history, but from now on, we'll have *human* history."

"How very noble," said Virlomi. This was not going as she intended. "I think you don't understand what I'm offering you."

"You're offering me something I want very much—India in the FPE. But the price you want me to pay is too high."

"Price!" Was he really that stupid. "To have me is not a *price* you pay. It's a sacrifice *I* make."

"And who says romance is dead," said Peter. "Virlomi, you're a Battle Schooler. Surely you can see why it's impossible for me to marry my way into having India in the FPE."

Only then, in the moment of his challenge, did the whole thing become clear. Not the world as *she* saw it, centered on India, but the world as he saw it, with himself at the center of everything.

"So it's all about you," said Virlomi. "You can't share power with another."

"I can share power with *everybody*," said Peter, "and I already am. Only a fool thinks he can rule alone. You can only rule by the willing obedience and cooperation of those you supposedly rule over. They have to *want* you to lead them. And if I married you—attractive as the offer is on every count—I would no longer be seen as an honest broker. Instead of trusting me to lead the FPE's foreign and military policy to the benefit of the whole world, I would be seen as tilting everything toward India."

"Not everything," she said.

"More than everything," said Peter. "I would be seen as the *tool* of India. You can be sure that Caliph Alai would immediately declare war, not just on India, which has his troops all over it, but on the FPE. I'd be faced with bloody war in Sudan and Nubia, which I don't want."

"Why would you fear it?"

"Why wouldn't I?" he said.

"You have *Bean*," she said. "How can Alai stand against you?"

"Well," said Peter, "if Bean is so all powerful and irresistible, why do I need *you?*"

"Because Bean can never be as fully trusted as a wife. And Bean doesn't bring you a billion people."

"Virlomi," said Peter, "I'd be a fool to trust you, wife or not. You wouldn't be bringing India into the FPE, you'd be bringing the FPE into India."

"Why not a partnership?"

"Because gods don't need mortal partners," said Peter. "You've been a god too long. There's no man you can marry, as long as you think you're elevating him just by letting him touch you."

"Don't say what you can't unsay," said Virlomi.

"Don't make me say what's so hard to hear," said Peter. "I'm not going to compromise my leadership of the whole FPE just to get one country to join."

He meant it. He actually thought his position was above hers. He thought he was greater than India! Greater than a god! That he would *diminish* himself by taking what she offered.

But now there was nothing more to say to him. She wouldn't waste time with idle threats. She'd show him what she could do to those who wanted India for an enemy.

He rose to his feet. "I'm sorry that I didn't anticipate your offer," said Peter. "I wouldn't have wasted your time. I had no desire to embarrass you. I thought you would have understood my situation better."

"I'm just one woman. India is just one country."

He winced just a little. He didn't like having his foolish, arrogant words thrown in his face. Well, you'll have more than that thrown at you, Ender's Brother.

"I brought two others to see you," said Peter. "If you're willing."

He opened a door and Colonel Graff and a man she didn't know entered the room. "Virlomi, I think you know Minister Graff. And this is Mazer Rackham."

She inclined her head, showing no surprise.

They sat down and explained their offer.

"I already have the love and allegiance of the greatest nation on Earth," said Virlomi. "And I have not been defeated by the most terrible enemies that China and the Muslim world could hurl against me. Why should I wish to run and hide in a colony somewhere?"

"It's a noble work," said Graff. "It's not hiding, it's building."

"Termites build," said Virlomi.

"And hyenas tear," said Graff.

"I have no need for or interest in the service you offer," said Virlomi.

"No," said Graff, "you just don't *see* your need yet. You always were hard to get to change your way of looking at things. It's what held you back in Battle School, Virlomi."

"You're not my teacher now," said Virlomi.

"Well, you're certainly wrong about one thing, whether I'm your teacher or not," said Graff.

She waited.

"You have not yet *faced* the most terrible enemies that China and the Muslim world can hurl against you."

"Do you think Han Tzu can get into India again? I'm not Tikal Chapekar."

"And he's not the Politburo or Snow Tiger."

"He's *Ender's Jeeshmate*," she said in mock awe.

"He's not caught up in his own mystique," said Rackham, who had not spoken till now. "For your own sake, Virlomi, take a good hard look in the mirror. You're what megalomania looks like in the early stages."

"I have no ambition for myself," said Virlomi.

"If you define India as whatever you conceive it to be," said Rackham, "you'll wake up some terrible morning and discover that it is not what you *need* it to be."

"And you say this from your vast experience of governing . . . what country was it, now, Mr. Rackham?"

Rackham only smiled. "Pride, when poked, gets petty."

"Was that already a proverb?" asked Virlomi. "Or should I write it down?"

"The offer stands," said Graff. "It's irrevocable as long as you live."

"Why don't you make the same offer to Peter?" asked Virlomi. "He's the one who needs to take the long voyage."

She decided she wasn't going to get a better exit line than that, so she walked slowly, gracefully, to the door. No one spoke as she departed.

Her sailors helped her back into the rowboat and cast off. Peter did not come to the rail to wave her off; just another discourtesy, not that she would have acknowledged him even if he had. As for Graff and Rackham, they'd soon enough be coming to her for funding—no, for *permission* to operate their little colony ministry.

The dhow took her back to a different fishing village from the one she had sailed from—no point in making things easy for Alai, if he had discovered her departure from Hyderabad and followed her.

She rode a train back to Hyderabad, passing for an ordinary citizen—if any Muslim soldiers should be so bold as to search the train. But the people knew who she was. Whose face was better known in all of India? And not being Muslim, she didn't have to cover her face.

The first thing I will do, when I rule India, is change the name of Hyderabad. Not back to Bhagnagar—even though it was named for an Indian woman, the name was bestowed by the Muslim prince who destroyed the original Indian village in order to build the Charminar, a monument to his own power, supposedly in honor of his beloved Hindu wife.

India will never again be obliterated in order to appease the power lust of Muslims. The new name of Hyderabad will be the original name of the village: Chichlam.

She made her way from the train station to a safe house in the city, and from there her aides helped get her back inside the hut where she had supposedly been meditating and praying for India for the three days she had been gone. There she slept for a few hours.

Then she arose and sent an aide to bring her an elegant but simple sari, one that she knew she could wear with grace and beauty, and which would show off her slim body to best advantage. When she had it arranged to her satisfaction, and her hair was arranged properly, she walked from her hut to the gate of Hyderabad.

The soldiers at the checkpoint gawped at her. No one had ever expected her to try to enter, and they had no idea what to do.

While they went through their flurry of asking their superiors inside the city what they should do, Virlomi simply walked inside. They dared not stop her or challenge her—they didn't want to be responsible for starting a war.

She knew this place as well as anyone, and knew which building housed Caliph Alai's headquarters. Though she walked gracefully, without hurry, it took little time for her to get there.

Again, she paid no attention to guards or clerks or secretaries or important Muslim officers. They were nothing to her. By now they must have heard Alai's decision; and his decision was obviously to let her pass, for no one obstructed her.

Wise choice.

One young officer even trotted along ahead of her, opening doors and indicating which way she should go.

He led her into a large room where Alai stood waiting for her, with a dozen high officers standing along the walls.

She walked to the middle of the room. "Why are you afraid of one lone woman, Caliph Alai?"

Before he had time to answer the obvious truth—that far from being afraid, he had let her pass unmolested and uninspected through his headquarters complex and into his own presence—Virlomi began to unwrap her sari. It took only a moment or two before she stood naked before him. Then she reached up and loosened her long hair, and then swung it and combed her fingers through it. "You see that I have no weapon hidden here. India stands before you, naked and defenseless. Why do you fear her?"

Alai had averted his eyes as soon as it became clear that she was undressing. So had the more pious of the other officers. But some apparently thought it was their responsibility to make sure that she was, in fact, weaponless. She enjoyed their consternation, their embarrassment—and, she suspected, their desire. You came here to ravish India, didn't you? And yet I am out of your reach. Because I'm not here for you, underlings. I'm here for your master.

"Leave us," Alai said to the other men.

Even the most modest of them could not help but glance at her as they shuffled out of the room, leaving the two of them alone.

The door closed behind them. She and Alai were alone.

"Very symbolic, Virlomi," said Alai, still refusing to look at her. "*That* will get talked about."

"The offer I make is both symbolic and tangible," she said. "This upstart Peter Wiggin has gone as far as he should go. Why should Muslim and Hindu be enemies, when together we have the power to crush his naked ambition?"

"His ambition isn't as naked as you are," said Alai. "Please put on clothing so I can look at you."

"May not a man look at his bride?"

Alai chuckled. "A dynastic marriage? I thought you already told Han Tzu what he could do with that idea."

"Han Tzu had nothing to offer me. You are the leader of the Muslims of India. A large portion of my people torn away from mother India in fruitless hostility. And why? Look at me, Alai."

Either the force of her voice had power over him, or he could not resist his desire, or perhaps he simply decided that since they were alone, he need not keep up the show of perfect rectitude.

He looked her up and down, casually, without reaction. As he did, she raised her arms above her head and turned around. "Here is India," she said, "no longer resisting you, no longer evading you, but welcoming you, married to you, fertile soil in which to plant a new civilization of Muslim and Hindu united."

She faced him again.

He continued to look at her, not bothering to keep his eyes only on her face. "You do intrigue me," he said.

I should think so, she answered silently. Muslims never have the virtue they pretend to have.

"I must consider this," he said.

"No," she said.

"You think I'll make up my mind in an instant?"

"I don't care. But I will leave this room in moments. Either I'll do it dressed in that sari, as your bride, or I'll do it naked, leaving my clothing behind. Naked I'll pass through your compound, and naked I'll return to my people. Let them decide what they think was done to me within these walls."

"You'd provoke such a war as that?" said Alai.

"Your presence in India is the provocation, Caliph. I offer you peace and unity between our peoples. I offer you the permanent alliance that will enable us, together, India and Islam, to unite the world in a single government and along the way cast Peter Wiggin aside. He was never worthy of his brother's name; he's wasted enough of the time and attention of the world."

She walked closer to him, until her knees touched his.

"You have to deal with him eventually, Caliph Alai. Will you do it with India in your bed and by your side, or will you do it while most of your forces have to remain here to keep us from destroying you from behind? Because I'll do it. Either we're lovers or enemies, and the time to choose is now."

He made no idle threat to detain her or kill her—he knew that he could no more do that than let her walk out of the compound naked. The real question was whether he would be a grudging husband or an enthusiastic one.

He reached out and took her hand.

"You've chosen wisely, Caliph Alai," she said. She leaned down and kissed him. The same kiss she had given Peter Wiggin, and which he had treated as if it were nothing.

Alai returned it warmly. His hands moved on her body.

"Marriage first," she said.

"Let me guess," he said. "You want the wedding now."

"In this room."

"Will you dress so we can show video of the ceremony?"

She laughed and kissed his cheek. "For publicity, I'll dress."

She started to walk away, but he caught her hand, drew her back, kissed her again, passionately this time. "This is a good idea," he said to her. "It's a bold idea. It's a dangerous idea. But it's a good one."

"I'll stand beside you in everything," she said.

"Not ahead," he said. "Not behind, not above, not below."

She embraced him and kissed his headdress. Then she pulled it off his head and kissed his hair.

"Now I'll have to go to all the trouble of putting that back on," he said.

You'll take whatever trouble I want you to take, she thought. I have just had a victory here today, in this room, Caliph Alai. You and your Allah may not realize it, but the gods of India rule in this place, and they have given me victory without another soldier dying in useless war.

Such fools they were in Battle School, to let so few girls in. It left the boys helpless against a woman when they returned to Earth.

# 18

# YEREVAN

From: PetraDelphiki@FreePeopleOfEarth.fp.gov
To: DinkMeeker@colmin.gov
Re: Can't believe you're at this address

When Bean told me what happened at that meeting, I thought: I know one guy who's never going to go along with any plan of Graff's.

Then I got your letter informing me of your change of address. And then I thought some more and realized: There's no place on Earth where Dink Meeker is going to fit in. You have too much ability to be content anywhere that they're likely to let you serve.

But I think you were wrong to refuse to be the head of the colony you're joining. Partly it's because: Who's going to do it better than you? Don't make me laugh.

But the main reason is: What kind of living hell will it be for the colony leader to have Mr. Insubordinate in his colony? Especially because everybody will know you were in Ender's Jeesh and they'll wonder why you AREN'T leader . . .

I don't care how loyal you think you're going to be, Dink. It's not in you. You're a brat and you always will be. So admit what a lousy follower you are, and go ahead and LEAD.

And just in case you don't know it, you stupidest of all possible geniuses: I still love you. I've always loved you. But no woman in her right mind would ever marry you and have your babies because NOBODY COULD STAND TO RAISE THEM. You will have the most hellish children. So have them in a colony where there'll be someplace for them to go when they run away from home about fifteen times before they're ten.

Dink, I'm going to be happy, in the long run. And yes, I did set myself up for hard times when I married a man who's going to die and whose children will probably have the same disease. But Dink—nobody ever marries anybody who ISN'T going to die.

God be with you, my friend. Heaven knows the devil already is.

Love, Petra

---

Bean held two babies and Petra one on the flight from Kiev to Yerevan—whichever one was hungriest got mama. Petra's parents lived there now; by the time Achilles died and they could return to Armenia, the tenants in their old home in Maralik had changed it too much for them to want to return.

Besides, Stefan, Petra's younger brother, was quite the world traveler now, and Maralik was too small for him. Yerevan, while not what anyone would call one of the great world cities, was still a national capital, and it had a university worth studying at, when he graduated from high school.

But to Petra, Yerevan was as unfamiliar a city as Volgograd would have been, or any of the cities named San Salvador. Even the Armenian that was still spoken by many on the street sounded strange to her. It made her sad. I have no native land, she thought.

Bean, however, was drinking it all in. Petra got into the cab first, and he handed her Bella and the newest—but largest—of the babies, Ramón, whom he had picked up in the Philippines. Once Bean was inside the taxi, he held Ender up to the window. And since their firstborn son was beginning to show signs that he understood speech, it wasn't just a matter of playfulness.

"This is your mama's homeland," said Bean. "All these people look just like her." Bean turned back to the two that Petra was holding. "You children all look different, because half your genetic material comes from me. And I'm a mongrel. So in your whole life, there'll be no place you can go where you'll look like the locals."

"That's right, depress and isolate the children from the start," said Petra.

"It's worked so well for me."

"You weren't depressed as a child," said Petra. "You were desperate and terrified."

"So we try to make things better for our children."

"Look, Bella, look, Ramón," said Petra. "This is Yerevan, a city with lots of people that we don't know at all. The whole world is full of strangers."

The taxi driver spoke up, in Armenian: "Nobody in Yerevan is a stranger to Petra Arkanian."

"Petra Delphiki," she corrected him mildly.

"Yes, yes, of course," he said in Common. "I just meaning that if you want a drink in a tavern, nobody let you pay!"

"Does that go for her husband?" asked Bean.

"Man big like you?" said the driver. "They don't tell you the price, they ask you what you wanting to give!" He roared with laughter at his own joke. Not realizing, of course, that Bean's size was killing him. "Big man like you, little tiny babies like these." He laughed again.

Think how amused he'd be if he knew that the largest baby, Ramón, was the youngest.

"I knew we should have walked from the airport," said Bean in Portuguese.

Petra grimaced. "That's rude, to speak in a language he doesn't know."

"Ah. I'm glad to know that the concept of rudeness *does* exist in Armenia."

The taxi driver picked up on the mention of Armenia, even though the rest of the sentence, being in Portuguese, was a mystery to him. "You wanting a tour of Armenia? Not a big country, I can take you, special price, meter not running."

"No time for that," said Petra in Armenian. "But thanks for offering."

The Arkanian family now lived in a nice apartment building—all balconies and glass, yet upscale enough that there was no hanging laundry visible from the street. Petra had told her family she was coming, but asked them not to meet her at the airport. They had gotten so used to the extraordinary security during the days when Petra and Bean were in hiding from Achilles Flandres that they accepted this unquestioningly.

The doorman recognized Petra from her pictures, which appeared in the Armenian papers whenever there was a story about Bean. He not only let them go up unannounced, but also insisted on carrying their bags.

"You two, and three babies, this all the luggage you have?"

"We hardly ever wear clothes," said Petra, as if this were the most sensible thing in the world.

They were halfway up in the elevator before the doorman laughed and said, "You joking!"

Bean smiled and tipped him a hundred-dollar coin. The doorman flipped it in the air and pocketed it with a smile. "Good thing *he* give me! If Petra Arkanian give, my wife never let me spend!"

After the elevator doors closed, Bean said, "From now on, in Armenia *you* tip."

"They'd *keep* the tip either way, Bean. It's not like they give it back to us."

"Oh, eh."

Petra's mother could have been standing at the door, she opened it so quickly. Maybe she was.

There were hugs and kisses and a torrent of words in Armenian and Common. Unlike the cabdriver and doorman, Petra's parents were fluent in Common. So was Stefan, who had cut his high school classes today. And young David was obviously being raised with Common as his first language, since that's what he was chattering in almost continuously from the moment Petra entered the flat.

There was a meal, of course, and neighbors invited in, because it might be the big city, but it was still Armenia. But in only a couple of hours, it was just the nine of them.

"Nine of us," said Petra. "Our five and the four of you. I've missed you."

"Already you have as many children as we did," said Father.

"The laws have changed," said Bean. "Also, we didn't exactly plan to have ours all at once."

"Sometimes I think," said Mother to Petra, "that you're still in Battle School. I have to remind myself, no, she came home, she got married, she has babies. Now we finally get to see the babies. But so small!"

"They have a genetic condition," said Bean.

"Of course, we know that," said Father. "But it's still a surprise, how small they are. And yet so . . . mature."

"The really little ones take after their father," said Petra, with a wry smile.

"And the normal one takes after his mother," said Bean.

"Thank you for letting us use your flat for the unofficial meeting tonight," said Bean.

"It's not a secure site," said Father.

"The meeting is unofficial, not secret. We expect Turkish and Azerbaijani observers to make their reports."

"Are you sure they won't try to assassinate you?" asked Stefan.

"Actually, Stefan, they brainwashed *you* at an early age," said Bean. "When the trigger word is said, you spring into action and kill everybody at the meeting."

"No, I'm going to a movie," said Stefan.

"That's a terrible thing to say," said Petra. "Even as a joke."

"Alai isn't Achilles," said Bean to Stefan. "We're friends, and he won't let Muslim agents assassinate us."

"You're friends with your enemy," said Stefan, as if it were too incredible.

"It happens in some wars," said Father.

"There *is* no war yet," Mother reminded them.

They took the hint, stopped talking about current problems, and reminisced instead. Though since Petra had been sent to Battle School so young, it's not as if she had that much to reminisce about. It was more like they were briefing her about her new identity before an undercover mission. *This* is what you should remember from your childhood, if you'd had one.

And then the Prime Minister, the President, and the Foreign Minister showed up. Mother took the babies into her bedroom, while Stefan took David out to see a movie. Father, being Deputy Foreign Minister, was allowed to stay, though he would not speak.

The conversation was complex but friendly. The Foreign Minister explained how eager Armenia was to join the FPE, and then the President echoed everything he had said, and then the Prime Minister began another repetition.

Bean held up a hand. "Let's stop hiding from the truth. Armenia is a landlocked country, with Turks and Azerbaijanis almost completely surrounding you. With Georgia refusing to join the FPE at present, you worry that we couldn't even supply you, let alone defend you against the inevitable attack."

They were obviously relieved that Bean understood.

"You just want to be left alone," he said.

They nodded.

"But here's the truth: If we don't defeat Caliph Alai and break up this strange and sudden union of Muslim nations, then Caliph Alai will eventually conquer all the surrounding nations. Not because Alai himself wants to, but because he can't remain Caliph for long if he isn't aggressively pursuing an expansionist policy. He says that's not his intent, but he'll certainly end up doing it because he'll have no choice."

They didn't like hearing this, but they kept listening.

"Armenia will fight Caliph Alai sooner or later. The question is whether you'll do it now, while I still lead the forces of the FPE in your defense, or later, when you stand utterly alone against overwhelming force."

"Either way, Armenia will pay," said the President grimly.

"War is unpredictable," said Bean. "And the costs are high. But *we* didn't put Armenia where it is, surrounded by Muslims."

"God did," said the President. "So we try not to complain."

"Why can't Israel be your provocation?" asked the Prime Minister. "They are militarily much stronger than we are."

"The opposite is true," said Bean. "Geographically their position is and always has been hopeless. And they have integrated so closely with the Muslim nations surrounding them that if they now joined the FPE, the Muslims would feel deeply betrayed. Their fury would be terrible, and we could not defend them. While you—let's just say that over the centuries, Muslims have slaughtered more Armenians than they ever did Jews. They hate you, they regard you as a terrible intrusion into their lands, even though you were here long before any Turks came out of central Asia. There's a burden of guilt along with the hatred. And for you to join the FPE would infuriate them, yes, but they wouldn't feel *betrayed*."

"These nuances are beyond me," said the President skeptically.

"They make an enormous difference in the way an army fights. Armenia is vital to forcing Alai to act before he's ready. Right now the union with India is still merely formal, not a fact on the ground. It's a marriage, not a family."

"You don't need to quote Lincoln to me."

Petra inwardly winced. The quote about "a marriage, not a family" did not come from Lincoln at all. It came from one of her own Martel essays. It was a bad sign if people were getting Lincoln and Martel confused. But of course it was better not to correct the misattribution, lest it appear that she was way too familiar with the works of Martel and Lincoln.

"We stand where we've stood for weeks," said the President. "Armenia is being asked too much."

"I agree," said Bean. "But keep in mind that we're asking. When the Muslims finally decide that Armenia shouldn't exist, they won't ask."

The president pressed his fingers to his forehead. It was a gesture that Petra called "drilling for brains." "How can we hold a plebiscite?" he asked.

"It's precisely the plebiscite that we need."

"Why? What does this do for you militarily except overextend your forces and draw off a relatively small part of the Caliph's armies?

"I know Alai," said Bean. "He won't want to attack Armenia. The terrain here is a nightmare for a serious campaigning. You constitute no serious threat. Attacking Armenia makes no sense at all."

"So we won't be attacked?"

"You will absolutely be attacked."

"You're too subtle for us," said the Prime Minister.

Petra smiled. "My husband is *not* subtle. The point is so obvious that you think it couldn't be *this* that he means. Alai will not attack. But Muslims will attack. It will force his hand. If he refuses to attack, but other Muslims do attack, then the leadership of the jihad moves away from him to someone else. Whether he strikes down these free-lance attackers or not, the Muslim world is divided and two leaders compete."

The President was no fool. "You have higher hopes than this," he said.

"All warriors are filled with hope," said Bean. "But I understand your lack of trust in me. For me it's the great game. But for you, it's your homes, your families. That's why we wanted to meet here. To assure you that it is our home and our family as well."

"To sit and wait for the enemy to act is the decision to die," said Petra. "We ask Armenia to make this sacrifice and take this risk because if you don't, then Armenia is doomed. But if you join the Free People of Earth, then Armenia will have the most powerful defense."

"And what will that defense consist of?"

"Me," said Petra.

"A nursing mother?" asked the Prime Minister.

"The Armenian member of Ender's Jeesh," she answered. "I will command the Armenian forces."

"Our mountain goddess versus the goddess of India," said the Foreign Minister.

"This is a Christian nation," said Father. "And my daughter is no goddess."

"I was joking," said Father's boss.

"But the truth that underlies the joke," said Bean, "is that Petra herself is a match for Alai. So am I. And Virlomi is no match for any of us."

Petra hoped that this was true. Virlomi now had years of experience in the field—if not in the logistics of moving huge armies, then in exactly the kind of small operations that would be most effective in Armenia.

"We have to think about it," said the President.

"Then we're where we were before," said the Foreign Minister. "Thinking."

Bean rose to his feet—a formidable sight, these days—and bowed to them. "Thank you for meeting with us."

"Wouldn't it be better," said the Prime Minister, "if you could get this new Hindu-Muslim . . . thing . . . to go to war against China?"

"Oh, that would eventually happen," said Bean. "But when? The FPE wants to break the back of Caliph Alai's Muslim League now. Before it grows any stronger."

And Petra knew they were all thinking: Before Bean dies. Because Bean is the most important weapon.

The President rose from his seat, but then laid a restraining hand on the other two. "We have Petra Arkanian here. And Julian Delphiki. Couldn't we ask them to consult with our military on our preparations for war?"

"I notice there are no military men here," said Petra. "I don't want them to feel that we've been thrust on them."

"They won't feel that way," said the Foreign Minister blandly. But Petra knew that the military was not represented here because they were eager to join the FPE, precisely because they did not feel adequate, by themselves, to defend Armenia. There would be no problems with a tour of inspection.

After the top leadership of Armenia left the Arkanian flat, Father and Petra flung themselves down on the furniture and Bean stretched out on the floor, and at once began discussing what had just happened and what they thought *would* happen.

Mother came in as the conversation was winding down. "All asleep, the little darlings," she said. "Stefan will drop David off after the movie, but we have a little while, just us grown-ups."

"Well, good," said Father.

"We were just discussing," said Petra, "whether it was a waste of time for us to come here."

Mother rolled her eyes. "How can it be a waste of time?" And then, to everyone's surprise, she burst into tears.

"What is it?" At once she was enveloped in the concern of her husband and daughter.

"Nothing," she said. "I just . . . you didn't come here and bring these babies because you had negotiations. Nothing happened here that couldn't have happened by teleconference."

"Then why do you think we're here?" asked Petra.

"You came to say good-bye."

Petra looked at Bean and, for the first time, realized that this might be true. "If we are," she said, "it wasn't our plan."

"But it's what you're doing," said Mother. "You came in person because you might not see us again. Because of the war!"

"No," said Bean. "Not because of the war."

"Mother, you know Bean's condition."

"I'm not blind! I can see that he's giraffed up so he can hardly get into houses!"

"And so are Ender and Bella. They have Bean's same condition. So once we get all our other children, we're going out into space. At lightspeed. So we can take advantage of relativistic effects. So that Bean will be alive when they finally find a cure."

Father shook his head.

"Then we'll be dead before you come home," said Mother.

"Pretend I'm away at Battle School again," said Petra.

"I get these grandchildren, but . . . then I don't get them." Mother cried again.

"I won't leave," said Bean, "until we've got Peter Wiggin safely in control of things."

"Which is why you're in such a hurry to get this war started," said Father. "Why not just tell them?"

"We need them to have confidence in me," said Bean. "Telling them that I might die in mid-campaign won't reassure them about joining the FPE."

---

"So these babies will grow up on a starship?" asked Mother, skeptically.

"Our joy," said Petra, "will be to see them grow old—without any of them growing as big as their father."

Bean raised one enormous foot. "These are tough shoes to fill."

"It really is true," said Petra, "that this war—in Armenia—is the one we want to fight. All these hills. It will go slowly."

"Slowly?" asked Father. "Isn't that the opposite of what you want?"

"What we want," said Bean, "is for the war to end as soon as possible. But this is one case where going slow will speed us up."

"You're the brilliant strategists," said Father, heading for the kitchen. "Anybody else want something to eat?"

---

That night, Petra couldn't sleep. She went out onto the balcony and looked out over the city.

Is there anything in this world that I can't leave?

I've lived apart from my family for so much of my life. Does that mean I'll miss them more or less?

But then she realized that this had nothing to do with her melancholy. She couldn't sleep because she knew that war was coming. Their plan was to keep the conflict in the mountains, to make the Turks pay for every meter. But there was no reason to think that Alai's forces—or whatever Muslim forces they were—would shrink from bombing the big population centers. Precision bombing had been the rule for so long—ever since Mecca was nuked—that a sudden reversion to anti-population, saturation bombing would come as a demoralizing shock.

Everything depends on our being able to get and keep control of the air. And the FPE doesn't have as many planes as the Muslim League.

Damn those short-sighted Israelis for training the Arab air forces to be among the most formidable in the world.

Why was Bean so confident?

Was it only because he knew that he'd soon leave Earth and wouldn't have to be here to face the consequences?

That was unfair. Bean had said he'd stay until Peter was Hegemon in fact as well as name. Bean did not break his word.

What if they never find a cure? What if we sail on through space forever? What if Bean dies out there with me and the babies?

She heard footsteps behind her. She assumed it would be Bean, but it was her mother.

"Awake without the babies waking you?"

Petra smiled. "I have plenty to keep me from sleeping."

"But you *need* your sleep."

"Eventually, my body takes it whether I like it or not."

Mother looked out over the city. "Did you miss us?"

She knew her mother wanted her to say, Every day. But the truth would have to do. "When I have time to think about anything at all, yes. But it's not that I miss you. It's that . . . I'm glad you're in my life. Glad you're in this world." She turned to face her mother. "I'm not a little girl anymore. I know I'm still very young and I'm sure I don't know anything yet, but I'm part of the cycle of life now. I'm no longer the youngest generation. So I don't cling to my parents as I once would have liked to. I missed a lot up there in Battle School. Children need families."

"And," said Mother sadly, "they make families out of whatever they have at hand."

"That will never happen to my children," said Petra. "The world isn't being invaded by aliens. I can stay with them."

Then she remembered that some people would claim that some of her children *were* the alien invasion.

She couldn't think that way.

"You carry so much weight in your heart," said Mother, stroking her hair.

"Not as much as Bean. Far less than Peter."

"Is this Peter Wiggin a good man?"

Petra shrugged. "Are great men ever really good? I know they *can* be, but we judge them by a different standard. Greatness changes them, whatever they were to start with. It's like war—does any war ever settle anything? But we can't judge that way. The test of a war isn't whether it *solved* things. You have to ask, Was fighting the war better than not fighting it? And I guess the same kind of test ought to be used on great men."

"*If* Peter Wiggin is great."

"Mother, he was Locke, remember? He stopped a war. Already he was great before I came home from Battle School. And he was still in his teens. Younger than I am now."

"Then I asked the wrong question," said Mother. "Is a world that he rules over going to be a good place to live?"

Petra shrugged again. "I believe he means it to be. I haven't seen him being vindictive. Or corrupt. He's making sure that any nation that joins the FPE does it through the vote of the people, so nothing is being forced on them. That's promising, isn't it?"

"Armenia spent so many centuries yearning to have our own nation. Now we have it, but it seems the price of keeping it is to give it up."

"Armenia will still be Armenia, Mother."

"No, it won't," she said. "If Peter Wiggin wins everything he's trying to win, then Armenia will be . . . Kansas."

"Hardly!"

"We'll all speak Common and if you go from Yerevan to Rostov or Ankara or Sofia, you won't even know you've gone anywhere."

"We all speak Common *now*. And there'll never be a time you can't tell Ankara from Yerevan."

"You're so sure."

"I'm sure of a lot of things. And about half the time, I'm right." She grinned at her mother, but her mother's return smile wasn't real.

"How did you do it?" asked Petra. "How did you give up your child?"

"You weren't 'given up,' " said Mother. "You were taken. Most of the time I managed to believe it was all for a good cause. The other times I cried. It wasn't death because you were still alive. I was proud of you. I missed you. You were good company almost from your first word. But so ambitious!"

Petra smiled a little at that.

"You're married now," said Mother. "Ambition for yourself is over. It's now ambition for your children."

"I just want them to be happy."

"*That* is something you can't do for them. So don't set that as your goal."

"I don't have a goal, Mother."

"That's nice. Then your heart will never break."

Mother looked at her with a deadpan expression.

Petra laughed a little. "You know, when I've been away for a while, I forget that you know everything."

Mother smiled. "Petra, I can't save you from anything. But I want to. I would if I could. Does that help? To know that somebody wants you to be happy?"

"More than you know, Mother."

She nodded. Tears slipped down her cheeks. "Going off into space. It feels like closing yourself in your own coffin. I know! But that's how it feels to *me*. I just know that I'm going to lose you, as sure as death. You know it too. That's why you're out here saying good-bye to Yerevan?"

"To Earth, Mother. Yerevan's the least of it."

"Well, Yerevan won't miss you. Cities never do. They go on and we don't make any difference to them at all. That's what I hate about cities."

And that's true of the human race, too, thought Petra. "I think it's a good thing, that life goes on. Like water in a pail. Take some out, the rest fills in."

"When it's my child that's gone, nothing fills in," said Mother.

Petra knew that Mother was referring to the years that she spent without Petra, but what flashed into Petra's mind was the six babies they still hadn't found. The two ideas put together made the loss of those babies—if they even existed—too painful to contain. Petra began to cry. She hated crying.

Her mother put her arms around her. "I'm sorry, Pet," she said. "I wasn't even thinking. I was missing one child, and you have so many and you don't even know whether they're alive or dead."

"But they aren't even real to me," said Petra. "I don't know why I'm crying. I've never even met them."

"We're hungry for our children," said Mother. "We *need* to take care of them, once we bring them into existence."

"*I* didn't even get to do *that,*" said Petra. "Other women got to bear all but the one. And I'm going to lose *him.*" And suddenly her life felt so terrible it could not be borne. She sobbed as her mother held her.

"Oh, my poor girl," her mother kept murmuring. "Your life breaks my heart."

"How can I complain like this?" said Petra, her voice high with crying. "I've been part of some of the greatest events in history."

"When your babies need you, history doesn't bring much comfort."

And as if on cue, there was a faint sound of a baby crying inside the flat. Mother made as if to go, but Petra stopped her. "Bean will get her." She used the hem of her shirt to dab at her eyes.

"You can tell from the crying which baby it is?"

"Couldn't you?"

"I never had two infants at the same time, let alone three. There aren't many multiple births in our family."

"Well, I've found the perfect way to have nonuplets. Get eight other women to help." She managed a feeble laugh at her own black humor.

The baby cried again.

"It's definitely Bella, she's always more insistent. Bean will change her, and then he'll bring her to me."

"I could do that and he could go back to sleep," Mother offered.

"It's some of our best time together," said Petra. "Caring for the babies."

Mother pecked her on the cheek. "I can take a hint."

"Thanks for talking to me, Mother."

"Thanks for coming home."

Mother went inside. Petra stood at the edge of the balcony. After a while, Bean came padding out in bare feet. Petra pulled her T-shirt up and Bella started slurping noisily. "Good thing your brother Ender got my milk factory started," said Petra. "Or it would have been the bottle for you."

As she stood there, nursing Bella and looking out over the night-time city, Bean's huge hands held her shoulders and stroked her arms. So gentle. So kind.

Once as tiny as this little girl.

But always a giant, long before his body showed it.

# 19

# ENEMIES

From "Note to Hegemon: You Can't Fight an Epidemic With a Fence"
By "Martel"
Posted on "Early Warning Network"

The presence of Julian Delphiki, the Hegemon's "enforcer," in Armenia might look like a family vacation to some, but some of us remember that Delphiki was in Rwanda before it ratified the FPE Constitution.

When you consider that Delphiki's wife, Petra Arkanian, also one of Ender's Jeesh, is Armenian, what conclusion can be reached except that Armenia, a Christian enclave nearly surrounded by Muslim nations, is preparing to ratify?

Add to that the close ties between the Hegemon and Thailand, where Wiggin's left-hand man, General Suriyawong, is now "consulting" with General Phet Noi and Prime Minister Paribatra, newly returned from Chinese captivity, and the FPE's position in Nubia—and it looks like the Hegemon is surrounding Caliph Alai's little empire.

Many pundits are saying that the Hegemon's strategy is to "contain" Caliph Alai. But now that the Hindus have gone over to the Muslim bed—er, I meant to say, "camp"—containment is not enough.

When Caliph Alai, our modern Tamerlane, decides he wants a nice big pile of human skulls (it's *so* hard to get good decorators these days), he can field huge armies and concentrate them wherever he wants on his borders.

If the Hegemon sits passively waiting, trying to "contain" Alai behind a fence of alliances, then he'll find himself facing overwhelming force wherever Alai decides to strike.

Islam, the bloodthirsty "one-way religion," has a track record only slightly less devastating to the human race than the Buggers.

It's time for the Hegemon to live up to his job title and take decisive, preemptive action—preferably in Armenia, where his forces will be able to strike like a knife into the neck of Islam. And when he does, it's time for Europe, China, and America to wake up and join him. We need unity against this threat as surely as we ever needed it against an alien invasion.

From: PeterWiggin%personal@FreePeopleOfEarth.fp.gov
To: PetraDelphiki%getlost@FreePeopleOfEarth.gov
Re: Latest Martel essay

Encrypted using code: ******
Decrypted using code: *********

"Strike like a knife into the neck of Islam" indeed. Using what enormous army? What vast air force to neutralize the Muslims AND airlift that enormous army over the mountainous terrain between Armenia and the "neck" of Islam?

Fortunately, while Alai and Virlomi will know that Martel is full of kuso, the Muslim press is famous for its paranoia. THEY should believe there's a threat. So now the pressure is on and the game's afoot. You're a natural rabble-rouser, Petra. Promise me you'll never run against me for anything.

Oh, wait. I'm hegemon-for-life, aren't I . . .

Good work, mommy.

Caliph Alai and Virlomi sat beside each other at the head of a conference table in Chichlam—which the Muslim press still called Hyderabad.

Alai couldn't understand why it bothered Virlomi that he refused to insist that the Muslims call the city by its pre-Muslim name. He had problems enough to worry about without a needlessly humiliating name change. After all, the Indians hadn't *won* their independence. They had married their way to self-government. Which was a far better method than war—but without having won a victory on the field of battle, it was unseemly for Virlomi to insist on tokens of triumph like making your undefeated conquerors change the name *they* used to refer to their own seat of government.

In the past few days, Alai and Virlomi had met with several groups. At a conference of heads of Muslim states they had listened to the woes and suggestions of such widely separated peoples as Indonesians, Algerians, Kazakhs, and Yemenis.

At a much quieter conference of Muslim minorities, they had indulged the revolutionary fantasies of Filipino, French, Spanish, and Thai would-be jihadists.

And in between, they had put on banquets for—and listened to stern counsel from—the French, American, and Russian foreign ministers.

These lords of the ancient, weary empires—hadn't they noticed that their nations had long since retired from the world? Yes, the Russians and Americans still had a formidable military, but where was their will to empire? They thought they could still boss around people like Alai, who had power and knew how to use it.

But it did Caliph Alai no harm to pretend that these nations still mattered in the world. Placate them with wise nods and palliative words, and they would go home and feel good about having helped promote "peace on Earth."

Alai had complained to Virlomi afterward. Wasn't it enough for the Americans that the whole world used their dollar and let them dominate the I.F.? Wasn't it enough for the Russians that Caliph Alai was keeping his armies away from their frontier and was doing nothing to support Muslim rebel groups inside their borders?

And the French—what did they expect Alai to *do* when he heard what their government's opinion was? Didn't they understand that they were spectators now in the great game, by their own choice? The players were not going to let the fans call the plays, no matter how well they played back in their day.

Virlomi listened benignly and said nothing in all these meetings. Most of the visitors came away with the impression that she was a figurehead, and Caliph Alai was in complete control. This impression did no harm. But as Alai and his closest advisers knew, it was also completely false.

Today's meeting was far more important. Gathered at this table were the men who actually ran the Muslim empire—the men Alai trusted, who made sure that the heads of the various Muslim states did what Alai needed them to do, without chafing at how thoroughly they were under the Caliph's thumb. Since Alai had the ecstatic support of most of the Muslim people, he had enormous leverage in gaining the cooperation of their governments. But Alai did not yet have the clout to set up an independent system of finance. So he was dependent on contributions from the various republics and kingdoms and Islamic states that served him.

The men at this table made sure that the money flowed inward toward Hyderabad, and obedience flowed outward, with the least possible friction.

The most remarkable thing about these men was that they were no richer now than they had been when he appointed them. Despite all their opportunities to take a bribe here or exact a bit of a kickback there, they had remained pure. They were motivated by devotion to the Caliph's cause and pride in their positions of trust and honor.

Instead of one wazir, Alai had a dozen. They were gathered at this table, to counsel him and hear his decisions.

And every single one of them resented Virlomi's presence at the table.

And Virlomi did nothing to help alleviate this. Because even though she spoke softly and briefly, she persisted in using the quiet voice and enigmatic attitude that had played so well among Hindus. But Muslims had no goddess tradition, except perhaps in Indonesia and Malaysia, where they were especially alert to stamp out such tendencies where they found them. Virlomi was like an alien being among them.

There were no cameras here. The role wasn't working for this audience. So why did she persist in acting the goddess here?

Was it possible she believed it? That after years of playing the part in order to keep Indian resistance alive she now believed that she was divinely inspired? Ridiculous to think she actually believed she was divine herself. If the Muslim people ever believed she thought *that,* they would expect Alai to divorce her and have done with this nonsense. They accepted the idea that the Caliph, like Solomon of old, might marry women from many kingdoms in order to symbolize the submission of those kingdoms to Islam as a wife submits to a husband.

She couldn't believe she was a goddess. Alai was sure of that. Such superstitions would have been stamped out in Battle School.

Then again, Battle School was over years ago, and Virlomi had lived in isolation and adulation during most of that time. Things had happened that would change anybody. She had told him about the campaign of stones in the road, the "Great Wall of India," how she had seen her own actions turn into a vast movement. About how she first became a holy woman and then a goddess in hiding in eastern India.

When she taught him about Satyagraha, he thought he understood. You sacrifice anything and everything in order to stand for what's right without causing harm to another.

And yet she had also killed men with a gun she held in her own hand. There were times when she did not shrink from war. When she told him of her band of warriors who had stood off the whole Chinese army, preventing them from flooding back into India, from even resupplying the armies that Alai's Persians and Pakistanis were systematically destroying, he realized how much he owed to her brilliance as a commander, as a leader who could inspire incredible acts of bravery from her soldiers, as a teacher who could train peasants to be brutally efficient soldiers.

Somewhere between Satyagraha and slaughter, there had to be a place where Virlomi—the girl from Battle School—actually lived.

Or perhaps not. Perhaps the cruel contradictions of her own actions had led her to put the responsibility elsewhere. She served the gods. She was a god herself. Therefore it was not wrong for her to live by Satyagraha one day, and wipe out an entire convoy in a landslide the next.

The irony was that the longer he lived with her, the more Alai loved her. She was a sweet and generous lover, and she talked with him openly, girlishly, as if they were friends in school. As if they were still children.

Which we are, aren't we?

No. Alai was a man now, despite being in his teens. And Virlomi was older than he was, not a child at all.

But they had had no childhood. Alone together, their marriage was more like *playing* at being husband and wife than anything else. It was still fun.

And when they came to a meeting like this, Virlomi could switch off that playfulness, set aside the natural girl and become the irritating Hindu goddess that continued to drive a wedge between Caliph Alai and his most trusted servants.

Naturally, the counsel was worried about Peter Wiggin and Bean and Petra and Suriyawong. That Martel essay was taken very seriously.

So naturally, in order to be irritating, Virlomi dismissed it. "Martel can write what he wants, it means nothing."

Careful not to contradict her, Hadrubet Sasar—"Thorn"—pointed out the obvious. "The Delphikis really are in Armenia and have been for a week."

"They have family there," said Virlomi.

"And they're on vacation taking the babies to visit grandfather and grandmother," said Alamandar. As usual, his irony was so dry you could easily miss the fact that he was utterly scornful of the idea.

"Of course not," said Virlomi—and her scorn was not subtle. "Wiggin *wants* us to think they're planning something. We withdraw Turkish troops from Xinjiang to invade Armenia. Then Han Tzu strikes in Xinjiang."

"Perhaps al-Caliph has some intelligence indicating that the Emperor of China is in alliance with the Hegemon," said Thorn.

"Peter Wiggin," said Virlomi, "knows how to use people who don't know they're being used."

Alai listened to her and thought: That principle might as easily apply to the Armenians as to Han Tzu. Perhaps *they're* being used by Peter Wiggin without their consent. A simple matter to send Bean and Petra to visit the Arkanians, and then plant a false story that this means the Armenians are about to join the FPE.

Alai raised a hand. "Najjas. Would you compare the language in the Martel essays with the writings of Peter Wiggin, including the Locke essays, and tell me if they might be written by the same hand?"

A murmur of approval around the table.

"We will not take action against Armenia," said Caliph Alai, "based on unsubstantiated rumors from the nets. Nor based on our longstanding suspicion of the Armenians."

Alai watched their reaction. Some nodded approvingly, but most hid their reactions. And Musafi, the youngest of his wazirs, showed his skepticism.

"Musafi, speak to us," said Alai.

"It makes little difference to the people," said Musafi, "whether we can prove that the Armenians are plotting against us or not. This isn't a court of law. They are being told by many that instead of gaining India peacefully by marriage, we lost it the same way."

Alai did not look at Virlomi; nor did he sense any stiffening or change in her attitude.

"We did nothing when the Hegemon humiliated the Sudanese and stole Muslim land in Nubia." Musafi raised his hand to the inevitable objection. "The people *believe* the land was stolen."

"So you fear that they will think the Caliph is ineffective."

"They expected you to spread Islam throughout the world. Instead, you seem to be losing ground. The very fact that Armenia cannot be the source of a serious invasion also means that it's a safe place to take some limited action that will assure the people that the Caliphate is still watching over Islam."

"And how many men should die for this?" said Alai.

"For the continued unity of the Muslim people?" asked Musafi. "As many as love God."

"There's wisdom in this," said Alai. "But the Muslim people are not the only people in the world. Outside of Islam, Armenia is perceived as a heroic victim nation. Isn't there a chance that any kind of action in Armenia will be seen as proof that Islam is expanding, just as Martel charges? Then what happens to the Muslim minorities in Europe?"

Virlomi leaned forward, looking each of the counselors boldly in the face, as if she had authority at this table. Her stance was more aggressive than Alai ever showed to his friends. But then, these were not her friends. "You care about unity?"

"It's always been a problem in the Muslim world," said Alamandar. Some of the men chuckled.

"The 'Free People' can't invade us because we're more powerful than they are at any point where they might attack," said Virlomi. "Is our goal to unite the world under the leadership of Caliph Alai? Then our great rival is not Peter Wiggin. It's Han Tzu. He came to me with plots against Caliph Alai. He proposed marriage with me, so India and China could unite against Islam."

"When was this?" asked Musafi.

Alai understood why he was asking. "It was before Virlomi and I even considered marriage, Musafi. My wife has behaved with perfect propriety."

Musafi was satisfied; Virlomi showed no sign that she even cared what the interruption had been about. "You don't fight wars to enhance domestic unity—to do that, you pursue economic policies that make your people fat and rich. Wars are fought to create safety, to expand borders, and to eliminate future dangers. Han Tzu is such a danger."

"Since he has taken office," said Thorn, "Han Tzu has taken no aggressive action. He has been conciliatory with all his neighbors. He even sent home the Indian prime minister, didn't he?"

"That was no conciliatory gesture," said Virlomi.

"The expansionist Snow Tiger is gone, his policies failed. We have nothing to fear from China," said Thorn.

He had gone too far, and everyone at the table knew it. It was one thing to make suggestions, and quite another to flatly contradict Virlomi.

Pointedly, Virlomi sat back and looked at Alai, waiting for him to take action against the offender.

But Thorn had earned his nickname because he would say uncomfortable truths. Nor did Alai intend to start banishing advisers from his council just because Virlomi was annoyed with them. "Once again, our friend Thorn proves that his name is well chosen. And once again, we forgive him for his bluntness—or should I say, sharpness?"

Laughter . . . but they were still wary of Virlomi's wrath.

"I see that this counsel prefers to send Muslims to die in cosmetic wars, while the real enemy is allowed to gather strength unmolested, solely because he has not attacked us yet." She turned directly to Thorn. "My husband's good friend Thorn is like the man in a leaky boat, surrounded by sharks. He has a rifle, and his fellow passenger says, 'Why don't you shoot those sharks! Once the boat sinks and we're in the water, you won't be able to use the rifle!'

" 'You fool,' says the man. 'Why should I provoke the sharks? None of them has bit me yet.' "

Thorn seemed determined to press his luck. "The way I heard the story, the boat was surrounded by dolphins, and the man shot at them until he ran out of ammunition. 'Why did you do that?' his friend asked, and the man said, 'because one of them was a shark in disguise.'

" 'Which one?' said his companion.

" 'You fool,' says the man. 'I told you he's in disguise.' Then the blood in the water drew many sharks. But the man's gun was empty."

"Thank you all for your wise counsel," said Alai. "I must now think about all that you have said."

Virlomi smiled at Thorn. "I must remember your alternate version of the story. It's hard to decide which one is funnier. Maybe one is funny to Hindus, and the other to Muslims."

Alai stood up and began shaking hands with the men around the table, in effect dismissing each one in turn. It had already been rude for Virlomi to continue the conversation. But still she would not let up.

"Or perhaps," she said to the group as a whole, "Thorn's story is funny only to the sharks. Because if *his* story is believed, the sharks are safe."

Virlomi had never gone this far before. If she were a Muslim wife, he could take her by the arm and gently lead her from the room, then explain to her why she could not say such things to men who were not free to answer.

But then, if she were a Muslim wife, she wouldn't have been at the table in the first place.

Alai shook hands with the rest of them, and they showed their deference to him. But he also saw a growing wariness. His failure to stop Virlomi from giving such outrageous offense—to a man who had admittedly gone too far himself—looked like weakness to them. He knew they were wondering just how much influence Virlomi had over him. And whether he was truly functioning as Caliph any more, or was just a henpecked husband, married to a woman who thought she was a god.

In short, was Caliph Alai succumbing to idolatry by being married to this madwoman?

Not that anyone could say such a thing—even to each other, even in private.

In fact, they probably weren't thinking it, either.

I'm thinking it.

When he and Virlomi were alone, Alai walked out of the room to the conference room toilet, where he washed his face and hands.

Virlomi followed him inside.

"Are you strong or weak?" she asked. "I married you for your strength."

He said nothing.

"You know I'm right. Peter Wiggin can't touch us. Only Han Tzu stands between us and uniting the world under our rule."

"That's not true, Virlomi," said Alai.

"So you contradict me, too?"

"We're equals, Virlomi," said Alai. "We can contradict each other—when we're alone together."

"So if I'm wrong, who *is* a greater threat than Han Tzu?"

"If we attack Han Tzu, unprovoked, and it looks as if he might lose—or he does lose—then we can expect the Muslim population of Europe to be expelled, and the nations of Europe will unite, probably with the United States, probably with Russia. Instead of a mountain border that Han Tzu is not threatening, we'll have an indefensible border thousands of kilometers long in Siberia, and enemies whose combined military might will dwarf ours."

"America! Europe! Those fat old men."

"I see you're giving my ideas careful consideration," said Alai.

"Nothing's certain in war," said Virlomi. "This *might* happen, that *might* happen. I'll tell you what *will* happen. India will take action, whether the Muslims join us or not."

"India, which has little equipment and no trained army, will take on China's battle-hardened veterans—and without the help of the Turkish divisions in Xinjiang and the Indonesian divisions in Taiwan?"

"The Indian people do what I ask them," said Virlomi.

"The Indian people do what you ask them, as long as it's *possible*."

"Who are you to say what's possible?"

"Virlomi," said Alai. "I'm not Alexander of Macedonia."

"*That* much is abundantly clear. In fact, Alai, what battle have you *ever* fought and won?"

"You mean before or after the final war against the Buggers?"

"Of course—you were one of the sacred Jeesh! So you're right about everything forever!"

"And it was my plan that destroyed the Chinese will to fight."

"Your plan—which depended on *my* little band of patriots holding the Chinese army at bay in the mountains of eastern India."

"No, Virlomi. Your holding action saved thousands of lives, but if every single Chinese they sent over the mountain had faced us in India, we would have won."

"Easy to *say*."

"Because my plan was for the Turkish troops to take Beijing while most of the Chinese forces were tied up in India, at which point the Chinese troops would have been called back from India. Your heroic action saved many lives and made our victory quicker. By about two weeks and an estimated hundred thousand casualties. So I'm grateful. But you've never led large armies into combat."

Virlomi waved it away, as if such a gesture could make the fact of it disappear.

"Virlomi," said Alai. "I love you, and I'm not trying to hurt you, but you've been fighting all this time against very bad commanders. You've never come up against someone like me. Or Han Tzu. Or Petra. And definitely no one like Bean."

"The stars of Battle School!" said Virlomi. "Ancient test scores and membership in a club whose president got outmaneuvered and sent into exile. What have you done lately, Caliph Alai?"

"I married a woman with a bold plan," said Alai.

"But what did I marry?" asked Virlomi.

"A man who wants the world to be united in peace. I thought the woman who built the Great Wall of India would want the same thing. I thought our marriage was part of that. I never knew you were so bloodthirsty."

"Not bloodthirsty, realistic. I see our true enemy and I'm going to fight him."

"Our *rival* is Peter Wiggin," said Alai. "He has a plan for uniting the world, but his depends on the Caliphate collapsing into chaos and Islam ceasing to be a force in the world. That's what the Martel essay was designed to do—provoke us into doing something stupid in Armenia. Or Nubia."

"Well, at least you see through *that*."

"I see through all of it," said Alai. "And you don't see the most obvious thing of all. The longer we wait, the closer we come to the day when Bean will die. It's a cruel and terrible fact, but when he's gone, then Peter Wiggin loses his greatest tool."

Virlomi looked at him with withering scorn. "Back to the Battle School test scores."

"All the kids in Battle School were tested," said Alai. "Including you."

"Yes, and what did that get any of them? They sat here in Hyderabad like passive slaves while Achilles bullied them. *I* escaped. *Me*. Somehow I was different. But did that show up on any of their tests in Battle School? There are things they didn't test for."

Alai did not tell her the obvious: She was different only because Petra asked her for help, and not someone else. She would not have escaped without Petra's request.

"Ender's Jeesh didn't come from the tests," said Alai. "We were chosen because of what we *did*."

"Because of what you did that *Graff* thought was important. There were qualities that he didn't know were important, so he didn't watch for them."

Alai laughed. "What, you're jealous because you weren't in Ender's Jeesh?"

"I'm disgusted that you still believe that Bean is irresistible because he's so 'smart.' "

"You haven't seen him in action," said Alai. "He's scary."

"No, you're just scared."

"Virlomi," said Alai, "don't do this."

"Don't do what?"

"Don't force my hand."

"I'm not forcing anything. We're equals, right? You'll tell your armies what to do, and I'll tell mine."

"If you send your troops on a suicide attack against China, then China will be at war with me, too. That's what our marriage *means*. So you're committing me to war whether I like it or not."

"I can win without you."

"Don't believe your own propaganda, my beloved," said Alai. "You aren't a god. You aren't infallible. And right now, you're so irrational that it scares me."

"Not irrational," said Virlomi. "*Confident*. And determined."

"You studied where I did. You already know all the reasons why an attack against China is insane."

"That's why we'll achieve surprise. That's why we'll win. Besides," said Virlomi, "our battle plans will be drawn up by the great Caliph Alai. And *he* was a member of Ender's Jeesh!"

"What happened to the idea of our being equals?" said Alai.

"We *are* equals."

"I never forced you to do anything."

"And I'm not forcing you, either."

"Saying that over and over won't make it true."

"I'm doing what I choose, and you're doing what you choose. The only thing I want from you is—I want your baby inside me before I lead my troops to war."

"What do you think this is, the middle ages? You don't lead your troops to war."

"I do," said Virlomi.

"You do if you're a squad commander. There's no point when you have an army of a million men. They can't *see* you so it doesn't help."

"You reminded me a minute ago that you aren't Alexander of Macedon. Well, Alai, I *am* Jeanne d'Arc."

"When I said I'm not Alexander," said Alai, "I wasn't referring to his military prowess. I was referring to his marriage to a Persian princess."

She looked irritated. "I studied his *campaigns.*"

"He returned to Babylon and married a daughter of the old Persian Emperor. He made his officers marry Persians, too. He was trying to unite the Greeks with the Persians and form them into one nation, by making the Persians a little more Greek, and the Greeks a little more Persian."

"Your point?"

"The Greeks said, We conquered the world by being Greek. The Persians lost their empire by being Persian."

"So you aren't trying to make your Muslims more Hindu or my Hindus more Muslim. Very good."

"He tried to combine soldiers of Persia and soldiers of Greece into one army. It didn't work. It fell apart."

"We're not making those mistakes."

"Exactly," said Alai. "I'm not going to make mistakes that destroy my Caliphate."

Virlomi laughed. "All right, then. If you think invading China is such a mistake, what are you going to do? Divorce me? Void our treaty? What then? You'll have to retreat from India and you'll look like even more of a zhopa. Or you'll try to stay and then I'll go to war against *you.* It all comes crashing down, Alai. So you're not going to get rid of me. You're going to stay my husband and you're going to love me and we'll have babies together and we'll conquer the world and govern it together and do you know why?"

"Why?" he said sadly.

"Because that's how I want it. That's what I've learned over the past few years. Whatever I think of, if I decide I want it, if I do what I know I need to do, then it happens. I'm the lucky girl whose dreams come true."

She came to him, wrapped her arms around him, kissed him. He kissed her back, because it would be unwise of him to show her how sad and frightened he was, and how little he desired her now.

"I love you," she said. "You're my best dream."

# 20
# PLANS

From: ImperialSelf%HotSoup@ForbiddenCity.ch.gov
To: Weaver%Virlomi@MotherIndia.in.net, Caliph%Salaam@caliph.gov
Re: Don't do this

Alai, Virlomi, what are you thinking? Troop movements can't be hidden. Do you really want this bloodbath? Are you bent on proving that Graff is right and none of us belong on Earth?

Hot Soup

From: Weaver%Virlomi@MotherIndia.in.net
To: ImperialSelf%HotSoup@ForbiddenCity.ch.gov
Re: Silly boy

Did you think that Chinese offenses in India would be forgotten? If you don't want bloodshed, then swear allegiance to Mother India and Caliph Alai. Disband your armies and offer no resistance. We will be far more merciful to the Chinese than the Chinese were to India.

From: Caliph%Jeeshman@caliph.gov
To: ImperialSelf%HotSoup@ForbiddenCity.ch.gov
Re: Look again

Take no precipitate action, my friend. Things will not go as they appear to be going.

Mazer Rackham sat across from Peter Wiggin in his office in Rotterdam.

"We're very concerned," said Rackham.

"So am I."

"What have you set in motion here, Peter?"

"Mazer," said Peter, "all I've done is keep pressing, using what small tools I have. *They* decide how to respond to that pressure. I was prepared for an invasion of Armenia or Nubia. I was prepared to take advantage of a mass expulsion of Muslims from some or all European nations."

"And war between India and China? Are you prepared for that?"

"These are *your* geniuses, Mazer. Yours and Graff's. You trained them. You explain to me why Alai and Virlomi are doing something so stupid and suicidal as to throw badly armed Indian troops against Han Tzu's battle-hardened, fully equipped, revenge-hungry army."

"So that's not something you did."

"I'm not like you and Graff," said Peter, irritated. "I don't think I'm some master puppeteer. I've got *this* amount of power and influence in the world, and it doesn't amount to much. I have a billion or so citizens who have *not* yet become a genuine nation, so I have to keep dancing just to keep the FPE viable. I have a military force which is well trained and well equipped, has excellent morale, and is so small it wouldn't even be noticed on a battlefield in China or India. I have my personal reputation as Locke and my not-so-empty-anymore office as Hegemon.

And I have Bean, both his actual abilities and his extravagant reputation. That's my arsenal. Do you see anything in that list that would allow me to even *think* of starting a war between two major world powers over whom I have no influence?"

"It just played into your hands so nicely, we couldn't help but think you had something to do with it."

"No, *you* did," said Peter. "You made these kids crazy in Battle School. Now they're all mad kings, using the lives of their subjects as playing pieces in a tawdry game of one-upmanship."

Rackham sat back, looking a little sick. "We didn't want this either. And I don't think they're crazy. Somebody must see some advantage in starting this war, and yet I can't think who. You're the only one who stands to gain, so we thought . . ."

"Believe it or not," said Peter, "I would not start a war like *this*, even if I thought I could profit from picking up the pieces. The only people who start wars that are bound to depend on human waves getting cut down by machine guns are fanatics or idiots. I think we can safely rule out idiocy. So . . . that leaves Virlomi."

"That's what we're afraid of. That she's actually come to believe her image. God-blessed and irresistible." Rackham raised an eyebrow. "But you knew that. You met with her."

"She proposed marriage to me," said Peter. "I turned her down."

"Before she went to Alai."

"I have a feeling that she married Alai on the rebound."

Rackham laughed. "She offered you India."

"She offered me an entanglement. I turned it into an opportunity."

"You knew when you turned her down that she'd be angry and do something stupid."

Peter shrugged. "I knew she'd do something spiteful. Something to show her power. I had no idea she'd try Alai, and I certainly had no idea he'd actually fall for it. Didn't he know she was crazy? I mean, not clinically, but drunk on power."

"You tell *me* why he did it," said Rackham.

"He was one of Ender's Jeesh," said Peter. "You and Graff must have so much paper on Alai that you know when he scratches his butt."

Rackham only waited.

"Look, I don't know why he did it, except maybe he thought he could control her," said Peter. "When he came home from Eros, he was a naive and righteous Muslim boy who's been sheltered ever since. Maybe he just wasn't ready to deal with a real live woman. The question now is, how will this play out?"

"How do *you* think it will play out?"

"Why should I tell you what I think?" said Peter. "What possible advantage will I get from you and Graff knowing what I'm expecting and what I'm preparing to do about it?"

"How will it hurt?"

"It'll hurt because if you decide your goals are different from mine, you'll meddle. Some of your meddling I've appreciated, but right now I don't want either the I.F. or ColMin doing one damn thing. I'm juggling too many balls to want some volunteer juggler to come in and try to help."

Rackham laughed. "Peter, Graff was so right about you."

"What?"

"When he rejected you for Battle School."

"Because I was too aggressive," said Peter wryly. "And look what he actually *accepted.*"

"Peter," said Rackham. "Think about what you just said."

Peter thought about it. "You mean about juggling."

"I mean about why you were rejected for Battle School."

Peter immediately felt stupid. His parents had been told that he was rejected because he was too aggressive—dangerously so. And he had wormed that information out of them at a very young age. Ever since then, it had been a burden he carried around inside—the judgment that he was dangerous. Sometimes it had made him bold; more often, it had made him not trust his own judgment, his own moral framework. Am I doing this because it's right? Am I doing this because it will really be to my benefit? Or only because I'm aggressive and can't stand to sit back and wait? He had forced himself to be more patient, more subtle than his first impulse. Time after time he had held back. It was because of this that he had used Valentine and now Petra to write the more dangerous, demagogic essays—he didn't want any kind of textual analysis to point to him as the author. It was why he had held back from any kind of serious arm-twisting with nations that kept playing with him about joining the FPE—he couldn't afford to have anyone perceive him as coercive.

And all this time, that assessment of him was a lie.

"I'm not too aggressive."

"It's impossible to be too aggressive for Battle School," said Rackham. "Reckless—now, that would be dangerous. But nobody has ever called you reckless, have they? And your parents would have known that was a lie, because they could have seen what a calculating little bastard you were, even at the age of seven."

"Why thanks."

"No, Graff looked at your tests and watched what the monitor showed us, and then he talked to me and showed me, and we realized: You weren't what we wanted as commander of the army, because people don't love you. Sorry, but it's true. You're not warm. You don't inspire devotion. You would have been a good commander *under* someone like Ender. But you could never have held the whole thing together the way he did."

"I'm doing fine now, thanks."

"You're not commanding soldiers. Peter, do Bean or Suri *love* you? Would they die for you? Or do they serve you because they believe in your cause?"

"They think the world united under me as Hegemon would be better than the world united under anyone else, or not united at all."

"A simple calculation."

"A calculation based on trust that I've damn well earned."

"But not personal devotion," said Rackham. "Even Valentine—she was never devoted to you, and she knew you better than anyone."

"She pretty much hated me."

"Too strong, Peter. Too strong a word. She didn't trust you. She feared you. She saw your mind like clockwork. Very smart. She always figured you were six steps ahead of her."

Peter shrugged.

"But you weren't, were you?"

"Ruling the world isn't a chess game," said Peter. "Or if it is, it's a game with a thousand powerful pieces and eight billion pawns, and the pieces keep changing their capabilities, and the gameboard never stays the same. So just how far ahead can you possibly see? All I could do was put myself into a position with the most possible influence, and then exploit whatever opportunities came."

Rackham nodded. "But one thing was certain. Your off-the-charts aggressiveness, your passion to control events, we knew that you would place yourself in the center of everything."

It was Peter's turn to laugh. "So you left me home from Battle School so I would be what I am now."

"As I said, you weren't suited for military life. You don't take orders very well. People aren't devoted to you, and you aren't devoted to anyone else."

"I might be, if I found somebody I respected enough."

"The only person you ever respected that much is on a colony ship right now and you'll never see him again."

"I could never have followed Ender."

"No, you never could. But he's the only person you respected enough. The trouble was, he was your younger brother. You couldn't have lived with the shame."

"Well, all this analysis is nice, but how does it help us now?"

"We don't have a plan either, Peter," said Rackham. "We're also just moving useful pieces into place. Taking others out of play. We have some assets, just as you do. We have our arsenal."

"You have the whole I.F. You could put a stop to all of this."

"No," said Rackham. "Polemarch Chamrajnagar is adamant about it, and he's right. We could force the world's armies to come to a halt.

They would all obey us or pay a terrible price. But who would be ruling the world then?"

"The fleet."

"And who is the fleet? It's volunteers *from Earth.* And from that moment on, who would be our volunteers? People who love the idea of going out into space? Or people who want to control the government of Earth? It would turn us into an Earth-centered institution. It would destroy the colonization project. And the Fleet would be hated, because it would soon be dominated by people who loved power."

"Makes you sound like a bunch of nervous virgins."

"We are," said Rackham. "And that's a strange line, coming from a nervous virgin like you."

Peter didn't bother responding to that. "So you and Graff won't do anything that would compromise the purity of the I.F."

"Unless somebody brings out the nukes again. We won't let that happen. Two nuclear wars were enough."

"We never had a nuclear war."

"World War II was a nuclear war," said Rackham. "Even if only two bombs were dropped. And the bomb that destroyed Mecca was the end of a civil war within Islam being fought out through surrogates and terrorism. Ever since then, nobody has even considered using nukes. But wars that are ended by nukes are nuclear wars."

"Fine. Definitions."

"Hyrum and I are doing everything we can," said Rackham. "So is the Polemarch. And believe it or not, we're trying to help you. We want you to succeed."

"And now you're pretending that you've been rooting for me all along?"

"Not at all," said Rackham. "We had no idea whether you'd be a tyrant or a wise ruler. No idea of what method you'd use or what your world government would be like. We knew you couldn't do it by charisma because you don't have much. And I'll admit you emerged with greater clarity after we got a good look at Achilles."

"So you didn't really get behind me until you realized I was better than Achilles."

"Your achievements were so extraordinary that we were still wary of you. Then Achilles showed us that you were actually cautious and self-restrained, compared to what *could* have been done by somebody who was truly ruthless. We saw a tyrant on the make, and we realized you weren't one."

"Depending on how you define 'tyrant.' "

"Peter, we're trying to help you. We want you to unite the world under *civilian* government. Without any advice from us, you've determined to do it by persuasion and plebiscite instead of using armies and terror."

"I use armies."

"You know what I mean," said Rackham.

"I just didn't want you to have any illusions."

"So tell me what you're thinking. What you're planning. So we *won't* interfere with our meddling."

"Because you're on my side," Peter said scornfully.

"No, we're not 'on your side.' We're not really in this game, except insofar as it affects us. We're in the business of dispersing the human race to as many worlds as possible. But so far, only two colony ships have taken off. And it will be another generation before any of them lands. Far longer before we know whether the colonies will take hold and succeed. Even longer than that before we know if they'll become isolated worlds or trade will be profitable enough to make interstellar travel economically feasible. That's all we care about. But to accomplish it, we have to get recruits from Earth, and we have to pay for the ships—again, from Earth. And we have to do it without any hope of financial return for a hundred years at the best. Capitalism is not good at thinking a hundred years ahead. So we need government funding."

"Which you've managed to get even when I couldn't raise a dime."

"No, Peter," said Rackham. "Don't you understand? Everybody except the United States and Britain and a handful of smaller countries has stopped paying their assessments. We're living off our huge cash reserves. It's been enough to outfit two ships, to build a new class of gravity-controlled messenger ships, a few projects like that. But we're running out of money. We have no way to finance even the ships we already have under construction."

"You want me to win so I'll pay for your fleet."

"We want you to win so that the human race can stop spending its vast surpluses on ways to kill each other, and can instead send all the people that would have been killed in war out into space. And all the money that would have been spent on weapons can be spent on colony ships, and on trading ships, eventually. The human race has always produced a vast surplus of human beings and of wealth, and it has used up almost all of it either on stupid monuments like the pyramids or on brutal, bloody, pointless wars. We want you to unite the world so that this waste can finally stop."

Peter laughed. "You are such *dreamers*. Such idealists!"

"We were warriors and we studied our enemy. The Hive Queens. They failed because they were too unified. Human beings are a better design for a sentient species. Once we get over this war thing. What the Hive Queens tried, we can *do*. Spread out the species so it can develop truly new cultures."

"New cultures? When you insist that each colony be made up entirely of people from one nation, one language group?"

"We're not absolutely rigid on that, but yes. There are two ways of looking at species diversity. One is that every colony should contain a complete copy of the whole human race—every culture, every language, every race. But what's the point of that? Earth already has that! And look how well it's worked.

"No, the great colonies of the past have succeeded precisely because they were internally unified. People who knew each other, trusted each other, shared the same purposes, embraced the same laws. Each one monochromatic to begin with. But when we send out fifty monochromatic colony ships, but all different colors, so to speak—fifty different colonies, each with a separate cultural and linguistic root—*then* the human race can perform fifty different experiments. Real species diversity."

"I don't care what you say," said Peter, "I'm not going."

Rackham smiled. "We don't want you to."

"The two colony ships you've launched. One of them was Ender's."

"That's right."

"Who's the commander of the second ship?"

"Well, the *ship* is commanded by—"

"Who's going to rule the *colony*," said Peter.

"Dink Meeker."

So that was the plan. They meant to take Ender's Jeesh and anybody else who was dangerously talented in a military way and send them off into space. "So to you," said Peter, "this war between Han Tzu and Alai is your worst nightmare."

Rackham nodded.

"Don't worry," said Peter.

"Don't worry?"

"All right," said Peter. "Worry if you want. But your offer to Ender's Jeesh, to take them all off planet, to give them colonies—now I understand what it's about. You care about these kids whose lives you coopted. You want to get them off to worlds where there's no rival. They can use their talents to help a community triumph over a new world."

"Yes."

"But the most important thing is, they won't be on Earth."

Rackham shrugged.

"You knew that nobody could ever unite the world as you need it to be united while those highly trained, highly aggressive, publicly certified geniuses are still in it."

"We didn't see a way it could happen."

"Well, that's a lie," said Peter. "You saw the way it would happen, because it's obvious. One of *them* would be the ruler of Earth, and all the others would be dead."

"Yes, we saw that, but it wasn't an option."

"Why not? It's the human way of settling things."

"We love these kids, Peter."

"But love them or not, they'll all die eventually. No, I think you would have been content to let them work it out, if you thought it would work. If you thought one of them would emerge triumphant. What you couldn't stand was the knowledge that they were so evenly matched that none of them would win. They'd use up the resources of Earth, all that surplus population, and *still* there'd be no clear winner."

"That wouldn't help anything," said Rackham.

"So if you could have found a cure for Bean's condition, you wouldn't need me. Because Bean could do it. He could defeat the others. He could unite the world. Because he's so much better than they are."

"But he's going to die," said Rackham.

"And you love him," said Peter. "So you're going to try to save his life."

"We want him to help you win first."

"That's not possible," said Peter. "Not in the time he has left."

"By 'win,' " said Rackham, "I mean, we want him to help you get into a position where your victory is inevitable, given your abilities. Right now, you could be stopped by all kinds of chance events. Having Bean increases your power and influence. Another thing that would help is if we could get the rest of the Jeesh off this planet. If we've removed from the board all the pieces that could challenge you—if, in effect, you're the queen in a game of knights and bishops—then you won't need Bean anymore."

"I'll need somebody," said Peter. "I'm not trained for war the way these Battle School kids were. And as you said, I'm not the kind of guy that soldiers want to die for."

Rackham leaned forward. "Peter, tell us what you're planning."

"I'm not planning anything," said Peter. "I'm simply waiting. When I met Virlomi, I realized that she was the key to everything. She's volatile, she's powerful, and she's drunk. I knew that she'd do something destabilizing. Something that would break things apart."

"So you think the war between India and China will happen? And that Alai's Muslim League will be drawn into it?"

"That's possible," said Peter. "I hope it won't happen."

"But if it does, you'll be poised to attack Alai when his forces are tied up fighting China."

"No," said Peter.

"No?"

"We're not going to attack anybody," he said.

"Then . . . what?" said Rackham. "Whoever emerges from that war—"

"I don't think that war's going to amount to much," said Peter, "if it happens at all. But if it does happen, then both sides will be weakened by it. There's no shortage of ambitious nations ready to step in and pick up the pieces."

"So what do *you* think is going to happen?"

"I don't know," said Peter. "I wish you'd believe me. There's only one thing I'm sure of. Alai's and Virlomi's marriage is doomed. And if you want either or both of them to command any of your precious colonies, you'd better make sure you're ready to get them off planet fast."

"Are you planning something?" asked Rackham.

"No! Aren't you listening? I'm watching the whole damn thing just like you are! I've already played my cards—making the Muslim leadership suspicious of my intentions. Provoking them. Plus a little quiet diplomacy."

"With whom?"

"With Russia," said Peter.

"You're trying to get them to join with you in attacking Alai? Or China?"

"No, no, no," said Peter. "If I tried anything like that, word would get out, and then what Muslim nation would ever, *ever* join the FPE?"

"So what are you doing with your diplomacy?"

"Begging the Russians to stay out of it."

"In other words, pointing out the opportunity and telling them that you're not going to interfere in any way."

"Yes," said Peter.

"Politics is so . . . indirect."

"That's why conquerors rarely make great rulers."

"And great rulers are rarely conquerors."

"You closed the door on my becoming a conqueror," said Peter. "So if I'm to be the ruler of the world—a good one—then I have to win that position in such a way as not to have to keep killing people in order to stay in power. It does the world no good if everything depends on me, if it all collapses when I die. I need to build this thing piece by piece, bit by bit, with powerful institutions that have their own momentum, so that it will make very little difference who's at the head. It's what I learned from growing up in America. It was a nation created out of nothing—nothing but a set of ideals that they never measured up to. Now and then they had great leaders, but usually nothing but political hacks, and I mean right from the start. Washington was great, but Adams was paranoid and lazy, and Jefferson was as vile a scheming politician as a nation has ever been cursed with. I learned a lot from *him* about destroying your enemies with demagoguery conducted under pseudonyms."

"So you were praising him."

"I'm saying that America shaped itself with institutions so strong that it could survive corruption, stupidity, vanity, ambition, recklessness, and even insanity in its chief executive. I'm trying to do the same thing with the Free People of Earth. Base it on some simple but workable ideals. Bring nations into it because they freely choose to join. Unite them with a language and a system of laws, and give them a stake in institutions that take on a life of their own. And I can't do any of that if I conquer a single country and force it to join. That's a rule I can never violate. My forces will defeat enemies who attack the FPE, and we'll carry war into their territory to do it. But when it comes to joining the FPE, they can only do it if a majority of the people want to. If they choose to be subject to our laws and take part in our institutions."

"But you're not above getting other nations to do your conquering for you."

"Islam," said Peter, "has never learned how to be a religion. It's a tyranny by its very nature. Until it learns to let the door swing both ways, and permit Muslims to decide not to be Muslim without penalty, then the world has no choice but to fight against it in order to remain free. As long as Muslim nations remained divided, working against each other, they weren't going to be a problem for me, because I could pick them up one by one, especially after the FPE becomes large enough for them to see how the people within my borders prosper."

"But united under Alai—"

"Alai is a decent guy," said Peter. "I think he has some idea of liberalizing Islam from the top. But it can't be done. He's simply wrong. He's a general, not a politician. As long as ordinary Muslims believe it's their duty to kill any Muslim who tries to quit being a Muslim, as long as they think they have a holy duty to resort to arms to compel unbelievers to obey Islamic law—you can't liberalize that, you can't make it a decent system for anybody. Not even for Muslims. Because the cruelest, narrowest, most evil people will always rise to power because they'll always be the ones most willing to wrap themselves in the crescent flag and murder people in God's name."

"So Alai is doomed to fail."

"Alai is doomed to die. The moment the fanatics realize that he's not as fanatically pure a Muslim as they are, they'll kill him."

"And install a new Caliph?"

"They can install whoever they want," said Peter. "It won't matter to me. Without Alai, there's no Islamic unity, because only Alai can lead them to victory. And in defeat, Muslims don't stay united. They move like a great wave—until they meet a wall of rock that doesn't move. Then they crash and recede."

"As they did after Charles Martel defeated them."

"It's Alai who made them powerful," said Peter. "The only trouble is, Alai doesn't like the things he has to do in order to rule a totalitarian system like Islam. He's already killed a lot more people than he wanted to. Alai's not a killer, but he's become one, and he likes it less and less."

"You think he's not going to follow Virlomi into war."

"It's a race," said Peter. "Between followers of Alai who plan to kill Virlomi in order to free Alai from her influence, and fanatical Muslims who plan to kill Alai because he betrayed Islam by marrying Virlomi in the first place."

"Do you know who the conspirators are?"

"I don't have to," said Peter. "If there weren't any conspirators planning murder, it wouldn't be a Muslim empire. And there's another race. Can they kill Alai or Virlomi before China or Russia attacks? And even if they do kill one or both of them, will that stop China or Russia from attacking, or simply encourage them to think that victory will be more likely?"

"And is there any scenario where you'll go to war?"

"Yes," said Peter. "If they get rid of Virlomi, and Russia and China don't attack, then Alai—or his successor, if they kill him, too—will be pushed into attacking Armenia and Nubia. And *that's* a war I'm ready to fight. We'll destroy them. We'll be the rock against which Islam crashes and breaks into pieces."

"And if Russia or China does attack them before they can turn to you, then you still profit from the war as frightened nations unite with you against either Russia or China—whichever country is seen as the aggressive, dangerous one."

"It's like I said," Peter answered. "I have no idea how things will turn out. I just know that I'm ready to take advantage of every situation I can think of. And I'm watching very closely so that if something happens that I haven't foreseen, I can take advantage of it."

"So here's the key question," said Rackham. "It's the information I came here to get."

"I'm dying to hear."

"How long are you going to need Bean?"

Peter thought about that one for a while. "I've had to make my plans knowing that he was going to die. Or, once you made your offer, leave. So the answer is, as long as I have him, of course I'll use him, either to intimidate would-be enemies, or to command my forces when we go to war. But if he dies or leaves, I can make do. My plans don't depend on having Bean."

"So if he left in three months."

"Rackham, have you already found his other children? Is that what you're saying? Have you found them and you aren't telling him and Petra because you think I need Bean?"

"Not all of them."

"You're cold. You're such bastards," said Peter. "You're still using children as your tools."

"Yes," said Rackham. "We're bastards. But we mean well. Just like you."

"Give Bean and Petra their babies. And save his life, if you can. He's a good man who deserves better than to have you toy with him any longer."

# 21

# PAPERS

From: The Impaled One
To: HonestAbe%Lincoln@RailSplitter.org/WriteToTheAuthor
Re: God help me

Sometimes you give advice assuming that no one will take it. I just hope the man upstairs will forgive me and still find a place for me. Meanwhile, tell the big guy he's got to do something about the cup I broke.

From: PeterWiggin%private@hegemon.com
To: Graff%pilgrimage@colmin.gov
Fwd: Re: God help me

Dear Hyrum,

As you'll see from below, our Slavic friend has apparently offered suggestions to his government that they actually took, and he regrets it. Assuming that you're the guy upstairs, I would guess this open encryption suggests he wants out. My sources last put him in Florida but if they're watching him closely, they would have moved him to Idaho.

As for the cup he broke, I think he means that instead of Russia looking for a chance to attack Alai, they've made a deal with the Muslim League and while China looks south to fight India, Russia is going to move on Han Tzu from the north while the Turks move from the west, the Indonesians from Taiwan, and Virlomi's insane invasion will go on over the mountains. Not so insane now.

However, on the chance that by "the big guy" Russian Boy meant somebody other than "the man upstairs," he could only mean a certain giant we both know. I'll confer with him and Mrs. Giant about what, if anything, we can do to deal with the situation.

Peter

Alai had given his orders, and now he was going to make sure he was out of Hyderabad when they were carried out. The Caliph could not be tainted with the arrest of his own wife.

But the Caliph could not be ruled by her, either. Alai knew that the wazirs of his council hated her; if he did not have her arrested by men loyal to him, then she would certainly be killed.

Later, after things had settled down, after she had regained her senses and stopped thinking she was unstoppable, he would take her out of prison. He could not release her in India—that was out of the question. Maybe Graff would take her. She wasn't one of Ender's Jeesh, but by the same reasoning Graff had used in his invitation, the world would certainly be a safer place with her gone from it, while a colony might be lucky to have someone of such ability and ambition at its head.

Meanwhile, without Virlomi there was no reason for him to govern from Hyderabad. He would continue to respect his treaty with India and withdraw his forces. Let them try to rebuild without Virlomi's madness trying to throw them prematurely into war. India would not be in shape to mount a meaningful military campaign against anything more substantial than a flock of starlings for many years to come.

Alai would spend the next few years putting Islam's house in order and trying to forge a real nation out of this mishmash that history had left for him to deal with. If Syrians and Iraqis and Egyptians couldn't get along with each other and despised each other the moment they heard the other's accent, how could anyone expect Moroccans and Persians and Uzbeks and Malays to see the world in the same way just because a muezzin called them to prayer?

Besides, he had to deal with the stateless peoples—the Kurds, the Berbers, half the nomad tribes of ancient Bactria. Alai knew perfectly well that these Muslims would not follow a Caliph who kept the status quo—not when Peter Wiggin was tempting revolutionaries everywhere with his promise of statehood and the examples of Runa and Nubia.

We brought Nubia on ourselves, thought Alai. The ancient Muslim contempt for blackest Africa still seethed under the surface; if Alai had not been a member of Ender's Jeesh, it would have been inconceivable for him, as a black African, to be named Caliph. It was in Sudan, where the races met face to face, that the ugliness had emerged with so much virulence. The rest of Islam should have disciplined Sudan long ago. And now they all paid the price, with the humiliation of Sudan at the hands of the FPE.

So we have to give the Kurds and Berbers their own governments. Real ones, not sham "autonomous regions." That would not be popular in Morocco and Iraq and Turkey, Alai knew. That's why it was stupid in the extreme to imagine embarking on wars of conquest when there was no peace or unity inside the world of Islam.

Alai would govern from Damascus. It was far more central. He would be surrounded by Muslim culture instead of Hindu. It would be a civilian-centered government, not an obvious military dictatorship. And the world would see that Islam was not interested in conquering the world. That Caliph Alai had already liberated more people from oppressive conquerors than Peter Wiggin ever could.

As Alai left his office, two of the guards fell in step beside him. Ever since Virlomi simply walked into his office the day they got married, Alamandar had insisted that it not be so easy to walk into highly sensitive areas of the compound. "We *are* in occupied enemy country, my Caliph," he had said, and he was right.

Still, there was something that made Alai uneasy about having to be accompanied by guards as he moved about the compound. It felt wrong. The Caliph should be able to move among his own people with perfect trust and openness.

As Alai stepped through the door into the parking garage, two more guards joined the two who had walked with him from upstairs. His limousine sat idling at the curb. The back door opened.

He saw someone jogging toward him from among the parked cars.

It was Ivan Lankowski. Alai had rewarded him for his loyal service by putting him in charge of the administration of the Turkish nations of central Asia. What was he doing here? Alai had not called him back from service, and Ivan had not written or called about coming.

Ivan reached into his jacket. Where a gun would be, if he was armed with a shoulder holster.

And he *would* be armed; he had carried a gun for too many years to be comfortable without one now.

Alamandar got out of the open back door of the limo. As he rose to his feet, he shouted at the guards. "Shoot him, you fools! He's going to kill the Caliph!"

Ivan's gun was out. He fired, and the guard to Alai's left dropped like a rock. The sound was strange—the barrel had a silencer, but Alai was close to being directly in front of it, so it wasn't so much silenced as shaped.

I should drop to the ground, thought Alai. To save my life, I should get out of the line of fire. But he couldn't take the danger seriously. He didn't feel as though he were in danger at all.

The other guards had their guns out now. Ivan shot another one, but then the bullets—not silenced—flew in the other direction, and Ivan fell to the ground. His gun did not slip from his hand; he maintained his grip on it to the end of his life.

Or maybe he wasn't dead. Maybe he could spend his last moments explaining to Alai how he could betray him like this.

Alai walked to Ivan's body and felt for a pulse. Ivan's eyes were open. He was already dead.

"Come away, my Caliph!" shouted Alamandar. "There may be other conspirators!"

Conspirators. There was no possibility of other conspirators. Ivan didn't trust anybody enough to conspire with them. The only person Ivan absolutely trusted was . . .

Was me.

Ivan was a perfect shot. Even at a run, he could not have aimed at me and then clumsily hit two guards.

"My guards," said Alai, looking up at Alamandar. "The ones he shot—will they be all right?"

One of the other guards jogged back to look. "Both dead," he said.

But Alai already knew that. Ivan had not been aiming at Alai. He had come here with one purpose in mind, the purpose that had guided him for years. Ivan was here to protect his Caliph.

It flashed into Alai's mind with immediate clarity. Ivan had learned of a conspiracy against the Caliph, and it involved people so close to Alai that there was no way for Ivan to warn him from a distance without running the risk of alerting one of the conspirators.

Alai reached with one hand to close Ivan's eyes, while with the other he pulled Ivan's pistol from his slackened fingers. Still not taking his eyes off of Ivan's face, Alai fired the pistol upward into the guard who was standing over him. Then he calmly aimed at the guard who had gone back to the bodies and fired. Alai had never been as good a shot as Ivan. He could not have done this while running. But kneeling, he was all right.

The guard he had shot without looking was lying on the pavement, twitching. Alai shot him again, then turned to Alamandar, who was getting back into the limo.

Alai shot him. He fell into the car and it screeched away from the curb. But the door was not closed yet, and Alamandar was in no shape to close it. So as it passed Alai, there would be a brief moment when the driver would be unprotected by the heavy armoring and bulletproof glass. Alai laid down three quick shots in order to have a better chance of catching that moment.

It worked. The car did not turn. It ran into a wall.

Alai jogged over to the still-open back door of the car, where Alamandar was panting and holding his chest. His eyes were on fire with rage and fear as Alai leveled Ivan's pistol to fire.

"You are no Caliph!" gasped Alamandar. "The Hindu woman is more of a Caliph than you are, you black dog."

Alai shot him in the head and he fell silent.

The driver was unconscious, but Alai shot him, too.

Then he went back to the bodies of the guards, who were dressed in western business suits. Ivan had shot one of them in the head. He was larger than Alai but his clothing would do. Alai had his white robe off in a moment. Underneath he wore jeans as he always did. After wrestling with the corpse for a few moments, he got the shirt and jacket off the man, and without popping any of the buttons off.

Alai took the pistols from the two guards who had never gotten off a shot and dropped them into the pockets of the jacket he now wore. Ivan's silenced pistol had to be nearly out of bullets, so Alai slid it across the pavement back toward Ivan's body.

Where do I imagine an African man can hide in Hyderabad? No

one's face was more recognizable than the Caliph's, and those who didn't know his face knew his race. They would also know that he spoke no Hindi. He would not make it a hundred meters outside in Hyderabad.

Then again, there was no chance he could get out of the compound alive.

Wait. Think.

Don't wait. Get away from this murder scene.

Ivan jogged through the parked cars. The garage would have been cleared of any observers by Alamandar's men; that meant Ivan must have been hidden inside a car. Where was that car?

Keys in the ignition. Thank you, Ivan. You planned for everything. No time would be wasted fumbling with keys, as you dragged me to your car to get me out of here.

Where were you going to take me, Ivan? Whom do you trust?

Alamandar's last words rang in his ears. The Hindu woman is more of a Caliph than you are.

He thought they all hated her. But now he realized that she was the one advocating war. Expansion. The restoration of a great empire.

That's what they wanted. And all his talk of peace, of consolidation, of reforming Islam from the inside before reaching out to the rest of the world, of competing with Peter Wiggin using the same methods, inviting other nations to join the Caliphate without requiring them to become Muslim or live under Shari'a—they had listened, they had agreed, but they hated it.

They hated *him*.

So when they saw the break between him and Virlomi, they exploited it.

Or . . . was Virlomi behind this?

Was Virlomi pregnant with his child?

The Caliph is dead. But here is his baby, born after he died but infused with the gifts of God from his birth. In the name of the baby Caliph, the council of wazirs will rule. And since the mother of the new

Caliph is ruler of India, he will join the two great nations in one. With Virlomi as regent, of course.

No. Virlomi could not have wanted him *murdered.*

Ivan would have an airplane waiting. The airplane that brought him. With his own trusted crew.

Alai drove at a normal pace. But he did not drive to the checkpoint where he normally entered the airport grounds. In all likelihood, that place would be manned by the conspirators. Instead, he went to a service gate.

The guard sauntered over and started to tell him only authorized service vehicles could use this gate.

"I'm the Caliph, and I want to go through this gate."

"Oh," said the guard, looking confused. "I see. I—"

He pulled out a cellphone and started to punch at it.

Alai didn't want to kill this man. He was an idiot, not a conspirator. So he swung the door open, bumping into the man. Not hard. Just enough to get his attention. Then he closed the door and reached through the window. "Give me that cellphone."

The soldier gave it to him. Alai switched it off.

"I'm the Caliph. When I say to let me through, you don't have to ask *anyone* else's permission."

The soldier nodded and ran to the controls and the gate slid open.

As soon as Alai was through the gate, he saw a small corporate jet with Cyrillic lettering under the Common letters naming the corporation. The kind of plane Ivan would have used.

The engines started up as Alai approached. No, as Ivan's car approached.

Alai stopped the car and got out. The door of the jet was open, forming steps to the ground. Holding one hand on the pistol in his pocket—for he was taking this plane whether it was Ivan's or not—Alai walked up the steps.

A businessman—or so he seemed—waited for him inside. "Where's Ivan?" he asked.

"We're not waiting for him," said Alai. "He died saving me."

---

The man nodded once, then went to the door and pushed the button to raise it. Meanwhile he shouted, "Let's go!" and then said to Alai, "Please sit down and fasten your seat belt, my Caliph."

The plane began taxiing before the door was closed.

"Do nothing out of the ordinary," said Alai. "Nothing to alert them. There are weapons here that could easily shoot down this plane."

"Our plan exactly, sir," said the man.

What would the conspirators do, when they found out that Alai had escaped?

They would do nothing. They would say nothing. As long as Alai might turn up alive somewhere, they dared not be on record as saying anything.

In fact, they would continue to act in his name. If they followed Virlomi's plans, if her insane invasion went forward, then Alai would know they were with her.

When they were in the air—having waited for ordinary permission from the controllers—Ivan's man came back and stood diffidently two meters away.

"My Caliph, if I may ask?"

Alai nodded.

"How did he die?"

"He was busy shooting the guards surrounding me. He got two of them before they cut him down. I used his weapon to kill the others. Including Alamandar. Do you know how far the conspiracy went?"

"No sir," said the man. "We only knew that you would be killed on the airplane to Damascus."

"And this airplane? Where is it taking me?"

"It has a very long range, sir," said the man. "Where will you feel safe?"

---

Petra's mother was tending the babies while Petra and Bean oversaw the last preparations for the opening of hostilities. Peter's message had been terse: How busy can you keep the Turks, while watching out for Russians in the rear?

Turks and Russians allies, or potentially so. What game was Alai playing? Was Vlad in it? Trust Peter not to share any more information than he thought he had to—which was invariably less than other people actually needed.

Still, she and Bean had been spending every spare moment working out ways, using limited, undertrained, and underequipped Armenian forces to cause maximum disruption.

A raid on the most highly visible Turkish target, Istanbul, would enrage them without accomplishing anything.

Blocking the Dardanelles would be a harsh blow against all the Turks, but there was no way to project that much force from Armenia to the western shore of the Black Sea, and maintain it.

Oh, for the days when oil was strategically important! Back then, the Russian, Azerbaijani, and Persian wells in the Caspian would have been a prime target for disruption.

But now the wells had all been dismantled, and the Caspian was mostly used as a source of water, which was desalinated and pumped over to irrigate fields around the Aral Sea, with the runoff being used to replenish that once-dying lake. And to strike at the water pipeline would impoverish poor farmers without affecting the enemy's ability to wage war.

The plan they finally came up with was simple enough, once you bought the concept. "There's no way to strike the Turks directly," said Bean. "Nothing is centralized. So we'll strike Iran. It's highly urbanized, the big cities are all in the northwest, and there'll be an immediate demand for Iranian troops to come home from India to fight us. The Turks will be under pressure to help, and when they launch a very badly planned attack against Armenia, we'll be waiting."

"What makes you think it will be badly planned?" Petra asked.

"Because Alai isn't running the show on the Muslim side."

"When did *this* happen?"

"If Alai were in control," said Bean, "he wouldn't let Virlomi do what she's doing in India. It's too stupid and it will kill too many men. So . . . somehow he's lost control. And if that's the case, the Muslim enemy we're facing is incompetent and fanatic. They're acting out of anger and panic, with poor planning."

"What if this *is* Alai's doing, and you don't know him as well as you think?"

"Petra," said Bean. "We *know* Alai."

"Yes, and he knows us."

"Alai is a builder, like Ender. He always has been. An empire won through audacious and bloody conquest isn't worth having. He wants to build his Muslim empire the way Peter is building the FPE, by transforming Islam into a system that other nations will want, voluntarily, to join. Only somebody's decided not to follow his path. Either Virlomi or the hotheads within his own government."

"Or both?" asked Petra.

"Anything's possible."

"Except Alai controlling the Muslim armies."

"Well, it's simple enough," said Bean. "If we're wrong, and the Turkish counterattack is brilliantly planned, then we'll lose. As slowly as possible. And hope Peter has something else up his sleeve. But our assignment is to draw Turkish forces and attention away from China."

"And meanwhile, we'll be putting pressure on the Muslim alliance," said Petra. "No matter what the Turks do, the Persians won't believe they're doing enough."

"Sunni against Shi'ite," said Bean. "It's the best I could think up."

So for the past two days they had been drawing up plans for the quick, audacious airborne attack on Tabriz, and then, when the Iranians started to react to that, an immediate evacuation and airborne attack on Tehran. Meanwhile, Petra, in command of the defense of Armenia, would be prepared to make the Turkish counterattack pay for every meter of progress through the mountains.

Now everything was ready, awaiting only the word from Peter. Petra and Bean weren't really necessary while the troops began their deployment and the supplies were moved to depots in the areas where they'd be needed. Everything was in the hands of the Armenian military.

"What scares me," Petra told Bean, "is how they have absolute confidence that we know what we're doing."

"Why does that scare you?"

"Doesn't it scare *you?*"

"Petra, we *do* know what we're doing. We just don't know why."

It was in that lull, between planning and getting the order to go ahead, that Petra got a call on her cellphone. From her mother.

"Petra, they say they're friends of yours, but they're taking the babies."

Panic stabbed through her. "Who's with them? Put the one in charge on the phone."

"He won't. He just says, the 'teacher' says to meet them at the airport. Who's the teacher? Oh, God help us, Petra! This is like the time they kidnapped you."

"Tell them we'll be at the airport and if they've hurt the babies I'll kill them. But no, Mother, it's not the same thing at all."

Unless it was.

She told Bean what was happening, and they calmly made their way to the airport. They saw Rackham waiting at the curb and made the driver let them off there.

"I'm sorry to frighten you," said Rackham. "But we don't have time for arguments until we get on the plane. Then you can scream at me all you like."

"Nothing is so urgent you have to steal our babies," said Petra, putting as much venom into her voice as she could.

"See?" said Rackham. "Arguing instead of coming with me."

They followed him then, through back passages and out to a private jet. Petra protested as they went. "Nobody knows where we are. They'll think we ran out on them. They'll think we were kidnapped."

Rackham just ignored her. He moved very quickly for a man so old.

The babies were on the plane, each one being cared for by a separate nurse. They were fine. Only Ramón was still nursing, because the two with Bean's syndrome were eating more-or-less solid food now. So Petra sat down and fed him, while Rackham sat down opposite them in the luxury jet and, as the plane took off, began his explanation.

"We had to get you out of there now," he said, "because the airport at Yerevan is going to be blown to bits in an hour or two, and we need to be out over the Black Sea before it happens."

"How do you know?" demanded Petra.

"We have it from the man who planned the attack."

"Alai?"

"It's a Russian attack," said Rackham.

Bean blew up. "Then what was all that *kuso* about distracting the Turks!"

"It all still applies. As soon as we see the attack planes take off from southern Russia, I'll let you know and you can give the word to launch *your* attack on Iran."

"This is Vlad's plan," said Petra. "A sudden preemptive strike to keep the FPE from doing anything. To neutralize me and Bean."

"Vlad wants you to know he's very sorry. He's used to none of his plans actually being used."

"You've been talking to him?"

"We got him out of Moscow about three hours ago and debriefed him as quickly as possible. We think they don't know he's gone. Even if they do know, it's no reason for them not to go ahead with their plan."

The telephone beside Rackham's seat beeped once. He picked it up. Listened. Pressed a button and handed it over to Petra. "All right, the rockets have launched."

"I assume I need the country code?"

"No. Put in the number as if you were still in Yerevan. As far as they'll know, you are. Tell them that you're conferring with Peter and you'll rejoin them with the attack in progress."

"Will we?"

"And then call your mother and tell her you're all right and not to talk about what happened."

"Oh, *that's* about an hour too late."

"My men told her that if she called anyone but you until she heard from you again, she'd be very sorry."

"Thank you for terrifying her even more. Do you have any idea what this woman has been through in her life?"

"It always turns out all right, though. So she's better off than some."

"Thanks for your cheery optimism."

A few minutes later, the strike force was launched and a warning was given to evacuate the airport, reroute all incoming flights, evacuate the parts of Yerevan nearest the airport, and alert the men at all possible military targets inside Armenia.

As for Petra's mother, she was crying so hard—with relief, with anger at what had happened—that Petra could hardly make herself understood. But finally the conversation ended and Petra was more pissed off than ever. "What gives you the right? Why do you think you—"

"War gives me the right," said Rackham. "If I'd waited till you could come home and *get* your babies and then meet us at the airport, this plane would never have taken off. I have my men's lives to think of here, not just your mother's feelings."

Bean put a hand on Petra's knee. She accepted the need for calm, and fell silent.

"Mazer," said Bean, "what's this about? You could have warned us with a phone call."

"We have your other babies."

Petra was already emotional. She burst into tears. Quickly she controlled herself. And hated the fact that she had acted so . . . maternal.

"All of them? At once?"

"We've been watching some of them for several weeks," said Rackham. "Waiting for an opportune moment."

Bean waited only a moment before saying, "Waiting for Peter to tell you that it was all right. That you didn't need us any more for his war."

"He still needs you," said Rackham. "As long as he can have you."

"Why did you wait, Mazer?"

"How many?" said Petra. "How many are there?"

"One more with Bean's syndrome," said Rackham. "Four more without it."

"That's eight," said Bean. "Where's the ninth?"

Rackham shook his head.

"So you're still looking?"

"No, we're not," said Rackham.

"So you have definite information that the ninth wasn't implanted. Or it's dead."

"No. We have definite information that whether it's alive or dead, we have no search criteria left. If the ninth baby was ever born, Volescu hid the birth and the mother too well. Or the mother is hiding herself. The software—the mind game, if you will—has been very effective. We wouldn't have found any of the normal children without its creative searches. But it also knows when it has nothing more to try. You have eight of the nine. Three of them have the syndrome, five are normal."

"What about Volescu?" asked Petra. "Can we drug him?"

"Why not torture?" said Rackham. "No, Petra. We can't. Because we need him."

"For what? His virus?"

"We already have his virus. And it doesn't work. It's a bust. Failure. Dead end. Volescu knew it, too. He just enjoyed tormenting us with the thought that he had endangered the entire world."

"So what do you need him for?" demanded Petra.

"We need him to work on the cure for Bean and the babies."

"Oh, right," said Bean. "You're going to turn him loose in a lab."

"No," said Rackham. "We're going to put him in space, on an asteroid-based research station, closely supervised. He's been tried and is under sentence of death for terrorism, kidnapping, and murder—the murders of your brothers, Bean."

"There's no death sentence," said Bean.

"There is in military court in space," said Rackham. "He knows he's alive as long as he's making progress on finding a legitimate cure for you and the babies. Eventually, our team of co-researchers will know everything he knows. When we don't need him anymore . . ."

"I don't want him killed," said Bean.

"No," said Petra. "I want him killed *slowly.*"

"He might be evil," said Bean, "but I wouldn't exist if not for him."

"There was a day," said Rackham, "when that would be the biggest crime you charged him with."

"I've had a good life," said Bean. "Strange and hard sometimes. But I've had a lot of happiness." He squeezed Petra's knee. "I don't want you to kill him."

"You saved your own life—*from* him," said Petra. "You owe him nothing."

"It doesn't matter," said Rackham. "We have no intention of killing him. When he's no longer useful, he goes into a colony ship. He's not a violent man. He's very smart. He could be useful in understanding alien biota. It would be a waste of a resource to kill him. And there's no colony that will have equipment he could adapt to create anything . . . biologically destructive."

"You've thought of everything," said Petra.

"Again," said Bean, "you could have told us this over the telephone."

"I didn't want to," said Rackham.

"The I.F. doesn't send a team like this or a man like you on an errand like this just because you didn't want to use the phone."

"We want to send you now," said Rackham.

"In case you haven't been listening to yourself," said Petra, "there's a war on."

Bean and Rackham ignored her. They just looked at each other for a long time.

And then Petra saw that Bean's eyes were welling up with tears. That didn't happen very often.

"What's happening, Bean?"

Bean shook his head. To Rackham he said, "Do you have them?"

Rackham took an envelope out of his inside jacket pocket and handed it to Bean. He opened the envelope, removed a thin sheaf of papers, and handed them to Petra.

"It's our divorce decree," said Bean.

Petra understood at once. He wasn't taking her with him. He was leaving her behind with the normal children. He was going to take the three children with the syndrome out into space with him. He wanted her to be free to remarry.

"You are my husband," she said. She tore the papers in half.

"Those are copies," said Bean. "The divorce has legal force whether you like it or not, whether you sign them or not. You're no longer a married woman."

"Why? Because you think I'm going to *remarry?*"

Bean ignored her. "But all the children have been certified as legitimately ours. They aren't bastards, they aren't orphans, they aren't adopted. They're the children of divorced parents, and you have custody of five of them, and I have custody of three. If the ninth one is ever found, then you'll have custody."

"That ninth one is the only reason I'm listening to this," said Petra. "Because if you stay you'll die, and if we both go, then there might be a child who . . ."

But she was too angry to finish. Because when Bean planned this, he couldn't have known there'd be one child missing. He'd already *done* this and kept it secret from her for . . . for . . .

"How long have you been planning this?" asked Petra. Tears were streaming down her face, but she kept her voice steady enough to speak.

"Since we found Ramón and we knew there *were* normal children," said Bean.

"It's more complicated than that," said Rackham. "Petra, I know how hard this is for you—"

"No you don't."

"Yes I damn well do," said Rackham. "I left a family behind when I went out into space on the same kind of relativistic turnaround voyage that Bean's embarking on. I divorced my wife before I went. I have her letters to me. All the anger and bitterness. And then the reconciliation. And then a long letter near the end of her life. Telling me about how she and her second husband were happy. And the children turned out well. And she still loved me. I wanted to kill myself. But I did what I had to do. So don't tell me I don't know how hard this is."

"You had no choice," said Petra. "But I could go with him. We could take all the children and—"

"Petra," said Bean. "If we had conjoined twins, we'd separate them. Even if one of them was sure to die, we'd separate them, so that at least one of them could lead a normal life."

Petra's tears were out of control now. Yes, she understood his reasoning. The children without the syndrome could have a normal life on Earth. Why should they spend their childhood confined to a starship, when they could have the normal chance of happiness?

"Why couldn't you at least let me be part of the decision?" said Petra, when she finally got control of her voice. "Why did you cut me out? Did you think I wouldn't understand?"

"I was selfish," said Bean. "I didn't want to spend our last months together arguing about it. I didn't want you to be grieving for me and Ender and Bella the whole time you were with us. I wanted to take these past few months with me when I go. It was my last wish, and I knew you'd grant it to me, but the only way I could *have* that wish is if you didn't know. So now, Petra, I ask you. Let me have these months without you knowing what was going to happen."

"You already have them. You stole them!"

"Yes, so now I ask you. Please. Let me have them. Let me know that you forgive me for it. That you give them to me freely, now, after the fact."

Petra couldn't forgive him. Not now. Not yet.

But there was no later.

She buried her face in his chest and held him and wept.

While she cried, Rackham spoke on, calmly. "Only a handful of us know what's really happening. And on Earth, outside of the I.F., only Peter will know. Is that clear? So this divorce document is absolutely secret. As far as anyone else will know, Bean is not in space, he died in the raid on Tehran. And he took no babies with him. There were never more than five. And two of the normal babies that we've recovered are also named Andrew and Bella. As far as anyone knows, you will still have all the children you ever did."

Petra pulled back from her embrace of Bean and glared savagely at Rackham. "You mean you're not even going to let me grieve for my babies? No one will know what I've lost except you and *Peter Wiggin*?"

"Your parents," said Rackham, "have seen Ender and Bella. It's your choice whether to tell them the truth, or to stay away from them until enough time has passed that they can't tell that there's been a change."

"Then I'll tell them."

"Think about it first," said Rackham. "It's a heavy burden."

"Don't presume to teach me how to love my parents," said Petra. "You know and I know that at every point in this you've decided solely on the basis of what's good for the Ministry of Colonization and the International Fleet."

"We'd like to think we've found the solution that's best for everyone."

"I'm supposed to have a funeral for my husband, when I know he's not dead, and that's best for me?"

"I will be dead," said Bean, "for all intents and purposes. Gone and never coming back. And you'll have children to raise."

"And yes, Petra," said Rackham, "there *is* a wider consideration. Your husband is already a legendary figure. If it's known that he's still alive, then everything Peter does will be ascribed to him. There'll be legends about how he's going to return. About how the most brilliant graduate of Battle School really planned out everything Peter did."

"This is about *Peter?*"

"This is about trying to get the world put together peacefully, permanently. This is about abolishing nations and the wars that just won't stop as long as people can pin their hopes on great heroes."

"Then you should send *me* away, too, or tell people *I'm* dead. I was in Ender's Jeesh."

"Petra, you chose your path. You married. You had children. Bean's children. You decided that's what you wanted more than anything else. We've respected that. You have Bean's children. And you've had Bean almost as long as you would have had him if we had never intervened. Because he's dying. Our best guess is that he wouldn't make it another six months without going out into space and living weightlessly. We've done everything according to *your* choice."

"It's true that they didn't actually requisition our babies," Bean said.

"So live with your choices, Petra," said Rackham. "Raise these babies. And help us do what we can to help Peter save the world from itself. The story of Bean's heroic death in the service of the FPE will help with that."

"There'll be legends anyway," said Petra. "Plenty of dead heroes have legends."

"Yes, but if they *know* we put him in a starship and trundled him off into space, it won't be just a legend, will it? Serious people would believe in it, not just the normal lunatics."

"So how will you even keep up the research project?" demanded Petra. "If everybody thinks the only people who need the cure are dead or never existed, why will it continue?"

"Because a few people in the I.F. and ColMin *will* know. And they'll be in contact with Bean by ansible. He'll be called home when the cure is found."

They flew on then, as Petra tried to deal with what they'd told her. Bean held her most of the time, even when her anger surged now and then and she was furious with him.

Terrible scenarios kept playing themselves out in her mind, and at the risk of giving Bean ideas, she said to him, "Don't give up, Julian Delphiki. Don't decide that there's never going to be a cure and end the voyage. Even if you think your life is worthless, you have my babies out there too. Even if the voyage goes on so long that you really are dying, remember that these children are like you. Survivors. As long as somebody doesn't actually kill them."

"Don't worry," said Bean. "If I had the slightest tendency toward suicide, we would never have met. And I would never do anything to endanger my own children. I'm only taking this voyage for them. Otherwise, I'd be content to die in your arms here on Earth."

She wept again for a while after that, and then she had to feed Ramón again, and then she insisted on feeding Ender and Bella herself, spooning the food into their mouths because when would she ever get a chance to do it again? She tried to memorize every moment of it, even though she knew she couldn't. Knew that memory would fade. That these babies would become only a distant dream to her. That her arms would remember best the babies she held the longest—the children she would keep with her.

The only one she had borne from her own body would be gone.

But she didn't cry while she was feeding them. That would have been a waste. Instead she played with them and talked to them and teased them to talk back to her. "I know your first word isn't going to be too long from now. How about a little 'mama' right now, you lazy baby?"

It was only after the plane had landed in Rotterdam, and Bean was supervising the nurses as they carried the babies down onto the tarmac, that Petra stayed back in the plane with Rackham, long enough to put her worst nightmare into words.

"Don't think that I'm not aware of how easy it would be, Mazer Rackham, for this fake death of Bean's not to be a fake at all. For all we know there is no ship, there is no project to find a cure, and Volescu is going to be executed. The threat of this new species replacing your precious human race would be gone then. And even the widow would be silent about what you've done to her husband and children, because she'll think he's off in space somewhere, traveling at lightspeed, instead of dead on a battlefield in Iran."

Rackham looked as if she had slapped him. "Petra," he said. "What do you think we *are?*"

"What you are," said Petra, "is *not denying it.*"

"I deny it," said Rackham. "There *is* a ship. We *are* seeking a cure. We *will* call him home."

Then she saw the tears streaming down his cheeks.

"Petra," said Rackham, "don't you understand that we love you children? All of you? We already had to send Ender away. We're sending them all away, except for you. *Because* we love you. *Because* we don't want any harm to you."

"So why are you leaving *me* here?"

"Because of your babies, Petra. Because even though they don't have the syndrome, they're also Bean's babies. He's the only one who had no hope of a normal life. But thanks to you, he had one. However briefly, he got to be a husband and a father and have a family. Don't you know how much we love you for giving him that? As God is my witness, Petra, we would never harm Bean, not for any *cause* and certainly not for our *convenience*. Whatever you think we are, you're wrong. Because you children are the only children we have."

She wasn't going to feel sorry for *him*. It was her turn right now. So she pushed past him and went down the stairs and took the hand of her husband and followed the nurses that were carrying her children toward a closed van.

There were five new children that she hadn't met yet, waiting for her and Bean. Her life hadn't ended yet, even though it felt like she was dying with every breath she took.

# 22

# RUMORS OF WAR

From: Graff%pilgrimage@colmin.gov
To: PeterWiggin%private@FreePeopleOfEarth.fp.gov
Re: debriefing

Attached are the data to the division level, including names of commanders. But the gist is simple enough: Russia is gambling everything on the quiescence of eastern Europe. They're all supposed to be terrified of a newly aggressive Russia. This is the move they thought they were going to be able to make when they had Achilles with them and kidnapped all of Ender's Jeesh.

What you can tell them, with authority, is this: Russia IS newly aggressive, they ARE bent on proving they're a world power again. They're dangerous. But:

1. They don't have Vlad. They have his plan, but can't adapt to any changes.

2. We have Vlad's plan, so we can anticipate every move they make while they follow it, and the generals in command are going to follow it with religious devotion. Expect no flexibility, even after they know we have it. Vlad knows the men in command. In the Russian military these days, any leaders with the imagination to improvise don't rise to the level where it will matter.

3. Han Tzu is being provided with their plan, so their main army will meet with disaster in the East.

4. They stripped their western defenses. A fast-moving army, competently led, should take St. Petersburg in a walk and Moscow in a week. That's Vlad's opinion. Bean has been over this information and concurs. He suggests you take Petra out of Armenia and put her in charge of the campaign in Russia.

When Suriyawong got the word from Peter, he was ready. Prime Minister Paribatra and Minister of Defense Ambul had kept their affiliation with the FPE secret for just this occasion. Now, armed with Burmese and Chinese permission to pass through their territory, the Thai army was going to have the chance to face the Indians who had begun all this nonsense with their vicious, unprovoked invasion of Burma and Thailand.

The troops went by train all the way into Chinese territory; Chinese trucks with Chinese drivers ferried them the rest of the way to the spots that Suriyawong had mapped out as soon as Peter suggested it as a contingency. At the time, Peter had said, "It's a remote possibility, because it requires incredible stupidity on the part of some nonstupid people, but be ready."

Ready to defend China. That was the irony.

But Han Tzu's China was not the China that had embraced Achilles's treacherous plan and crushed everyone, carrying away the entire Thai leadership and Suriyawong's parents. Han Tzu promised friendship, and Bean vouched for him. So Suriyawong had been able to persuade his top leadership, and they had persuaded his men, that defending China was nothing more or less than a forward defense of Thailand.

"China has changed," Suriyawong told the officers, "but India has not. Once again, they're pouring over the border of a nation that believes itself to be at peace with them. This goddess they follow, Virlomi—she's just another Battle School graduate, like me. But *we* have what she doesn't have. We have Julian Delphiki's plan. And we *will* win."

Bean's plan, however, was simple enough. "The only way to end this once and for all is to make it a disaster. Like Varus's legions in the Teutoburger Wald. No guerrilla action. No chance of retreat. Virlomi alive if possible, but if she insists on dying, oblige her."

That was the plan. But Suriyawong needed no more than that. The mountainous country of southwestern China and northern Burma was ambush country. Virlomi's ill-trained troops were advancing on foot—ridiculously slowly—in three main columns, following three river valleys with three inadequate roads. Suriyawong's own plans called for a simple, classical ambush on all three routes. He hid relatively small but heavily armed contingents at the heads of the valleys, where they would be passed by the Indian troops. Then far, far down the valley, he had far larger contingents with plenty of transport to move up the valley upon command.

Then it was a matter of waiting for two things.

The first thing came on the second day of waiting. The southernmost outpost notified him that their column had entered the valley and was moving briskly. This was no surprise—they had had a much easier trip than the two northern armies.

"They're not careful about probing ahead," said the general in charge of that contingent. "Raw troops, marching blind. As I watched them, I kept thinking, this must be an attempt to deceive us. But no—they keep passing, with large gaps in the line, stragglers, and only a few regiments that put out scouts. None of them came close to finding us. They haven't put a single observer on either ridge. They're *lazy*."

When, later in the day, the other two hidden contingents reported a similar story, Suriyawong relayed the information back to Ambul. While he waited for the next triggering event, he had his lookouts make a particular point of searching for any sign that Virlomi herself was traveling with any of the three armies.

There was no mystery about it. She was traveling with the northernmost Indian army, riding in an open jeep, and the troops cheered when she passed, moving up and down the line—slowing down her own army's advance in the process, since they had to move off the road for her.

Suriyawong heard this with sadness. She had been so brilliant. Her assessment of how to undo the Chinese occupation had been dead on. Her holding action to keep the Chinese from returning to India or resupplying when the Persians and Pakistanis invaded had been of Thermopylaean proportions. The difference was that Virlomi was more careful than the Spartans—she had already covered all the back roads. Nothing got past her Indian guerrillas.

She was beautiful and wise and mysterious. Suriyawong had rescued her once, and cooperated in the little drama that made the rescue possible—and played upon her reputation as a goddess.

But in those days, she had known she was just acting.

Or had she? Perhaps it was her intimations of godhood that had caused her to reject Suriyawong's overtures of friendship and more-than-friendship. The blow had been painful, but he wasn't angry with her. She had an aura of greatness about her that he had seen in no other commander, not even Bean.

The troop deployments she was showing here were not what he would have expected from the woman who had been so careful of her men's lives in all her previous actions. Nor from the woman who had wept over the bodies of the victims of Muslim atrocities. Didn't she see that she was leading the soldiers to disaster? Even if there were no ambush in these mountains—though it was absolutely predictable that there would be—an army this ragged could be destroyed at will by a trained and determined enemy.

As Euripides wrote, Whom the gods would destroy, they first make mad.

Ambul, knowing how Suriyawong felt about Virlomi, had offered to let him command only that part of the army that wouldn't face her directly. But Suri refused. "Remember what Bean said Ender taught. 'To know the enemy well enough to defeat him requires that you know him so well you can't help but love him.' "

Well, Suriyawong already loved this enemy. And knew her. Well enough that he even thought he understood this madness.

She wasn't vain. She never thought she'd survive. But all her plans kept succeeding. She couldn't believe that it was because of her own ability. So she thinks that she has some kind of divine favor.

But it *was* her abilities and training, and she isn't using them now, and her army is going to pay for it.

Suriyawong had left plenty of room for the Indians to move down the valleys before they reached the ambush. They weren't traveling at the same pace, so he had to make sure all three ambushes were sprung at the same time. He had to make sure all three armies passed through the top of the trap in their entirety. His instructions to his men were clear: Accept the surrender of any soldier who throws down his weapon and puts up his hands. Kill anyone who doesn't. But let no one out of the valley. *All* killed or captured.

And Virlomi alive, if she lets us.

Please let us, Virlomi. Please let us bring you back to reality. Back to *life*.

---

Han Tzu went among his troops. There was no nonsense about an invisible emperor. The soldiers of the Chinese army had chosen him and sustained his authority. He was theirs, and they would see him often, sharing their privations, listening to them, explaining to them.

It was what he had learned from Ender. If you give orders and explain nothing, you might get obedience, but you'll get no creativity. If you tell them your purpose, then when your original plan is shown to be faulty, they'll find another way to achieve your goal. Explaining to your men doesn't weaken their respect for you, it proves your respect for *them.*

So Han Tzu explained, chatted, pitched in and helped, shared the meals of common soldiers, laughed at their jokes, listened to their complaints. One soldier had complained about how no one could sleep on ground like this. Han Tzu promptly took over the man's tent and slept in it himself, exactly as it was, while the man took Han Tzu's tent. In the morning, the man swore that Han Tzu's bed was the worst one in the army, and Han Tzu thanked him for his first good night's sleep in weeks. The story made its way through the army before nightfall.

Han Tzu's army did not love him any more than Virlomi's loved her. And there was no hint of worship in it. The key difference was that Han Tzu had worked to train this army, had made sure that it was as well equipped as possible, and they knew the stories about the last war, when Han Tzu had constantly warned his superiors about all their mistakes before they made them. The belief was that if Han Tzu had been emperor all along, they would not have lost the lands they conquered.

What they didn't understand was that if Han Tzu had been their emperor, there would have been no conquests to lose. Because Achilles would have been arrested the moment he entered China and turned over to the I.F., under whose authority he had been confined to a mental hospital. There would have been no invasion of India and southeast Asia, only a holding action to block the Indian invasion of Burma and Thailand.

A real warrior hates war, Han Tzu well understood. He had seen how devastated Ender was when he learned that the last game, the final exam, had been the real war, and that his enemy had been utterly destroyed by Ender's victory.

So his men trusted him as Han Tzu kept retreating, farther and farther into China, moving from one strong position to another, but never allowing his army to engage with the Russian invaders.

He heard what the men said, the questions they asked. His answers were honest enough. "The farther they come, the longer their supply lines." "We want them so deep inside China that they can't get home again." "Our army grows the deeper we move back into China, and theirs shrinks, as they have to leave men behind to guard their route."

And when they asked him about the rumors of a huge Indian army invading in the south, Han Tzu only smiled and said, "The madwoman? The only Indian who ever conquered China was Gautama Buddha, and he did it with teachings, not artillery."

What he couldn't tell them was that they were waiting.

For Peter Wiggin.

---

Peter Wiggin stood in front of the microphones in Helsinki. Beside him stood the heads of government of Finland, Estonia, and Latvia.

Aides were on secure cellphones connected to diplomats in Bangkok, Yerevan, Beijing, and many capitals in eastern Europe.

Peter smiled at the gathered reporters.

"At the request of the governments of Armenia and China, both of which were the victims of simultaneous unprovoked aggression by Russia, India, and the Muslim League of Caliph Alai, the Free People of Earth have decided to intervene.

"We are joined in this effort by many new allies, many of which have agreed to hold plebiscites to determine whether or not to ratify the Constitution of the FPE.

"Emperor Han Tzu of China assures us that his armies are capable of dealing with the combined Russian and Turkish forces that are now operating well within the Chinese border in the north.

"In the south, Burma and China have opened their borders to safe passage for an army led by our old friend General Suriyawong. Right now, in Bangkok, Prime Minister Paribatra is holding a press conference to announce that Thailand will hold a plebiscite on ratification, and that as of this moment, the Thai Army is regarded as being under the provisional command of the FPE.

"In Armenia, where it is not possible to hold a press conference right now because of the exigencies of war, a nation under attack has turned to the FPE for help and leadership. I have placed the Armenian military under the direct command of Julian Delphiki, where they are resisting unprovoked Turkish and Russian aggression and have carried the war deep inside Muslim territory, in Tabriz and Tehran.

"And here in eastern Europe, where Finland, Estonia, Latvia, Lithuania, Slovakia, Czechland, and Bulgaria had already joined the FPE, we are joined by our new allies Poland, Rumania, Hungary, Serbia, Austria, Greece, and Belarus. They have all repudiated the Warsaw Pact, which never obligated them to join in an offensive war in any event.

"Under the command of Petra Delphiki, the combined allied armies are already making rapid progress toward capturing key targets inside Russia. They have met little resistance so far, but they are prepared to deal with any forces the Russians care to throw against them.

"We call upon the aggressors—Russia, India, and the Muslim League—to lay down their arms and accept an immediate ceasefire. If this offer is not accepted within the next twelve hours, then a ceasefire will only be accepted by us upon our terms and at a time of our choosing. The enemies of peace can expect to lose all the forces they have committed to this immoral war.

"I would now like to play for you a video that was recently recorded at a safe haven. In case you don't recognize him, since the Russians have kept him under wraps for many years now, the speaker is Vladimir Denisovitch Porotchkot, a citizen of Belarus who until several days ago was kept against his will in the service of a foreign power, Russia. You may also remember him as one of the team of young warriors who defeated the enemy that threatened the existence of the human race."

Peter stepped away from the microphone. The room was darkened; the screenwall came alive.

There stood Vlad, in front of what looked like an ordinary office in an ordinary room on Earth. Only Peter knew that this was recorded in space—in the old Battle School space station, as a matter of fact, which was now the Ministry of Colonization.

"I offer my apologies to the people of Armenia and China, whose borders were violated and citizens were killed by Russians who were using plans I created. I assumed that the plans were for contingency only, in response to aggression. I did not know that they would actually be used, and without the slightest provocation. As soon as I understood that this was how my work was to be used, I escaped from Russian custody and am now in a safe place, where I can finally speak the truth.

"It came to my knowledge just before I left my captivity in Moscow that the leaders of Russia, India, and the Muslim League have divided up the world among them. To India will go all of southeast Asia and most of China. To Russia will go part of China and all of eastern and northern Europe. To the Muslim League will go all of Africa and the western European countries with large Muslim populations.

"I repudiate this plan. I repudiate this war. I refuse to let my work be used to enslave innocent people who did no harm and do not deserve to live under tyranny.

"Therefore I have provided to the Free People of Earth a complete knowledge of all the plans I drew up for Russian use. There is no movement they are now making which is not completely anticipated by the forces acting in concert with the FPE.

"And I urge the people of Belarus, my true homeland, to vote to join the Free People of Earth. Who else has stood relentlessly against aggression and in favor of freedom and respect for every nation and every citizen?

"As for me—my talents and training are entirely geared toward warfare. I will no longer put my abilities at the service of any nation. I gave my childhood to fighting an alien enemy that was trying to destroy the human race. I did not fight off the Buggers so that millions of humans could be slaughtered and hundreds of millions conquered and enslaved.

"I am on strike. I urge every other graduate of Battle School except those who serve the FPE to join me in that strike. Do not plan war, do not wage war, except to help the Hegemon Peter Wiggin to destroy the armies of the aggressors.

"And to the common soldiers I say, Do not obey your officers. Surrender at the first opportunity. Your obedience makes war possible. Take responsibility for your own actions and join me in my strike! If you surrender to the forces of the FPE, they will make every effort to spare your life and, at the earliest opportunity, to return you to your families.

"Again, I beg the forgiveness of those whose lives were lost because of plans I drew. Never again."

The video ended.

Peter strode back to the microphone. "The Free People of Earth and our allies are now at war with the aggressors. We have already told you everything we can say without compromising ongoing military operations. There will be no questions."

He walked away from the microphone.

---

Bean stood in the midst of the small wheeled beds that held his five normal children. The ones he would never see again, once he left them today.

Mazer Rackham put a hand on his shoulder. "It's time to go, Julian."

"Five of them," said Bean. "How will Petra manage?"

"She'll have help," said Rackham. "The real question is, how will *you* manage on that messenger ship? They'll outnumber you three to one."

"As I can attest, children with my particular genetic defect become self-sufficient at a very early age," said Bean.

He touched the bed of the baby named Andrew. The same name as the eldest of the siblings. But this Andrew was a normal infant. Not undersized for his age.

And this second Bella. She would lead a normal life. As would Ramón and Julian and Petra.

"If these five are normal," Bean said to Rackham, "then the ninth child—it's most likely . . . defective?"

"*If* the odds are fifty-fifty of the traits getting passed on, and we know that five of the nine didn't get them, then it stands to reason that the missing one has a higher likelihood of having the traits. Though as any expert on probability would tell you, the probability for each child was fifty-fifty, and the distribution of the syndrome among the other infants will have no effect on the outcome for the ninth."

"Maybe it's better if Petra never finds . . . the last one."

"My guess, Bean, is that there is no ninth baby. Not every implantation works. There could easily have been an early miscarriage. That would be a complete explanation of the lack of any record that was traceable by the software."

"I don't know whether to be comforted or appalled that you would think I'd find that the death of one my children might be comforting."

Rackham grimaced. "You know what I meant."

Bean took an envelope from his pocket and laid it under Ramón. "Tell the nurses to leave that envelope there, even if he leaks and wets all over the thing."

"Of course," said Rackham. "For what it's worth, Bean, your pension will also be invested, like Ender's, and run by the same software."

"Don't," said Bean. "Give it all to Petra. She'll need it, with five babies to raise. Maybe six someday."

"What about when you come home, when they find the cure?"

Bean looked at him as if he were crazy. "Do you really think that will happen?"

"If you *don't,* why are you going?"

"Because it might," said Bean. "And if we stay here, early death is certain for all four of us. *If* the cure is found, and *if* we come home, then we can talk about a pension. I'll tell you what. After Petra dies, after these five all grow old and die, then start paying my pension into a fund controlled by that investor software."

"You'll be back before then."

"No," said Bean. "No, that's . . . no. Once we're ten years out—and there's no hope of a cure before that—then even if you find the cure, don't call us back until . . . well, until Petra would be dead before we got here. Do you understand? Because if she remarries—and I want her to—I don't want her to have to face me. To face me looking as I do right now, the boy she married—the *giant* boy. This is cruel enough, what we're doing now. I'm not going to cause her one last torment before she dies."

"Why don't you let her decide?"

"It's not her choice," said Bean. "Once we leave, we're dead. Gone forever. She can never have back the life that will have been lost. But I'm not worried, Mazer. There *is* no cure."

"You know that?"

"I know Volescu. He doesn't want to find a cure. He doesn't think it's a disease. He thinks it's the hope of humanity. And except for Anton, nobody else knows enough to proceed. It was an illegal field of study for too long. It's still tainted. The methods Volescu used, the whole process surrounding Anton's Key—nobody's going to turn that key again, and therefore you're not going to have any scientists who know what they're doing in that area. The project will have less and less importance for your successors. Someday—not too long from now—somebody will look at the budget item and say, We're paying for *what?* And the project will die."

"It won't happen," said Mazer. "The Fleet doesn't forget its own."

Bean laughed. "You don't get it, do you? Peter is going to succeed. The world is going to be united. International war will end. And along with it, the sense of loyalty among the military will also die. There'll just be . . . colony ships and trading ships and scientific research institutes that will be scandalized at the thought of wasting money doing a personal favor for a soldier who lived a hundred years ago. Or two hundred. Or three hundred."

"The funding won't be contingent," said Rackham. "We're funding it using the same investment software. It's really good, Bean. This is going to be one of the best-funded projects ever, in a few years."

Bean laughed. "Mazer, you just don't understand how far people will go to get their hands on money that they think is being wasted on pure research. You'll see. But no, I take that back. You won't see. It'll happen after you're dead. *I'll* see. And I'll raise a glass to you, among my little children, and I'll say, Here's to you, Mazer Rackham, you foolish old optimist. You thought humans were better than they are, which is why you went to all the trouble of saving the human race a couple of times."

Mazer put an arm around Bean's waist and clinched tight for a moment. "Kiss the babies good-bye."

"I will not," said Bean. "Do you think I want them to have nightmares of a giant bending over them and trying to eat them?"

"*Eat* them!"

"Babies fear being eaten," said Bean. "There's a sound evolutionary reason for it, considering that in our ancestral homeland in Africa hyenas would always have been happy to carry off a human baby and eat it. I guess you've never read the child-rearing literature."

"Sounds more like Grimm's Fairy Tales."

Bean walked from bed to bed, touching each child in return. Perhaps spending a bit longer with Ramón, since he had spent so much time with him, compared to mere minutes with the others.

Then he left the room and followed Rackham out to the enclosed van that was waiting for him.

---

Suriyawong heard the report and the order: The press conference has been held; Thai participation in the FPE has been announced; now begin active operations against the enemy.

Suri timed the departure of all six contingents so that they would arrive simultaneously, more or less. He also ordered the Chinese battle choppers into position, ready to join in the battle as soon as surprise was achieved.

One of them would take him to where Virlomi would be.

If there are any gods looking out for her, thought Suriyawong, then let her live. Even if a hundred thousand soldiers die for her pride, please let her live. The good she did, the greatness in her, should count for something. The mistakes of generals can kill many thousands, but they're still mistakes. She set out for victory, not destruction. She should be punished only for her intent, not the result.

Not that her intent was all that good.

But you—you gods of war! Shiva, you destroyer!—what was Virlomi, ever, except your servant? Will you let your servant be destroyed, solely because she was so good at her job?

---

St. Petersburg had fallen more quickly than anyone expected. The resistance hadn't even been enough to count as "token." Even the police had fled, and the Finns and Estonians ended up working to maintain public order rather than fight a determined enemy.

But that was all just a matter of reports to Petra, who was improvising her way across Russia. Without a huge air force, there was no way to airlift her army of Brazilians and Rwandans to Moscow. So she was bringing them in on passenger trains, carefully watching from what looked like recreational aircraft so she'd know as soon as there was any kind of problem. The heavier ordnance was being carried on the highway by big Polish and German moving vans, of the kind that plied the highways across Europe all the time, stopping only to eat and pee and visit roadside whores. Now they carried the war that the Russians had begun straight to Moscow.

If the enemy was determined, they would be able to track Petra's army's progress. After all, there was no concealing what the trains were carrying as they raced through stations without stopping and demanded that the tracks be cleared in front of them "or we'll blast you and your station and your stupid little village of baby-killing Russians to smithereens!" All rhetoric—a single telephone pole dropped across the tracks here and there would have slowed them down considerably. And they weren't about to start killing civilians.

But the Russians didn't know that. Peter had told her that Vlad was sure the commanders who were left in Moscow would panic. "They're runners, not fighters. That doesn't mean nobody will fight—but it will be local people. Scattered. Wherever you meet resistance, just go around. If the Russian army in China is stopped and international vids show Moscow and St. Petersburg in your hands, either the government will sue for peace or the people will revolt. Or both."

Well, it had worked for the Germans in France in 1940. Why not here?

The loss of Vlad had a devastating effect on Russian morale. Especially because the Russians all knew that Julian Delphiki himself had planned the counterattack, and Petra Arkanian was leading the army that was "sweeping across Russia."

More like "chugging across Russia."

At least it wasn't winter.

---

Han Tzu gave the orders, and his retreating troops moved to their positions. He had timed his retreat exactly right, to lure the Russians to the exact spot he needed them to reach at the exact time he wanted them there. Well ahead of Vlad's original schedule—the only deviation from his plan.

The satellite information forwarded to him by Peter Wiggin assured him that the Turks had withdrawn westward, heading toward Armenia. As if they could get there in time to make any difference at all! Caliph Alai had apparently not solved the perpetual problem of Muslim armies. Unless they were under iron control, they were easily distracted. Alai was supposed to *be* that control. It made Han Tzu wonder if Alai was even in command anymore.

No matter. Han Tzu's objective was the huge, overextended, weary Russian Army that was still rigidly following Vlad's plan despite the fact that their pincer movements had encountered an empty Beijing, with no Chinese forces to crush or Chinese government to seize. And despite the fact that panicky reports must be coming from Moscow as they kept hearing rumors of Petra's advance without knowing where she was.

The Russian commander he was facing was not wrong to persist in his campaign. Petra's advance on Moscow was ultimately cosmetic, as Petra no doubt knew: designed to cause panic, but without sufficient force to hold any objective for long.

In the south, too, Suri's Thai army would do important work, but India's army wasn't a serious threat in the first place; Bean, in Armenia, had drawn off the Turkish armies, but they could easily come back.

Everything came down to this battle.

As far as Han Tzu was concerned, it had better not be a battle at all.

They were in the wheatfield country near Jinan. Vlad's plan assumed that the Chinese would seize the high ground to the southeast of the Hwang Ho and dispute the river crossing. Therefore the Russians were prepared with portable bridges and rafts to move across the river at unexpected places and then surround the supposed Chinese redoubt.

And, just as Vlad's plan predicted, Han Tzu's forces were indeed gathered on that high ground, and were shelling the approaching Russian troops with reassuring ineffectiveness. The Russian commander had to feel confident. Especially when he found the bridges over the Hwang Ho ineptly "destroyed," so repairs were quick.

Han Tzu couldn't afford to have a grinding battle, matching gun for gun, tank for tank. Too much materiel had been lost in the previous wars, and while Han's soldiers were battle-hardened veterans, and the Russian army hadn't fought in years, Han's inability to get his army back to full material strength in the short time he had been emperor would inevitably be decisive. Han was not going to use human waves to overwhelm the Russians with numbers. He couldn't afford to waste this army. He had to keep it intact to deal with the much more dangerous Muslim armies, should they get their act together and join in the war.

The Russian drones were easily a match for the Chinese; both commanders would have an accurate picture of the battlefield. This was wheatfield country, perfect for the Russian tanks. Nothing Han Tzu did could possibly surprise his enemy. Vlad's plan was going to work. The Russian commander had to be sure of it.

His forces that had been concealed behind the Russian advance now reported that the last of the Russians had passed the checkpoints without realizing what the small red tags on fences, bushes, trees, and signposts signified.

For the next forty minutes, Han Tzu's army had only one task: To confine the Russian army between those little red flags and the highlands across the Hwang, while none of the Chinese army strayed into that zone.

Didn't the Russians notice that every single civilian had been evacuated? That not a civilian vehicle was to be found? That the houses had been emptied of belongings?

Hyrum Graff had once taught a class in which he told them that God would teach them how to destroy their enemy, using the forces of nature. His prime example was the way God used a flood of the Red Sea to destroy Pharaoh's chariots.

The little red flags were the highwater mark.

Han Tzu gave the order for the dam to be blown up. It would take the wall of water forty minutes to reach the Russian army and destroy it.

---

The Armenian soldiers had achieved all their objectives. They had forced a panicky Iranian government to demand the recall of their troops from India. Soon an overwhelming force would arrive and they would all be lost.

They thought, when the black choppers came flying low over the city, that their time had come.

Instead, the soldiers that emerged from the choppers were Thais in the uniform of the FPE. The original strike force trained by Bean and led in so many raids by him or Suriyawong.

Then Bean himself stepped out of the chopper. "Sorry I'm late," he said.

Within minutes, the FPE troops had secured the perimeter and the Armenian troops were embarking on the choppers. "You're going to be taking the long way home," one of the Thais said, laughing.

Bean made a big deal about how he was going to go down the hill to see how things were going with the forward defense. The Armenians watched as Bean ducked to go through the door of a half-bombed-out building. A few moments later, the building blew up. Nothing left standing. No walls, no chimney. And no Bean.

The chopper took off then. The Armenians were so happy to have been rescued that it was hard to remember the terrible news they were going to have to take to Petra Arkanian. Her husband was dead. They'd seen it. There was no way anyone in that building could have survived.

# 23

# COLONIST

From: BlackDog%Salaam@IComeAnon.com
To: Graff%pilgrimage@colmin.gov
Encrypted using code: *******
Decrypted using code: *********
Re: Vlad's farewell message

Why I'm writing to you from hiding should be obvious; I'll give you the detailed story at a later date.

I want to take you up on your invitation, if it's still open. I learned recently that while I'm a real whiz at military strategy, I'm a dimwit about what motivates my own people—even those I thought were closest to me. For instance, who would have guessed that they would hate a modernizing, consensus-building black African Caliph a lot more than they hated a dictatorial, idolatrous, immodest Hindu woman?

I was going to simply disappear from history, and was feeling quite sorry for myself in my exile, while grieving for a dear friend who gave his life to save mine in Hyderabad, when I realized that the news reports that endlessly replayed Vlad's message were showing me what I needed to do.

So I've made arrangements to make a vid inside a nearby mosque. In a country where I'll be safe showing my face, so don't worry. I'm not going to let this one be released through you or Peter—that would discredit it immediately. It's going to move out through Muslim channels only.

The thing I realized is this: I may have lost the support of the military, but I'm still Caliph. It's not just a political office, it's also a religious one. And not one of those clowns has the authority to depose me.

Meanwhile, I know now what they called me behind my back. "Black dog." They're going to hear those words back from me, you can be sure.

When the vid is released, then I'll let you know where I am. If you're still willing to take me.

Randi watched the news reports avidly. It seemed so hopeful at first, when they heard that Julian Delphiki had been killed in Iran. Maybe the enemies hunting her baby would be crushed, and she'd be able to come out in the open and proclaim that she was carrying Achilles's son and heir.

But then she realized: the evil in this world would not die just because a few of Achilles's enemies were killed or defeated. They had done too good a job of demonizing him. If they knew who her son was, he would at least be scrutinized and tested constantly; at worst, they'd take him away from her. Or kill him. They'd stop at nothing to erase Achilles's legacy from the earth.

Randi stood by her son's little traveling bed in the former motel room that now was as cheap a one-room hot-plate apartment as northern Virginia offered. A traveling bed was all he needed. He was so small.

His birth had taken her by surprise. Months too early. And he came so fast. She couldn't get to a hospital. Not that they would have taken her. She was in the midst of changing her identity. She had no health insurance.

But because he was so small, the birth was easy. He just . . . came out. And small as he was, he didn't have any problems. He didn't even look like one of those premature babies, the ones who looked so . . . fetal. Fishlike. Not her boy. He was beautiful, completely normal looking. Just . . . small.

Small and brilliant. It almost frightened her sometimes. He had said his first word just a couple of days ago. "Mama," of course—who else did he know? And when she spoke to him, explained things to him, told him about his father, he seemed to be listening intently. He seemed to understand. Was that possible?

Of course it was. Achilles's child would be wiser than normal. And if he was small, well, Achilles himself had been born with a twisted foot. An abnormal body to contain extraordinary gifts.

Secretly, she had named the baby Achilles Flandres II. But she was careful. She didn't write that name anywhere but in her heart. Instead the birth certificate called him Randall Firth. She was going by the name Nichelle Firth now. The real Nichelle Firth was a retarded woman in a special school where she had worked as an aide. Randi looked old enough, she knew, to pass for the right age—being on the run and working so hard and worrying all the time gave her a kind of tired look that aged her. But what did she care about vanity? She wasn't trying to attract a man. She knew men well enough to know that none of them would want to marry a woman only to have her spend all her care on another man's baby.

So she made herself up only enough to be hirable in decent jobs that didn't require a long resume. They'd say, Where have you worked before, and she'd say, Nothing since college, they wouldn't even remember me, I was a stay-at-home mom, but my husband wasn't a sleep-at-home guy, so here I am, no resume except my baby's healthy and my house is clean and I know how to work like my life depended on it cause now it does. That line got her hired anywhere she bothered to apply. She'd never be an executive but she didn't want to be. Just put in her hours, get "Randall" out of daycare, and then talk to him, sing to him, and study about how to be a good mother and raise a healthy, confident baby who would have the strength of character to overcome the bigotry against his father and take on the whole world.

But these wars, and Peter Wiggin's hideous face on the camera, announcing *this* nation was now in the FPE and *that* nation was allied with the FPE, it worried her. She couldn't hide forever. Her fingerprints couldn't be changed, and there was that shoplifting arrest when she was in college. It was so stupid. She really had sort of forgotten that she took the thing. If she'd remembered she would have changed her mind and paid for it, like the other times. But she forgot and they stopped her outside the store so she had actually done the theft, they said, and she wasn't a minor so she got the whole arrest treatment. They let her off, but her prints were in the system. So someday somebody would know who she really was. And the man who approached her, who gave her Achilles's baby—how could she be sure he wouldn't tell them? Between what he told them and her fingerprints, they could find her no matter how often she changed her name.

That was when she decided that for the first time in human history, when a person was not safe anywhere on Earth, he had somewhere else to go.

Why should her little Achilles Flandres II be raised here, in hiding, with bloodthirsty monsters out to kill him in order to punish his father for being better than them? When instead he could grow up on a clean new colony world, where no one would care that the baby wasn't really hers or that he was small, if he was smart and worked hard and she raised him right? They promised that there would be trade back and forth between colony worlds, and visits from starships. When the time was right for Achilles II to claim his heritage, his legacy, his *throne,* she would bring him aboard one of those starships and they'd come back to Earth.

She had studied the relativistic effects of star travel. It might be as much as a hundred years or more—fifty years out and fifty years back, say—but it would only be three or four years of voyaging. So all of Achilles's enemies would be long since dead. Nobody would bother spreading vicious lies about him anymore. The world would be ready to hear of him with fresh ears, with open minds.

She couldn't leave him alone in the apartment. It was a drizzly afternoon, though. Was it worth risking him catching cold?

She bundled him well and carried him in a sling in front of her. He was so *small,* it felt like he was lighter than her purse. Her umbrella shielded them both from the rain. They'd be fine.

It was a long walk to the Metro station, but that was the best—and the driest—way to get to the liaison office of the Ministry of Colonization, where she could sign up. That would be a risk, of course. They might fingerprint her. They might run a check. But . . . surely they knew that many people would choose to go on a colony ship because they needed to get away from their old lives. And if they found that she had changed her name, the shoplifting arrest might explain it. She had been drifting into crime and . . . what would they assume? Drugs, probably . . . but now she wanted a fresh start, under a new name.

Or maybe she should use her real name.

No, because under *that* name she had no baby. And if they questioned whether "Randall" was really hers and ran a genetic test, they'd find that he had none of her genes. They'd wonder where she had kidnapped him. He was so small they'd think he was a newborn. And the birth had been so easy, there'd been no tearing—did they have tests to determine if she had ever given birth? Nightmares, nightmares. No, she'd give them her new name and then be prepared to run if they came looking for her. What else could she do?

It was worth the risk, to get him off planet.

On the way to the Metro she walked past a mosque, but there were cops outside, directing traffic. Had there been a bombing? Those were happening in other places—Europe, she kept hearing—but not in America, surely. Not *lately,* anyway.

No, not a bombing. Just a speaker. Just . . .

"Caliph Alai." She heard someone say it, almost as if they had been speaking to her.

Caliph Alai! The one man on Earth who seemed to have the courage to stand against Peter Wiggin.

Luckily she had a scarf over her head—she looked Muslim enough for this secular town, where plenty of Muslims wore no special clothing at all. Nobody challenged her, a woman with a baby, though they did make everybody leave things like umbrellas and purses and jackets at the security counter.

She walked into the women's section of the mosque. She was surprised at how the carved and decorated latticework interfered with her ability to see what was going on in the men's part of the mosque. Apparently even liberal American mosques still thought women did not need to see the speaker for themselves. Randi had heard about such things, but the only church she had ever attended was Presbyterian and families sat together there.

There were cameras all over the men's section, so maybe the view from here was as good as most men were getting. She wasn't converting to Islam, anyway, she just wanted to catch a glimpse of Caliph Alai.

He was speaking in Common, not Arabic. She was glad of that.

"I remain Caliph, no matter where I live. I will take with me in my colony only Muslims who believe in Islam as a religion of peace. I leave behind me the bloodthirsty false Muslims who called their Caliph a black dog and tried to murder me so they could make war on their harmless neighbors.

"Here is the law of Islam, from the time of Muhammed and forever: God gives permission to go to war only when we are attacked by an enemy. As soon as a Muslim raises his hand against an enemy who has not attacked him, then he is not engaged in jihad, he has become shaitan himself. I declare that all those who plotted the invasion of China and Armenia are not Muslims and any good Muslim who finds these men must arrest them.

"From now on Muslim nations may only be governed by leaders who were freely elected. Non-Muslims may vote in these elections. It is forbidden to molest any non-Muslim, even if he used to be a Muslim, or deprive him of any of his rights, or put him at any disadvantage. And if a Muslim nation votes to join the Free People of Earth and abide by its constitution, that is permitted by God. There is no offense in it."

Randi was heartsick. This was just like Vlad's speech. A complete capitulation to Peter Wiggin's phony "ideals." They had apparently blackmailed or drugged or frightened even Caliph Alai.

She picked her way carefully over and around the woman seated and standing and leaning in the packed women's chamber. Many of them looked at her as if she were sinning by leaving; many others were looking toward Caliph Alai with love and longing.

Your love is misplaced, thought Randi. Only one man was pure in his embrace of power, and that was my Achilles.

And to one woman who glared at her with special ferocity, Randi pointed to baby Achilles's diaper and made a face. The woman at once relaxed her grimace. Of course, the baby had messed himself, a woman had to take care of her baby even before she heard the words of the Caliph.

If the Caliph cannot stand against Peter Wiggin, then there is nowhere on Earth for me to raise my son.

She walked the rest of the way to the Metro as the rain came down harder and harder. Her umbrella did its job, though, and the baby stayed dry. Then she was in the Metro station and the rain had stopped.

That's how it will be in space. All the sheltering of this baby will be needless then. I can put away the umbrella and he will have nothing to fear. And on the new world, he can walk in the open, in the light of a new sun, like the free spirit he was born to be.

When he returns to Earth, he will be a great man, towering over these moral dwarfs.

By then, Peter Wiggin will be dead, like Julian Delphiki. That's the only disappointment—that my son will never be able to face his father's murderers directly.

# 24

# SACRIFICE

From: Mosca%Molo@FilMil.gov.ph
To: Graff%pilgrimage@colmin.gov
Re: My ticket

Just when things were getting interesting here on Earth, I keep getting this nagging feeling that you were right. I hate it when that happens.

They came to me today, excited as babies. Petra took Moscow with a ragtag army traveling by passenger train! Han Tzu wiped out the entire Russian Army without taking more than a few dozen casualties! Bean was able to decoy the Turkish forces toward Armenia and keep them from getting involved in China! And of course Bean also gets the credit for Suriyawong's victory in China—everybody wants to assign all glory to the boys and girl of Ender's Jeesh.

You know what they wanted from me?

I'm supposed to conquer Taiwan. No joke. I'm supposed to draw up the plans. Because, you see, my poor little ragtag island nation has *me*, Jeeshboy, and that makes them a great power! How dare those Muslim troops remain on Taiwan!

I pointed out that now that Han Tzu had won against the Russians and the Muslims probably wouldn't dare attack, he'd probably be looking to put Taiwan back in his fold. And even if he didn't, did they really think Peter Wiggin would sit idly by while the Philippines committed an act of unprovoked aggression against Taiwan?

They wouldn't listen. It was: Do as you're told, genius boy.

So what's left for me, Hyrum? (I feel so wicked calling you by your first name.) Do as Vlad did, and draw up their plans, and let them fall into their own pit? Do as Alai did and repudiate them openly and call for revolution? (That is what he did, isn't it?) Or do as Han did and stage an internal coup and become Emperor of the Philippines and Master of the Tagalog-Speaking World?

I don't want to leave my home. But there's no peace for me on Earth. I'm not sure I want the burden of running a colony. But at least I won't be drawing up blueprints for death and oppression. Just don't put me in the same colony with Alai. He thinks he's *so* the man because he's the successor of the Prophet.

Even the tanks had been washed downstream, some of them for kilometers. Where the Russians had been spreading out for their offensive against Han Tzu's forces on the high ground, there was nothing, not a sign that they had been there.

Not a sign that the villages and fields had been there either.

It was a muddy version of the moon. Except for a couple of deep-rooted trees, there was nothing. It would take a long time and a lot of work to restore this land.

But now there was work to do. First, they had to glean the survivors, if there were any, from the countryside downstream. Second, they had to clean up the corpses and gather up the tanks and other vehicles—and, most important, the live armaments.

And Han Tzu had to swing a large part of his army north, to retake Beijing and sweep away whatever remnants of the Russian invasion might be left behind. Meanwhile, the Turks might decide to come back.

The work of war wasn't over yet.

But the grinding, bloody campaign he had feared, the one that would tear China apart and bleed a generation to death, that had been averted. Both here in the north and in the south as well.

And then what? Emperor of China indeed. What would the people expect? Now that he had won this great victory, was he supposed to go back and subjugate the Tibetans again? Force the Turkic-speakers of Xinjiang back under the Chinese heel? Spill Chinese blood on the beaches of Taiwan to satisfy old claims that the Chinese had some inherent right to rule over the racially-Malay majority on that island? And then invade any nation that mistreated its Chinese minorities? Where would it stop? In the jungles of Papua? Back in India? Or at the old western border of Genghis's empire, the lands of the Golden Horde on the steppes of Ukraine?

What frightened him most about these scenarios was that he knew he could do it. He knew that with China he had a people with the intelligence, the vigor, the resources, and unified will—everything a ruler needed to go out into the world and make everything he saw his own. And because it was possible, there was a part of him that wanted to play it out, see where this path led.

I know where it leads, thought Han Tzu. It leads to Virlomi leading her pathetic army of half-armed volunteers to certain death. It leads to Julius Caesar bleeding to death on the floor of the Senate, muttering about how he was betrayed. It leads to Adolf and Eva dead in an underground bunker while their empire crumbles in explosions above their corpses. Or it leads to Augustus, casting about him for a successor, only to realize that it all has to be handed over to his revolting pervert of a . . . stepson? What *was* Tiberius, really? A sad statement about how empires are inevitably led. Because what rises to the top in an empire are the bureaucratic infighters, the assassins, or the warlords.

Is that what I want for my people? I became Emperor because that's how I could bring down Snow Tiger and keep him from killing me first. But China doesn't need an empire. China needs a good government. The Chinese people need to stay home and make money, or travel through the world and make even more money. They need to do science and create literature and be part of the human race.

They need to have no more of their sons die in battle. They need to have no more of them cleaning up the bodies of the enemy. They need peace.

The news of Bean's death spread slowly out of Armenia. It came to Petra, incredibly enough, on her cellphone in Moscow, where she was still directing her troops in the complete takeover of the city. The news of Han's devastating victory had reached her, but not the general public. She needed to be in complete control of the city before the people learned of the disaster. She needed to make sure they could contain the reaction.

It was her father on the telephone. His voice was very husky, and she knew at once what he was calling to tell her.

"The soldiers who were rescued from Tehran. They came back by way of Israel. They saw . . . Julian didn't come back with them."

Petra knew perfectly well what had happened. And, more to the point, what Bean would have made sure people thought they had *seen* happen. But she let the scene play out, saying the lines expected of her. "They left him behind?"

"There was . . . nothing to bring back." A sob. It was good to know that her father had come to love Bean. Or maybe he only wept in pity for his daughter, already widowed, and only barely a woman. "He was caught in the explosion of a building. The whole thing was vaporized. He could not have lived."

"Thank you for telling me, Father."

"I know it's—what about the babies? Come home, Pet, we—"

"When I'm through with the war, Father, then I'll come home and grieve for my husband and care for my babies. They're in good hands right now. I love you. And Mother. I'll be all right. Good-bye."

She cut off the connection.

Several officers around her looked at her questioningly. What she had said about grieving for her husband. "This is top-secret information," she said to the officers. "It would only encourage the enemies of the Free People. But my husband was . . . he entered a building in Tehran and it blew up. No one in that building could possibly have survived."

They did not know her, these Finns, Estonians, Lithuanians, Latvians. Not well enough to say more than a heartfelt but inadequate, "I'm sorry."

"We have work to do," she said, relieving them of the responsibility to care for her. They could not know that what she was showing was not iron self-control, but cold rage. To lose your husband in war, that was one thing. But to lose him because he refused to take you with him. . . .

That was unfair. In the long run, she would have decided the same way. There was one baby unfound. And even if that baby was dead or had never existed—how did they know how many there were, except what Volescu told them?—the five normal babies shouldn't have their lives so drastically deformed. It would be like making a healthy twin spend his life in a hospital bed just because his brother was in a coma.

I would have chosen the same *if I'd had time.*

There was no time. Bean's life was too fragile already. She was losing him.

And she had known right from the start that one way or another, she would lose him. When he begged her not to marry him, when he insisted he wanted no babies, it was to avoid having her feel as she felt now.

Knowing it was her own fault, her own free choice, all for the best—it didn't ease the pain one bit. If anything, it made it worse.

So she was angry. At herself. At human nature. At the fact that she was a human and therefore had to *have* that nature whether she wanted it or not. The desire to have the babies of the best man she knew, the desire to hold on to him forever.

And the desire to go into battle and win, outwitting her enemies, cutting them off, taking all their power away from them and standing astride them in victory.

It was a terrible thing to realize about herself—that she loved the contest of war every bit as much as she missed her husband and children, so that doing the one would take her mind off the loss of the others.

---

When the gunfire began, Virlomi felt a thrill of excitement. But also a sick sense of dread. As if she knew some terrible secret about this campaign that she had not allowed herself to hear until the gunfire brought the message to her consciousness.

Almost at once, her driver tried to take her out of harm's way. But she insisted on heading toward the thick of the fighting. She could see where the enemy was gathered, in the hills on either side. She immediately recognized the tactics that were being used.

She started to issue orders. She ordered them to notify the other two columns to withdraw up their valleys and reconnoiter. She sent her elite troops, the ones that had fought with her for years, up the slopes to hold the enemy off while she withdrew the rest of her troops.

But the mass of untrained soldiers were too frightened to understand their orders or execute them under fire. Many of them broke and ran—straight up the valley, where they were exposed to fire. And Virlomi knew that not far behind them would be the trailing force which they had carelessly passed by.

All because she didn't expect Han Tzu, preoccupied with the Russians, to be able to send a force of any size here to the south.

She kept reassuring her officers—this is only a small force, we can't let them stop us. But the bodies were falling steadily. The firing only seemed to increase. And she realized that what she was facing was not some aging Home Guard unit thrown together to pester them as they marched. It was a disciplined force that was systematically herding her troops—her hundreds of thousands of soldiers—into a killing ground along the road and the riverbank.

And yet the gods still protected her. She walked among the cowering troops, standing upright, and not a bullet struck her. Soldiers fell all around her, but she was untouched.

She knew how the soldiers interpreted it: The gods protect her.

But she understood something completely different: The enemy has given orders not to harm me. And these soldiers are so well trained and disciplined that they are obeying the order.

The force opposing them was not huge—the firepower wasn't overwhelming. But most of her soldiers weren't shooting at all. How could they? They couldn't see a target to shoot at. And the enemy would concentrate its fire on any force that tried to leave the road and get up the hills to sweep over the enemy lines.

As far as she could see, if any of the enemy had died, it was by accident.

I am Varus, she thought. I have led my troops, as Varus led the Roman Legions, into a trap, where we will all die. Die without even damaging the enemy.

What was I thinking? This terrain was made for ambush. Why didn't I see that? Why was I so sure the enemy couldn't attack us here?

Whatever you're sure the enemy *can't* do, but which would destroy you if they did it anyway, you must plan to counter. This was elementary.

No one from Ender's Jeesh would have made such a mistake.

Alai knew. He had warned her from the start. Her troops weren't ready for such a campaign. It would be a slaughter. And here they were now, dying all around her, the whole highway thick with corpses. Her men had been reduced to piling up the dead as makeshift bulwarks against enemy fire. There was no point in her issuing commands, because they would not be understood or obeyed.

And yet her men fought on.

Her cellphone rang.

She knew at once that it was the enemy, calling her to ask her to surrender. But how could they know her cellphone number?

Was it possible that Alai was with *them?*

"Virlomi."

Not Alai. But she knew the voice.

"This is Suri."

Suriyawong. Were these FPE troops? Or Thai? How could Thai troops get across Burma and all the way up here?

Not Chinese troops at all. Why was it suddenly so clear now? Why hadn't it been clear before, when Alai was warning her? In their private talks, Alamandar said it would all work because the Russians would have the Chinese army fully involved in the north. Whichever attack Han Tzu defended against, the other side would be able to rampage through China. Or if he tried to fight both, then each would destroy that part of his army in turn.

What neither of them had realized was that Han Tzu was just as capable of finding allies as they were.

Suriyawong, whose love she had spurned. It felt like so many years ago. When they were children. Was this his vengeance, because she had married Alai instead of him?

"Can you hear me, Vir?"

"Yes," she said.

"I would rather capture these men," he said. "I don't want to spend the rest of the day killing them all."

"Then stop."

"They won't surrender while you're still fighting. They worship you. They're dying for you. Tell them to surrender, and let the survivors go home to their families when the war is over."

"Tell Indians to surrender to *Siamese?*"

As soon as she said it, she regretted it. Once she had cared first for the lives of her men. Now, suddenly, she found herself speaking out of injured pride.

"Vir," said Suri. "They're dying for nothing. Save their lives."

She broke the connection. She looked at the men around her, the ones that were alive, crouching behind piles of their comrades' bodies, searching for some kind of target out in the trees, up the slopes . . . and seeing nothing.

"They've stopped shooting," said one of her surviving officers.

"Enough men have died for my pride," said Virlomi. "May the dead forgive me. I will live a thousand lives to make up for this one vain, stupid day." She raised her voice. "Lay down your weapons. Virlomi says: Lay down your weapons and stand up with your hands in the air. Take no more lives! Lay down your weapons!"

"We will die for you, Mother India!" cried one of the men.

"Satyagraha!" shouted Virlomi. "Bear what must be borne! Today what you must bear is surrender! Mother India commands you to live so you can go home and comfort your wives and make babies to heal the great wounds that have been torn in the heart of India today!"

Some of her words and all of the meaning of her message were passed up and down the highway of corpses.

She set the example by raising her hands and walking out beyond the wall of bodies, into the open. Of course no one shot at her, because no one had during the whole battle. But soon others joined her. They lined up on the same side of the corpse wall that she had chosen, leaving their weapons behind them.

From out of the trees on both sides of the highway, wary Thai soldiers emerged, guns still at the ready. They were covered with sweat and the frenzy of killing was only just leaving them.

Virlomi turned and looked behind her. Emerging from the trees on the other side of the road was Suriyawong. She walked back over the walls of corpses to meet him in the grass on the other side. They stopped when they were three paces apart.

She gestured up and down the road. "So. This is your work."

"No, Virlomi," he said sadly. "It's yours."

"Yes," she said. "I know."

"Will you come with me to tell the other two armies to stop fighting? They'll only give up when you tell them to."

"Yes," she said. "Now?"

"Phone them and see if they obey. If I try to lead you away right now, these soldiers will take up arms again to stop me. For some reason they still worship you."

"In India we worship the Destroyer along with Vishnu and Brahma."

"But I never knew that you served Shiva," said Suriyawong.

She had no answer for him. She used her cellphone and made the calls. "They're trying to stop the men from fighting."

Then there was silence between them for a while. She could hear the barked commands of the Thai soldiers, forming her men into small groups and beginning their march down the valley.

"Aren't you going to ask about your husband?" said Suri.

"What about him?"

"Are you so sure your Muslim co-conspirators killed him, then?"

"Nobody was going to kill him," she said. "They were only going to confine him until after the victory."

Suri laughed bitterly. "You spent this long fighting the Muslims, Vir, and you still don't understand them any better than that? This isn't a chess game. The person of the king is not sacred."

"I never sought his death."

"You took away his power," said Suri. "He tried to stop you from doing *this* and you plotted against your own husband. He was a better friend to India than you ever were." His voice cracked with passion.

"You cannot say anything to me that's crueller than what I am now saying to myself."

"The girl Virlomi, so brave, so wise," said Suri. "Does she still exist? Or has the goddess destroyed her too?"

"The goddess is gone," said Virlomi. "Only the fool, only the murderer remains."

A field radio crackled at his waist. Something was said in Thai.

"Please come with me now, Virlomi. One army is surrendering, but the other shot the officer you telephoned when he tried to give the order."

A chopper approached them. Landed. They got on.

In the air, Suriyawong asked her, "What will you do now?"

"I'm your prisoner. What will *you* do?"

"You're Peter Wiggin's prisoner. Thailand has joined the Free People."

She knew what that would mean to Suriyawong. Thailand—even the name meant "land of the free." Peter's new "nation" had coopted the name of Suriyawong's homeland. And now, his homeland would no longer be sovereign. They had given up their independence. Peter Wiggin would be master of all.

"I'm sorry," she said.

"Sorry? Because my people will be free within their borders, and there'll be no more wars?"

"What about my people?" she asked.

"You're not going back to them," said Suri.

"How could I, even if you let me? How could I possibly face them?"

"I was hoping that you *would* face them. By vid. To help undo some of the damage you've done today."

"What could I possibly say or do?"

"They still worship you. If you disappear now, if they never hear of you again, India will be ungovernable for a hundred years."

Virlomi answered truthfully: "India has always been ungovernable."

"*Less* governable than ever," said Suri. "But if you speak to them. If you tell them—"

"I will not tell them to surrender to yet another foreign power, not after they've been conquered and occupied by Chinese and then Muslims!"

"If you ask them to vote. To freely decide whether to live in peace, within the Free People—"

"And give Peter Wiggin the victory?"

"Why are you angry with Peter? What did he ever do but help you win your nation's freedom in every way that was possible to him?"

It was true. Why was she so angry?

Because he had beaten her.

"Peter Wiggin," said Suriyawong, "has the right of conquest. His troops destroyed your army in combat. He showed mercy he didn't have to show."

"*You* showed mercy."

"I followed Peter's instructions," said Suriyawong. "He does not want any foreign occupiers in India. He wants the Muslims out. He wants only Indians to govern Indians. Joining the FPE means exactly that. A free India. But an India that doesn't need, and therefore doesn't *have,* a military."

"A nation without an army is nothing," said Virlomi. "Any enemy can destroy them."

"That's the Hegemon's work in the world. He destroys the aggressors, so peaceful nations can remain free. India was the aggressor. Under your leadership, India was the invader. Now, instead of punishing your people, he offers them freedom and protection, if they only give up their weapons. Isn't that Satyagraha, Vir? To give up what you once valued, because now you serve a greater good?"

"Now you teach *me* about Satyagraha?"

"Hear the arrogance in your voice, Vir."

Abashed, she looked away from him.

"I teach you about Satyagraha because I lived it for years. Hiding myself utterly so that I would be the one Achilles trusted in the moment when I could betray him and save the world from him. I had no pride at the end of that. I had lived in filth and shame for . . . forever. But Bean took me back and trusted me. And Peter Wiggin acted as if he had known all along who I really was. They accepted my sacrifice.

"Now I ask you, Vir, for your sacrifice. Your Satyagraha. Once you put everything on the altar of India. Then your pride nearly undid what you had accomplished. I ask you now, will you help your people live in peace, the only way that peace can be had in this world? By joining with the Free People of Earth?"

She felt the tears streaming down her face.

Like that day when she was making the video of the atrocities.

Only today she was the one who had caused the deaths of all these Indian boys. They came here to die because they loved and served her. She owed their families something.

"Whatever will help my people live in peace," she said, "I'll do."

# 25

# LETTERS

From: Bean@Whereverthehelliam
To: Graff%pilgrimage@colmin.gov
Re: Did we actually do it?

I can't believe you still have me hooked up to the nets. This continues by ansible after we're moving at relativistic speeds?

The babies are fine here. There's room enough for them to crawl. A library big enough I think they won't lack for interesting reading or viewing material for . . . weeks. It will only be weeks, right?

What I'm wondering is: did we do it? Did I fulfil your goal? I look at the map, and there's still nothing inevitable about it. Han Tzu gave his farewell speech, just like Vlad and Alai and Virlomi. Makes me feel cheated. They got to bid the world farewell before they disappeared into this good night. Then again, they had nations to try to sway. I never really had anybody who followed me. Never wanted them. That's the thing, I guess, that set me apart from the rest of the Jeesh—I was the only one who didn't wish I were Ender.

So look at the map, Hyrum. Will they buy Han Tzu's plan of dividing China into six nations and all of them joining the Free Peoples? Or will they stay unified and still join? Or look for another Emperor? Will India recover from the humiliation of Virlomi's defeat? Will they follow her advice and embrace the FPE? Nothing's assured, and I have to go.

I know, you'll tell me by ansible when anything interesting happens. And in a way, I don't care. I'm not going to be there, I'm not going to have any effect on it.

In another way, I care even less than that. Because I never did care.

Yet I also care with my whole heart. Because Petra is there with the only babies I actually wanted—the ones that don't have my defects. With me I have only the cripples. And my only fear is that I'll die before I've taught them anything.

Don't be ashamed when you see your life coming to an end and you haven't found a cure for me yet. I never believed in the cure. I thought there was enough of a chance to take this leap into the night, and cure or not, I knew that I didn't want my defective children to live long enough to make my mistake and reproduce, and keep this valuable, terrible curse going on, generation after generation. Whatever happens, it's all right.

And then it occurs to me. What if Sister Carlotta was right? What if God is waiting for me with open arms? Then all I'm doing is postponing my reunion. I think of meeting God. Will it be like when I met my father and mother? (I almost wrote: Nikolai's parents.) I liked them. I wanted to love them. But I knew that Nikolai was the child she bore, the child they raised. And I was . . . from nowhere. And for me, my father was a little girl named Poke, and my mother was Sister Carlotta, and they were dead. Who were these other people really?

Will meeting God be like that? Will I be disappointed with the real thing, because I prefer the substitute I made do with?

Like it or not, Hyrum, you were God in my life. I didn't invite you, I didn't even like you, but you kept MEDDLING. And now you've sent me into outer darkness with a promise to save me. A promise I don't believe you can keep. But at least YOU aren't a stranger. I know you. And I think that you honestly meant well. If I have to choose between an omnipotent God who leaves the world in this condition, and a God who has only a little bit of power but really cares and tries to make things better, I'll take you every time. Go on playing God, Hyrum. You're not bad at it. Sometimes you kind of get it right.

Why am I writing like this? We can email whenever we want. The thing is, nothing's going to happen here, so I'll have nothing to tell you. And nothing you have to tell me is going to matter to me all that much, the farther I get from Earth. So this is the right time for these valedictories.

I hope Peter succeeds in uniting the world in peace. I believe he's still got a couple of big wars ahead of him.

I hope Petra remarries. When she asks you what you think, tell her I said this: I want my children to have a father in their lives. Not some absent legend of a father—a real one. So as long as she chooses somebody who'll love them and tell them they've done ok, then do it. Be happy.

I hope you live to see colonies established and the human race thriving on other worlds. It's a good dream.

I hope these crippled children I have with me find something interesting to do with their lives after I'm dead.

I hope Sister Carlotta and Poke are there to meet me when I die. Sister Carlotta can tell me I told you so. And I can tell them both how sorry I am that I couldn't save their lives, after all the trouble they went to to save mine.

Enough. Time to switch on the gravity regulator and get this boat out to sea.

From: Graff%pilgrimage@colmin.gov
To: Bean@Whereverthehelliam
Re: You did enough

You did enough, Bean. You only had a little time, and you sacrificed so much of it to helping Peter and me and Mazer. All that time that could have belonged to Petra and you and your babies. You did enough. Peter can take it from here.

As for all that God business—I don't think the real God has as bad a track record as you think. Sure, a lot of people have terrible lives, by some measure. But I can't think of anybody who's had it tougher than you. And look what you've become. You don't want to give God the credit because you don't think he exists. But if you're going to blame him for all the crap, kid, you got to give him credit for what grows from that fertilized soil.

What you said about Petra getting a real father for your kids. I know you weren't talking about yourself. But I have to say it, because it's true, and you deserve to hear it.

Bean, I'm proud of you. I'm proud of myself because I actually got to know you. I remember sitting there after you figured out what was really going on in the war against the Buggers. What do I do with this kid? We can't keep a secret from him.

What I decided was: I'll trust him.

You lived up to my trust. You exceeded it. You're a great soul. I looked up to you long before you got so tall.

You did ok.

The plebiscite was over in Russia and it joined the FPE. The Muslim League was broken up and the most belligerent nations had been subdued, for now. Armenia was safe.

Petra sent her army home on the same civilian trains that had brought them to Moscow.

It had taken a year.

During that time she missed her babies. But she couldn't bear to see them. She refused to let them be brought to her. She refused to take even a brief leave to see them.

Because she knew that when she came home, there would only be five of them. And the two she knew the best and therefore loved the best would not be there.

Because she knew that she would have to face the rest of her life without Bean.

So she kept herself busy—and there was no shortage of important work to do. She told herself—next week I'll take a leave and go home.

Then her father came to her and bulled his way past the aides and clerks that fenced her off from the outside world. Truth to tell, they were probably glad to see him and let him through. Because Petra was hell on wheels and terrified everybody around her.

Father came to her with an attitude of steel. "Get out of here," he said.

"What are you talking about?"

"Your mother and I lost half your childhood because they *took you away.* You're cheating yourself out of some of the sweetest time in the lives of your children. Why? What are you afraid of? The great soldier, and babies terrify you?"

"I don't want this conversation," she said. "I'm an adult. I make my own decisions."

"You don't grow out of being my daughter." Father said. Then he loomed over her, and for a moment she had a childish fear that he was going to . . . to . . . *spank* her.

All he did was put his arms around her and hug her. Tight.

"You're suffocating me, Papa."

"Then it's working."

"I mean it."

"If you have breath to argue with me, then I'm not done."

She laughed.

---

He let her out of the hug but still held her shoulders. "You wanted these children more than anything, and you were right. Now you want to avoid them because you think you can't bear the grief of the ones that aren't there. And I tell you, you're wrong. And I *know.* Because I was there for Stefan, during all the years you were gone. I didn't hide from *him* because I didn't have *you.*"

"I know you're right," said Petra. "You think I'm stupid? I didn't decide *not* to see them. I just kept putting it off."

"Your mother and I have written to Peter, begging him to *order* you home. And all he said was, She'll come when she can't help it."

"You couldn't listen to him? He *is* the Hegemon of the whole world."

"Not even half the world yet," said Father. "And he might be Hegemon of nations, but he's got no authority inside my family."

"Thank you for coming, Papa. I'm demobilizing my troops tomorrow and sending them home across borders where they won't need passports because it's all part of the Free People of Earth. I did something while I was here. But now I'm done. I was going home anyway. But now I'll do it because you told me to. See? I'm willing to be obedient, as long as you order me to do what I was going to do anyway."

---

The Free People of Earth had four capitals now—Bangkok had been added to Rwanda, Rotterdam, and Blackstream. But it was Blackstream—Ribeirão Preto—where the Hegemon lived. And that was where Peter had had her children moved. He hadn't even asked her permission and it made her furious when he informed her what he had done. But she was busy in Russia and Peter said that Rotterdam wasn't home to her and it wasn't home to him and he was going home, and keeping her kids where he could make sure they were getting cared for.

So it was Brazil she came home to. And it did feel good. Moscow's winter had been a nightmare, even worse than Armenia's winters. And she liked the feel of Brazil, the pace of life, the way they moved, the football in the streets, the way they were never quite dressed, the music of the Portuguese language coming out of the neighborhood bars along with batuque and samba and laughter and the pungent smell of pinga.

She took a car part of the way but then paid him and told him to deliver her bags to the compound and she walked the rest of the way. Without actually planning it, she found herself walking past the little house where she and Bean had lived when they weren't inside the compound.

The house had been changed. She realized: It was connected to the house next door by a couple of rooms added in, and the garden wall between them had been torn down. It was one big house now.

What a shame. They can't leave well enough alone.

Then she saw the name on the little sign on the wall beside the gate.

Delphiki.

She opened the gate without clapping hands for permission. She knew now what had happened, but she also couldn't believe that Peter had gone to such trouble.

She opened the door and walked in and . . .

There was Bean's mother in the kitchen, making something that had a lot of olives and garlic in it.

"Oh," said Petra. "I'm sorry. I didn't know you—I thought you were in Greece."

The smile on Mrs. Delphiki's face was all the answer Petra needed. "Of course you come in, it's your house. I'm the visitor. Welcome home!"

"You came to—you're here to take care of the babies."

"We work for the FPE now. And our jobs brought us here. But I couldn't stand to be away from my grandchildren. I took a leave of absence. Now I cook, and change nasty diapers, and scream at the empregadas."

"Where are the . . ."

"Naptime!" said Mrs. Delphiki. "But I promise you, little Andrew, he's only faking. He *never* sleeps, whenever I go in his eyes are just a little tiny bit open."

"They won't know me," said Petra.

She dismissed that with a wave. "Of course not. But you think they're going to remember that? Nothing that happens before age three."

"I'm so glad to see you. Did . . . did he say good-bye to you?"

"He wasn't sentimental that way," said Mrs. Delphiki. "But yes, he called us. And sent us nice letters. I think it hit Nikolai harder than us, because he knew Julian better. From Battle School, you know. But Nikolai is married now, did you know? So pretty soon, maybe another grandchild. Not that we have a shortage. You and Julian did *very* well by us."

"If I'm very quiet and don't wake them, can I go see them?"

"We divided them into two rooms. Andrew shares one room with Bella, because he never sleeps, but she can sleep through anything. Julian and Petra and Ramón are in the other room. They need it dimmer. But if you wake them, it's not a problem. All their cribs have the sides down because they climb out anyway."

"They're walking?"

"Running. Climbing. Falling off things. They're more than a year old, Petra! They're normal children!"

It almost set her off, because it reminded her of the children who weren't normal. But that wasn't what Mrs. Delphiki meant, and there was no reason to punish her for a chance remark by bursting into tears.

So the two who bore the names of the children she grieved for most were sharing a room. She had courage enough to face this. She went there first.

Nothing about these babies reminded her of the ones who were gone. They were so big. Toddlers, not babies now. And, true to reputation, Andrew's eyes were already open. He turned to look at her.

She smiled at him.

He closed his eyes and pretended to be asleep.

Well, let him retreat and decide what he thinks of me. I'm not going to demand that they love me when they don't even know me.

She walked to Bella's crib. She was sleeping hard, her black curls tight and wet against her head. The Delphiki genetic heritage was *so* complicated. Bella really showed Bean's African roots. Whereas Andrew looked Armenian, period.

She touched one of Bella's curls and the girl didn't stir. Her cheek was hot and damp.

She's mine, thought Petra.

She turned and saw that Andrew was sitting up in bed, regarding her soberly. "Hello, Mama," he said.

It took her breath away.

"How did you know me?"

"Picture," he said.

"Do you want to get up?"

He looked at the clock on the top of the dresser. "Not time."

These were *normal* children?

How would Mrs. Delphiki know what normal was, anyway? Nikolai wasn't exactly stupid.

Though they weren't *so* brilliant. They were both wearing diapers.

Petra walked over to Andrew and held out her hand. What do I think he is, a dog that I give my hand to sniff?

Andrew took hold of a couple of her fingers, just for a moment, as if to make sure she was real. "Hello, Mama."

"May I kiss you?"

He lifted his face and puckered up. She leaned down and kissed him.

The touch of his hands. The feel of his little kiss. The curl on Bella's cheek. What had she been waiting for? Why had she been afraid? Fool. I'm a fool.

Andrew lay back down and closed his eyes. As Mrs. Delphiki had warned, it was completely unbelievable. She could see the whites of his eyes through the partly-open slits.

"I love you," she whispered.

"Loveyoutoo," murmured Andrew.

Petra was glad that someone had said those words to him so often that the answer came by rote.

She crossed the hall into the other room. It was much darker. She couldn't see well enough to dare to cross the room. It took a few moments for her eyes to grow used to the dark and make out the three beds.

Would she know Ramón when she saw him?

Someone moved to her left. She was startled, and she was a soldier. In a moment she was in a defensive crouch, ready to spring.

"Only me," whispered Peter Wiggin.

"You didn't have to come and—"

He held a finger to his lips. He walked over to the farthest crib. "Ramón," he whispered.

She came and stood over the crib.

Peter reached down and flipped something. A paper.

"What is it?" she asked. In a whisper.

He shrugged.

If he didn't know what it was, why had he pointed it out to her?

She pulled it out from under Ramón. It was an envelope, but it didn't contain much.

Peter took her gently by the elbow and guided her out the door. Once they were in the hall, he said softly, "You can't read in that light. And when Ramón wakes up, he's going to look for it and be very upset if it isn't there."

"What is it?"

"Ramón's paper," said Peter. "Petra, Bean put it there before he left. I mean, not *there.* It was in Rotterdam. But he tucked it under Ramón's diaper as he was lying asleep in bed. He meant you to find it there. So it's been there every night of his life. It's only been peed on twice."

"From Bean."

The emotion she could deal with best was anger. "You knew he had written this and—"

Peter kept the both of them moving out of the hall and into the parlor. "He didn't give it to me or anyone else to deliver. Unless you count Ramón. He gave it to Ramón's butt."

"But to make me wait a year before—"

"Nobody thought it would be a year, Petra." He said it very gently, but the truth of it stung. He always had the power to sting her, and yet he never shrank from doing it.

"I'll leave you alone to read it," he said.

"You mean you didn't come here for my homecoming so you could find out what was in it?"

"Petra." Mrs. Delphiki stood in the doorway to the parlor. She looked mildly shocked. "Peter didn't come here for *you*. He's here all the time."

Petra looked at Peter and then back and Mrs. Delphiki. "Why?"

"They climb all over him. And he puts them down for their nap. They obey him a *lot* better than me."

The thought of the Hegemon of Earth coming over to play with her children seemed freakish to her. And then it seemed worse than freakish. It seemed completely unfair. She pushed him. "You came to *my* house and played with *my* children?"

He didn't show any reaction; he also stood his ground. "They're great kids."

"Let me find that out, will you? Let me find it out for myself!"

"Nobody's stopping you."

"*You* were stopping me! I was doing your work in Moscow, and you were *here* playing with my kids!"

"I offered to bring them to you."

"I didn't want them in Moscow, I was busy."

"I offered you leave to come home. Time after time."

"And let the work fall apart?"

"Petra," said Mrs. Delphiki. "Peter has been very good to your children. And to me. And you're behaving very badly."

"No, Mrs. Delphiki," said Peter. "This is only *slightly* badly. Petra's a trained soldier and the fact that I'm still standing—"

"Don't tease me out of this." Petra burst into tears. "I've lost a year of my babies' lives and it was my own fault, do you think I don't know that?"

There was a crying sound from one of the bedrooms.

Mrs. Delphiki rolled her eyes and went down the hall to rescue whoever it was that needed rescuing.

"You did what you had to do," said Peter. "Nobody's criticizing you."

"But *you* could take time for my children."

"I don't have any of my own," said Peter.

"Is that my fault?"

"I'm just saying I had time. And . . . I owed it to Bean."

"You owe more than that."

"But this is what I can do."

She didn't want Peter Wiggin to be the father figure in her children's lives.

"Petra, I'll stop if you want. They'll wonder why I don't come, and then they'll forget. If you don't want me here, I'll understand. This is yours and Bean's, and I don't want to intrude. And yes, I did want to be here when you opened that."

"What's in it?"

"I don't know."

"Didn't have one of your guys steam it open for you?"

Peter just looked a little irritated.

Mrs. Delphiki came into the room carrying Ramón, who was whimpering and saying, "My paper."

"I should have known," said Peter.

Petra held up the envelope. "Here it is," she said.

Ramón reached for it insistently. Petra handed it to him.

"You're spoiling him," said Peter.

"This is your mama, Ramón," said Mrs. Delphiki. "She nursed you when you were little."

"He was the only one that wasn't biting me by the time . . ." She couldn't think of a way to finish the sentence that wouldn't involve speaking of Bean or the other two children, the ones that had to go on solid food because they got teeth so incredibly young.

Mrs. Delphiki wasn't giving up. "Let your mama see the paper, Ramón."

Ramón clutched it tighter. Sharing was not yet on his agenda.

Peter reached out, snagged the envelope, and held it out to Petra. Ramón immediately began to wail.

"Give it back to him," said Petra. "I've waited this long."

Peter got his finger under the corner, tore it open, and extracted a single sheet of paper. "If you let them get their way just because they cry, you'll raise a bunch of whiny brats that nobody can stand." He handed her the paper, and gave the envelope back to Ramón, who immediately quieted down and started examining the transformed object.

Petra held the paper and was surprised to see that it was shaking. Which meant her hand was shaking. She didn't *feel* like she was trembling.

And then suddenly Peter was holding her by her upper arms and helping her to the sofa and her legs weren't working very well. "Come on, sit here, it's a shock, that's all."

"I've got your snack all ready," said Mrs. Delphiki to Ramón, who was trying to get his whole forearm inside the envelope.

"Are you all right?" Peter asked.

Petra nodded.

"Want me to go now so you can read this?"

She nodded again.

Peter was in the kitchen saying good-bye to Ramón and Mrs. Delphiki as Andrew padded down the hall. He stopped in the archway of the parlor and said, "Time."

"Yes, it's time, Andrew," said Petra.

She watched him toddle on toward the kitchen. And then a moment later she heard his voice. "Mama," he announced.

"That's right," said Mrs. Delphiki. "Mama's home."

"Bye, Mrs. Delphiki," Peter said. A moment later, Petra heard the door open.

"Wait a minute, Peter!" she called.

He came back inside. He closed the door. As he came back into the parlor she held the paper out to him. "I can't read it."

Peter didn't ask why. Any fool could see the tears in her eyes. "You want me to read it to you?"

"Maybe I can get through it if it isn't his voice I hear," she said.

Peter opened it. "It isn't long."

"I know."

He started reading aloud, softly so only she could hear.

"I love you," he said. "There's one thing we forgot to decide. We can't have two pairs of children with the same name. So I've decided that I'm going to call the Andrew that's with me 'Ender,' because that's the name we called him when he was born. And I'll think of the Andrew that's with you as 'Andrew.' "

The tears were streaming down Petra's face now and she could hardly keep herself from sobbing. For some reason it tore her apart to realize that Bean was thinking about such things before he left.

"Want me to go on?" asked Peter.

She nodded.

"And the Bella that's with you, we'll call Bella. Because the one that's with me, I've decided to call her 'Carlotta.' "

She lost it. Feelings she'd had pent up inside her for a year, feelings that her underlings had begun to think she didn't have, burst out of her now.

But only for a minute. She got control of herself, and then waved to him to continue.

"And even though she isn't with me, the little girl we named after you, when I tell the kids about her, I'm going to call her 'Poke' so they don't get her confused with you. You don't have to call her that, but it's because you're the only Petra I actually know, and Poke ought to have somebody named after her."

Petra broke down. She clung to Peter and he held her like a friend, like a father.

Peter didn't say anything. No "It's all right" or "I understand," maybe because it wasn't all right and he was smart enough to know he couldn't understand.

When he did speak, it was after she was much calmer and quieter and another of the children had walked past the archway and loudly proclaimed, "Lady crying."

Petra sat up and patted Peter's arm and said, "Thank you. I'm sorry."

"I wish his letter had been longer," said Peter. "It was obviously just a last-minute thought."

"It was perfect," said Petra.

"He didn't even sign it."

"Doesn't matter."

"But he was thinking of you and the children. Making sure you and he would think of all the children by the same names."

She nodded, afraid of starting again.

"I'm going to go now," said Peter. "I won't come back till you invite me."

"Come back when you usually do," she said. "I don't want my homecoming to cost the children somebody they love."

"Thanks," he said.

She nodded. She wanted to thank him for reading it to her and being so decent about her crying all over his shirt, but she didn't trust herself to speak so she just sort of waved.

It was a good thing she had cried herself out. When she went into the kitchen and washed her face and listened to little Petra—to Poke—say, "Lady crying" again, she was able to be very calm and say, "I was crying because I'm so happy to see you. I've missed you. You don't remember me, but I'm your mama."

"We show them your picture every morning and night," said Mrs. Delphiki, "and they kiss the picture."

"Thank you."

"The nurses started it before I came," she said.

"Now I get to kiss my boys and girls myself," she said. "Will that be all right? No more kissing the picture?"

It was too much for them to understand. And if they wanted to keep kissing the picture for a while, that would be fine with her, too. Just like Ramón's envelope. No reason to take away from them something that they valued.

By your father's age, Petra said silently, he was on his own, trying not to starve to death in Rotterdam.

But you're all going to catch up with him and pass him by. When you're in your twenties and out of college and getting married, he'll still be sixteen years old, crawling through time as his starship races through space. When you bury me, he'll not have turned seventeen yet. And your brothers and sister will still be babies. Not as old as you are. It will be as if they never change.

Which means it's exactly as if they had died. Loved ones who die never change, either. They're always the same age in memory.

So what I'm going through isn't something so different. How many women became widows in the war? How many mothers have buried babies that they hardly had time to hold? I'm just part of the same sentimental comedy as everyone else, the sad parts always followed by laughter, the laughter always by tears.

It wasn't until later, when she was alone in her bed, the children asleep for the night, Mrs. Delphiki gone next door—or, rather, to the other wing of the same house—that she was able to bring herself to read Bean's note again. It was in his handwriting. He had done it in a hurry and in spots it was barely legible. And the paper was stained—Peter hadn't been joking about Ramón peeing on the envelope a couple of times.

She turned the light out and meant to go to sleep.

And then something occurred to her and she switched on the light again and fumbled for the paper and her eyes were so bleary she could hardly read, so maybe she had actually fallen asleep, and this thought had woken her out of a sound slumber.

The letter began, "There's one thing we forgot to decide."

But when Peter read it, he had started with "I love you."

He must have scanned over the letter and realized that Bean never said it. That it was just a note that Bean had jotted at the last moment, and Peter worried that she might be hurt by the omission.

He couldn't have known that Bean just didn't put that kind of thing in writing. Except obliquely. Because the whole note said "I love you," didn't it?

She turned the light off again, but still held the letter. Bean's last message to her.

As she drifted off again, the thought passed briefly through her mind: When Peter said it, he wasn't reading at all.

# 26

# SPEAK FOR ME

From: PeterWiggin%hegemon@FreePeopleOfEarth.fp.gov
To: ValentineWiggin%historian@BookWeb.com/AuthorsService
Re: Congratulations

Dear Valentine,

I read your seventh volume and you're not just a brilliant writer (which we always knew) but also a thorough researcher and a perceptive and honest analyst. I knew Hyrum Graff and Mazer Rackham very well before they died, and you treated them with absolute fairness. I doubt they would dispute a word of your book, even where they did not come off as perfect; they were always honest men, even when they lied their zhopas off.

The work of the Hegemon's office is pretty slight these days. The last actual military ventures that were needed took place more than a decade ago—the last gasp of tribalism, which we managed to mostly put down with a show of force. Since then I've tried to retire half a dozen times—no, wait, I'm talking to a historian—twice, but they don't believe I mean it and they keep me in office. They even ask my advice sometimes, and to return the favor I try not to reminisce about how we did things in the early days of the FPE. Only the good old USA refuses to join the FPE and I have hopes they'll get off their "don't tread on me" kick and do the right thing. Polls keep saying that Americans are sick of being the only people in the world who don't get a chance to vote in the world elections. I may see the whole world formally united before I die. And even if I don't, we've got peace on earth.

Petra says hi. Wish you could have known her, but that's star travel. Tell Ender that Petra is more beautiful than ever, he should eat his heart out, and our grandchildren are so adorable that people applaud when we take them out for walks.

Speaking of Ender. I read The Hive Queen. I heard about it before, but never read it till you included it at the end of your last volume—but before the index, or I would never have seen it.

I know who wrote it. If he can speak for the buggers, surely he can speak for me.

Peter

Not for the first time, Peter wished they made a portable ansible. Of course it would make no economic sense. Yes, they miniaturized it as much as possible to put it on starships. But the ansible only made an important difference in communication across the void of space. It saved hours for within-system communication; decades, for communication with the colonies and the ships in flight.

It just wasn't a technology designed for chatting.

There were a few privileges that came with the vestiges of power. Peter might be over seventy—and, as he often pointed out to Petra, an *old* seventy, an *ancient* seventy—but he was still Hegemon, and the title had once meant enormous power, it once meant attack choppers in flight and armies and fleets in motion; it once meant punishment for aggression, collection of taxes, enforcement of human rights laws, cleaning up political corruption.

Peter remembered when the title was such an empty joke they gave it to a teenage boy who had written cleverly on the nets.

Peter had brought power to the office. And then, because he gradually stripped away its functions and assigned them to other officials in the FPE—or "EarthGov" as people now called it as often as not—he had returned the position to a figurehead position.

But not a joke. It was no longer a joke and never would be again.

Not a joke, but not necessarily a good thing, either. There were plenty of people left alive who remembered the Hegemon as the coercive power that shattered their dream of how Earth ought to be (though usually their dream was everyone else's nightmare). And historians and biographers had often had at him and would do it again, forever.

The thing about the historians was, they could arrange the data all neatly in rows, but they kept missing what it was for. They kept inventing the strangest motives for people. There was the biography of Virlomi, for instance, that made her an idealistic saint and blamed Suriyawong, of all people, for the slaughter that ended Virlomi's military career. Never mind that Virlomi herself repudiated that interpretation, writing by ansible from the colony on Andhra. Biographers were always irritated when their subject turned out to be alive.

But Peter hadn't bothered to answer any of them. Even the ones that attacked him quite savagely, blaming him for everything that went badly and giving others the credit for everything that went well . . . Petra would fume over some of them for days until he begged her not to read them anymore. But he couldn't resist reading them himself. He didn't take it personally. Most people never had biographies written about them.

Petra herself had only had a couple about her, and they were both of the "great women" or "role models for girls" variety, not serious scholarship. Which bothered Peter, because he knew what they seemed to neglect—that after all the other members of Ender's Jeesh left Earth and went out to the colonies, she stayed and ran the FPE defense ministry for almost thirty years, until the position became more of a police department than anything else and she insisted on retiring to play with the grandchildren.

She was there for *everything*, Peter said to her when he was griping about this. "You were Ender's and Bean's friend in Battle School—you taught Ender how to *shoot*, for heaven's sake. You were in his Jeesh—"

But at those points Petra would shush him. "I don't want those stories told," she said. "I wouldn't come off very well if the truth came out."

Peter didn't believe it. And you could skip all of that and start when she returned to Earth and . . . wasn't it Petra who, when the Jeesh was almost all kidnapped, found a way to get a message out to Bean? Wasn't she the one who knew Achilles better than anybody that he didn't succeed in killing? She was one of the great military leaders of all time, and she also married Julian Delphiki, the Giant of legend, and then Peter the Hegemon, another legend, and on top of all that raised five of the children she had with Bean and five more that she had with Peter.

And no biography. So why should he complain that there were

dozens about him and every one of them got simple, obvious things wrong, things that you could actually *check*, let alone the more arcane things like motive and secret agreements and . . .

And then Valentine's book on the Bugger wars started to come out, volume by volume. One on the first invasion, two on the second—the one Mazer Rackham won. Then four volumes on the Third Invasion, the one that Ender and his Jeesh fought and won from what they thought was a training game on the asteroid Eros. One whole volume was about the development of Battle School—short biographies of dozens of children who were pivotal to the improvements in the school that eventually led to truly effective training and the legendary Battle Room games.

Peter saw what she wrote about Graff and Rackham and about the kids in Ender's Jeesh—including Petra—and even though he knew part of her insight came from having Ender right there with her in Shakespeare colony, the real source of the book's excellence was her own keen self-questioning. She did not find "themes" and impose them on the history. Things happened, and they were connected to each other, but when a motive was unknowable, she didn't pretend to know it. Yet she understood human beings.

Even the awful ones, she seemed to love.

So he thought: Too bad she isn't here to write a biography of Petra.

Though of course that was silly—she didn't have to be there, she had access to any documents she wanted through the ansible, since one of the key provisions of Graff's ColMin was the absolute assurance that every colony had complete access to every library and repository of records in all the human worlds.

It wasn't until the seventh volume came out and Peter read The Hive Queen that he found the biographer that made him think: I want him to write about me.

The Hive Queen wasn't long. And while it was well written, it wasn't particularly poetic. It was very simple. But it painted a picture of the Hive Queens that was as they might have written it themselves. The monsters that had frightened children for more than a century—and continued to do so even though all were now dead—suddenly became beautiful and tragic.

But it wasn't a propaganda job. The terrible things they did were recognized, not dismissed.

And then it dawned on him who wrote it. Not Valentine, who rooted things in fact. It was written by someone who could understand an enemy so well that he loved him. How often had he heard Petra quote what Ender said about that? She—or Bean, or somebody—had written it down. "I think it's impossible to really understand somebody, what they want, what they believe, and not love them the way they love themselves."

That's what the writer of The Hive Queen, who called himself Speaker for the Dead, had done for the aliens who once haunted our nightmares.

And the more people read that book, the more they wished they had understood their enemy, that the language barrier had not been insuperable, that the Hive Queens had not all been destroyed.

The Speaker for the Dead had made humans love their ancient enemy.

Fine, it's easy to love your enemies after they're safely dead. But still. Humans give up their villains only reluctantly.

It had to be Ender. And so Peter had written to Valentine, congratulating her, but also asking her to invite Ender to write about him. There was some back and forth, with Peter insisting that he didn't want approval of anything. He wanted to talk to his brother. If a book emerged from it, fine. If the book painted him to be a monster, if that's what Speaker for the Dead saw in him, so be it. "Because I know that whatever he writes, it'll be a lot closer than most of the kuso that gets published here."

Valentine scoffed at his use of words like *kuso*. "What are you doing using Battle School slang?"

"It's just part of the language now," Peter told her in an answering email.

And then she wrote, "He won't email you. He doesn't know you anymore, he says. The last he saw of you, he was five years old and you were the worst older brother in the world. He has to talk to you."

"That's expensive," Peter wrote back, but in fact he knew the FPE could afford it and would not refuse him. What really held him back was fear. He had forgotten that Ender had only known him as a bully. Had never seen him struggle to build a world government, not by conquest, but by free choice of the people voting nation by nation. He doesn't know me.

But then Peter told himself, Yes he does. The Peter that he knew is part of the Peter who became Hegemon. The Peter that Petra agreed to marry and permitted to raise children with her, that Peter was the same one that had terrorized Ender and Valentine and was filled with venom and resentment at having been deemed unworthy by the judges who chose which children would grow up to save the world.

How much of my achievement was the acting out of that resentment?

"He should interview Mother," Peter wrote back. "She's still lucid and she likes me better than she used to."

"He writes to her," said Valentine. "When he has time to write to anyone. He takes his duties here very seriously. It's a small world, but he governs it as carefully as if it were Earth."

Finally Peter swallowed his fears and set a date and time and now he sat down at vocal interface of the ansible in the Blackstream Interstellar Communication Center. Of course, BICC didn't communicate directly with any ansible except ColMin's Stationary Ansible Array, which relayed everything to the appropriate colony or starship.

Audio and video were so wasteful of bandwidth that they were routinely compressed and then reinflated at the other end, so despite the instantaneity of ansible communications, there was a noticeable timelag between sides of the conversation.

No picture. Peter had to draw the line somewhere. And Ender hadn't insisted. It would be too painful for both of them—for Ender to see how much time had passed during his relativistic voyage out to

Shakespeare, and for Peter to be forced to see how young Ender still was, how much life he still had ahead of him while Peter was looking coolly at his own old age and approaching death.

"I'm here, Ender."

"It's good to hear your voice, Peter."

And then silence.

"No small talk, is there?" said Peter. "It's been too long a time for me, too brief a time for you. Ender, I know I was a slumbitch to you as a kid. No excuses. I was full of rage and shame and I took it out on you and Valentine but mostly on you. I don't think I ever said a kind thing to you, not when you were awake anyway. I can talk about that if you want."

"Later maybe," said Ender. "This isn't a family therapy session. I just want to know what you did and why."

"Which things I did?"

"The ones that matter to you," said Ender. "What you choose to tell me is as important as what you say about those events."

"There's a lot. My mind is still clear. I remember a lot."

"Good. I'm listening."

He listened for hours that day. And more hours, more days. Peter poured out everything. The political struggles. The wars. The negotiations. The essays on the nets. Building up intelligence networks. Seizing opportunities. Finding worthwhile allies.

It wasn't until near the end of their last session that Peter dredged up memories of when Ender was a baby. "I really loved you. Kept begging Mom to let me feed you. Change you. Play with you. I thought you were the best thing that ever existed. But then I noticed. I'd be playing with you and have you laughing and then Valentine would walk into the room and you'd just rivet on her. I didn't exist anymore.

"She was luminous, of course you reacted that way. Everybody did. *I* did. But at the same time, I was just a kid. I saw it as, Ender loves Valentine more than me. And when I realized you were born because they regarded me as a failure—the Battle School people, I mean—it was just one more resentment. That doesn't excuse anything. I didn't have to be a bastard about it. I'm just telling you, I realize now that's where it started."

"OK," said Ender.

"I'm sorry," said Peter. "That I wasn't better to you as a kid. Because, see, my whole life, all the things I've told you about in all these incredibly expensive conversations, I would find myself thinking, that was OK. I did OK that time. Ender would like that I did that."

"Please don't tell me you did it all for me."

"Are you kidding? I did it because I'm as competitive a marubo as ever was born on this planet. But my standard of judgment was: Ender would like that I did that."

Ender didn't answer.

"Aw, hell, kid. It's way simpler than that. What you did by the time you were twelve made my whole life's work possible."

"Well, Peter, what you did while I was voyaging, that's what made my . . . victory worth winning."

"What a family Mr. and Mrs. Wiggin had."

"I'm glad we talked, Peter."

"Me too."

"I think I can write about you."

"I hope so."

"Even if I can't, though, it doesn't mean I wasn't glad. To find out who you grew up to be."

"Wish I could be there," said Peter, "to see who *you* grow up to be."

"I'm never going to grow up, Peter," said Ender. "I'm frozen in history. Forever twelve. You had a good life, Peter. Give Petra my love. Tell her I miss her. And the others. But especially her. You got the best of us, Peter."

At that moment, Peter almost told him about Bean and his three children, flying through space somewhere, waiting for a cure that didn't look very promising now.

But then he realized that he couldn't. The story wasn't his to tell.

---

If Ender wrote about it, then people would start looking for Bean. Somebody might try to contact him. Someone might call him home. And then his voyage would have been for nothing. His sacrifice. His Satyagraha.

They never spoke again.

Peter lived for some time after that, despite his weak heart. Hoping the whole time that Ender might write the book he wanted. But when he died, the book was still unwritten.

---

So it was Petra who read the short biography called, simply, The Hegemon, and signed Speaker for the Dead.

She wept all day after reading it.

She read it aloud at Peter's grave, stopping whenever any passersby came near. Until she realized that they were coming in order to hear her reading. So she invited them over and read it aloud again, from the beginning.

The book wasn't long, but there was power in it. To Petra, it was everything Peter had wanted it to be. It put a period on his life. The harm and the good. The wars and the peace. The lies and the truth. The manipulation and the liberty.

The Hegemon was a companion piece, really, to The Hive Queen. The one book was the story of an entire species; and so was the other.

But to Petra, it was the story of the man who had shaped her life more than any other.

Except one. The one who lived now only as a shadow in other people's stories. The Giant.

There was no grave, and there was no book to read there. And his story wasn't a human one because in a way he hadn't lived a human life.

It was a hero's life. It ended with him being taken away into heaven, dying but not dead.

I love you, Peter, she said to him at his grave. But you must have known that I never stopped loving Bean, and longing for him, and missing him whenever I looked in our children's faces.

Then she went home, leaving both her husbands behind, the one whose life had a monument and a book, and the one whose only monument was in her heart.

# ACKNOWLEDGMENTS

Thanks to Joan Han, M.D., who works in pediatric endocrinology at the National Institutes of Health in Bethesda, for advice on what kinds of legitimate therapy might be tried to stop Bean's unstoppable growth. Along the same lines, M. Jack Long, M.D., brought up the ideas that became Volescu's suggestions for how Bean might live a long life. My thanks to Dr. Long—along with my relief that he realized they were truly appalling ideas. (His letter ended "Yikes—I hope not!")

Thanks to Danny Sale for suggesting that Bean might have a hand in the decision to convert the Fantasy Game from Battle School into the program that eventually became Jane. Farah Khimji of Lewisville, Texas, reminded me of the need for a world currency—and the fact that the dollar already is one. Andaiye Spencer let me know that I could not let the old Battle School relationship between Petra Arkanian and Dink Meeker die without at least some mention.

Mark Trevors of New Brunswick reminded me that Peter and Ender conversed once before Peter died, and expressed the wish that he could see that scene more fully, and from Peter's point of view. Since this idea was *much* better than the one I had for ending the book, I seized upon it immediately, with gratitude. I also had reminders and help from Rechavia Berman, my Hebrew translator, and from David Tayman.

I'm not good with calendaring my books or aging my characters. I don't pay attention to those things in real life, and so I have a hard time keeping track of the passage of time in my fiction. In response to a plea at our Hatrack River Web site (www.hatrack.com), Megan Schindele, Nathan Taylor, Maureen Fanta, Jennifer Rader, Samuel Sevlie, Carrie Pennow, Shannon Blood, Elizabeth Cohen, and Cecily Kiester all pitched in and sorted through all the age and time references in *Ender's Game* and the other *Shadow* books to help sort it out for me. In addition, Jason Bradshaw and C. Porter Bassett caught a continuity error between the original *Ender's Game* and this novel. I'm grateful for readers who know my books better than I do.

I'm grateful for the willingness of my good friends Erin Absher, Aaron Johnston, and Kathy Kidd, who set aside many other more important concerns in order to join my wife, Kristine, in giving me quick feedback on each chapter as it was written. It never ceases to amaze me how many errors—not just typos, but also continuity lapses and outright contradictions—can slip past me and three or four very careful readers, only to be caught by the next. If there are such mistakes still in this book, it's not their fault!

Beth Meacham, my editor at Tor, went the extra mile on this book. Still in pain from major surgery and drugged to the gills, she read this manuscript while the bits and bytes were still sizzling, and gave me excellent advice. Some of the best scenes in this book are here because she suggested them and I was smart enough to recognize a great idea when I heard it.

The whole production team at Tor went to extraordinary lengths to help us bring out this book in time for a good publishing window, and I appreciate their patience with an author whose estimate of the time needed to complete this book was so laughably wrong.

And Tom Doherty may just be the most creative publisher in the business. There's no idea too wacky for him to at least consider it; and when he decides to do something unusual—like a series of "parallel novels"—he puts everything behind it and makes it happen.

Barbara Bova's creativity and dedication as my agent have blessed my family for most of my career. And I haven't forgotten that the Ender saga first reached the public because, even before she became an agent, her husband, Ben Bova, found a novella called "Ender's Game" on his slushpile and, with a few small changes, agreed to publish it in the August 1977 *Analog* magazine. That one decision (and it wasn't a no-brainer—other editors turned it down cold) has been putting bread on my table and opening the door for readers to find my other work ever since.

But when the writing day is done and I come down out of my garret room, it's finding my wife, Kristine, and my daughter Zina there that makes it all worth doing. Thanks for the love and joy in my life each day. And to my other kids as well, for leading lives that I'm proud to be connected with.